AWAKENER

AWAKENER

Persimmon

Podium

To Giordano,

for always being there whenever I needed you.

This is a work of fiction. Names, characters, places, and incidents are either products of the author's imagination or used fictitiously. Any resemblance to actual events, locales, or persons, living, dead, or undead, is entirely coincidental.

Cover design by Mario Teodosio

ISBN: 978-1-0394-7509-0

Published in 2025 by Podium Publishing
www.podiumaudio.com

AWAKENER

CHAPTER ONE

Good evening, ladies and gentlemen. We interrupt your regular programming for an astonishing breaking news story out of Little Rock, Arkansas, where the unimaginable has just occurred. After seven dead and fifty-four injured, the A-rank dungeon that mysteriously appeared downtown has been cleared by an elite team of Awakeners.

"Little Rock's guilds were taken by surprise, as such powerful dungeons aren't known to appear within human settlements, but Team Nightshade delved into the abyss and emerged victorious, defeating the boss, a named [Lava Golem].

"City officials say this miraculous intervention has averted a disaster that could have had apocalyptic consequences for Little Rock and perhaps even the entire state.

"Tonight, the city rests easy, its skyline intact, its people safe—thanks to the efforts of the heroic Awakeners. We will mourn those we lost and look forward to a bright new day.

"And for that, Little Rock is eternally grateful. Back to you."

The presenter's image faded away as the TV returned to its regular programming. Soon, soft classical music permeated the entirety of Brooklyn's Home Depot again.

Everyone went about their business without a hitch, as if nothing out of the ordinary had happened.

"Thank you for stopping by!" James called, waving at the retreating backs of a newlywed couple. It wasn't every day that he managed to bag such a big sale, and his customers happened to be two lovely people.

"If you keep grinning like that, your face is gonna get stuck," a feminine voice called from behind him.

James turned, feeling his grin get even wider, if possible. "Things just seemed to go well for me today. What can I say, I was due some good luck," he replied, winking at the girl.

Sally was the kind of beauty that you'd expect to see on the cover of a magazine, not working at a Home Depot next to Coney Island. Her long brown hair was let loose out of her usual braid. The barest hint of eyeliner made her big brown eyes pop and gave her a doe-like look. She had evidently made some effort, and James's cheeks warmed at the knowledge that it was for him.

Her smile could light up the room, and even though she never bothered to put on much makeup, she was by far the prettiest everywhere she went.

And she knows it, he thought, watching her sashay away with an impish smile.

The retail job was supposed to be a short-term deal for James, just a way to earn some cash while figuring out his life. His granddad hadn't been happy about his decision to skip college, but he gave in, hoping James would make the right choice eventually.

The economy was a mess; it had been since the world ended eleven years ago. Despite political promises of a bright future beyond the Mana Apocalypse, James knew better. Good jobs were out there but mostly for Awakeners, and he hadn't felt a hint of mana within him, no matter how much he wished otherwise.

That just leaves more manual labor, or things you need to be a genius for. And since I'm not one, no matter what Grandma says, I needed to look reality in the face.

It always depressed him, considering his future. The world was a shitty place, and it didn't hold nineteen-year-old young men in high regard.

Still, today was different. Not only had he managed to close quite the sale, but it was worth enough money to replace his old, battered computer—it still ran on electricity and circuits—with a new one and to pay for his upcoming date after his shift.

Going on a date with Sally sounded more like one of his daydreams if he was being honest with himself. Still, in a moment of courage, he had asked her out that morning, and after giving him a once over that felt more like an X-ray, she said yes, on the condition that she could choose the location.

Since that freed him of the burden of thinking about where to take her, James readily agreed, and so he had spent the whole day quietly bursting with excitement.

Finally, the clock struck five, the little jingle sounding almost solemn. The store wouldn't close for another five hours, but that was a problem for those suckers with the evening shift, and James was most certainly not one of them.

Changing out of his orange uniform felt like liberation, and James took the few minutes he knew he had—as Sally always needed at least ten before she was ready to come out of the locker room. He checked himself in the slightly dirty mirror that hung over the fake porcelain sink.

Energetic green eyes stared back at him. He ran his hand through his hair, mussing up the dark locks until they fell artfully over his forehead. His lips were plumper than normal because he had spent the whole day chewing on them, but he didn't mind the look.

He knew he was a bit of a pretty boy, and though he had the hints of what would one day be a decent beard, he preferred shaving completely for the moment, as the scraggly mess that would otherwise grow wasn't flattering.

"His nose is straight, his teeth white, and his dimples lovely." Well, that's what Mrs. Johnson says, but that woman will compliment a tree if you'd allow her. Not a good metric for what college girls like, unfortunately.

Still, he thought he made a decent sight. James wasn't one to put too much stock in his appearance, but he was well aware that it was an essential factor in any relationship. If he wanted to have a shot at having more than a singular date with Sally, he would need to make sure he was always presentable.

Reassured that he wouldn't send the girl screaming, he put on his black-and-green jacket and exited the building, stopping below the big orange sign that read THE HOME DEPOT to wait for his date.

Not even five minutes later, Sally emerged from the backdoor. She wore an all-black outfit—a tank top and a pair of leggings—with a complementing white ribbon that kept her hair out of her face.

She wasn't as dressed up as some of the other girls he had gone out with during high school, but to James, she was much better looking than them. Having a style of your own and rocking with it no matter the circumstance was much cooler than bowing to social pressure, after all.

"Well, I'm ready to follow you everywhere!" he exclaimed, making her laugh.

"Then shut up and walk, lucky boy," she teased, passing him by and moving toward Cropsey Avenue's bridge. Coney Island Creek didn't make for much of a romantic sight, but James didn't mind as he jogged to catch up.

"So what do you have planned? Are you going to finally reveal that you're a serial killer and want to dispose of me?" he jokingly questioned. Sally stumbled, turning to look at him with a surprised look. Then she burst out laughing, holding her belly.

James stood there, bemused, as he didn't really think that his lame joke was that funny. *Well, a win is a win. If she's laughing this hard now, things might be looking up even more than I thought.*

Sally finally gathered herself, holding on to the bridge's handrail. She was a bit flushed, with chuckles still occasionally shaking her frame, but to James, she had never been more beautiful.

"Man, that was funny." She then caught his hand in hers and tugged him forward.

They walked for a few minutes, mainly discussing what classes Sally was thinking of taking the next semester at college and the latest gossip at work.

Neptune Avenue wasn't James's ideal date spot in New York due to its lack of allure, but its proximity to work and Sally's home weighed in for safety amid a world fraught with violence.

In a world rife with violent crime, women often had to be cautious, even with familiar faces, as harrowing news stories constantly reminded them.

When can they stop talking about Awakeners, monsters, and the System anyway? I think they're important too, but it shouldn't be all everyone can talk about.

Finally, they reached their first destination. Millennium Bodega was a classic spot in Coney Island, and its chopped cheese had few rivals. Though the place was dirty and greasy, no one could complain about its food, and these days, that kind of atmosphere was common almost everywhere, unless you ventured into the shiny side of Manhattan.

There, titanic high-rises were still being built, towering over the city like giants. They always looked jarring to James. As if they were a slap to the face to all those who were suffering. People's standards of living declined thanks to the Mana Apocalypse—but as long as there was money to be made, New York City would always funnel some of it into new construction.

The two didn't stop at the bodega, merely picking up a couple of sandwiches and drinks before moving toward Kaiser Park. In the summer, it wasn't much more than a few sports fields and dry grass, which kept the foot traffic low as people flocked to the beach. That gave them some privacy. They chose to sit on one of the cleaner benches, and they ate while chatting. As always, Sally managed to be funny, charming and witty. She could easily discuss the newest developments in the reclaiming of the land, or simply gossip about the two coworkers they had both noticed were sweet on each other.

I don't think I'm putting the cart before the horses here. We had some good food and she chose to come to the park. That sounds like it might lead to some action! Or am I? Ugh!

For all his thoughts, James hadn't done much with his dates before; most of his previous ones ended with a kiss on the cheek after he accompanied the girls back home.

Still, he was determined not to fuck this up. Sally was beautiful, intelligent, and considering her college major—mana engineering was complex, especially for ordinary people!—she had a bright future ahead. If he could show her that he was a good guy and that he'd treasure and respect her, he might have a shot at an actual relationship.

"You've been quiet," she commented as she finished her chopped cheese.

James shook himself out of his thoughts, deciding that he could wait until he was back home to hyperanalyze his behavior.

"Sorry, I'm just really happy that you agreed to come on a date. It means a lot that you gave me a chance," he explained, smiling as he looked at her.

Sally rolled her eyes. "You are an idiot," she stated, not elaborating further.

James blinked. He didn't understand her meaning.

Seeing him make a very good impression of a stunned goldfish, the girl patted his cheek.

"You're lucky you are pretty. Not much going on up there, is it?"

It would be better for him to simply shut up and allow the very pretty lady to keep touching him, so James just smiled.

"Yeah, that's a good boy."

Whelp, that did something to me.

* * *

Walking Sally back home turned out to be a more involved endeavor than he would have expected. They were taking side streets, twisting and turning through Coney Island in places that James hadn't even known about.

"Sorry again about this. It's just that those annoying guys from the Radiant Guild are patrolling the neighborhood, and they take way too much pleasure in stopping every woman to 'inspect' them," Sally explained. She made suggestive air quotes when she got to the last part.

It was an unfortunate reality they all had to contend with that, since there simply weren't enough personnel from the Awakeners Association—or, the AA for short—to deal with every new dungeon that popped up. So most of the supernatural security had to be given to private guilds. They usually abused that power, which surprised no one, but it was the price to pay to be safe from monsters.

"Radiant . . . Isn't that the one your ex is from?" James asked, thinking about the blond jock he had seen at the beginning of the year. He was a strong Awakener, if he remembered correctly, but also insufferable.

"Yeah, he's the reason why I'm making us take this whole convoluted path. He won't directly acknowledge me, but he'll make his mooks harass me if he sees me," she explained grimacing.

James's blood boiled. To him, guilds were already leeches sucking life out of humanity. Seeing their members abuse their power for trivial nonsense made it all the more unbearable.

"Unfortunately," she continued, "he's actually pretty strong. Became F-rank in a few years, if I remember correctly, which means they definitely won't do anything about it even if I were to report it."

Before anything more could be said, there was a *screech* as a sewer cover was ripped open. The two looked at each other in dread and then slowly turned to the sound.

There, an ugly, dirty creature was climbing out. It resembled a rat, in theory, if that rat was the size of a Rottweiler and ten times as aggressive. An oily substance covered its fur, and its eyes were pools of darkness. When it noticed them, it made a sound that was close to a roar, though more high pitched.

James took one look at the beast and immediately grabbed Sally's hand, pulling her away as quickly as he could. "RUN!"

CHAPTER TWO

The rat's body was enormous, far too large to be naturally grown. Its skin was stretched thin over its frame, with matted fur clumped with dirt. Its glowing red eyes promised suffering as they stared straight at him.

Mana warped the beast into something more than it had once been, turning a normal sewer rat into a creature capable of murdering a human.

All the lessons he had been given throughout his life—how to avoid monsters and quickly reach safe zones—flashed in James's mind. They should have avoided dark, damp alleys while there was an ongoing search for a possible dungeon. Unfortunately, they hadn't and were now paying the consequences.

Pulling Sally along, James considered their chances. The girl wasn't in good shape to successfully escape the rat, which was rapidly gaining ground. For a moment, he seriously considered using himself as bait, letting the monster get him so that his crush could live, but common sense immediately reasserted itself.

He couldn't leave Sally behind, as she'd be doomed. He couldn't stay still because he'd surely die. A monster, even a weak one, could still kill a man; given his current condition, he didn't think he could last long enough to let her get to safety.

That left just one option. Inside James was a fiery determination; he had known it existed all his life. Rather than flickering and dying down, it blazed up and grew into an inferno.

He gritted his teeth, grinding them hard enough that he could hear it. His fists closed tightly, and strength flooded his limbs. James might have been doomed, but at that moment, he decided he wouldn't go down lightly. He wouldn't let harm come to Sally and wouldn't allow this *thing* to destroy his newfound happiness.

This world is shit. My life is probably going to be shit. But if you stupid bastards think I'll allow you to kill me without even putting up a fight, then I'll show you. I'll fucking show you how James Summers dies.

As he had his moment of revelation, the rat finally closed the distance. It wasted no time, squeaking angrily and jumping at him with murderous intent.

Sally screamed as she threw herself aside and pulled James away from danger. It was slow enough that they barely managed to avoid its charge. Instinctively, James grabbed the trash can nearby and started using its contents as projectiles, slowing down the monster's charge.

In his left hand, the metal lid served as an improvised shield. Remembering his coach's words, James dropped into an approximation of a stance and prepared to charge.

"Getting so close to a monster that it attacks you means you're already as good as dead. If you can, you should run away as far as possible. Better if you get to a guild building and alert them. If, for whatever reason, you can't, you should try to surprise it. Use everything around you as a weapon; try and stop its movements enough that you can hit it once; and then do so again and again. Just to be clear, this should be the absolute last resort."

Last resort it is, then. Thank you, Coach Humbly. I'll never make fun of your pot-belly and bald head again if I make it out of here because of you.

A guttural yell came from James's throat as he ran toward the beast. His heart pounded loud enough that he couldn't even hear the answering bellow; he knew he was far too committed now to back away.

The rat made for his legs, attempting to incapacitate him, but he had expected it and turned that weakness into a strength. With a kick that should have, by all rights, landed him a spot on the football team, James's foot connected with the monster's head and sent it crashing into the opposite wall.

Knowing he couldn't lose the initiative now, he advanced on his fallen foe. However much he would have liked for it to be already over, he was all too aware that monsters had much greater durability than normal animals, and so he attacked again.

As the rat picked itself up, James came down upon it with his improvised shield, sending it crashing back down. Then, he started whaling on it.

Desperate strength flooded his limbs as he felt close to victory, and he brought his weapon on its head again, screaming in terror and euphoria.

It took a dozen hits before the rat stopped moving and then a few more until he felt safe enough that it was truly down for the count.

His arm ached in a way that told him he would feel it for a week. Then his legs gave out from under him, sending him sprawling back on the hard cement.

"James! NO!"

The blood-chilling shout forced him up. He barely managed to turn before he saw something he was sure would stay with him for the rest of his life.

Another rat, bigger and oilier than the first, had somehow sneaked up on them. It charged at James, an attack that would surely end James's life. That was, if Sally hadn't thrown herself at it, bodily pushing the large dog-sized monster away with a strength he couldn't believe she possessed.

Unfortunately, the thing righted itself quickly, resuming its attack with a different target.

James scrambled up; he moved faster than he ever had. But still too late.

"AAAAHHH!!!" Sally screamed in pain as the monster clamped down on her foot. Its teeth sheared through muscle and bone alike as if they were cardboard.

With a furious yell, the boy tackled it away from Sally. His fists glowed with otherworldly light as he hit it, blood splattering everywhere as his hands and the rat's head crunched. James raged on, undaunted by the damage he was inflicting on himself, until he was absolutely sure the monster was dead, bits of its brain stuck to his clothes.

The boy gathered himself, tired beyond words, but somehow pushed on. The fire within him didn't waver; instead, it strengthened as he carefully picked up the quietly sobbing Sally in his arms.

He'd save her, even if he had to run all the way to the hospital.

Thankfully, that didn't end up being the case. A group of patrolling Awakeners found them as soon as they got out of the back alleys, and the Awakeners immediately brought them to a nearby clinic, where emergency care was administered.

James felt like he was in a dream as the events of the evening kept repeating themselves in front of his eyes. If only he had been more careful, stronger, faster, they wouldn't be in the situation they were in.

It wasn't so much the extent of the injuries that worried James, as that had been taken care of with a simple potion for him, and with a much more expensive elixir therapy for Sally. Her foot would need time to fully regrow, and the cost would be enough to pay for her entire college tuition, but she'd get her foot back.

No, he worried about the trauma the girl had gone through. Her foot had been eaten, all because she saved him.

"Well, this is all I can do for you two tonight." The doctor's voice shook him out of his contemplations, and James managed to smile—brittle as it was—as he thanked him.

"Don't worry too much about her," the balding man added. "She'll get through it. She's a fighter."

Watching the girl of his dreams get carried off by her parents, James felt only emptiness. Her father had been kind enough to thank him for his help, but he had also firmly stated that she'd need time to recover and that they would appreciate him keeping his distance.

James had wanted to put up a fight, but after seeing Sally scream in terror, desperate to escape the night's pain and trauma, he was listless.

Still, he gathered himself up, not wanting to incur more expenses than he already had. As it was, all of his day's bonus was used up to pay for his treatment, since his hands were damaged by the fight. The potion had burned, but it had been a distant feeling.

Now that he was outside, the cold sea breeze sobered him that he noticed he was being followed. Unafraid, James stopped beneath a streetlight, waiting for the person tailing him to reveal themselves.

Finally, someone stepped under the light, the shiny blond hair, bright green eyes, and strong jaw immediately identifying him as Sally's ex-boyfriend, Callum.

"You seem to be doing pretty well, Summers."

James just looked at him, waiting for the Awakener to get to the point.

Seeing that he wasn't getting the reaction he wanted, the blond scoffed, "What, the rat got your tongue? I thought you used Sally as a shield well enough that you were uninjured."

"You thought wrong. If you people had done your job, this whole thing wouldn't have happened, Wright."

The older blond suddenly got into his personal space, bending down slightly so as to bring their eyes to the same level. "Listen up, you little shit. Not only did you get Sally crippled, but now you want to act like it's my fucking fault? I better not see you sniffing around her anymore, unless you want me to put you in the hospital for good."

James's fists clenched tightly, anger warring with wisdom. He knew very well that the older boy was just waiting for the opportunity to attack him without consequences. If he fell for the provocation, no one would be able to gainsay Wright. An Awakener attacking a normal person out in the open, where cameras would record everything, was still too much, even for a band of thugs like the Radiant Guild.

"Coward," the blond scorned, pulling away when it was apparent James wasn't about to attack him.

Only when he left did James address the slight pressure in his mind, as if a part of his brain was trying very hard to remind him of something important he had forgotten.

As soon as he concentrated on that, a transparent window popped up in his vision, startling him. "Aargh! What the hell? What the fuck?!"

A bolt of realization then hit him, and his eyes widened like saucers as he took in the window's content.

CONGRATULATIONS, AWAKENER!

The light of your soul shined brightly today, and its might was enough to Awaken you! The System is here to guide your path forward as you grow into the best possible version of yourself!

Be ready for joy and strife, Awakener, because the world is now open to you.

It was a message James was painfully familiar with. He read about it everywhere, from classes in high school to the Internet—and he even saw it on the TV.

The words appeared before the few blessed ones that Awakened, who'd become the bastions of humanity's survival and enter the highest class in society.

It was what James wished he'd seen for years, ever since his father had died and a sense of complete helplessness had overtaken him.

He had begged and prayed to gods he didn't believe in for the chance to gain agency in a world where only the strongest could decide their future.

It almost felt ridiculous that it would happen now, but a small part of him realized that it was precisely because he Awakened that he managed to kill the two rats. The guild members had done little investigating, satisfied with the knowledge that the two rats had been H-ranks from a newly formed dungeon. Now, he knew the truth as to how he had made it.

James took a deep breath and then uttered the word that was impressed upon everyone who had even a passing interest in Awakeners: "Status."

Another window popped up, replacing the welcome message that shook him so much.

STATUS WINDOW	
Name	James Summers
Age	19
Awakening	1st
Talent	Thakinesis
Title	
Level	2
MP	6/10
STR	5
VIT	5
AGI	6
SEN	4
MND	7
STAT POINTS	2

CHAPTER THREE

With misty eyes, James took in the words that would change his life forever. He angrily scrubbed at his face, feeling as if he should be more manly about it, but he felt overwhelmed.

I awakened… Fuck, I actually did it. I spent so long praying for this day to come that it feels absurd to have my dream finally realized.

Still dazed by everything that had just happened, he postponed the decision about what to do with the two free stat points for later, when he would be more in control of his faculties. The flight, the fight, and the consequences emotionally exhausted him, and he simply wasn't in the right state of mind.

For the moment, he focused more on the fifth line. Talents were what made or broke Awakeners, differentiating between those who would be relegated to the back lines and those who would guide the path forward for humanity, pushing back against the madness that befell the world eleven years before.

Unfortunately, James had no idea what Thakinesis might be. He scrambled for his phone to search it up, but it decided this was the perfect moment to die. *Oh well, I'll just look it up when I get home, then.* Halfway across Coney Island, James remembered there was more to the System that he almost forgot to check.

With a mental push, he brought up the status window.

This time, however, he didn't stop there.

"Skills," he spoke in the quiet of the evening.

SKILLS	LEVEL	DESCRIPTION
Thakinetic Empowerment	1	(Active): Utilize your Willpower to temporarily raise STR - VIT - AGI.
Thakinetic Awareness	1	(Active/Passive): Expand your SEN to feel others' wills.
Thakinetic Resistance	1	(Active/Passive): Empower your MND to defend yourself against foreign influences.

There they were. The powers he received from the System thanks to his Talent. They would determine his future as an Awakener, and in the confusion and tiredness of the moment, he had almost forgotten about them.

So it's something to do with willpower. It would explain the surge of strength I felt when fighting the rats. Yeah, that has to be it. I somehow used my skills without even knowing what they were, and they saved my ass. James hadn't been trained to battle against monsters, even the lowest rung of them, and his survival being owed to more than just blind luck actually made sense.

Skills were what constituted an Awakener's power, and once you had them, they became a part of you. He had studied this in school, but it always remained a nebulous subject. To have it happen to him felt absurd, but the glowing blue window said otherwise.

Awakening only happened to few people, generally in moments of great distress—though not always. If he remembered correctly from his old classes, scientists believed that around 10 percent of the human population had the potential to manipulate mana and that they should reach that number in the next few years.

James was now one of those privileged few, which gave him butterflies in his stomach, but he shelved those dreams of glory until he got home.

Though he did not intend to hide his status from the Awakeners Association, James wanted to get there in due time after talking with his grandparents about his future and taking some time to reflect.

Being noticed now meant representatives from various guilds knocking on his door to quickly make him offers. Not all of them were as sleazy as Callum Wright's Radiant Guild, but enough of them were that he'd need to be very careful.

It took him another fifteen minutes of walking before he finally got to Brighton Beach, where he and his family lived. Meanwhile, he noticed that his mana ticked up until it read 10/10, implying that he had used some during the fight.

Of course, it must have happened when I subconsciously used my skills. They require mana to be used, I know that. But I thought I would feel something . . . Well, I wasn't paying much attention, to be honest.

James barely had the time to knock on the door, too tired to look for his keys, before it swung open, revealing his grandmother in all her '70s nightgown glory. Her hair was done up in short curls, and a pair of silver eyeglasses framed her green eyes, complementing them nicely. Her worried expression, however, made his heart squeeze. The woman barely stopped to check that it was him before she threw herself at James, hugging him tightly.

"Grandma, you're squeezing too tight," he complained, but something in him relaxed at the familiar warmth.

The day had been a rollercoaster for James, and his grandmother's hug was simply the last straw. Almost without his notice, a few tears slipped down his cheeks, and he broke the embrace to angrily swipe at them.

"Sorry, sorry, I don't know what came over me."

"Oh, James." The elderly woman sighed. "I don't know what happened to you, but you have to know that you can allow yourself to feel. We're your family. You don't have to hide anything from us."

Behind her, a gruff voice agreed, "We're here for you, James. Whatever you need, even if it's to go fight some punk that took your lunch money."

That startled a laugh out of the boy, and he composed himself.

"Let's do this inside. I don't want to make a spectacle out of it."

Others would have avoided telling the gruesome story of their fight with the monster rats to their sweet grandmothers, but Rosa Summers was made of sterner stuff. As a nurse who had spent many years in the emergency room, especially during the chaotic years following the 2012 Mana Apocalypse, she had seen a lot. She led him to the living room, a warm environment that helped James relax slightly. Rosa sat James down and bustled off once she was sure he was comfortable, coming back with a warm cup of tea.

Larry, his grandfather, grunted in surprise when James revealed that he had defeated two monsters. He wasn't a soft man, and his quick mind immediately grasped the implications. Unless immense luck was involved, it was improbable for an ordinary, unarmed person to defeat a monster, and since James wasn't sporting obvious injuries beyond looking a bit dirty, the leap was quickly made.

"You Awakened," he said, causing his wife to gasp reflexively.

James just nodded, not seeing the benefit of hiding it. "We were attacked near Kaiser Park. I didn't even realize until the fight was over, but after, it became obvious that something happened."

"I'll drive you down to the Awakeners Association tomorrow morning, then," the old man said, turning around to leave.

That was how he was, gruff and to the point, but in a way, James was glad for it. Given the day he had just had, a tiny bit of normalcy could only help.

"Wait, what do you mean 'we'? Who else was with you?" Rosa asked, stopping her husband in his tracks.

The boy grimaced, not really wanting to get into the mess that his relationship with Sally had become. Still, he decided not to hide anything important, and so he quickly told of how exactly he had wandered into the rat's territory.

His grandparents both had stony expressions, making him worry they'd be mad at him. Quickly, it became apparent that was not the case.

"What a foolish girl. I can understand not wanting to get harassed by those guild hooligans, but taking dimly lit alleys while there's an ongoing hunt for a dungeon is the stupidest thing I've heard in a while. It'd be better for you to let her go." Surprisingly, the harsh statement came from Rosa rather than Larry.

Even more surprising, it was Larry that tried to defuse the situation. "Now don't go all mama bear on the boy. He can make that choice by himself." When it was obvious his wife was about to interrupt, he placated, "Yes, it was stupid, but I think he learned that lesson. Haven't you, James?"

James nodded vigorously. He'd definitely think twice before following pretty girls down shady alleyways.

With an uncharacteristic hard look, Rosa told him that he needed to clean himself, as the blood and grime sticking to him might make him ill. James didn't put up a fuss. The day's events had taken a toll on him, and a long hot shower sounded divine.

Upstairs, he quickly disrobed once he reached his bathroom, taking care not to have his dirty clothes touch the clean floor. He put them in the wicker basket beneath his sink and decided that cleaning those would be a tomorrow problem.

The shower, it turned out, was truly as magnificent as he expected. The water ran brown, then red, and finally, after almost five minutes of scrubbing himself with a loofah that looked entirely done with its lot in life, it turned clear.

The thought of going down to eat something—his grandmother always had a stocked pantry and a fridge filled to the brim; the consequences of living through the end of the world—made his stomach rebel.

He had already eaten enough during his date—he was glad he hadn't thrown up, and chancing it didn't feel like a good idea.

James put on his softest pajamas, the ones he kept for special occasions; they were difficult to find for cheap these days. The baby-blue color wasn't particularly flattering, but since he was by himself, he didn't worry about it.

Instead, he dropped on his bed, a heavy sigh leaving him.

His life had changed irreparably, he knew, but coming to terms with it wasn't easy. Awakeners lived entirely different lives than ordinary people, and though their work made sure that society could still run, even after the craziness of 2012, they weren't exactly present in the average person's daily life.

Of course, the news talks about them. The Silver Eye Guild cleared this dungeon, and Mark Kelly II broke up a ring of smugglers. But it's not something you think about much beyond that.

With a thought, the System interface popped up, an undeniable reminder that he, too, would now be part of that world.

He still had two free stat points to assign, and he knew from his classes that it was better to do so as early as possible—an Awakener never knew when their next fight would come, and it was important to acclimate to the power boost. However, he first wanted to learn more about his power.

That could wait for tomorrow. The Awakeners Association served several purposes, and though it had been gutted by Congress and was a far cry from what its founders envisioned, it was still a very useful place for a new Awakener.

Instead, what he wanted to do now was decide what kind of path he'd walk.

James, like all teenagers, had always dreamed of one day waking up with incredible powers. He'd break up crime syndicates, save cats from trees, and heal society.

Unfortunately, now that the prospect of making a difference was real, he felt it wasn't that simple. He could do things like that by himself, a lone avenger in the night, but statistically speaking, most of those died within the first two months.

That was hard to contest when it was corroborated by hundreds of papers from the US's top scientists. It was something everyone who had ever taken Awakener studies knew about.

It was also why guilds swallowed up all up-and-coming talents. Why their power and influence grew every day, as the government's and the people's shrank.

A few mighty people controlled everything, from industries to television. Everyone knew about it, but not much could be done. They needed those people to save them from the powerful monsters, be they human or not.

But James didn't want to simply become another cog in the system. He didn't want to get assigned a team by a middling guild and spend his life toiling for contribution points.

His father had been an agent. He'd never been sure of what agency, and his grandparents told him they didn't know either, but he had worked for the betterment of society and died for it.

He died because the government was weak and ineffective. But he had also believed that a few good apples still existed and that it was worth fighting so the people's voices could be heard.

James believed that too.

CHAPTER FOUR

This has to be some sort of record. I told myself I'd be responsible and wait until I got to the AA to delve deeper into the System, and yet here I am, in the middle of the night, doing just that.

James, it turned out, wasn't as patient as he believed himself to be. He managed a few hours of sleep before the image of Sally screaming in pain woke him up.

He cared deeply for her, and his inability to protect her would stick to him for a long time. He could only hope she'd recover soon, and maybe they'd be able to see each other again. For now, he would respect her father's request.

Fortunately, he had a shiny new toy to distract him. The System was the single most important thing to an Awakener, he knew that much, and getting acquainted with it was fundamental.

Thakinesis, he already learned, meant willpower manipulation. According to the Internet, there weren't any active users of the same exact Talent—which wasn't a surprise, as unique Talents were by definition very rare—but he could cobble up enough information from similar powers.

Basically, it boils down to using my willpower to enhance my actions. I can empower my body, senses, or mind with it. At higher levels, I should be able to do some very nifty things, but for the moment, it's just a slightly better Warrior Talent.

He was being uncharitable, he knew. Warrior was one of the most common Talents out there, and though some Awakeners could rise to high ranks with it, it was considered a pretty bad one.

When he realized that his Thakinesis was unique, or at least rare enough to be unheard of, he got very excited.

People like Michael Towers, the highest-ranking Awakener in America, were well known for their unique Talents. Son of War was such a cool power that everyone knew who it was linked to.

With it, Towers had broken the siege of Tampa by the crocodilians and defeated innumerable enemies. His visage was plastered everywhere, even in James's room. That was a true powerhouse.

He looked at the lightly armored man. Towers was dressed more for fashion—like a modern superhero, he remembered reading on a forum once. Then the boy sighed. He wouldn't be the Unstoppable Juggernaut from the beginning, but then again, Towers didn't begin his career as the monster he now was.

James, too, had to slowly grind his level up. He had to fight countless monsters, probably many of whom were even more disgusting than the sewer rats he had faced.

Though you couldn't find information online about a high-ranker's level, the web was rife with speculation. Some would claim the most outlandish numbers—like, 6666? Not even good trolling. But a few serious people attempted to infer the real numbers with thorough observation and compounded their conclusion with data.

There were no official level requirements to reach a specific ranking given by the AA; everyone knew that depending on one's talent, their destructive power would widely vary, even at the same level. However, unofficial ranges were easy to find. Every fifty levels or so, an Awakener's ranking could be expected to increase. The scale started at H, with level 50 being the cap, and then on and on like that.

The most accredited people agreed that Towers had to have surpassed level 400, making him an S-rank Awakener. One of the very few around the world.

Considering how the growth rate decreased the higher the level, S-rank was a monstrously tall order to achieve in little more than ten years. Projections estimated Towers to reach the 600s toward the end of his career, if he survived that long. Given what the eggheads thought about the possible effects of the vitality stat on the human life span, it was very likely he'd do so.

Of course, the average Awakener was nowhere close to that. Most reached E- or D-rank after years of effort and were content with their lot in life. That kind of person was revolting to James. He couldn't understand having the world at your fingertips and wasting it.

Their guilds would send them on easy extermination missions, where they would barely get any experience, and they'd be lucky to get a few levels per year.

People, James knew, got used to their lot in life quite easily. The 2012 apocalypse had shown how adaptable humans were. When the world turned on them, people collectively panicked but soon shrugged and went back to their lives, slowly but surely getting most of it back under control.

It was one of the fundamental qualities of humanity. But it also meant that if there was no external push to greatness, many would simply stop growing.

On the other hand, James knew just how low one could go without the ray of hope offered by the System. Just like how its appearance had pulled humanity out of its death spiral and into a new age, it saved him too.

And I won't let it go to waste. I have the chance to make a difference, and I'd never forgive myself if I didn't take it. Dad wouldn't forgive me.

Shaking his head, James refocused on why he wasn't able to sleep. The two points banked in his status window burned something fierce.

It was commonly shared advice for new Awakeners to wait until they got picked up by a guild and received some guidance before they assigned their first stat points. Depending on the path they chose, they'd have to prioritize different attributes, and without the resources of a guild, making the right choice was like tossing a coin.

However, James had little intention of participating in the guild system. Beyond the personal issues he had because of his father, he genuinely believed that allowing private organizations with little to no oversight to run society was a recipe for disaster.

And even if there is little I can do about it now, at least I don't want to take part in it.

Which meant he would have to take the risk of choosing without that guidance.

His research online yielded more than he feared, but less than he had hoped for. When it came to mind-oriented Talents like Telekinesis, putting aside strength and vitality stats was the easy choice. For others, like Warrior, mind and sense stats made little sense to invest in beyond the minimum.

His Thakinesis, however, wasn't that easily defined. Each of his skills touched a different attribute, and his main draw of power, his will, wasn't given a numerical value. It seemed to depend entirely on how much he wanted something and how strong his focus on that thing was.

Ultimately, the only thing he could count on was the enhancement his skills would have on his attributes. It took some finicking, but James eventually understood how to activate them.

The results were, to put it lightly, awesome. Level 1 of Thakinetic Empowerment lifted his strength, vitality, and agility by at least 10 percent, which, while not as impressive as the skills of high-ranking Awakeners, made a world of difference to a previously average human. Especially considering that he wasn't in a situation where his willpower was stimulated.

Putting it to the test, James tried to lift his dumbbells with and then without the enhancement. Concentrating on the specific skill and willing it to happen seemed to do the trick, and he easily lifted his twenty-five-pound weights, doing a full set with little to no strain. Without the Empowerment, he felt his muscles working.

James wasn't obsessed with weightlifting, but he had bought the dumbbells to try and keep up a decent level of fitness. However, simply willing himself to be stronger had more of an effect than a month of hard work.

There's the fact that it's temporary. Once he'd finished the task, James felt the strength leaving his limbs. More than anything, that seemed to be the main limitation of his power. He needed to keep wanting to do something; otherwise, it'd turn off.

It makes sense, what with it being Willpower Enhancement, but still . . . It'd be cool if I were a magic swordsman who can buff himself and not worry about anything else.

Thakinetic Awareness, on the other hand, was a different beast. Twisting his mind to feel more turned out to be more complex than expected. He first tried by focusing on something he knew was beyond his physical senses—his bathroom sink—and wasted a lot of time.

Only by rereading the skill text did he realize that it wasn't a simple enhancement, unlike his physical stats. Awareness worked by empowering his senses to feel other beings. A bathroom sink did not have a mind, which made it ineligible for the skill to work.

When he focused on his grandparents' room, where he knew they would be sleeping, he finally felt something. A faint knowledge, coming from the recesses of his mind, informed him of where exactly they were lying. It was almost instinctive, which explained how he had used it during the fight with the rats without even noticing.

The last skill refused to answer his call, though admittedly, he didn't try that hard. It sounded like the kind of thing he'd be able to use only when there was a real need for it, and his worries about the future didn't seem to count as a mental attack.

At last, knowing he'd have to go to sleep soon if he wanted to be presentable tomorrow when he went to register with the Awakeners Association, James turned to assigning his stat points.

Since his build didn't seem to be focused on anything in particular, he'd probably have to keep an even spread between all his attributes. Still, for the moment, his mind stat could be left aside, at least until he figured out just how much it influenced his willpower.

I don't think it's as connected as it looks like at first glance. The mind stat governs a person's brain capacity, in both processing power and versatility. It does nothing to help someone with a lousy personality, which makes me think willpower is not wholly dependent on it.

He'd experiment in the future as soon as he got a few more levels under his belt, but for now, he simply decided to put one point in strength and one in sense, thus bringing them respectively to six and five.

James knew that raising one's stats could feel very odd, but he was still unprepared for the surge of electricity that touched every fiber of his being. His hair rose all over his body, and he felt his muscles twitching as they expanded and then contracted again.

The process took only a couple of seconds to finish, but when it did, James opened his eyes a changed man. The increase in power was tiny compared to what he'd achieve in time, but for the first time, he felt himself grow in real time. This sensation, he knew, was one he'd chase after his whole life.

The AA building in Downtown Manhattan was as sleek and well maintained as always. In the heart of the financial center, it gave the impression of being one of the country's true powers.

James knew that, though it was initially conceived to be influential, because of greed and corruption, the guilds stripped the AA of all the powers it should have.

The glass facade shimmered with countless protections, meant to serve as a last-resort shelter for the entire New York City government in case of disaster. They had enough power that even as a normal person, James was able to feel it.

Now that he had unlocked the System, however, it was like a flashlight in the dark.

James took a deep breath, then exhaled his anxieties. A grin crept up on his face, excitement taking over, and he stepped forth into the unknown.

CHAPTER FIVE

Just like a perfectly wrapped Christmas gift that fell short of a child's expectations, the Awakeners Association building was extremely disappointing when seen from the inside.

Oh, the sleek, clean interiors could fool anyone who lived with their head in the ground, but James knew exactly how little power these offices held.

The AA should have been, by all rights, one of the most powerful agencies in the US, standing alongside the DOD and the CIA, but due to heavy lobbying, Congress had passed laws to strip it of its oversight powers and to remove much of its funding, in favor of tax cuts for established guilds. The AA was smothered in its infancy.

These days, the AA served mostly as the gateway into the supernatural world for new Awakeners and little more beyond that.

Well, they still employ a few elite teams for dungeon clearing duty, but even those are likely to disappear in a few years, with how quickly the money is draining.

Still, for all the frustration James felt, the AA was the place to go to get registered as an Awakener. Then, he could start earning money by cleaning up dungeons and selling off monster parts and mana stones. It also had state-of-the-art facilities to evaluate rankings and Talents, which James intended to fully take advantage of.

The lobby was relatively empty, with only a dozen people milling about. Once their number appeared on the screen, positioned above the front desk, they would go up to speak with the receptionist. Getting the hint, James quickly strode toward one of the small, softly glowing machines and, after tapping a couple buttons, got his own number.

Thirteen, huh? I suppose I shouldn't be surprised, what with my luck lately. Still, it shouldn't take too long for my turn. There aren't that many new Awakeners every day, and the older ones who want to get retested to increase their rank go through a different process.

He had managed to convince his grandfather not to wait around for him, as the process of getting tested could take a little while, but only after promising he'd call home as soon as he was done.

The nervousness he had expected to feel never materialized. Instead, James took the time to examine all the other new Awakeners.

There was no rhyme or reason to someone unlocking the System. A middle-aged salaryman stood before the desk, asking questions about the test he was about to receive. A bored-looking teenage girl was accompanied by what he believed to be her older brother, given the resemblance between the two.

Well, there's no old people, but not because they can't Awaken. They usually enjoy the benefits of a stronger body, but they have no desire to take the test and risk their lives fighting monsters.

Luckily, the line moved pretty quickly, as several rooms were dedicated to evaluating new Awakeners. It only took half an hour of waiting before his number was called. James promptly moved to the front desk, where the receptionist, a pretty blonde with a bob cut and bright red nails and lips, smiled professionally.

"Room 4. You'll just have to answer a few questions, show off your powers a bit, and you'll be free to go, ay?" She graced him with a wink, probably reserved for the younger testees. James, too focused on the next part, barely remembered to acknowledge her, grunting a "Thank you."

As he followed the brightly illuminated directions that littered the place, James walked deeper into the building, observing the sterile white walls that were given some life by some art pieces from the local kindergarten. He didn't know whose idea that was, but he could appreciate its efficacy. It made the AA feel less like a nameless government agency and more like an integrated part of society.

Eventually, he reached a warmly colored wooden door with the number 4 stamped in softly glowing ink. Before entering the room, James used his Thakinetic Awareness, curious about what he'd find inside.

Within, two presences glowed to his senses. One, whom he believed to be his examiner, sat toward the back of the room. The other, much fainter and harder to distinguish, stood at the other end; they didn't seem to be doing anything but constantly escaped his perception.

I haven't felt anything like this before. Is it a stealth skill? Or something else?

With a deep breath, James put those thoughts aside. He'd find out soon enough. He pushed the door, walking in on his Awakener test.

"Good morning!" he greeted, his customer service smile coming out unbidden. The biggest presence, which was facing him directly, turned out to be a large old man with a shaved bald head and a full white mustache. Kind eyes regarded him, though James was immediately set on edge by something in his pose.

He sat behind a wooden desk with the same warm tone as the door; it was the only splash of individuality in an otherwise unremarkable room. To the right was a statuesque figure covered with a cloth—the only other thing of note.

Having lived with his grandparents since he was orphaned, James was well acquainted with how the elderly moved and behaved. Unseen aches and joints in poor condition made all their steps and shifts stiff and, at times, painful.

The old man before him didn't show any sign of that as he got up to greet him with an extended hand. He possessed a fluidity that would have been enviable in an Olympic gymnast back before the apocalypse, a sense of hidden strength as he carefully took James's hand, as if barely containing his strength from crushing James.

Most elderly Awakeners stay at home and only use the System enough to live a more comfortable life. That's common knowledge. But there are a few who take to it like fish to water. Forced into stillness by their age, they jump at the chance of finally getting their bodies and lives back. Those rare few are dangerous and should be treated with all due respect.

The life of an Awakener was a dangerous business; to make it as either a very old or very young person, one had to be special.

"Welcome to your first test in the AA," the old man said, his voice calm and soothing. "I'm Marcus Bethany, your examiner, and I'll be conducting this test. If you have truly Awakened, you'll get an official ID and the clearance necessary to operate in the Supernatural Market as more than just a buyer."

This was all rote, but it felt like the newly named Marcus was imparting the most important information in the world. Still, James paid attention. He didn't want to miss anything and fail because of that.

"As I said before, this will be your first test of many. To advance in rank and get access to higher, more dangerous missions or areas, you'll have to come back here and get certified. I'm sure you already know this, but your rank doesn't necessarily depend on your level, though there is some correlation between the two. A person with a Talent not suited for fighting might get a lower rank, even though they are of a higher level than someone who has Warrior or Fire Mage," Marcus continued, explaining basic but fundamental things about his future life.

James wasn't particularly worried about being held back by his Talent. Thakinesis was a weird one, for sure, but it still allowed him to fight off two monsters without any training whatsoever. He might not have the flashy factor of an Elemental Mage, but it still worked well enough, and he was confident he'd be able to grow with it.

"Now, with all the official spiel done, we can get to the interesting bit." Immediately, James refocused. Now was not the time to get lost in his theories.

Marcus walked over to the cloth-covered figure. His steps didn't make a sound despite his massive frame. One large hand reached over and gripped the white cotton, lifting it with a flourish to reveal a human-shaped dummy made of some kind of gel.

James's mind quickly made the connection to the practice targets he had seen before. In one of the few public training videos released by Towers's team, the man went through a golden dummy like a knife through butter.

"This is a slime dummy, made of a material inspired by the old ballistic gel but enhanced with mana. It can hold up to anything a G-rank can throw at it, so it's almost overkill," the old man explained, giving the dummy a tap to show how it jiggled with the force.

"Since this is your first exam, and you're aiming to get an H-rank clearance, you just need to show me something that a normal, baseline human can't do. From your next one forward, the requirements will be steeper."

Nodding to show he understood, James focused on his skills. The more he used them, the better he became at calling upon them. The need to show off and get a good result also aided him as he focused his will.

"Give it a go when you feel ready. A good, solid hit will do. Unless you have something more indirect, like a Poison Handler Talent." Even as he said so, Marcus was already walking back to his seat, having assessed that James would be a more straightforward Awakener.

"I'll be punching it, sir," the boy answered. Meanwhile he focused his mana on his limbs, trying to keep it from dispersing all over his body.

Thakinetic Empowerment was a seemingly simple skill, but the more he used it, the more James realized that a lot of finicky details were hidden in the System's short explanation. In the future, he might be able to focus it on single points in his body, or even on just one attribute, rather than all three physical ones.

Still, he just had to show something beyond standard human ability for the moment. That should be easy enough, since he had already killed two monsters and leveled up, enhancing his body beyond his base level.

With a deep breath, James pushed all distractions aside and centered himself, coming to a stop before the dummy. Flexing his will, he coalesced mana through the medium of his skill into his upper body—the limitations of how much he could do with Empowerment at level 1.

When the feeling of power coursed through him, he wasted no time. His right fist shot forward, his stance clear and steady, thanks to his grandfather's teachings.

The impact against the slime dummy produced a very satisfying *whack*, making the gel jiggle for a couple of seconds, until it finally settled down.

Suddenly feeling exhausted, James turned to his examiner, to find him peering at the dummy with a fascinated look. "Was it okay?" he asked, hating how insecure he sounded.

"Mmh? Oh yes, that was wonderful. I dare say you passed with flying colors. A fascinating approach to a frontline role. Yes, I think I'll keep my eye on you, Mr. Summers." Marcus stamped a paper on his desk and proffered it to James.

"Take that to the reception, and they'll file it and give you your new ID card. I hope to see you here again soon." The smile the old man gave him this time was more genuine yet less reassuring.

A bit confused but quite happy with the result, James took it and quickly left the room after one last "Thank you" to the examiner.

It was only when he was back in the lobby, waiting to get his new ID issued, that he remembered that he had felt another person's presence inside the room before entering.

CHAPTER 5.5 – INTERLUDE

Marcus Bethany

Marcus exhaled as soon as the door shut, running a hand over his meticulously groomed mustache. "So, what do you think?"

Out of nowhere, a feminine voice tinged with interest answered, "It looked like a straightforward enhancement type. Not Warrior or Berserk, as those have a few obvious signs, but something like that. I don't see why you asked for my presence with such urgency."

Chuckles shook the elderly man's frame, sending small tremors through the room. He didn't need to hold back his strength now. "Even if that was true, we aren't exactly in the condition of rejecting anyone here. The guilds will just snap up anyone with even a hint of being special."

Suddenly, a woman materialized in front of his desk. The small, gleeful tightening of her eyes was the only indication of her pride for fooling his senses for so long. She wore a dark uniform with red highlights, the Awakeners Association symbol proudly emblazoned on her chest. Though a black mask covered most of her face, her crimson eyes and delicate features made for a remarkable sight.

"That doesn't mean we have to lower our standards, though. I think we might have to be even stricter, to avoid getting bogged down by useless people," she answered.

Marcus waved away her words, not moved. "The times have changed, and we have to change with them, or get left behind. What few funds we receive get sent to the guilds when we call on them to clean up problems we don't have the resources to solve. If we start being too tight on recruitment, we'll just become a rubber stamp agency."

By the slumping of his interlocutor's shoulders, she knew this reality all too well. "Still," she refocused, pushing the sad situation the AA was in to the side for the moment, "I don't understand what made you call me down here. This James Summers might become something in the future if he dedicates himself to training and finds a good guild to nurture him, but for now, he's just one amongst many. Nothing that would require my attention."

Marcus's mustache twitched up in a grin. "I can see that you still have that same habit of dismissing those who aren't outwardly as impressive as you are, dear Leila. You, of all people, should know that not all things are as they seem."

Unbothered by the reprimand, the woman merely raised an eyebrow, evidently waiting for the real answer.

"If you really must pry all the secrets from a defenseless old man," he finally conceded, ignoring the disbelieving scoff, "I felt something very interesting from that young man. It's not bravado or even a particular level of strength, though I wouldn't be surprised if he already leveled up once. No, it's that Talent of his that I immediately noticed as soon as he walked into the building. I don't know if he's even aware of it, but the moment he stepped foot in the lobby, he already categorized every single person and subconsciously shifted away from the less dangerous ones and toward where one of the hidden guards was. That, coupled with what I felt during his examination, makes me think he must have a very eclectic Talent."

This time, Leila seemed to take his words much more seriously. Marcus knew that for all the walls she put up around herself, his old student cared. She cared for the AA and its destitute future; she cared for him and all the other Awakeners who put in long hours of sweat and blood to prevent their agency from slipping even further.

A young talent like Mr. Summers wouldn't change much in the grand scheme of things, but if I can give her something else to concentrate on, she might be able to relax just a little. And who knows, they might help each other grow. God knows I did when I first started teaching.

"So you think he might have a high-tier Talent and that it's understated enough that the guilds wouldn't challenge us too much if we tried to recruit him," Leila summarized, looking thoughtful now that she was following his logic.

"Indeed. After all, we both know that the moment the evaluation papers touch the front desk, they'll find their way to at least a dozen different guilds," Marcus agreed. He was well used to the way things were, and if, for once, he could use the corruption in the system to their advantage, he would. "I might have avoided mentioning any of those observations in the official papers, which coincidentally might mean that they'd simply approach him as if he were a Warrior type."

His grin looked a bit too devious to be appropriate on his kind old face, but if he couldn't enjoy sticking it to the parasites suckling at his life's work, he might just quit.

"Of course," he continued, "that doesn't mean he won't accept any of their offers, even though they will lowball him. Most kids these days think about nothing but joining up with a guild. It's even the preferred path on those online guides that have become so popular."

"But something you know makes you think he won't join them," Leila finished for him.

Marcus grinned, reaching for a desk drawer and taking out a wad of papers. Given the many red stamps that screamed classified, Leila could easily deduce that it wasn't a simple document.

"This is what I found when I looked up the kid's family history," the old man explained, passing the stack to his student.

The next few minutes were spent in silence as the woman went through the papers with great speed. From the widening of her eyes, she was finally getting where his confidence was coming from.

"But how did you get these so quickly? And what made you want to look for them in the first place?" she finally asked, handing the papers back.

"It's a little habit of mine to run a check on all the candidates who stand out to my eye. And you should know, by now, that I have my ways. Though the AA isn't nearly as well funded and is held in low regard amongst the federal agencies, we still operate as one, and we have access to the internal network of the United States. That, more than anything, is our greatest remaining strength."

Leila mulled over it for a couple of seconds before seemingly shrugging her surprise off. "All right, so we know the kid won't go with just any guild that comes calling. And that he might end up a good asset in the future. That still doesn't explain why you asked *me* to come down here."

"Isn't it obvious? The higher-ups managed to scrounge the funds to build a new team of rookies; they want us to take in the most inexperienced people possible and make them into gems. Mr. Summers fits in perfectly," Marcus explained, his leading tone implying something more was about to be revealed. "Considering how you've been put on leave after that last mission . . . Well, trying your hand at teaching them wouldn't be the worst thing."

When he saw how Leila's expression was closing off and the temperature in the room was rising sharply, the mustached man hurried to continue, "Successfully taking a team of rookies up a few ranks will show the higher-ups that you've matured enough that they should rethink their stance on your path forward. And when they get good enough, even if the guilds eventually snatched them, they would have to pay us much more than if they were just H-ranks."

From the quick cooling of the air, Marcus deduced his reasoning had worked well enough. He didn't show any discomfort, knowing that his student would pounce on any weakness she could sense.

When nothing happened for the next few seconds, she sighed. "All right, I'll give it a try. It sounds like a real pain, but if it truly goes the way you said it will, I guess it'd be worth it."

She then got up, looking pensive but resolute enough that Marcus didn't feel he needed to push more.

With a careless wave, Leila stepped forward. A dark shadow appeared beneath her feet and, in a blink, swallowed her whole, leaving nothing behind.

The old man, however, didn't react at all, perfectly used to his former student's Talent and weird skills. Only after she was gone did he allow himself to sigh in relief.

That girl. All that power and so little patience with anything that doesn't involve fighting. Well, she might finally learn some, dealing with a bunch of brats. If she doesn't kill them all immediately, that is.

Marcus eyed the melted slag cooling on the floor, the sad remains of his second office chair's arms. The front of his wooden desk was warped and blackened, and the floor looked to have suffered under the intense heat.

With a huff, he tapped one of his fingers on the desk, causing the entire room to ripple. In but a second, everything shifted back to what it once was, restored to a pristine state.

I'll have to keep an eye on Leila and Mr. Summers. If what's hinted at in his file is even just half-true, we will see some big waves soon.

CHAPTER SIX

James took the metro back home on autopilot, his mind firmly stuck on the shiny new card sitting in his hands.

Generally, he would have been more careful with something that precious. New York was a relatively safe place compared to the rest of the world, but petty theft still happened regularly. However, everyone should recognize his new treasure for what it was.

The AA ID card had his face printed on it, with a softly glowing H on the top right corner. Though he wasn't a high-ranker, his new status made it clear that he wasn't someone to be messed with.

Most gangs, these days, had reorganized into guilds and operated, at least in part, as legitimate businesses. No one with the strength to take it from him would feel it worth their time.

Still, James clutched at it like a lifeline. Everything had happened quickly, and though he had spent most of the past night thinking and researching, he still found it hard to believe that this was his life now.

Getting off at his usual stop, James briefly looked toward the bridge in the distance, where he had walked just the day before with Sally. Just thinking of her sent a pang to his heart, still raw with emotion. The image of her last look at him, as she lay groaning on the clinic's bed, her eyes desperate with pain and fear—it would stick with him for a long time.

Shaking that thought off, James hurried back home. His grandparents would be waiting for him. He'd already sent a text to tell them he'd passed, but he was sure they'd want to hear him recount the whole experience.

After the talk with his grandparents, James escaped to the beach. As he walked, he took advantage of the overcast skies to have the area to himself.

He contemplated his next moves, trying to give shape to the nebulous thoughts he had come up with the night before.

Becoming stronger is obviously the correct choice. I can't really go back to my previous life now . . . There's nothing for me there. But how to do so is the question.

The most common thing for a new Awakener to do would be to look for a guild. They'd have the resources and teachers necessary to guide him as he started his journey. But James had no intention to go begging for scraps at their door. Not only was he ideologically opposed to how modern guilds operated, but since his Talent wasn't particularly flashy, they wouldn't offer him anything more than the basic recruitment package.

A decent salary, a few training sessions, and a team with whom to go on dungeon raids. It wasn't a bad life, but the strings attached made it unpalatable. He'd be contributing to the rot overtaking the country, and he wouldn't be able to look at his father's pictures if he fell that low.

Considering how poorly they had handled the whole mess with the rat dungeon, James wasn't inclined to be charitable.

That meant either going back to the AA and begging them to take him on, which he wasn't inclined to do, given how low the possibility of them having an open spot would be; or going it alone.

This last option was something he was seriously considering. It was the most dangerous of the three; he'd have no backup during fights. *And I'll have to fight if I want to level up. Skills can take a long time to improve if there's no external stimulus, so I can't just hole up in my room and spam them like I'd do in an RPG.*

Fighting monsters was a dangerous business, however, and he'd have to take as many precautions as possible before proceeding. Finding a low-level dungeon would be a priority so that he could cut his teeth on something manageable before he went after stronger prey. Being a lone wolf would severely hamper his growth, but he didn't see any other possibility at the moment. Maybe one day he'd find others, but for now, he was by himself.

First, I need to get some experience fighting monsters, and if I can find a newborn H-rank dungeon somewhere, I'll be able to get it without immediately risking my life.

He knew of one such place already: the sewers connected to the back alley where he had fought the rat monsters. However, the thought of going back there sent a shiver down his spine and made his stomach churn.

It wasn't that he was scared of what he'd find there. After all, he had managed to kill the rats without even knowing he had Awakened. No, the emotional block he was feeling had a different origin.

I'll have to go back there one day, if only so I don't get stuck mentally. But finding a place that won't unsettle me as much for the first dive is probably better.

"Dungeon" was the commonly used term to describe Mana Sinks. Places where the power would naturally pool and mutate all nonsapient life within. It was a phenomenon that could range from mildly annoying H-rank dungeons—that police officers armed with small-caliber guns could take care of—to dangerous S-rank ones—that had to be immediately evacuated and quarantined, and where the entire might of a nation was necessary to deal with it. Clearing those was often not worth the sacrifice of the best Awakeners.

Fortunately, S-rank dungeons were extremely rare, and only about a dozen were active worldwide. Even better, the higher the rank of the Mana Sink, the more stable it was, meaning fewer monsters would leave it as they got used to the plentiful natural mana that was lacking in the outside world.

If that weren't the case, I'm pretty sure humanity would have been doomed. We only managed to claw back as much of the world as we have because top-tier monsters generally don't leave their territories.

Conversely, that meant it was common for monsters to exit low-level dungeons, causing death and destruction. It made identifying and dealing with them a priority for any surviving nation, and means had been implemented to promptly alert the populace when they were found.

Looking through his phone notifications, James easily found the one he was looking for. He'd have to retake the metro, but if he left immediately, he was pretty sure he'd be able to get back before midafternoon.

ALERT! H-rank Squirrel Dungeon found within a grove in Central Park. All citizens are not to approach it and are to wait for a dedicated Awakener team to clear it. ETA 7h 53m, the message read.

Compared to the higher-ranked dungeons with powerful monsters ready to destroy entire blocks, this specific one was only given a high priority because it sat in the heart of the Big Apple.

The ETA meant that the AA was estimating it'd take almost eight hours for an adequate team to tackle it, which gave him more than enough time to try his hand at it.

If, for any reason, he thought he couldn't actually do it, he'd retreat immediately. He promised himself he'd be careful, as he didn't want to have to be subjected to his grandmother's worried expression more than he needed to.

With a grunt, James pushed off the sand, his path much clearer now. He'd hurry back home, put on his father's old ballistic vest and gloves, and go hunt some squirrels.

He ended up not putting the vest on immediately. Not because he didn't want to be caught by his grandparents—he had told them what he was up to and held strong under their combined questioning. But he didn't want to look weird while walking around the city. James knew most Awakeners wore gaudy and peculiar armor, made with high-ranking monster materials, but he felt uncomfortable at the thought of being stared at.

Therefore, he put his father's vest in his backpack, alongside the lunch his grandma had forcefully shoved on him, and set off, giving one last nod to his stoic grandpa.

It probably would've been easier not to tell them anything, but if I started lying to them now, I'd never stop. This is my life, and it's important they understand it immediately. Also, I don't intend on getting hurt at all this time. Really.

During his first fight with a monster, he had been entirely unprepared, mentally and physically.

Now, however, he was stronger than before. Thanks to the System, he had access to skills and was looking for a fight knowingly. That alone changed everything.

Getting off at 103rd Street, James looked around. Few people seemed to be out and about in this part of the park. Still, even just a few hundred feet away, the usual hubbub resumed, New Yorkers going about their day as if there wasn't a nest of murderous squirrels sitting next to them.

Huffing a laugh at the weirdness of his city, James quickly walked over the Great Hill. He passed the quiet brook with his Thakinetic Awareness activated.

I'm not about to get ambushed again. This time, I'm the hunter.

Soon enough, he got the first sign that the regular Central Park fauna had been replaced with something more dangerous.

A squirrel the size of a cat was resting on a branch high up a tree, guarding the path leading to the center of the hill. It had seen him already, James noticed, but seemed uninterested in attacking him. That would surely change the moment he tried stepping foot into its territory.

He took the time to gear up. Once he put his backpack down, he quickly opened it and took out the vest, gloves, and face mask he had decided to use.

Unfortunately, it made him look like an edgy teenager trying to cosplay as a villain, but the protection afforded wasn't something he could say no to. The face mask, the kind robbers would use, wouldn't defend him from direct hits, but it should allow him to avoid getting scratched up if he had to drop on the ground and roll.

His gloves, also from his father's old gear, were reinforced with titanium, lending his blows a little more *oomph*. James had briefly contemplated taking more weapons, his father's tactical knife being the first thing that came to mind, but he had never been trained in their use, and since he hadn't mastered his skills yet, he preferred using them in ways he was sure would work.

Trying to strengthen his baseball bat with Thakinetic Empowerment would have exhausted him immediately without any result. Therefore, he decided to go with what already worked once before.

James took a deep breath and put his backpack under a bench, hiding it from view. This was an essential step for him, as the results would determine exactly how viable this lonely path forward was.

If he managed to clear the dungeon, it'd be a green light. But he didn't consider this to be realistic, as the boss monster should be beyond his capabilities, and it would mean risking himself in ways he wasn't comfortable with.

He'd consider it a yellow light if he trounced several monsters but was forced to retreat before the boss. It would mean he could go through it, but he'd have to be careful. This was the most likely result.

A red light would mean running away at the first or second encounter. James sincerely hoped this wouldn't happen, as it'd be a death sentence for his career. He'd be forced to rethink his approach and possibly even bend his morals and accept a guild's offer.

Yeah, let's make sure that doesn't happen. I'm gonna show these squirrels who the real boss is.

CHAPTER SEVEN

At the end of the day, there wasn't much else James could do besides charge in. He had no stealth skill, nor was his Talent useful for long-range attacks. Fighting hand to hand was all he was good for currently, and though the monstrous squirrels looked to have wickedly sharp claws at the end of their paws, he was pretty sure they'd still feel it if he kicked them in the head.

The moment he left the safe zone and entered the base of the hill, the sentinel that had been lazily keeping an eye on him went berserk. Its reddish fur glowed—signifying an active skill being used—and it charged down the tree with a screech.

Having steeled his heart, James was still beset by a moment of hesitation at the sight. But with a grunt, he pushed it aside, focusing on the swiftly approaching enemy.

Once the squirrel was halfway down the tree trunk, it jumped off, its claws extended to skewer him in one hit. James called upon his Talent, manifesting his willpower into reality. His limbs flooded with strength, becoming more resilient, stronger, and faster.

He met the squirrel's claws with his fist, his eyes clear and unafraid. If he got defeated by a measly sentinel now, he'd have to give up entirely, which was unacceptable.

Fueled by his resolve, his fist easily overpowered the creature, hitting it in the chest with the power of a strongman. For all its unnatural robustness, it must have felt the hit because it let out a pained whimper as it rolled on the ground, barely able to stand back up.

The dissonance between this fight and his desperate one against the rat was great, and the thought of having grown so much in such a short amount of time made James grin widely.

Stop it. Now isn't the time to get lost in congratulating myself. I need to kill this thing before it can call more of its kind.

With swift strides, James approached the limping creature that was still shaking off the blow. He kicked its head with all his might, earning a wet crunch as its skull was fractured beyond help.

Not wanting it to suffer needlessly, for all that it was an unnatural monster, James quickly stomped down again, ending its life. At the edge of his vision, he saw a blue window pop up, which stated that he had killed a [Mutated Red Squirrel - Runt], which granted him [+5 EXP].

While it wasn't enough to push him to the next level, he could feel that fighting a few more would, so James put it out of his mind. More importantly, he defeated his third monster, earning not even a scratch.

The squirrel was evidently much weaker than the rats, given its status as the runt of the litter, relegated to the outskirts of their little realm.

On the other hand, his first two enemies had been well fed and within the parameters of what an adult [Mutated Sewer Rat] from the *Monster Encyclopedia* should be. It was clear that he couldn't lower his guard simply because he had an easy win.

I need to keep my head in the game. Its screech might not have called anything, but it must have alerted them that something is here.

He gave one last look at the squirrel's body. He had decided beforehand to not stop and collect his victim's mana stone unless he was entirely safe. It would be a pity to get ambushed simply because he had gotten greedy.

As he pushed farther up the forested hill, James quickly located his next opponents. A couple of squirrels, looking quite a bit larger than the runt, were chittering at each other, casually eating nuts.

Having to fight multiple opponents by himself was his greatest problem in solo diving, but it wasn't something he had an answer to. His Talent didn't allow for the taming of a monster, nor for him to call upon elementals to fight for him. He had no team and likely wouldn't for a while. This all meant that his strategizing was done with those limitations in mind. Thus, he set about creating the conditions necessary for his win.

The one advantage he had over the average Awakener with a Warrior Talent, as far as James was aware, was the versatility afforded by Thakinesis. It strengthened him physically, which would likely remain his main mode of attack for a long time. But more than that, it granted him a sense of where all sentient life was, not just the general bloodlust sensing that Warriors unlocked after the second Awakening.

His Thakinetic Awareness was his most significant advantage, and he had spent a long time trying to find a way of using it beyond the obvious. Had he also had a stealth skill, he could have gone for Rogue tactics, but he had all the grace of a bull in a fine china shop.

So he had to think simpler. He had never held a firearm in his life, and using one on his first dungeon dive was a good way to kill himself. Archery required too much time to develop into something useful. That left good old-fashioned rock throwing.

James took advantage of the two squirrels' inability to see him from their positions, and he situated himself so that only foliage stood between them. After grabbing a rock from the ground, he tossed it in his hand a couple of times, willing himself to remember all the hours he spent playing baseball so he could make his grandpa happy.

With his new sixth sense locked in on the position of his victims, James charged his limbs with willpower and took a stance.

His right leg shifted back, his left forward. His torso twisted. Then, in an explosive movement, he unleashed all the stored energy, launching the stone at incredible speed.

It shredded the foliage as if it wasn't even there, hitting the closest squirrel in the chest with a powerful *thump!* and launching it from the tree and into the distance.

The second monster wasn't flabbergasted for long. It screeched angrily at the fate of its companion and jumped toward the projectile's origin.

There, James lay waiting. As soon as he felt it closing in, he started running. That decision paid off when the squirrel squeaked as it was beset by a very determined human.

When James's foot came into contact with the beast, the force folded the squirrel in half before shooting it toward a solid trunk with a painful smash. Not letting it have the time to right itself, he was on top of it, whaling powerful punches until its chest caved in.

Only then did he allow himself to stop. He stood up with a sigh and walked to the flickering presence of the beast he had hit with the stone.

It glared hatefully, red fur matted with blood and claws weakly trying to reach him, to rip into his flesh and leave a sign. James didn't allow it, using his willpower to empower his limbs again and crush it once and for all.

Though he wanted to immediately push forward, one look at his status—he only had 3 MP left—told James that he needed to take a moment to recover. So he grabbed the two mangled corpses, grunting in disgust at the blood on his gloves. As he quickly retraced his steps, he remembered to also pick up the runt.

I'm not about to leave any mana stone here for others to loot. No such thing as free money.

The process of dressing a carcass was a difficult and tedious one, especially since James had no experience with it. He'd have to get used to it soon enough, though, so he didn't complain beyond grumbling at how mangled the bodies were.

Considering how he was the one to leave them in such a state, he had no one else to blame.

In the end, little of the bodies could be salvaged, though James still wrapped them up in gauze and put them next to his rucksack. He could sell them. The mana stones, on the other hand, were intact. The size of the first one was quite lacking due to the squirrel's runt nature. The other two, however, were bigger and should fetch more money than he had ever made in a single day. Mana stones, after all, were always in high demand. They powered the protections of public and private buildings alike, as well as artifacts, which were becoming a common sight even in normal households.

I could stop here. I should stop here. I achieved all my goals. I'm now certain that, with the proper precautions, I can run dungeons by myself. I've proven that monsters don't scare me. If I go back in, I could get seriously injured.

The problem was that James wanted to not only prove that his Talent and mettle were sufficient, but deep within, he held a yearning to become stronger. And the three squirrels he killed were insufficient to get him even to level 3.

"Just one more should be enough. I'll deal with one, and if I find more, I'll ignore them and run away." Even as he was saying it, James knew it was horseshit. The tremor of fear and hesitation in his limbs had been replaced with one of excitement. Fighting the squirrels felt good, and he couldn't deny it.

After being stuck in a limbo and experiencing a traumatic night, plus losing contact with his crush who possibly hated him, James found something he was apparently good at.

With a huff, he dropped the three mana stones in his backpack, carefully hid it again, and marched back into the thicket.

It took only a couple of minutes to find another squirrel, this time a bigger, meaner variant, whose muscle made it resemble a pit bull more than any rodent.

It was also more intelligent than its companions. It sniffed the air curiously before homing in on his presence. Where the previous ones had screeched, this one roared. It fell on all fours and charged at where James was hiding behind a rock, its fur taking on an unnatural color.

Not wanting to be open to attacks should his throw fail, James lightly tossed the rock he had picked up. Then he crouched down, his muscles coiled for an explosive strike.

When the squirrel jumped over the rock, claws extended and fur glowing a blood red, James pounced, his gloved fist burying into the beast's stomach, sending it flying away.

He repeated his earlier tactics and ran to it, not wanting to allow it any respite. This time, however, the squirrel wasn't half-dead, but rather it righted itself swiftly.

With another bloodthirsty sound, it launched forward, paws digging deep into the soft loam. When it got to James, they clashed, willpower-enhanced fists against red-glowing claws.

Ignoring the damage he was taking, he focused on the beast, his mind locked in on crushing it once and for all.

He stopped only when his fist met the ground, having carved through the thing. What had once been a ferocious beast that met his blows was now a gory mash of blood and flesh on the grass.

James was horrified. Then vomit rose up his throat, and he was forced to hunch over, spewing his stomach's contents over his dead opponent.

He took a moment to breathe, surprised at just how much he was affected by the fight. The ease with which he'd dealt with the previous squirrels had fooled him, he realized. Real fights were messy affairs, and he'd have to get used to it soon.

He looked at his vest, where deep furrows had damaged the reinforced Kevlar, and at the three bloody scratches on his arms. Luckily, they seemed shallow enough, but losing himself like that wasn't a repeatable tactic.

Sitting on the moss beside the mess, he glanced to the side, where a softly glowing notification told him he finally reached level 3.

CHAPTER EIGHT

I t was common knowledge on the Internet that many aspiring Awakeners, even those with promising Talents, were felled inside a dungeon because they underestimated it.

Increasing one's stats without anyone to serve as a lookout while in a hostile environment was, it turned out, a perfectly good way to kick the bucket.

Still, as James looked at his status window, the pull of a quick jump in strength was simply too great. He knew he should retreat and be content with what he achieved so far, but with how easy it was to deal with the squirrels, James thought he had a real chance at clearing the dungeon.

Since it was a newly established H-rank one, there shouldn't be too many monsters, and the boss should still be well within his capabilities.

Had it been an older dungeon, he wouldn't have dared his luck, but things seemed to be working well for him.

Thus, he decided to assign his free points, since even he wasn't foolhardy enough to believe he could take the boss with level 2 stats.

STATUS WINDOW	
Name	James Summers
Age	19
Awakening	1st
Talent	Thakinesis
Title	
Level	3
MP	12/15
STR	7
VIT	5
AGI	6
SEN	6
MND	7
STAT POINTS	0

Again, the weird sensation of muscle and mind expanding overtook him, leaving him defenseless to the outside world. In a stroke of luck, no monster approached him for the few seconds he was busy writhing and panting on the ground.

Thus, James completed the change, and he stood up with a satisfied grin. He opened and closed his hands, feeling new strength fill them.

This is such a heady feeling. It's no wonder so many people throw themselves at danger if these are the rewards.

That wasn't even touching on the massive wealth that could be accrued by dungeon diving. An H-rank one, like the one he was in currently, wasn't worth the time for experienced Awakeners, but it'd still rack in more than two months' pay in his last job.

Considering that a G-rank Awakener could clear it in an hour, the trade-off was simply amazing.

The reason the squirrels hadn't been dealt with already, despite the money that could be made, was that better opportunities were available elsewhere.

In the cities, mana struggled to concentrate in significant amounts, resulting in weaker dungeons than what could be found outside them.

In the American wilderness, where you could go for hours by car without meeting anyone, Mana Sinks grew to massive size, resulting in a C- or B-rank. Professional Awakeners loved to raid those.

Coming back to reality, James put away all his dreams about taking part in those expeditions, aware that he'd need to at least complete his second Awakening—possibly even reaching the third—before he could be considered for any such team, even in a support role.

I could be a good scout, with Thakinetic Awareness allowing me to feel any monster around. Speaking of . . .

Two squirrels, though luckily not as large as the one he had just dealt with, were rapidly approaching his position. They must have been drawn in by the sounds of fighting.

Taking up his stance, James decided to face the monsters head-on, without any trick this time. The power-up might be making him more reckless, he realized, but he needed to see how much he could push himself in a straight fight, and enemies as weak as these were not going to be easy to find in the future.

Twin screeches heralded their arrival, and the squirrels wasted no time jumping at him, claws drawn and murderous looks promising death.

Though he hadn't raised his agility, which he promised himself to do next, James was able to easily dodge the first one, bending low beneath its jump. Its glowing claws barely touched his hair before he set his left foot forward, using his momentum to empower a heavy punch.

Filled with his will, the blow sent the second squirrel flying, its ribcage cracking.

With one momentarily dealt with, James rolled to the side, avoiding a charge from the first squirrel by a hairbreadth. It quickly righted itself as it screeched out a challenge. This time, it jumped between rocks and trees, making its trajectory more confusing to follow.

Surprised by the show of intelligence by an otherwise dumb creature, James couldn't entirely avoid its next attack. A line of searing pain scored his arm, next to the scratches from his previous opponent.

He hissed but didn't allow himself to get distracted. Thanks to that, he was able to track the beast's movements using his Awareness skill. Therefore, he was ready when it repeated its maneuver, jumping in a zigzag.

A devastating punch to the head sent it rolling away, and James quickly followed that with even more blows, ending its life. After wiping away a few droplets of blood that splattered his mask, he rose from his crouch and walked over to where he could feel the last squirrel.

It was in bad shape. The hit to the ribcage damaged its internal organs that it could only lay there, breathing laboriously. James ended its suffering with an empowered stomp, crushing its throat. That over, he sighed, disgusted at how quickly he had gotten used to the gory mess.

A quick sweep with Thakinetic Awareness revealed that one more squirrel was approaching. It was similar in size to the biggest one he had encountered so far.

James grabbed the still-warm corpse and threw it in the direction the beast was pouncing from. It was forced to roll away, its charge interrupted.

Unfortunately for it, no second chances were available.

Dealing with a dozen murderous squirrels took more time than he would have liked, but it brought him all the way to the brink of level 5.

After assigning his two stat points to agility and strength once he was sure the coast was clear, James felt more prepared to deal with what was waiting for him in the center of the grove.

I know that a boss isn't the same as the ones I've been fighting so far. They're the strongest and most influenced by the mana, which makes them smarter too. Taking it on at level 4 might be too much, but this dungeon is extremely new, which makes me think it shouldn't have had the time to grow enough. I'll just take a peek.

First, he removed the corpses, gathering them all behind the bench where he had hid his backpack. He drank some water, then checked on the few wounds he had. Thanks to his first aid skills, they weren't bleeding anymore, so he reentered the dungeon.

Nothing stopped his path this time, signifying that he must have dealt with all the dungeon's denizens but one.

Fifteen monsters is at the lowest point of the scale. Really, even calling this a dungeon is a bit of a stretch. But I guess it works in my favor. Had it been more populated and with stronger creatures, I wouldn't have made it this far.

The top of the hill was crowned by one large oak tree. Its thick trunk was decorated with slashes, as if attempting to warn interlopers of the resident's might.

In its branches, James spied his quarry. The boss was a fair bit bigger than even the muscular squirrels he had fought, telling him that even without it using skills—and he doubted he'd be so lucky—it would be much harder to defeat.

His biggest problem was that he had trouble inflicting lethal damage quickly. His strength and skill usage were better than any of these monsters, but he needed to spend a lot of time ending each one.

Even when James empowered his punches and used reinforced gloves, he only broke bone and bruised flesh. He might end the fight on the spot if he got a good hit in, but it was more a matter of luck than skill.

Still, the boss rested within its tree in a lax manner, as if unaware of what was going on in its domain. It made James think it wasn't as bright as he had feared.

The whole dungeon was turning out easier than expected, and though he didn't want to put the cart before the horse, he believed he might have a good shot at clearing it entirely on his first try.

It's literally the weakest dungeon possible, but not many people get to say they cleared one by themselves as an H-rank, even a newly born one. Without the support of a guild.

James grabbed another rock from the ground and considered it. He might have a shot if he managed to get a good hit in before the thing became aware of him.

It was still entirely possible that he would miss and then have to contend with a large-dog-sized murder squirrel that was intent on tearing him to ribbons. His speed had increased, but he didn't think he'd be able to run away from it.

He should give up. Let the rock fall from his hands, go back to his loot, and relish in having accomplished the goal he had set for himself. Be safe.

Instead, his hand rose up unbidden; he started pumping mana to his limbs with his skill. His choice was made without even a hint of hesitation.

My goal is too big to give up now. I can't possibly think of tackling the corruption of the guild system if I give up before a newborn H-rank dungeon.

Thanks to his latest level, the strength he could exert had increased again, and the point in agility would serve him well in aiming his shot.

With his Awareness locked in on the boss and his muscles coiled tight, James set his mind to the task, the resoluteness of his decision flooding his limbs with additional energy.

His arm shot forward like a rocket, inhuman strength flinging the rock at a speed he would have never been capable of even just a couple of days before.

It flew true, striking the boss in its ribs and sending it tumbling down the tree. It grunted in surprise and pain.

James used the momentum to run to it; he didn't want to give it time to reorient itself. Forcing even more of his dwindling mana reserves into his limbs, he quickly reached it as it was rolling on the ground, and mercilessly attacked.

This squirrel, however, was evidently much more resilient than its subordinates, for it withstood a kick that would have killed any of them. It clutched at

James's foot with a deadly grip, its glowing claws tearing into the shin guards and reaching the flesh beneath.

He screamed in pain and smashed his foot against the trunk of a nearby tree, aiming to dislodge the monster.

It took the blow; it stuck to his leg like glue. Even as James repeatedly smashed it against the hard trunk, it tore into his leg, mangling it with desperation fueled by the knowledge it was about to die anyway.

James growled, pain making his thinking hazy but somehow sharpening his focus. Every ounce of him was focused on getting the monster off his leg, so much so that he didn't even notice when Thakinetic Empowerment stopped working on all his limbs. Instead, the skill focused on the injured one, strengthening it well beyond what it used to be.

The image of Sally's foot being bit off was a powerful motivator, and James fought desperately to prevent the same fate befalling him.

Finally, with one last yell, he landed a blow to the squirrel's head, which made its grip go slack.

James wasted no time freeing himself and ending the boss's life. His fist blew through the monster's already dented skull, splattering bits everywhere.

Once it was over, James lay down beside it, softly weeping for his ruined leg.

"Well, I can't say I expected you to get here. Good thing I stuck around, eh?" came a feminine voice from above.

CHAPTER NINE

Watching his flesh regrow in real time was a trippy sight. It fascinated and disgusted James.

Well, considering I'm caked in the blood and offal of almost twenty monsters, I'm feeling a bit desensitized right now.

His mysterious savior had given him a potion that looked as costly as elixirs, which could do anything from curing chronic conditions to regrowing limbs with higher dosages and adequate supply—just like what Sally was receiving. Had he managed to get himself to a hospital before dying of blood loss, it would have cost him twice the earnings he'd make by selling all the loot from this harebrained expedition.

Miraculously, his leg was still attached, which meant one dose would be enough to put him back on his feet, but the process was uncomfortable and painful. Still, James kept his mouth shut, even though he really wanted to scream.

He already made a terrible first impression on what was undoubtedly a professional hunter. He didn't want to add being a crybaby to that.

"It should only take a couple of minutes to finish working. I've seen this kind of elixir put people back in the fight when they've been turned inside out," the red-eyed woman, dressed in black attire with a face mask, tried to reassure him. It wasn't particularly effective, mainly because James was busy gritting his teeth.

When the process finally ended, his leg an angry pink—he was reassured it would fade within the next hour or so—he managed to gather his wits enough to thank her. "I don't know what I would have done without your help. Thank you, you saved me."

If there was one thing his grandfather had taught him, it was that when you received help, you needed to make it clear that you understood your debt and would try to repay it immediately. "Long-term debt can cripple a person's mind, James. It can turn them into a shell of themselves as they work to the bone to repay it. Be it a favor or money, if you can't help but take them, do your best not to let it hang on you for too long." Larry Summers's words echoed in his mind, and James rapidly thought about what he could offer the woman.

"You can take the loot from the dungeon and the credit for clearing it. The prize, alongside the rest, should be worth most of the elixir's cost. If you tell me how much is left, I'll cover it as soon as possible," he said as he gingerly pushed himself up.

It was his fault he had ended up in this situation, so he wouldn't do his savior the disservice of thinking this was all an elaborate entrapment scheme. It was an unfortunately common tactic for the sleazier guilds to offer new Awakeners loans of gear and provision, only to use that debt to force them to join.

The woman seemed to quickly realize where his mind went because she waved her hands rapidly, as if to ward off any suspicion. "I'm not doing this because I wanted you to repay me. You could say it's my fault even, for letting it go this far. I saw you go through the entire dungeon, but I should have stepped in before the boss."

So, she has been observing me all along. Is she a guild recruiter, then? This is actually making me more suspicious.

When his expression closed off, the woman huffed, taking out an easily recognizable badge from the AA. It read, "Leila Walker, B-rank Agent."

With a gulp, James bowed his head, apologizing once again. "I'm sorry, ma'am. I didn't mean to imply you were doing anything suspicious."

A huff of frustration made him raise his head, and he saw the high-level Awakener ruffle her hair. "I'm not trying to put you on edge, kid. I just wanted to show you I'm not one of those guild bastards."

At that, James relaxed a bit. His savior was poor at making herself understood, but he wouldn't hold it against her. Still, even if she was trying to pass off giving him an elixir like that, he couldn't accept it. His morals wouldn't allow it. "At least take the boss monster's core and body. I wouldn't be able to go on knowing that I owe you that much."

Leila gave him the stink eye for a moment, before conceding with a defeated sigh. "All right, kid. If that makes you feel better, I'll take the boss. We can call it even then, right?"

James nodded quickly, happy not to have put himself in debt with a powerful figure. Really, considering that he was now hale and healthy and had crossed level 5 to reach even level 6, the whole expedition could be counted as a win. *Well, if it wasn't for her, I would need to drag myself out of here, hoping I didn't die of blood loss first. And then I'd be in debt with the hospital. Probably not a flawless run, eh?*

Once James tested his newly healed leg and saw that it had no problem holding his weight, he turned to face the AA-affiliated ranker. "Could I ask why you were observing me, then? Were you just in the area, or did I steal your dungeon?"

He had checked the AA site just before entering. No one had claimed the squirrel dungeon, so it was left to the assigned team, who would have arrived in about five hours. But with great power, people became a bit quirky. It wouldn't be strange if the woman had simply not cared to register if she wanted the dungeon for herself.

Luckily, the answer was negative: "No, no. I don't care one whit about this place. I'm here because I recognized you from your test at the AA while walking around. Since I should have approached you in a couple of days anyway, I decided to deal with that immediately."

It was a relief for James to know that he hadn't inadvertently stolen her dungeon, especially since he wouldn't have any recourse, because *he* hadn't requested it for himself either. *Well, they wouldn't have accepted the request. A newly Awakened H-rank taking on a dungeon in Central Park all by himself? No way.*

The last part of her statement, however, made him still. "What do you mean you would have approached me anyway? And why would a high-ranking hunter like you remember me?"

James was skirting a dangerous territory here, as more than one person online warned that the more powerful the Awakener, the less they enjoyed explaining themselves to weaker people. Still, this Leila Walker had been nothing if not polite and approachable, so he dared to ask.

"Your examination went pretty well. So well, in fact, that Marcus recommended you for a new team we're building from the ground up. I meant to come to your house in a couple of days, after you had the time to acclimate to being an Awakener, but since I saw you here, I thought it'd be easier to just get it over with now," she answered easily, shocking him even more.

She then continued, not giving him the time to elaborate, "I have your email on file, so I'll send you the contract to review soon. You have four days to think about it, since the official offer starts in forty-eight hours. I'll attach my number so you can ask me questions at any time. I might not respond immediately, but I'll do my best."

Stunned by all the information being dumped on him, James seized on one thing. "What do you mean a new team?"

Though her mouth was covered, her crinkled eyes conveyed her smile. "We're trying something new. Rather than taking in established hunters, we want to build fresh ones from the ground up. That way, you'll be less likely to be immediately poached."

"Do you even have the money for that?" As soon as he said it, James realized it was a very rude thing to say to an AA agent, but it was the truth. Nurturing new Awakeners into something useful was expensive, and those resources generally went into other, more helpful programs with immediate results.

Luckily, she didn't take offense, instead seeming amused at his concern. "Well, normally, you'd be correct, but my bosses seemingly managed to get a small budget exactly for this kind of thing, arguing that in the long term it would save us money. So it's pretty important that you're committed if you accept."

That said, she brushed herself off, even though not a speck of dirt had touched her. "Well, I really need to go. Don't worry, I'll take care of things on my end so that you can claim the reward for clearing this dungeon without flagging any attention."

Before he could answer, thank her, or defend himself, the woman disappeared before his eyes. One moment, she was there, and the next, suddenly not.

"Wait, the boss . . ." James trailed off, noticing that even the carcass was gone without him seeing anything. Even when he activated Thakinetic Awareness to sweep his surroundings, nothing pinged. She had vanished without a trace.

Since he had no intention of taking all the squirrel corpses back home, James gathered them all up in one large garbage bag and, helped by his newly gained strength, easily hauled them to the closest appropriate shop.

I kinda want to put all four points in strength; it'd be even more of a breeze, then. But I need to seriously think about what I'll do in the future before I do that, and there's no pressing need that requires me to get stronger immediately.

The man at the shop, just off the 104th, sniffed imperiously at his bedraggled appearance, but those dealing with Awakeners returning from dungeon runs rarely expected clean clothes and pleasant smells, so he didn't say anything.

The price he offered was a bit less than James would have gotten had he removed all the mana stones and dressed the corpses himself, but he couldn't be bothered at the moment. It was still more than he had ever made in a single setting, and the promise of getting the reward for clearing the dungeon also put him in a good enough mood that he didn't waste time haggling.

Dragging himself back home was a weird experience, as his body was completely fine, helped by the expensive elixir and his higher stats, but mentally, James was done for the day.

He could easily keep going physically. Hell, he could go on a run with how energetic he felt. But the psychological toll of having to fight for his life was significant, and though he had been saved from any consequence by the AA agent, it still scared him shitless.

When he finally got home, his grandparents only had to take one look at him to realize he had gone through the wringer, but luckily, they decided to let him clean himself and have a nap before they started with the interrogation.

As he was falling asleep, he gave one last look at his status, smiling in satisfaction at what he had accomplished.

STATUS WINDOW	
Name	James Summers
Age	19
Awakening	1st
Talent	Thakinesis
Title	
Level	6
MP	29/30
STR	8

VIT	5
AGI	7
SEN	6
MND	7
STAT POINTS	4

SKILLS	LEVEL	DESCRIPTION
Thakinetic Empowerment	2	(Active): Utilize your Willpower to temporarily raise STR - VIT - AGI.
Thakinetic Awareness	1	(Active/Passive): Expand your SEN to feel others' wills.
Thakinetic Resistance	1	(Active/Passive): Empower your MND to defend yourself against foreign influences.

CHAPTER TEN

James pushed himself out of bed, still feeling groggy, when he saw the morning sun streaming through the window. He was dumbfounded. His quick nap had unexpectedly turned into a night's sleep.

He had been exhausted when he got back, but he hadn't expected to sleep for so long, considering how he had returned home before dinnertime.

I must have looked like a mess since they didn't wake me up. I know they must be dying to ask questions.

After a quick stop to the bathroom to freshen up, James finally walked downstairs, where he could feel his grandparents waiting in the living room trying to go through the motions of their morning routine. Knowing them, James wouldn't be surprised to find that they had been up for hours, debating what to ask him. Despite that, their nervous energy filled the room.

The moment he set foot off the stairs, his grandfather stood up, only to be stopped by Rosa. "Oh, Larry, he's not going anywhere. Let him eat something; he must be starving since he didn't have dinner yesterday."

James's stomach rumbled in agreement, and he grinned embarrassedly, quickly shuffling to the table that was still laden with scrambled eggs, fresh bread—one of his grandfather's fixations, as he said the classic American sandwich bread was an abomination—fruit, and, thankfully, coffee.

Drinking from his mug with great gulps, James finally started feeling human again. He knew that coffee couldn't have possibly already worked its magic, but he was content with his placebo-induced wakefulness.

Once he was done scarfing down double of what he usually would have eaten, James quickly washed the dishes under his grandparents' gaze, all too aware that he would need to explain himself soon.

Technically, I didn't do anything wrong. They know I'm an Awakener, and it's just common sense to expect one to go on dungeon runs. But I wasn't very forthcoming and then came back all dirty with crusted blood and torn clothes . . .

With his task finally done, he couldn't delay anymore, so he took his place on his favorite couch, meeting his grandfather's eyes for the first time that morning.

Surprisingly, he found very little anger or disappointment. Instead, worry and sadness were the main emotions, mixed in with something else, a bittersweet twist to his lips that he couldn't exactly place.

"As you might imagine, I went to a dungeon and fought the monsters inside," James began, deciding to cut to the chase.

"I was actually successful at clearing it," he added, and he got surprised looks. Even clearing just an H-rank dungeon was a great accomplishment for a new Awakener, especially one who just got his powers less than a week before.

James continued, "It was the squirrel dungeon in Central Park, so the very weakest one available. I managed to defeat the boss by myself, and then I was helped by an AA agent, who gave me a potion to recover from the cuts it inflicted."

This was the bit he enjoyed the least. He wasn't about to lie to his family, especially because they knew him too well. Still, if he went into detail about the extent of his injuries, and more importantly, how much the elixir he had been given was worth, he'd never hear the end of it.

"I realize that it was reckless of me," he said, gaining a scoff of disbelief from Larry, who then gestured for him to continue with an errant hand wave. "I know. I took many precautions and still went in for the boss because I got overconfident. It would have sucked to go to the hospital because of that, so I'm very grateful to Miss Walker for her help."

"And what did she want in return?" Larry asked, homing in on the crux of the matter.

"She followed me in because she recognized me from the AA test I took the other day, and she's been assigned the leadership of a new team of rookies they're forming, which she wants me to join," James explained, pulling out his phone to check his email.

As expected, one leilawalker@aa.gov had sent him a message with a document attached. Inside the file was a contract a dozen pages long, and from a quick skim, it was more or less what he expected it to be.

He showed them the contract was real, and when his grandmother, who'd been silent so far, extended her hand, he passed her his phone. James settled back, waiting for their judgment.

"What did you have to give her in exchange for the potion she used on you? Those things are mighty expensive," his grandfather asked, returning to the topic he felt the most strongly about.

James sighed, having known it would be a point of contention. "I gave her the boss monster and its mana stone in repayment. She didn't want anything at first, but I insisted, not wanting there to be a debt between us, just like you taught me."

A hint of a proud smile flickered across Larry's face. It might have been an illusion with how quickly it passed, but James knew the old man well enough to realize it was real.

"This is a generous contract, dear," Rosa finally interjected, handing the phone back. "If you want to consider it more seriously, though, we should have someone look at it." She gave Larry a look. He stood up with a grunt, then walked over the landline to grab the black agenda where they kept all their numbers.

"Thomas should be perfect for this," he commented, finger skimming the pages until it stopped over a name.

"Wait, I still haven't even thought about this! I need time before committing to such a huge decision," James complained, not liking how quickly things were moving. He wasn't necessarily against it, but his main concerns with working for the AA were the lack of funding and their overall submissive attitude to the guilds. Still, if the first problem was resolved, at least in the specific instance of his future team, James might seriously look at it. That didn't mean he wanted to choose now!

"Yes, dear. No one is making you do anything. But it's important to know whether it's a legitimate offer. Only then can you truly start thinking about it," his grandmother explained calmly.

"No use wasting time if this thing is a trap or scam of some kind," her husband agreed, punching in the numbers.

Before the call could go through, a series of strong knocks at the front door stole their attention. Considering how it was Saturday morning, and they weren't expecting anyone, this was a surprise.

Extending his Awareness, James found two presences, much stronger and more noticeable than the average person.

Immediately, this put him on high alert. "Two Awakeners. Do you have any idea who they might be?" he asked, even though he already had a suspicion.

"Absolutely not," Larry replied, putting the phone down for the time being. He made to go for the back, where his firearms were stashed, but James stopped him.

"I think they might be guild recruiters. I've read many times that the AA leaks like a sieve, so they might have already gotten access to my data," he explained. Greeting two guild members with a gun wasn't the best idea. While firearms were still useful up to C-rank, especially high-caliber ones, starting a confrontation like that was an excellent way to make an enemy they couldn't afford.

One of the reasons James hated the guild system so much was that they basically operated like gangs or mafia families, with grudges and acts of revenge they constantly enacted on each other.

"Let's see what they want first. We might be able to send them away without resorting to that," he added when seeing that the old man wasn't convinced.

Larry sighed, acquiescing to his grandson's request.

When James finally opened the door, it was to find two well-dressed men in expensive-looking suits, with what looked like gold Rolexes on their wrists.

Jesus. This is such low-level manipulation. Who do they think I am, some bumpkin ready to throw away my rights simply for some money?

Still, he kept a friendly smile thanks to his customer service training. "Hello, how may I help you, gentlemen?"

The taller of the two, a blond man with a well-groomed full beard and bright blue eyes, extended a hand holding a paper card. On it was the golden emblem of the Golden Sun Guild, one of the top ten such organizations in New York City.

"My name is Bradley Esposito, and this is my colleague, Jeremy Truss. We come from the Golden Sun Guild because we have heard tales of your Talent, Mr. Summers," he said. The man gestured to his shorter companion, a hook-nosed and stoic man who merely inclined his head.

"We don't want to take too much of your time, as you might be busy preparing to run another dungeon," Bradley added, immediately revealing that they knew everything that was on his file at the AA. "We're here simply because we want to offer you a very generous entrance package if you accept entering Golden Sun. This isn't a common offer, as we would place you in one of our subsidiaries to nurture you into a high-ranker worthy of standing with us."

Bradley flashed a professional smile, like a devil bartering a poor man's soul. Even had James not been ideologically and personally against joining a guild, the sheer smarminess Bradley exuded would have turned him against it.

"A copy of our standard contract, which includes the bonus package, should be arriving shortly, both to your email and that of your grandparents. You do well in valuing their wisdom so much, Mr. Summers. Grandparents are always missed greatly when they are no longer there," the blond finished with a colder tone. It wasn't enough to be threatening, but James wasn't inclined to be charitable, considering that Bradley explicitly referenced things he shouldn't have access to and had come to his house uninvited.

Before he could respond, however, the other man motioned to his watch, showing Esposito the time. The blond grimaced before turning to James and giving a very shallow nod. "I'm sorry to say that we have to cut this short. I would've liked to speak with you more and tell you all about the wonderful things you'll have access to in Golden Sun, from fantastic trainers to powerful equipment and access to even better dungeons, but we have to run."

The conversation ended without James getting a word in as the two Awakeners were enveloped in a shiny gold light. With a wave, they shot up into the sky, their speed so fast that James immediately lost track of their ascent.

The whole thing couldn't have lasted longer than a minute, but from the sweat collecting on his back, James could have sworn it was much longer.

So the carrot is the benefits, the money, and the image of wealth and power they displayed. The stick was showing me that they knew exactly who I am and who my family is, where we live, and a vague reference to their possible deaths. Fucking guild bastards. Golden Sun's subsidiaries are the Eclipse and the Radiant Guilds . . . Yeah, no.

It took James a couple of minutes to calm his anger. Before, he'd kept himself in check because he knew anything he tried would be useless against the Awakeners who had to be C-rank. Now, he wouldn't be surprised if smoke were billowing out of his ears. He stomped back in, closing the door with more force than strictly necessary.

"Well?" asked his grandmother, who was pale faced and clutching at the armrest.

James turned to his grandfather, motioning toward the phone.

"Let's make that call."

CHAPTER ELEVEN

His second time at the AA building, James knew what to expect. He was still nervous, as today was the day he'd meet the team he would go on dungeon dives with, but it was a less pervasive emotion. There was no chance he'd be rejected and thus return to his dreary days as a retail worker.

He'd taken the leap to sign the contract with the federal agency, initially motivated by spite and a desire for protection that he couldn't give his family. Once he cooled off and had a long chat with his grandparents' lawyer friend, he realized that the conditions the AA offered were even better than Miss Walker had initially hinted at.

From his bit of snooping into online forums, it seemed something hush-hush was happening at the AA—it was common knowledge within the guilds—but no one seemed to know exactly what.

Some believed that the AA received an order to finally let go of the last dregs of autonomy they had, thus releasing their elite teams from their contracts, but that seemed by far the most fringe theory.

Others understood that rather than collapsing, the AA was preparing to fight on some level. Discussion still abounded on whether it was the agency's death throes or a new resurgence.

Thomas Abramowitz, his grandparents' lawyer, had seen something promising within the lines of James's contract. Indeed, Thomas believed that the AA might have gotten the funding to do much more than just establish a team of rookies in New York. The contract was standardized and generous enough—especially for a notoriously penny-pinching organization—that it had to be a nationwide effort.

Well, whether it's truly the start of a new phase for the AA or not, I still appreciate all the resources they're putting into this. Once I've grown enough to stand on my feet, I'll see what to make of it.

The reception at the AA was less crowded than the last time he had been here, probably because it was a Tuesday morning. Still, he was quickly directed toward the fifteenth floor, where the orientation would take place.

In the elevator, he was joined by a pretty redheaded girl with Eastern European features, her hair kept in a loose bun. James spied heavy bags under her eyes despite her makeup. She looked close to his age, and given that her presence positively blazed to his Thakinetic Awareness, she seemed to be an Awakener too.

"Which floor?" James asked since he was by the buttons.

She glanced at the panel, where only one number was lit up. "I'm good. I need to get off at the fifteenth too."

A suspicion quickly formed that she'd be one of his new teammates. Still, he kept his mouth shut, having been warned not to speak of it to anyone beyond his immediate family, on pain of contractual penalties.

From the contemplative looks she threw at him, she might have the same idea.

Soon enough, they both got off the elevator and stepped into a sterile corridor. On the wall, there was a glowing sign that read ROOKIE TEAM MEETING, ROOM 5 with an arrow pointing the way.

James became certain of his suspicion when they both started walking in that direction, which was further confirmed when the redhead finally opened her mouth.

"So, it looks like we'll be on the same team, huh?"

"It seems so. Signed up a couple of days ago. I'm James Summers, by the way. Pleasure to meet you," he said, extending a hand while keeping his eyes firmly on hers.

First impressions were not the end-all and be-all, but overcoming a bad one was complex and lengthy. Better to just start off on a good foot.

She smiled, revealing pearly white teeth, and took his hand in a firm grip. "Maria Olegova, the pleasure is all mine."

They soon reached room 5. James looked at Maria, who shrugged, so he tried the door. The handle twisted under his hand, and he opened the door for Maria before following her in. Three people sat waiting on a comfortable-looking sofa. With no sign of Miss Walker, James went to greet his new teammates, who stood up.

The closest to him, and tallest person in the room by far, was a young Black man called Daniel Smith. His voice was smooth and calm, and he had kind eyes. James noticed a scar below his right eye from what looked like a knife cut.

Next, standing at least three inches shorter than James, was another boy, this time very pale and with curly, messy hair. Ezekiel Bogdanoff was evidently very excited to be here as he almost vibrated. His sharp features, coupled with the mole above his lips, gave him a noble look.

The last person, the shortest but also the oldest at twenty-three, was an Italian American girl named Lauren Digiovanni. She had a strong Brooklyn accent, a loud voice, and was quite busty. For all that, her presence was the brightest to his senses, and James made a note not to underestimate her.

From what he understood, his Thakinetic Awareness didn't necessarily pick up on a person's power but rather the strength of their will. That didn't necessarily translate into a danger rating, but it was still useful information.

Once everyone had greeted each other and they all took a spot on the sofas, the lights in the room dimmed as shadows started converging to the small stage set in front of the projector. The darkness churned and they all watched in awe and wariness, until it finally coalesced into a familiar figure.

Miss Walker, the high-rank Awakener who had saved James after his foolhardy dungeon run, stepped through the shadows, dispersing them with an errant wave of the hand.

The lights immediately returned to normal, though they all remained silent, waiting with bated breath for the woman to speak.

"Well, at least you have some manners," she began expressionlessly, thanks to the face mask and armor she wore. "As you all can imagine, you're here because you decided to take part in the new AA program, the Dawn Initiative!"

Seeing that she had their full attention, Miss Walker continued, "I've been authorized to inform you that you aren't the only team we are building, as the higher-ups took a liking to the idea of taking entirely fresh rookies and turning them into rankers. They pulled some strings, threatened some people, begged others, and we've finally received enough funding to do something more than scrape by."

The tension in the room suddenly rose as the woman twitched, somehow sending shivers down all their spines. "That should tell you the level of importance this program has. No failure can be accepted here, so if you feel you're not up for it, now is the time to go back home to your simple, slow lives."

Her eyes, the only part of her face visible, glowed fiery red like embers. They were deadly serious, a stark contrast with the easygoing and, at times, clumsy person James had first met.

This is a high-level Awakener. Not someone to be messed with, to be sure. She's not doing anything but it feels hard to breathe just being in her presence.

Content that her message had gotten across, she relaxed minutely, and the tension released.

Daniel and Ezekiel slumped, while James and the two girls sighed in relief. It didn't feel like a skill had been used, as no mana had moved at all, but it hadn't been a pleasant experience.

"Very well, now that you're all committed, we can start with the boring stuff."

An extensive orientation followed, an overview that would be expanded upon in the following months. It covered the rules and regulations for how they should behave within the headquarters and in public, as they were now technically AA agents and part of federal law enforcement.

Miss Walker took pity on them two hours later, seeing their bored expressions. "We'll stop here with the introduction to your duties for the moment. Now, who wants to do something practical?"

A cheer rose as they scrambled away from the room. The group doggedly followed their teacher down the hallways until they reached a blast door. After Miss Walker put her hand on a display and injected her mana into it, the door slid open.

An enormous room, tall enough to cover three floors and with reinforced walls strong enough to withstand a natural disaster, greeted them. "This is training room 7. It'll be your home away from home, so make sure to get comfortable," Miss Walker said, gesturing toward one of the corners, where a glowing glass wall separated a parlor from the rest of the room. Cozy-looking couches, a wide-screen TV, and a cooking area were all present.

"I mean it when I say you'll be here a lot. You'll spend some time in the morning following tactics and legal lessons in the room we just left, but the rest of your time not on duty outside will be here with me," the masked woman continued as she walked toward the opposite corner of the parlor, where an armory with all kinds of weapons had been set up.

"Before we begin with the practical side of the day, does any of you have questions?"

Immediately, Ezekiel raised his hand, drawing chuckles from all.

"Yes, Ezekiel? Despite all the lessons, you don't need to act like this is school. You're all adults here, and though you don't have much experience in the field, you still deserve at least that recognition," Miss Walker said, motioning with her hand for the curly-haired boy to go ahead.

"Are you going to be our only teacher? Will we have assigned roles in the team? Are there other people we will learn from? When is our first mission? Is this room truly all for us? Do we have to reveal our status to each other? Do we have lessons every day?"

Once he was done, the boy looked a bit out of breath and scratched his head embarrassedly. "Sorry, sometimes I get too excited."

Shaking her head in amusement, Miss Walker answered, "No, I won't be your only teacher. I did the theory lesson today since it was orientation, but most of the time, someone else will hold them. And theory lessons will be held only two to three times a week, depending on your duties. When we're sure you know enough, we'll just do tactics once a week. No, I don't know who your other teachers are. As for the team composition, it's only you five, and the room is really just for you. Though it's not required to show your status, revealing your Talent and skills will go a long way to help you make good strategies."

After the long explanation, the teacher picked up a staff. The end was wrapped with cloth, padded with a soft substance, so it wouldn't cause much injury upon impact.

"Now that the boring bits are done, we can get to the interesting part of the day. One by one, come with me to the middle of the room. We'll have a spar so that your companions and I can learn a bit of what you are capable of."

The way her eyes squinted in happiness should have been cute, but James only felt a cold shiver go down his spine. Still, he steeled himself, not wanting to make a poor showing.

Before he could speak up, the shortest member of their team followed their teacher, a bright grin on her face.

"Very well then, Digiovanni. Show me what you can do," Miss Walker said, holding her staff at the ready.

As soon as she finished, Lauren disappeared from their sight.

CHAPTER TWELVE

I t took James a second to locate Lauren again, but by then, she was already clashing with Miss Walker, her knife pushing against the older Awakener's armored forearm.

When Lauren realized the woman hadn't budged at all, she jumped back, clearing ten feet in a single movement.

It was immediately apparent to all watching that Lauren Digiovanni had a reason to be so confident. She might have been slightly older than the rest, but she must have spent some time as an Awakener to have developed such attributes.

Not one to be so easily deterred, the short brunette jumped around the room, mixing in feints and probing attacks to test the waters.

Of course, they all knew that if Miss Walker wanted to, she'd end the fight in an instant, but this was about showcasing their skills rather than trying to defeat her.

It really wouldn't be a contest. She hasn't budged an inch the whole time, and Lauren's actually pretty strong. Better than me, at least. She's likely close to level 10.

Levels, of course, weren't the end-all, be-all, but they still were the best indication given by the System, alongside the tiers of Awakening.

Considering how good she must be to be assigned responsibility over our team, she's likely well past her second Awakening. Maybe even into her third. B-rank is supposed to begin at level 300 and reach all the way to 400. . .

A high-ranker like that had to be part of an elite team. Taking her off the roster would cost the AA as much as developing the entire group of rookies for a year. It showed just how seriously they were taking the Dawn Initiative.

Meanwhile, the fight had devolved into a stall. Nothing Lauren could do seemed enough to make Miss Walker move, but she was too fast to get caught in the retaliatory strikes of the older Awakener.

Finally, the girl seemed to have had enough. She charged up a skill of some kind, her knife becoming even harder to distinguish by sight. The metallic ring it made when it hit the high-ranker's gloved hand was loud, but even that was stopped in its tracks.

"All right, that's good enough. Good job, Lauren, you can rejoin the others," Miss Walker said before gesturing for James to take her place.

He startled, then hurried to get in the ring. James had nothing in his arsenal that would surprise the masked woman, especially since she had seen him fight against the squirrel boss a few days ago, but he wasn't about to give up like that.

The determination to make a good showing flowed within him; the clear purpose enhanced his Thakinetic Empowerment.

Once she gave him a nod, James rushed at her, his speed greatly aided by his skill. When he got into close range, he threw a punch strong enough that it would have caved in the head of any of the squirrels he had fought, save the boss.

A gentle touch to his inner forearm was enough to throw him off completely, though he managed to avoid falling over. Again, he tried attacking, even as she easily deflected his blows. When he decided to mix things up by adding a sweeping kick that should have, by all rights, broken her shins, she surprised him again.

Rather than jumping up like James had expected—it had been his goal to force her from her position, since he knew he couldn't possibly win the spar—she took the blow, not showing any outward reaction. He, on the other hand, was forced to hop back. James barely kept himself from groaning in pain.

Not only was she much sturdier than he was, but her clothes were all heavily armored; it felt like kicking a steel wall.

From the amused squinting of her eyes, Miss Walker knew what he was feeling very well.

A surge of shame and anger forced James back into the fray. He wouldn't allow himself to be made a fool of, even in such an unequal fight. That determination stirred up his willpower, providing additional strength to his skills. When his fist hit her open palm, the *whack* it made was even louder; then, she made to grab him, but he was quicker at dodging. It happened again and again, forcing her to up the ante.

This continued for a couple of minutes before his mana started dwindling. Frustrated by his inability to do anything more than be swatted away like an errant fly, James was about to assign his free points, though he knew it would be a foolish thing to do in a fight, when Miss Walker ended the spar.

"That's enough. Good job, James, you're growing quickly."

Her eyes were kind enough that he managed to calm down, breathing out his frustrations and letting go of his skills. *This isn't a fight I can win. I'm here to learn and show her where I'm at so she can help me grow.*

Daniel, the tall and heavyset Black young man, took James's place, giving him a nod of acknowledgment that made him feel better about himself.

Back on the sidelines, James settled in a lotus position, too tired to keep standing, and watched the next fight unfold. It was immediately evident that his new teammate was hesitant to strike a much smaller woman, even though he had to know that she was stronger than all of them combined.

When his hesitance continued for a few more seconds, Miss Walker sighed, moving away from her chosen spot for the first time. Daniel watched her approach with evident apprehension. Only when she stopped right before him, a fist cocked as if to strike him, did he react.

He closed his arms together, and a shield of light appeared before them, the first genuinely supernatural skill used that day. When the masked woman's fist struck, it rang like a gong, cracking and shattering in a shower of golden light.

Before she could strike again, Daniel finally made his move, one of his large hands making as if to grab her fist around the wrist. Surprisingly to everyone, he managed to complete his maneuver, which in an equal fight would have signified a win.

Instead, Miss Walker's fist kept going as if nothing was stopping it, folding the large boy like a paper tissue. He let out a grunt of pain and surprise, dropping to his knees while clutching his stomach, gasping for air.

"Kindness and good manners are important, but refusing to fight another Awakener, one stronger than you by leagues, could be taken as an insult. Let this be a lesson to all of you." The woman's voice was much harder than it had been, pressure returning to imprint on their mind that she wasn't one to be messed with.

She kept it up for a few seconds, seeking and meeting everyone's eyes to ensure they understood. When she was satisfied, they were released from her metaphysical grip, and they sagged in unison.

"All right, next up is Ezekiel. I know you have White Mage as a Talent, but you still have to be able to fight. So come at me with what you can."

The boy in question, who had been bouncing on his heels while waiting for his turn, quickly took Daniel's place. He flashed a grin, quite sure of himself. It was more than what James would have expected from a noncombatant Mage Talent.

Mages are such a weird class of Awakeners. They operate on the same rules as us but have much more customization and uniqueness for skills, even amongst the same exact Talents. White Mage isn't directly oriented toward combat, though they can have shields and buffs. And Su Yang the Pale Crane should have made it clear that they aren't harmless. That woman retook control of the whole Hunan province by herself.

Indeed, his suspicions were quickly proved right. Ezekiel cast two different skills around himself, buffing up his attributes to a high enough level that he moved as quickly as James himself had.

The fight turned out to be nothing special besides the enthusiasm with which the youngest of their group attacked their instructor. Ezekiel tried different maneuvers and angles without ever letting up.

A couple of minutes later, the soft white glow around him faded away, leaving him defenseless against a light push that sent him sprawling.

"That should leave Maria, then. Please come over here. Don't worry about collateral damage. Your teammates will be protected by the room's defenses."

With that ominous statement, the last fight of the day began. It became obvious why Miss Walker had felt the need to specify that Maria shouldn't be afraid of hitting them. Because Maria conjured a basketball-sized sphere of flames before lobbing it at the teacher.

It, too, was easily dodged by the masked woman. Miss Walker tilted her head to the side, letting it pass harmlessly. When the fireball splashed against the wall, it resulted in an explosion of flames, though it left no sign behind.

Now that it was revealed she was a Fire Mage, Maria started spamming fireballs, all slightly lesser than the first, but in such a barrage that it was impossible to avoid.

Unsurprisingly, Miss Walker had no trouble dealing with them. She lifted a glowing hand and, with extreme speed, slapped the spells away, sending some of them toward the group of new Awakeners.

Before they could panic, a glowing blue shield sprang up between them and the incoming danger, protecting them from any harm. James stared at it, surprised as he hadn't expected the AA to give them such a high-tech room. Training barriers like these were commonly seen in viral videos of high-rankers' spars, since the barriers served to protect the bystanders from the immensely powerful skills being used. Of course, the one he was looking at was weaker than those, but it was still quite expensive.

Refocusing on the fight, James noticed a flabbergasted look on Maria's face. Her arms were limp, and a sheen of sweat covered her skin. The girl had completely exhausted herself by going so hard.

Well, it's a legitimate strategy. At least Miss Walker had to react more than she did any of us.

Seeing that the girl was done, the masked woman clapped her hands. "Well, that was a pretty good showing. At least all of you are capable of some form of attack skill, and you should complement each other fairly well."

The high-ranker seemed entirely unfazed by having faced all five of them, as if she had just taken a leisurely walk. "For the next few days, we'll review regulations and basic tactics to employ in a dungeon. After that, we'll find you an easy one to take on by yourselves, so you can get some experience."

She then turned to look at James directly, her gaze piercing. "Please refrain from going on a dive alone until then. We'll provide guidance on the path you can take with your Talent and attributes, which tactics are better suited to you, and how to deal with any specific monster."

That said, she walked over to the parlor and turned on the large TV. A recording of the fights played as if she had already set up the whole thing.

They hurried over, still stunned at how easily she had handled them all.

Once satisfied with how they arranged themselves around the TV, she started the footage, beginning with Lauren, and started giving her pointers on how to better utilize her Talent.

I admit, I was slightly skeptical about this whole thing, but they might actually want us to make it.

CHAPTER THIRTEEN

It turned out to be surprisingly easy to fall into the new routine. James woke up at the same time he would to go to Home Depot for work, but instead of walking through Brooklyn, he'd take the metro to Manhattan alongside all the commuters. He'd spend a couple hours with different instructors—various bureaucrats who had the free time to go over protocol and the limits of their authority while acting as AA agents. And then he'd go train in the spacious room that was reserved for Team 0.

They were apparently the pilot to the whole Dawn Initiative, the origin point that drove the higher-ups to push for more funds, which meant they were stuck with that name.

To be honest, it feels too cool for what we are right now. It's like we should all be A-rank Awakeners. Not H-rank rookies trying to not hit each other during practice.

That was the main focus of Miss Walker's lessons. She also had a more personalized program for each of them, and James already reaped the benefits, finally bringing his Thakinetic Awareness and Resistance to level 2.

The first time he used Resistance turned out to be almost involuntary. Miss Walker was pushing her aura on them again, to temper them against any high-ranker that might want to intimidate them, when the effect suddenly lessened.

Once the passive effects of Resistance kicked in, he was able to supplement it with additional mana, and repeated instances of being subjected to the masked woman's intent increased the skill's level.

On the other hand, Awareness leveled up when he managed to keep his attention on all four of his teammates and the target, thus avoiding getting in the way of their attacks.

Beyond that, Miss Walker took each of Team 0's members to the side and showed them an in-depth analysis of their current status and possible future paths. It was kept mostly private, but the generalities were then shared with everyone else to develop strategies together.

For him, his teacher laid down three different possibilities. He could continue as he was doing and become a sort of Warrior-slash-Rogue hybrid—the type to push through every obstacle before him while keeping the battlefield under control. Or he could shift to a more mind-oriented path, focusing mostly on his mental skills and using his empowerment to deal precise blows. Alternatively, he could become a more archetypal physical attacker, with Thakinetic Empowerment as his primary skill.

James quickly chose the first, as the style came to him organically. He was bullheaded by nature. Plus, since the basis of his Talent was applying his willpower through mana, becoming anything he wasn't fully committed to was a recipe for disaster.

By the end of the first week, he was finally allowed to assign the free stat points he had banked.

STATUS WINDOW	
Name	James Summers
Age	19
Awakening	1st
Talent	Thakinesis
Title	
Level	6
MP	30/30
STR	8
VIT	7
AGI	7
SEN	8
MND	7
STAT POINTS	0

SKILLS	LEVEL	DESCRIPTION
Thakinetic Empowerment	2	(Active): Utilize your Willpower to temporarily raise STR - VIT - AGI.
Thakinetic Awareness	2	(Active/Passive): Expand your SEN to feel others' wills.
Thakinetic Resistance	2	(Active/Passive): Empower your MND to defend yourself against foreign influences.

He would focus more on strength and sense stats once all his attributes reached a decent level. Since the threshold to G-rank was level 50, he should get another eighty-eight stat points before then, and with Miss Walker's guidance, he decided to assign so he'd reach twenty in both his main stats and sixteen in the rest.

The thought of focusing entirely on his two main stats had been quickly shot down. Apparently, that was a good way to grow out of balance; he'd risk hurting himself since his body and mind would be doing more than they could physically support.

The distance between the main stats and the lesser ones would grow with time as he got stronger and stronger, but Miss Walker was very clear that they shouldn't overly specialize. Their Talents and the benefits of reaching a new Awakening tier would do that for them.

Being almost twice as strong as he had been when he got his powers, James felt amazing. His body responded in ways it could have never done before, and everything felt more vivid. He threw himself into the training, using it as a crutch to not think about the night he received the System and what Sally must think of him. He tried to send her texts a couple of times, but no answer came, and he finally decided to acquiesce to her father's request.

He would give her all the time she needed to fully recover, but one day, they would meet again. He would accept it if she still wanted to have nothing to do with him, but he couldn't give up so easily.

"Oi, Summers, come back to us, will you?" Lauren's voice cut through James's contemplation, and he looked up to find his team waiting for him in the training room's parlor.

"We need to review all the info they gave us, possibly before noon, since we should start scouting the dungeon by then," the Italian American explained, holding up her tablet with a document opened.

"Yeah, I'm sorry. So which one did they give us?"

"A rat dungeon in Coney Island," Daniel commented, making James freeze in his tracks.

"What? Why did you make that face?" asked Maria, noticing the wild look in the James's eyes.

"Why is that dungeon still open? Was the Radiant Guild not supposed to clear it more than a week ago?" he asked instead as he slumped into his chair. He had been ready to let go of the trauma of that night, especially because he had been reassured several times that the rats would be taken care of quickly. That they wouldn't attack anyone else.

"Yeah, they were supposed to, but then a D-rank dungeon opened up in Long Island and they bought the rights for that too, so they ended up leaving the rat one to itself until the contract terms expired and it reverted back to the AA," Lauren explained distractedly, her finger a blur as she scrolled through the document to find the relative section.

"Aha! Here it is. They paid ten thousand dollars for the exclusive rights to Coney Island's H-rank rat dungeon for ten days, which should have been more than enough time for them to clear it, considering they have several D-ranks and many more E- and G-ranks." When she looked back up, she seemed confused at his expression. "But why that face? It doesn't look like a particularly dangerous dungeon, and it's not exactly uncommon for guilds to leave those be after they've made their money farming the mobs, especially if juicier prey turns up."

James took a deep breath, forcing himself to remain calm. "That dungeon should've been closed a long time ago. The rats have already started leaving it, and they knew it. They said they would take care of it."

Immediately, all four of his teammates understood the subtext in his words. Awakening was a profoundly personal experience. While it could only happen in moments of great stress or personal change, the specifics changed greatly depending on the person. Some could Awaken while in the throes of grief for losing a loved one, while others, like James, did so when under direct threat.

It was why they had never spoken about how they all gained access to the System; it was taboo to ask in the Awakener community.

With a much gentler voice, Lauren asked, "Do you feel comfortable taking on this mission? We could get assigned to a dozen different dungeons if we ask. It wouldn't be a problem for any of us."

James smiled bitterly. "Thank you, but no. Someone needs to clear that place before more people can get hurt, and this way, I'll be sure the job gets done well." *I should have known those filthy bastards wouldn't even clean up the mess they'd left behind.*

"All right, if you are sure . . ."

The questioning looks coming from everyone were a bit annoying, but James dealt with it. He had come to like these people, even if they were not friends yet. Still, they didn't deserve his anger. He should keep it for those who were at fault.

When he kept his silence, they resumed the meeting, reviewing the general information gathered for them. "Since it's been there for a while now, we should expect at least the boss and the monsters closest to the center to have gotten a bit stronger than the initial data suggests," Lauren commented, her finger hovering over a specific passage.

"They shouldn't be close to G-rank. Projections for the density of mana show that it would only happen in a month or so," Maria expanded.

Everyone nodded.

"There should be no long-range attacker presence, but there is a warning about possible infection if we get hit," Ezekiel read. "Well, living in the sewers is certainly not conducive to good health, I guess."

"The armor and equipment arrived this morning, too, so we should be good to go," Daniel added, gesturing toward the pile of boxes sitting in a corner of the room.

They quickly wrapped up the meeting, all generally confident that they should be able to tackle the dungeon, especially when working together.

"Finally! I can't wait to see how I look in mine," Lauren exclaimed, grabbing Maria's hand and pulling her to the women's changing room. The three boys looked at each other, a shared understanding passing through them.

Returning to the back alleys of Coney Island turned out to be easier than James had feared. The flames of anger, reignited when he found out the dungeon was still open, pushed away any lingering hesitation he might have felt, and he stalked ahead of the group, his Awareness scouring every inch for any life.

If you want a job done well, do it yourself. At least, I'll take pleasure in getting rid of these rats.

He wore sleek black-and-green armor, which hugged his body. It was made of treated monster leather, sourced from a D-rank dungeon the AA kept open to farm for the valuable parts. If he had been required to pay for it, James would have had to work for a few years before he could even think about affording it, but the agency had given each Team 0 member their own. It was one of the signing bonuses they were gifted, and it almost made the whole thing worth it by itself.

Maria's had red highlights, Daniel's gold, Ezekiel's white, and Lauren's was entirely black. Despite all being rookies, they cut quite the sight. After they were dropped off by the AA driver, a quiet man called Robinson, they quickly walked to the dungeon's main entrance.

Similar to the squirrel den James had defeated, this place had multiple access points, thanks to it being in the sewers. But the main one was right behind the lighthouse, where a packaging company had once had a depot. There, the sewer line had been chewed open in a wide hole, and numerous droppings all around made it clear they were entering the rats' territory.

"All right, we're here. Did anyone notice anything different from what we expected? Is the mana gauge still indicating this is an H-rank dungeon?" James asked Lauren, who was fiddling with the sleek apparatus that analyzed mana emissions.

"Yeah, no relevant changes from the last time it was checked. We should be good to go in," the busty brunette answered.

James gave his gear one last look over, fastened his new reinforced gloves, and carefully jumped into the darkness.

CHAPTER FOURTEEN

The fall turned out to be shorter than expected; it was at most seven feet deep. Considering Team 0's enhanced physique, it was no trouble.

Still, it was suspicious that it had looked like a steeper drop from the outside. Indeed, looking around, James noticed that it was unnaturally dark. Light streamed in occasionally through grates, making the visibility minimal. Thankfully, the new suits had built-in flashlights, which would illuminate the way.

That was something he had expected; it was common enough in dungeons. The denser the mana, the more the monsters evolved; and the process would further alter the environment.

The squirrel dungeon hadn't been old enough for any particular change to happen beyond the dampening of sound. The one he was in currently had been allowed to grow, so a few atmospheric effects were to be expected.

"Clear!" James called out, having swept the nearby area with his senses.

Next to him, Lauren's form was almost indistinguishable from the walls, her uniform and skills working in great synergy with the dungeon's atmosphere. "I wouldn't mind this place so much if it didn't stink," she commented, looking in distaste at the flow of dirty water in the canal next to them.

Thankfully, they could avoid walking through the worst of it, as a concrete platform ran the whole course of the sewers. Still, rat droppings and grime were everywhere, especially on the path they needed to take, and they wouldn't be able to avoid them.

"Ugh, and we just got these! We're gonna have to burn them once we clear this place," Maria complained, her boots already dirty with unspeakable things.

James chuckled. He was unsurprised that this dungeon business wasn't as glamorous as movies made it out to be, having already been in one, but for some of his companions, this would be a first.

Everyone had fought monsters, having a minimum level of five, but it was much different to enter and fight in the monsters' den than it was to battle in the open, in the middle of a grain field, or on the beach. They had all studied and trained hard for this moment, but he expected a few hiccups to still happen along the way.

Well, that's the reason they're sending all five of us to clear an H-rank dungeon. I don't think I'd be able to solo it, especially not in one go, but now that we've learned how to work together decently well, this shouldn't be too hard.

The image of Sally's foot being bitten off and swallowed by a rat, the feeling of its brain pulping under his fists—they sobered James up. He wouldn't lower his guard just because they should be superior on paper.

"All right, people, let's get this party started," he said once Maria gave the ok, having taken out a strip of paper from her kit and checked that the air was not flammable. James took point, closely followed by Daniel, who, as their Tank, would be the one to gather the monster's attention while James and the others attacked.

It might have seemed counterproductive for a person to never deal direct damage to monsters, but the System was constructed well enough to deal with things like that. In a group battle, experience points were divided by contribution. Since that was decided by the System itself, no one could complain. Tanks were known to gather quite a decent amount by bearing the brunt of a monster's attacks. It was the reason support mages like Ezekiel also gained experience from buffing more damage-oriented teammates.

They only walked for a few minutes before the first enemy came into sight. A rat—the same size as the first one James had killed—came from around a corner, sniffing the air as if looking for something that didn't belong. A cold hand gripped James's heart for a moment, before he refocused on the present, gritting his teeth and banishing the shadow.

Thankfully, they had known about it beforehand thanks to James's Awareness, and it was quickly dispatched by a single knife blow to the back of its neck.

"It'd be a pity to dull these pretty knives so soon, and their skulls are surprisingly strong," Lauren explained as she cleaned her weapon with a flick, inspecting it for damage. Since it was D-rank, James sincerely doubted it would dull so easily.

When she was satisfied, they kept going, carefully avoiding making too much noise.

The one with the least agility, Ezekiel, was especially circumspect. He was walking at the back of the group alongside Maria, the two mages having decided to cover them from any sneak attack thanks to the boy's buffs and debuffs.

Once he gets a bit stronger and has more mana to work with, he would be a game changer. For now, it's better if he keeps his power for when it's strictly necessary.

The sound of angry squeaking from the back alerted the team that a group of rats had found the corpse they had left behind. James cursed under his breath, annoyed that his sensory range was short enough that he hadn't felt them coming. He backtracked and hurried over, their entire formation shifting.

Three rats, bigger and meaner looking than the first, came bounding from the corner they had just turned, their forms barely visible in the unnatural darkness.

Ezekiel sent of bolt of light, searing the rats' eyes, attuned as they were to the shadows. In a flash, the rest of Team 0 took advantage of their weakness to end the fight before it could begin.

James activated Thakinetic Empowerment, strength flooding his limbs. He was on the first rat in three quick steps, a heavy overhand punch to the cranium flattening it to the ground. He didn't allow it any time to recover; two quick stomps with his monster-leather-reinforced boots ended its life.

Meanwhile, Daniel sent another one flying with a charge; it landed right where Lauren was, hidden in the shadows. A flick of her knife split its belly open, the sharp D-rank mana steel making short work of the monster's resilience.

The last rat died a gruesome death. After being blinded, deafened, and its movement speed reduced by Ezekiel's curses, it was burned alive by one well-placed fireball. Maria pumped her fist in glee, delighted that she managed to hit her target without any collateral damage.

Though the beast had been wet and dirty, the oily residue on its skin worked against it, instantly catching fire and accelerating its death. It took only a minute before it was gone, after which the redhead extinguished the blaze with a wave of her hand.

It's good that she took the time to test the flammability of the air, or we could have all blown up.

"Oh, I leveled up!" Ezekiel exclaimed, bouncing on his heels in excitement.

"Do it now before we meet another group. Something tells me these things might be more numerous than we expected," said Lauren.

James nodded in agreement with her. Though mana changed much of an animal's basic functioning, rats were well known for their ability to proliferate quickly. Since the dungeon had been mostly left to itself, with only a few initial cullings on record, they should expect a pretty long dungeon dive.

"Depending on the conditions, we might have to retreat and finish this tomorrow," he commented, getting a look of displeasure from everyone. "Hey, I'm just being the voice of reason here," James defended himself, feeling a little ironic, considering his previous dungeon experience.

"It's so annoying having to leave all these mana stones behind. We could quickly open them up and take them," Lauren groused, poking the rat closest to her with her boot.

"You know the rules." Daniel sighed. This was an old argument between them, but nothing could be done about it. Team 0 wasn't about to break regulations on their first-ever mission. They'd pick up the mana stones once they cleared the dungeon and not a moment sooner.

While they bickered, Ezekiel assigned his stat points; he massaged his head as the changes to his mind stat gave him a headache. Once the boy was combat ready, they resumed their trek in the semidarkness.

James took point again, keeping Thakinetic Awareness in its active state to prevent an ambush and to train the skill.

A minute later, they came to a fork in the tunnel, but before they could choose which path to take, James felt another group of rats approaching from the left. He quickly relayed this to the others, who all took position around the path's entrance.

Five rats, grimier than the last ones but thankfully no bigger, plodded out. The first one just had the time to let out a confused squeak at the unfamiliar smell before they were set upon.

Since the monsters were clumped together, the first shot was left to Maria, who gleefully threw a large fireball and ignited their oily fur.

As the confusion and pain scattered the rats, the team made short work of the monsters, with Ezekiel applying debuffs from the back. James ended up killing two. One in a single blow, his fist sending it crashing against a block of broken concrete with a rusted iron bar sticking out, which speared the rat through.

The second, he put out of its misery. It had been badly hurt by the fire but had managed to throw itself in the sewer water, which put out the fire. With burned flesh and blood leaking from where it scratched itself, it took only two stomps to end it.

By the time the fight was over, everyone but Ezekiel had leveled up, and they quietly cheered the accomplishment. James placed his two points in strength and sense, bringing both to nine. The weird sensation of his muscles and mind twisting and reforming passed quickly, and he felt he was slowly becoming more used to it.

Ezekiel, who served as a lookout while they assigned the points, whispered, "All done?"

James nodded, joining him in his guard while the others finished. "Yeah, it's getting easier. Also, the additional mana is always helpful."

"Now that, I can get behind. It's so annoying having to stop what you're doing because mana is running out, but if you hit rock bottom and try to push for more, you can actually hurt yourself badly," the curly-haired boy groused.

James was about to respond when Thakinetic Awareness alerted him that something was coming. He barely had the time to push Ezekiel to the side when a rat, smaller but faster than the others, jumped out of the sewers, its form entirely black, almost indistinguishable within the darkness.

Knowing that his companions were still incapable of defending themselves, James scrambled up and, in a surprising move, threw himself at it. The rat jumped back with a squeak.

Before it could resume its attack, he felt his strength and speed increasing even further than his Empowerment allowed, the distinct soft white glow of a buff telling him that Ezekiel had joined in.

The rat was taken by surprise by his burst of speed, and once he was on it, he didn't let it run. James grabbed its tail and launched it against the wall with enough strength to daze it. Then, with a powerful kick, he ruptured its insides. Then the rat disappeared from sight, likely engaging in a stealth skill similar to Lauren's, but James's senses told him it was merely crawling toward the dirty water.

A stomp later, the boy was busy scraping off rat grime from his boots, not wanting it to cake and stain.

A notification popped up, telling him that he defeated a [Mutated Sewer Rat - Assassin] and received a whopping [+50 EXP]. It was surprising, but he quickly concluded that the monster must have had a pretty high level, with skills completely focused on stealth. His skill countered it entirely, which had made the fight so easy, especially with the buff Ezekiel added on top.

Not one to look a gift horse in the mouth, James gratefully accepted the reward, especially since it already put him a third of the way to level 8.

"Thank you for that—you saved me," the curly-haired boy said, patting James on the shoulder. "I would have hated having to waste so much mana to heal myself so soon."

"No worries. Now, if we're all done, we can continue. Which way should we take?"

CHAPTER FIFTEEN

We need to clear the entire dungeon anyway, so it's not like it matters much," Lauren commented. "But if I had to choose, I'd go right. Since the rats came from the left, it could mean that more of them are that way. If we can get another level or two in the meantime, we'll be better off when we get closer to the boss."

Her words were met with nods of agreement by all. It wasn't like they had other information to go on. The reports left behind by the Radiant Guild were sparse, to say the least. It wasn't unexpected, as H-rank dungeons weren't considered relevant threats and could even be dealt with by regular law enforcement—with special equipment—if necessary, but it still would have been helpful for them to attach a map.

The group started walking right, leaving behind the rat corpses with only a little regret at not having extracted the mana stones.

Doing it once wouldn't be a problem, but if we started stopping for every single monster, we'd never end. I'd like to sleep in my own bed tonight.

The path they had chosen turned out to be a dead end, but not before they had to fight two more groups of rats, which they quickly dispatched.

"This is easier than I expected, given all the fearmongering about not going into dungeons alone," Maria commented as they walked back.

"Well, we are a team of five who've been training together for a week. While this isn't the weakest possible dungeon, as it's not newly formed, it's still at the bottom of the ranks." Daniel was always the voice of reason in these cases, trying to bring some perspective before the others could get too bigheaded.

"The boss, at least, should give us a challenge. We should expect it to use wide-area skills since the rats always move in groups. It'd need them for crowd control," James added, thinking back at how much stronger the squirrel boss had been than its minions.

"Yeah, let's not lower our guard here. We still have a lot of work to do," Ezekiel agreed.

Finally, they returned to the fork in the tunnel and took the rightmost path, the left fork from before. It took only a while before the sewer widened, becoming almost a chamber.

James halted their advance with a raised hand, having felt several presences scurrying in the dark. "They're coming," he murmured.

The team barely had the time to start their skills when a group of rats—much larger than any they had met before—charged them. The rats were as big as the [Rat - Assassin] James had dealt with but without its defining features.

Nevertheless, a swarm of two dozen Labrador-sized rats coming your way was an unpleasant sight, which made Maria's scream quite understandable. However, her ensuing decision to set fire to them all with a barrage of fireballs made things chaotic for everyone, as the swarm's momentum made it impossible for them to stop.

Still, at the AA, they had trained for such an occasion with the help of several automatons, which served as facsimiles of monsters when powered by mana stones. Dealing with swarms was a fundamental skill for any would-be dungeon diver, so they quickly employed the tactics they were taught.

Daniel placed himself at the front, acting as a shield against the screeching, burning rats. Behind him, James and Lauren, empowered by Ezekiel's buffs, crushed as many as possible while Maria dealt with those that managed to escape their reach. All the while, Ezekiel also cast debuffs on those few rats that managed to avoid the flames, thus slowing and confusing them enough that they were quickly defeated.

All in all, the whole thing took them only a few minutes, and the cleanup after the initial charge was a little more than that.

James shook his hands, trying to get the grime off his expensive gloves, very thankful that the D-rank leather had a self-cleaning property; no matter how many heads he had to break, not much stuck to the gloves. The swarm had been made up of weaker rats, but coupled with the groups they had defeated on the right fork, they all leveled up again, much to their happiness.

The sensation of his mana reserves increasing was exhilarating to James, enough that he knew it wouldn't be easy to give up his career as an Awakener now that he had felt it.

The team took turns assigning their points in preparation for the boss fight, which they had to be coming close to. Once it was James's turn, he put one point in sense and one in agility, wanting to be more mobile. They might find more assassin rats.

His fear turned out to be correct, as after dispatching another group of large rats, they were beset from two sides by the stealthy monsters.

Thakinetic Awareness proved its worth in gold, as it alerted him to their approach. But since he was the only one who could sense them, they soon suffered their first injury.

Lauren tackled the first of two monsters bearing on them due to her familiarity with stealth-based skills, while James handled the second. However, Lauren did not notice when her opponent faked a charge at her and instead went for Maria.

The rat managed to inflict a gash on Maria's cheek, just below her left eye—her face unprotected by the expensive armor—before Daniel bull-rushed it, crushing the rat against the wall.

Luckily, they had Ezekiel, who quickly started treating the wound and reassured Maria that it'd close up without any scar in only a couple of minutes.

Still, they were all shaken by the fight, having easily crushed all their opponents so far.

"Fuck, I'm sorry, I should have been more careful. This is my fault," Lauren apologized, holding her head low.

James understood that the girl, being the oldest and with the highest level, felt responsible for all of them, but in a dungeon, getting injured was to be expected. He said, "We knew this would happen, and we prepared for it. We should be good, since Maria still managed to prevent a serious injury. We just need to learn from this."

Rather than being shaken, like he feared she would be, Maria agreed vehemently, not allowing Lauren to blame herself. "He's right. We all messed up. I should have had a fireball ready to place between us, so let's put this behind us and focus on taking down the boss."

Once Ezekiel was done with the treatment, and Maria poked and prodded her cheek to see if she felt any pain, they resumed their walk. The curly-haired boy drank a mana potion, a relatively expensive brew that replenished one's reserves in a pinch.

"It's so annoying that healing takes much more mana than all my other skills. I almost ended up empty even after leveling up twice!" Ezekiel complained, though he kept his eye on the surroundings.

Soon enough, they reached the end of the sewers, where the waters would be redirected to be purified and then let out into the ocean.

It was a cavernous room, wide enough for three buses to sit in both directions. On the right side was where the waters accumulated, waiting to pass through the purifiers, while on the left, the platform they were on was wide enough to be a plaza.

Maria conjured a few orbs of fire, illuminating the room farther than their flashlights could. Grand arches held up the ceiling, while toward the end, the unnatural darkness pooled, somehow countering the light let out by the fireballs.

"No points for a guess as to where the boss is."

Chuckling at Lauren's joke, James took up his position, and they slowly advanced forward. Daniel led the way, his shield softly glowing.

That turned out to be an excellent idea, as a figure emerged from the darkness with a roar. It was by far the biggest rat James had ever seen, and if it stood up on its hind feet, he bet it would be as tall as him.

Its fur was oily with an indefinable quality as it blended in with the surroundings. Its breath misted, curling around it with intent, signifying an active skill.

Then, it shot forward, clearing the distance between them in two great leaps. Its limbs, longer than on a normal rat, thrust forward, crashing against Daniel's shield. The Tank was sent careening backward, though he achieved his goal of nullifying the blow.

Immediately, three fireballs shot at the boss, forcing it to jump away in an acrobatic display. James and Lauren were on it the moment it touched down, buffed by Ezekiel's spells. The girl jumped on top of it, using her wickedly sharp knives to pierce its hide, while James punched it in the head, stunning it.

"Scatter!" came the shout, and both Awakeners obliged, avoiding a fiery encounter. A fireball, larger than any Maria had cast before, exploded on the rat, sending it flying backward.

The boss, however, was not one to be defeated so easily, and it unfortunately had help. With a pain-filled screech, it called upon reinforcements, and a new swarm of smaller rats crawled out of the darkness, which had obfuscated their presence.

"We're on it!" Maria yelled, using magic alongside Ezekiel to contain the mass of monsters. The youngest of the team was cast another buff, this time on Daniel, who had recovered from the previous hit. With the boost, Daniel started dispatching the rats that weren't hit by the destructive fireballs.

Since their companions had the swarm handled, James and Lauren resumed their assault, running toward the boss rat to finish the fight. Its gambit failed, so the creature decided to go for broke. It roared again, a low sound that sent a tremble through the room.

It soon became evident what it had done. The unnatural shadows pooling in the back swarmed to the rat boss. Then, they rose from the ground, reformed as sinuous tendrils of shadow.

The new limbs shot toward the two, seeking to end them quickly. Seeing how desperate the boss was getting, James pumped more mana into his skill, concentrating his will on his hands.

Just as a shadow whip was about to hit him, he raised his hands and caught it, stunning the boss rat and causing it to squeak.

The grin on the boy's face was almost maniacal as he tugged on the shadow tendril, dragging the boss forward. With a kick that would have made a professional MMA fighter proud, James hit it in the snout with great force, only to pull the rat toward him again.

Bones crunched, and the rat finally released its skill, allowing the two to get close to it and finish the fight. This time, Lauren had no qualms about attacking the most lethal spot with her knife, burying it in the middle of its skull.

The boss twitched one last time before exhaling its final breath. Just to be certain, the girl stabbed it again, and only when it didn't move was she satisfied.

Meanwhile, the fight against the swarm had wrapped up, as the combined might of Maria's fire magic, Ezekiel's buffing spells, and Daniel's mighty physique crushed all resistance.

Seeing that it was over, Lauren mused, "Well, now that the fun part's over, we need to start with the cleanup. Who wants to start cutting up the boss?"

CHAPTER 15.5 – INTERLUDE

Leila

As she stalked her charges from the shadows, Leila mused about how much her life had truly changed these past few days. Not only had she been taken off the roster for anything but the most urgent tasks, but she had also been given babysitting duty over a group of rookies.

Now, as an elite high-ranker in the middle of her ascent, she would be perfectly justified in feeling sidelined and being unfairly treated. And to be honest, that was how Leila had felt at the beginning.

Her last mission might have ended up in much more collateral damage than strictly necessary, but the higher-ups knew very well why that had been the case, especially after she had warned them repeatedly that being forced to work with a guild as obnoxiously thuggish as Golden Sun would have consequences.

Still, she acquiesced to playing school out of respect for her old teacher; at least this way she could do something while her leave ran its course.

What she ended up finding, however, was a very interesting group of people. James Summers was the one who started the whole thing; his clearing of the squirrel dungeon intrigued her enough to accept. But he wasn't the only standout.

No, the AA pulled all the stops in this latest scheme. The Dawn Initiative was something she could have only dreamed about, and she had no idea how the chief director had managed to pull off getting so many funds, but if it worked, it would breathe new life into the agency.

Leila nodded in satisfaction, seeing that Team 0 was taking all the necessary precautions before lowering themselves into the dungeon.

She had already scouted the whole thing herself, of course; she couldn't allow the time she invested in these rookies go up in flames if they got done in because something unexpected mauled them.

Luckily for them, nothing seemed amiss beyond a surprising number of low-level rats. The boss was a creature attuned to shadows, but its level was so low that it couldn't possibly hope to feel her presence if she didn't want it to.

So it's swarms and stealth-based elites. If it had been any other team of rookies, this would be quite the challenge, but these guys should make it through easily. I'll be shocked if it takes them more than one day.

Considering the ridiculous sensory ability James Summers had, the rats didn't have any hopes of actually sneaking up on them.

Indeed, her prediction was quickly proved right. Team 0 easily dispatched the monsters they encountered, and though there was a little hiccup that led to Maria Olegova's injury—wasn't it trippy that she almost broke cover to go help the girl?—they arrived at the boss room with little trouble.

Thankful beyond words that she was immune to the stench while she stayed within the shadows, Leila watched as the rookies successfully managed to deal with the [Shadow Assassin Rat] and its minions, thus completely clearing the dungeon.

Though she would have liked to reveal herself now that they were done, to congratulate them on their first run, she stopped, knowing the importance of building confidence.

If I show them that they were in a controlled environment all along, they'll start expecting me to pull them out of sticky situations whenever they go inside a dungeon. That's a very good way of dying young.

Leila did one last sweep through the dungeon, just to be absolutely sure nothing else was about to come out, and left, satisfied with her kids' performance.

Once an Awakener got to a certain level, training only helped so much. It was still helpful to become more acquainted with one's skills or to try out different combinations, but there came a point where it simply wasn't cost effective anymore.

So it was uncommon for high-rankers to make use of their organization's facilities, no matter how high-tech they might be. Dungeons were much better, as the danger of losing one's life sharpened skills more efficiently than any detailed review a team of analysts might develop.

Reviews were still useful, so she usually wore a micro camera on her uniform when she went on official missions, but there were times when Leila just wanted to fight without any of the crap her role forced on her.

That was why she was currently shifting between shadows in the countryside, at the edges of Bear Mountain State Park. A C-rank dungeon had been found here, and since no one came to clear it, even after the Golden Sun Guild acquired the rights to it, she felt it would hurt no one if she let out some steam without worrying about any collateral damage.

To say that she was surprised to find a base camp at the dungeon's entrance would be an understatement, as no report of planned activity had been filed with the AA. And guilds, even powerful ones like Golden Sun, usually complied with that kind of regulation, as it was one of the few ways the AA had to keep a leash on them.

Heavy fines could be expected if they were found to have entered and used a dungeon without communicating it, and in the worst cases, their privileges would be revoked. Guilds were very careful when those were at stake.

I guess it's still possible that they literally just decided to go in and communicated it soon after I checked a couple of hours ago.

Leila's instincts, however, blared at her. And she had long since learned to listen to them.

That was why, instead of announcing herself like she usually would, she stayed in the shadows, observing the comings and goings for a while.

Nothing outwardly illegal seemed to be happening, allaying her worst fears, but one thing stood out. This was a C-rank dungeon, and a certain level of equipment was expected to clear it. What the members of Golden Sun were using would have been better suited in a B-rank one, which was surprising.

Considering how expensive D-rank equipment was and all the strings she had to pull to get it in time to Team 0, it was weird that a generally resource-efficient guild would use such expensive equipment without a reason. What she observed them use alone would be enough to outfit the rookie team a hundred times over.

Snooping around more, Leila found that the guild members had brought expensive elixirs, which furthered her suspicions.

All evidence pointed to this being a power-leveling training camp, which was known to be hideously costly and could only be maintained by the wealthiest guilds. Even then, only for a few select members.

More than a dozen people were participating, enough that it should have bankrupted Golden Sun within a couple of weeks. Considering that they had been holding the rights to this specific dungeon for almost a month, nearing the time limit before it would revert back to the AA—things weren't adding up.

More spying revealed nothing. Unfortunately, none of the members seemed inclined to speak about the specifics of their dealings, only caring about efficiently dispatching the [Direbears] and [Fungi Thralls] to gain more levels.

Still, Leila made a note of everyone present, her high mind stat easily allowing her to remember all their features, even after many years. She would check in the following days if a notice of use of the dungeon came in, but she strongly suspected nothing of the sort would arrive.

Not alerting the AA would allow Golden Sun to sell the mana stones and materials on the black market, thus making a tidy sum without paying taxes. That explained some of their wealth.

But not everything. It's just too much. Either they're doing this same thing on an absurd scale—though I refuse to think they could have gotten away with it, even after paying off their patsies in the AA—or it's just one piece of a much wider web of illegal activities.

Considering how much distaste she felt for the Golden Sun Guild, especially after the accident that forced her on leave, Leila was well inclined to think they were down to their elbows in shady business.

She'd have to shift a few things around and likely keep her mouth shut while she accumulated evidence—if it truly turned out to be what she thought it was—but if no one interfered, she might have found a way of eliminating one of the worst cancers in New York City.

CHAPTER SIXTEEN

utting the mana stones out of every last rat took them a couple of hours, and by the end they were numb. Disgusting as it might have been, rummaging through a monster's offal for the shiny prize was still worth it.

They would all receive a part of the reward money for clearing the dungeon, but since it had to be divided by five, the amount each of them would receive wasn't anything worth writing home about.

However, considering how many rats they had killed, their monetary gains from the whole expedition would still be satisfying. It wouldn't be the maximum amount of money, as most of the carcasses would have to be left behind—there simply wasn't much request for H-rank rat materials—but at least the rat boss should net them a decent bonus.

The creature had been attuned to darkness, a rare enough type that it should sell well on the market, especially now that the AA would take care of all those pesky bureaucratic annoyances for them.

All in all, I'm going to bring back home as much as when I cleared the squirrel dungeon by myself, but this time my leg didn't have to get mauled. Worth it.

As for the System gains, defeating the boss alongside Lauren ended up netting James a whole new level, bringing him up to level 9. That meant he got three levels from the run.

He decided not to immediately assign the stat points in agreement with his teammates. Since the danger was over, they could take the time to review their actions, reevaluate their mistakes, and learn from what others might have observed.

They'd all assign the points before the next dungeon run, after Miss Walker gave her opinion.

Since all the gains had to be divided between five people, James felt three levels was a fantastic result. Not all H-rank dungeons would be as densely populated as the one they had just completed, but if he could maintain a similar rhythm, he'd rank up in no time.

By the time they were done with the cleanup and the last sweep, just to make sure they hadn't missed anything, Team 0 was bone tired. Their attributes ensured their bodies and minds could still keep going, but the stress of fighting ugly, dirty monsters in a dimly lit, horribly smelly environment took a toll.

When they finally emerged from the dungeon, they barely had the wherewithal to high-five each other, unanimously deciding to leave the celebrations for tomorrow.

Unfortunately for them, someone seemed determined to stop them from getting their well-deserved rest.

"So this is where you scurried off to, Summers. It shouldn't have surprised me that you lived in the sewers, you little rat."

The sight of Callum Wright swaggering into the lighthouse's parking lot along with his cronies was not what James expected.

He was honestly too tired to deal with him but still managed to contain himself, knowing that the older boy would pounce on any perceived provocation.

"That's very funny," James deadpanned. "Unfortunately, as you can see, we just finished a job, so we really need to get going."

James could feel the confusion radiating from his teammates, but thankfully, they decided not to interfere for the moment.

"I can see you managed to beg your way into the AA. What, no decent guild wanted to take you on?"

Callum Wright was someone who never had to work a day in his life for what he had, and that was what annoyed James the most. He was born into a wealthy family, his father being a big-shot lawyer. He was tall and, objectively, handsome. When he Awakened, he was scouted by the Radiant Guild, a subsidiary of Golden Sun, and had been cultivated as a talent enough to have reached F-rank. It wasn't a world-shattering Talent, but it was enough that he could brag about it. Most Awakeners only reached F-rank after three or four years, compared to his two.

On top of his being dumped by Sally after a couple months of dating, it was no wonder he developed a nasty personality; he was obsessed with putting down people who defied him, which he considered the natural order of things.

James had never directly antagonized him, but his closeness with Sally, especially since she had agreed to go out with him after having rejected Callum for so long, must have immediately made him an enemy. Now that James had Awakened too, it couldn't have been more infuriating to Callum.

James understood all of this, but he sincerely didn't care. Callum could stay as the twisted, popular jock as long as he wanted, never addressing his problems, for all that he cared.

"That's exactly right. I had no choice but to go to the AA, and luckily, a spot opened up just in time." It wasn't so much that James cared enough to respond to him, but Miss Walker had been very clear in what they said that if any guild member ever asked them questions.

The AA was trying to let the Dawn Initiative fly under the radar for as long as possible, and James certainly wouldn't be the one to uncover them.

Seeing that he wasn't getting the reaction he wanted, Callum got closer to James so that he could glare down his nose. "I don't like your tone, boy. Lest you forget, this is Radiant's territory."

Sensing that his teammates were starting to lose their patience, James sighed. "We were here because your guild didn't clear this dungeon; nothing more. Now, if you please, we need to go. The driver is expecting us."

Callum refused to back off. Instead, his eyes got flintier and a wicked smile formed. "I can see that you worked hard, yes," he said, looking at where Daniel was lugging the boss monster's carcass. "Maybe we can help take some of the weight off you."

And there it is, extorting an AA team, why not. This is so damn stupid. If I didn't know that he could kick my ass without a sweat, I would've dropped him by now. But this bastard is quite strong, unfortunately.

"All right, that's enough. Do you think stealing directly from the AA is a good idea? Also, who the fuck are you, even?"

James sighed. Lauren wouldn't have been able to keep her mouth shut for long.

Callum's gaze left James and slowly roved over the Italian American girl, stopping languidly over her chest. "Now, now beautiful. There's no need for that tone. You see, me and Summers are old friends. I was just offering to help carry the heavy stuff, since you must be so tired from clearing the dungeon."

"As you can see, we have it perfectly handled. No need for you to dirty your hands," came the reply. Lauren didn't bat an eye at the smarmy tone Callum used.

"There is a problem, you see." One of the F-rank Awakener's goons joined in. "The time limit for our lease might have expired, but we couldn't make use of it because we had to ensure everyone's safety while we searched for every entrance. You only got to the boss thanks to our information, after all." His voice was so sleazy that James would have dismissed him out of hand, but this one had a glint of intelligence in his eyes that the others lacked.

"Yeah, Lucas is right. We did all the hard work, and now you swoop in and get the rewards. It's just not right," Callum added, smirking at his companion.

The most frustrating thing is that he already has more money than he can spend. He's just doing this because he's a thug and a bully.

The sound of something heavy being dropped made everyone turn, and they saw that Daniel had let go of the boss monster. He was readjusting his uniform, his shield unlatched, apparently preparing for a fight.

Seeing the questioning looks, Daniel shrugged. "They seem to want a fight. I don't think we'll be able to convince them otherwise."

"You are an idiot, then," Lucas the goon commented. "We're all G-rank, and Callum is F-rank. Rookies like you wouldn't even count as an appetizer for us."

It rankled James that he was right. That was the unfortunate reality of the world they lived in. Since strength was needed to protect human society from the ever-encroaching darkness, those who possessed it were afforded immense privileges.

Even amongst the Awakeners, the tyranny of rank still reigned supreme. An F-rank could do whatever they wanted to an H-rank unless the latter had substantial backing. And however much James would like to think that Miss Walker would have come to their rescue, she wasn't here now, and even then, her hands would be tied when clashing with an entire guild.

"Oh yes, I know that," Daniel added, unconcerned. "You swagger too much to be weaklings. But if I have to choose between being robbed blind of my hard work and at least putting up a fight, I'll take the second any day."

Callum snorted. "Well, at least he has some balls. But do the rest of you want to get beaten up so badly? You girls must know that it's not a good idea."

"Well, I'm not someone to abandon my friends in a time like this." Lauren sighed before smirking. "And at least, the harder you beat us, the worse it'll be for you. It's true that we wouldn't be able to do much if you just take our stuff, since a complaint will get lost in the bureaucracy. But physical signs of a fight are a different thing entirely."

Lucas's eyes narrowed, a snarl forming on his lips as he stalked closer to the girl. "If you think your pathetic little organization will be able to do anything to us beyond a slap on the wrist, you're mistaken. You'll be in the hospital for a long while by the time I'm done with you." The way he stared at her bust made it very clear what he intended to do.

James gritted his teeth, preparing for a surprise attack so that he could at least take the would-be rapist out before he could enact his plans, when a thunderous clap from above stopped them all.

There, wreathed in golden light, was the man who had come to his house to threaten and entice James into joining his guild. Which, if he remembered correctly, was the Radiant Guild, to be exact, while the man, Bradley Esposito, was part of Golden Sun, its parent guild.

"All right, kids, you had enough fun. This isn't the time nor the place to get into a scrap. Let the AA team leave—we all have better things to do."

Bradley wore an expensive-looking suit and kept glancing at his golden pocket watch. The mere fact that he could fly without aid meant he must be a high-ranker, and the Golden Sun emblem sewn into his waistcoat and tie made it clear what organization he belonged to.

With his superior unamused at his antics, Callum tsked, giving one last venomous look at James. "You won't always get this lucky, Summers."

Once again calling upon all his patience and willpower, James didn't respond, merely giving a curt nod and gesturing for his teammates to follow him.

"I'll explain when we get back," he murmured, getting nods from everyone, and they quickly moved past the Radiant members under Esposito's watchful gaze.

Robinson, the driver who had accompanied them, was still where they had left him, though he was holding a handkerchief to his forehead to wipe copious sweat. He had apparently witnessed the entire thing.

"Let's go back," James told him, spurring the man into action.

CHAPTER SEVENTEEN

"All right, spill."

James smiled ruefully; he knew that Lauren would be the one to hold him accountable first. They were sitting at the sofas in their training room's parlor, having showered and changed into their civilian clothes. Now that they were finally out of danger, James wanted to succumb to the drowsiness he felt, but it seemed his teammates had other plans.

"Well, there isn't that much to say," he started, receiving deadpan looks from everyone. "The F-rank who came up to me first is Callum Wright. I ended up befriending his ex and now he hates me."

"You don't think that's going to be enough, do you?"

James shook his head, sighing theatrically. "What else do you want me to say? He's a bully and a thug, but you could see that much for yourselves. He has it out for me because . . . Well, I went on a date with his ex two years after they broke up."

Yeah, sorry, but I'm not gonna share every little detail about Sally . . . It still hurts to think about her. I just hope she's feeling better now.

"But he never let go of her, so you became enemy number one. I know that type, unfortunately," Maria finished with a grimace.

The redhead had been quiet during the whole confrontation, which was surprising, given her usual temper, but it seemed that she, too, had had ugly experiences with overbearing Awakeners.

I suppose she must have had a reason not to go to a guild. Our benefits package is quite generous, and we know they want us to succeed, but initially, it did look dicey. She must have had a good reason to take the plunge.

"Yeah, that's about it. I honestly didn't want to bring you into my problems, but it was already too late when he saw us."

Daniel reached over the armchair and patted his hand. "Don't worry about it, Jimbo. We're all friends here. I know you would have done the same for any of us."

Jimbo? What? Well, all right, it's not that important. You can't really fight a nickname anyway.

"I would have, but still, you guys backing me up even while knowing we would have gotten our asses kicked means a lot to me."

Lauren snorted, tossing her long brown hair to the side. "I'll tell you what.

Next time we clash with those thugs, you leave the smarmy bastard to me. I need to pay him back with interest."

James chuckled, easily acquiescing. "He's all yours. Honestly, I wouldn't want to touch him anyways, even if it was to rearrange his features."

Laughter echoed through the room as the new friends let go of their anxieties and celebrated their first victory. Their dungeon run had been successful, only marred by a confrontation with the Radiant Guild at the end. They were all safe and sound, back in their room.

They were stronger than before, and it wouldn't be long before they wouldn't have to worry about Callum Wright and his cronies. James was certain.

The next day, Team 0 resumed their regular training schedule. In the morning, they had their usual lessons on law and regulation, and afterward, they were at Miss Walker's mercy.

"I'm proud of what you've achieved," their teacher began once James had finished recounting the day's events, "I expected nothing less, but it's always possible for a dungeon dive to go wrong. You've shown that my trust in you is not misplaced." Then, she sighed, "I'm sorry I couldn't be there to greet you on your return. Thugs like that need to be shown their place as soon as they start, or they'll never stop." Miss Walker seemed particularly frustrated by the fact that the confrontation happened as soon as they got out, but quickly refocused on the story, seeming perplexed that a high-ranker from Golden Sun had stepped in to help them.

"Well, technically, it's his duty to do so. Since his guild has a special relationship with the AA, they also have more rules to abide by, and keeping the peace between Awakeners is one of them. But they usually never stoop so low, especially if it's a scrap between rookies and one of their subsidiaries," she explained, fiddling with her armor's straps.

"Was there any weird behavior? Did he say anything that stood out to you?"

James tried to remember. He had been trying to avoid getting beat to a pulp, but he finally recalled something. "He was looking at his watch. He did it several times, even though the whole thing couldn't have lasted more than a couple of minutes."

Miss Walker hummed, also thinking it was pretty peculiar. "Nothing else? No? All right, if anything comes to mind, please tell me immediately."

She then stood up and moved toward the center of the training area. "We can't do much to reprimand the Radiant Guild members, especially since they didn't end up doing anything to you, but I can promise you something." Her eyes squinted in the way she did when she smiled. An ominous aura started seeping into the room, and the lights flickered. "The next time you meet them, you'll be able to stand up to them, even if I have to train you so hard that you vomit every day."

Team 0 members all exchanged glances before looking back at their mentor, trying to gauge how serious she was being.

"Oh, come on, I'm not that bad," the masked woman complained, as if she was pouting. "Now, come over here and let's have a mock boss battle. I want to see how much you've grown with all those new shiny stats."

They all groaned theatrically but quickly took their positions, using the standard boss formation they had used in the rat dungeon.

Rather than bowling them over completely with physical strength, like what they expected her to do, Miss Walker conjured arrows of solid shadows. It was clear that if they wouldn't close the distance, she was perfectly content keeping the fight at long range.

Since Maria was the only one who was adept at long-range fighting, and by herself, she wouldn't be more than an annoyance to their teacher, they changed tactics.

Daniel kept his position, his shield drawing in most of the arrows thanks to his skill, while Ezekiel and Maria served as artillery behind him.

While the youngest couldn't really do any damage directly, his healing skill manifested with a bright glow. Thanks to his ingenuity, he had developed the ability to cast it without any healing factor, concentrating all the power into the light.

It made for an excellent distraction, especially since it didn't take much mana, and if it hit the eyes, it could even blind a target. Coupled with his buffs cast on his allies and his debuffs on his enemies, Ezekiel was a force multiplier all by himself.

Maria's fireballs had also increased in strength, due to her leveling up the skill during the last fight with the swarm of rats. Now, her spells packed a serious punch, and the explosions when they hit the shadow arrows were enough to destroy all the nearby ones too.

Meanwhile, James and Lauren served as melee attackers. Buffed by Ezekiel's skills, they closed the distance quickly, taking different approaches.

James was the flashier one, charging directly at Miss Walker like a bull, Thakinetic Empowerment covering his limbs. His right fist crashed against a hastily constructed shield—well, hastily since the masked woman was keeping herself to an approachable level, otherwise she would have reacted much sooner. He rained heavy blows on it, cracking it with his increased power.

On the other side, Lauren used her stealth skills to sneak by. She waited for the perfect moment to slip her knife in.

She had to retreat when she fell for a fake opening and was almost hit by a shadow-strengthened punch. But Lauren eventually broke through, slipping her training knife against Miss Walker's ribs.

The surprise was enough that James managed to break the shield that kept him at bay and kicked her hard, sending her skidding on the ground.

Maria delivered the final blow with her enhanced fireballs exploding on the teacher. It had enough power that most H-rank bosses would have been dead.

"All right, good job!" The call came from the cloud of smoke left from Maria's attack. Completely uninjured and looking as fresh as a rose, Miss Walker strolled out, nodding in satisfaction. "Your synergy has increased a lot since your early days. Not only has the power you gained made you stronger, but you also managed to use it better. I'd say that this deserves an early day off."

When no one moved, she waved them off with a hand. "You are free, people!" And off they went, running toward the locker rooms.

"If we're quick enough, we'll be able to take the metro without the rush!" Lauren commented giddily.

"I really wanted to get some shopping done. My sister should be coming out of her piano lesson now," Ezekiel agreed, taking out his phone to shoot a text.

Daniel just shrugged. "I'm going to go play some games. God knows I miss it. I just don't have the time for it these days."

Maria snorted at that. "Yeah, maybe because your current life is more exciting than any game? And aren't most of them about Awakeners now anyway?"

Daniel shook his head, an exaggerated expression of distaste. "You are such a heathen. I don't play modern games, obviously. Vintage is where it's at, vintage, I tell you!"

Banter flowed easily between the team now that they had all risked their lives together. The confrontation with the Radiant Guild thugs had only made them feel more connected.

There were some things you simply couldn't go through without a sense of kinship forming, after all. James was still surprised at how quickly he became friends with them, having expected their relationship to remain standoffish for a long time.

This is something I don't mind being wrong about.

Shortly after, the training room was empty, except for two people. Miss Walker stayed behind to put things in order, even though the cleaning crew would pass by in a couple of hours, while James needed to do something.

"Miss, could you give me the authorization to access some files?" he asked, doing his best not to wring his hands. This was a fundamental part of his plan, as with his H-rank clearance, he couldn't find anything of worth on his target.

The masked woman stared at him for a moment, her gaze piercing. Evidently, she found what she was looking for, because she acquiesced, "I'll send you the code via message."

"Thank you!" he said giddily, already sprinting off toward the elevator. He needed some answers, and while he didn't believe he would find everything in the AA servers, it was the best starting point he could think of.

"James!" she called, stopping him in his tracks. "I'm here if you want to talk about anything."

Noticing how serious she was, James turned to face her. "Thank you, Miss Walker. I'll keep that in mind."

CHAPTER EIGHTEEN

JX45!HL223W.W" Aaand . . . *I'm in! Now, let's see what this bad boy has for me.*

Thankfully, the AA record room was almost completely digitized, or James would have had to spend the entire week sorting through reports before he got to anything concerning the Radiant Guild.

With the help of modern technology and a B-rank credential to open the way, he quickly managed to find the folders he sought.

He was tempted, for a moment, to look up his teacher's file and what the AA had on all of Team 0's members, but he quickly shook the thought away. He had been trusted with a high rank clearance, and if he immediately misused it, he'd lose Miss Walker's confidence.

That, and he simply didn't want to snoop into his new friends' private lives. If they had something they wanted him to know, they'd tell him, just like he had secrets of his own that he wasn't ready to share just yet.

Since he had a much more pressing interest anyway, it didn't bother him too much to leave that curiosity unaddressed.

Sorting through the Radiant Guild–related folders took a few more minutes until he found the reports related to their activities in Brooklyn and Coney Island. James set aside the reports concerning Brooklyn as a whole, which he'd return to if he didn't uncover anything in the others. Then he dived headfirst into the reading.

For monster-hunting reports, this is surprisingly dry.

There was very little effort made into making the files enjoyable. Instead, they focused on conveying the most information in the shortest time possible. It was clear that it was all done by the same person, as the style never changed.

They must have some poor mook they fobbed everything onto. I bet Wright doesn't draft his own reports, the bastard.

Still, when he read between the lines, a pattern became apparent. Four times in the last two years had a dungeon spawned in Coney Island, and Radiant had been given the lease over it every single time.

They should have cleared it immediately but didn't. Instead, they used the dungeon's presence as an excuse to conduct "patrols." Little imagination on James's part was needed to realize that they were purposefully risking an increase in rank just to maintain control over the neighborhood.

Of course, they couldn't have done it without someone on the inside willfully ignoring that their average clearing time was a month, which was longer than what was allowed for a lease. But since no AA team was available for dispatch on such low-tier dungeons, the terms were renewed without trouble after a week of lying fallow.

It also explained why Wright's team was so surprised to find them coming out of the dungeon, even though their lease had already expired.

They're used to doing whatever they want with impunity. And someone is allowing them to do so from the inside.

The name that came out repeatedly as the AA official monitoring the situation was one Julius Green. His signature was everywhere, from accepting the terms of the initial leases to the extensions, to even writing recommendations for the Radiant Guild to be paid extra for their neighborhood watch work.

That alone would have been enough for James to write them all off as criminals, but something more beyond that was present in the files. There were at least a dozen cases of false alarms, all with similar stories: a new dungeon had formed somewhere in Brooklyn, which required dispatching a team the AA simply didn't have the resources to send.

And who came in, then, eager to fill the void left by the federal government? No points for guessing the Radiant Guild.

Report after report detailed their long "searches," during which they had to send patrolling teams through the whole borough, and for which they received compensation from the AA.

It was enough to send a sane man to the madhouse. They were evidently manufacturing these alerts, because a quick little search in Queens showed that they had only 10 percent as many false alarms.

If he noticed this, James seriously doubted the higher-ups didn't know of it. Or at least, they had to suspect something when budget review time came.

Unless everyone who should have raised an alarm is either involved in this scheme or has been intimidated into silence. It wouldn't surprise me if that band of thugs sent their "patrols" to a particularly zealous bureaucrat's house to ensure they understood how things should be handled.

James wasn't surprised to find evidence of wrongdoing. He had known for many years that guilds didn't always operate in the light and were, more often than not, a drain on society.

But the sheer brazenness with which the Radiant Guild operated a racketeering ring stunned him. It was all here, out in the open, and no one did anything.

James made sure to send a copy of those incriminating files to a burner email he had set up specifically. Even if he couldn't do anything immediately, he wanted to keep a record for when he became stronger.

If that's how I need to operate, then that's what I'll do. Just wait, you bastards, I'll show you what happens when you cross the wrong person. Justice will be served, sooner or later.

He just finished sending the last folder, full of the "false alarm" reports, when a hand suddenly gripped his shoulder, sending his heart into a frenzy.

James shot up from his seat, sweat forming on his brow as a dozen scenarios about being discovered by a Radiant Guild's accomplice played out in his mind, and what he could do to mislead them.

When he saw who it was, a great breath of relief escaped him. In all her masked glory, Miss Walker looked at him in amusement, her red eyes crinkled. "I'm sorry, James. Was I too quiet? I didn't mean to scare you."

Sending her a weak glare only seemed to increase her mirth, so James decided that cleaning up his station and shutting down the computer were better ways to spend his time.

The masked woman waited in silence as he finished up, not asking questions even when he abused her credentials to clear the cache of his activities. The computer would only show that it had been used to check up on an old nonthreatening file he had picked at random.

Once he was done, he turned to face her, ready to answer the questions he was sure she might have.

Surprisingly, the high-ranker remained silent, looking at him as if waiting for something. Knowing the tactic for what it was, having experienced it a lot growing up with his grandparents, James sighed, "All right, I'll tell you everything, but let's move from here. I don't want anyone to suspect anything."

Again, the older woman acquiesced without complaint, following him until they were back in Team 0's room. There, they sat down at the parlor couches, one in front of the other.

James quickly explained what he suspected and what he found, growing more incensed as his retelling continued. By the end of it, his fists were clenched and his eyes hard as stone. "I can only conclude that a significant part of the AA bureaucracy is compromised by the guilds, if not all of it," he finished, almost ready to spit fire.

Miss Walker was silent for a minute, staring off into the distance. Finally, she returned to the present. "You aren't wrong. And your conclusion that this is an open secret is also correct. We all know that some guilds, though not all of them, abuse the system we have because the AA doesn't have the resources to pursue them. And even more, they've corrupted the agency enough to pass it off as ordinary business."

Something in the way she said it told James that this was an old wound for her. There was a bitter air around her, as if she was remembering a battle she had been forced away from.

"I'll now give you the speech that my superior gave me at the time I found out about this system, five years ago," she said, confirming James's suspicion.

Seeing that he had no questions, she continued, "We're losing the battle against time. Dungeons, especially higher-rank ones, are expected to keep growing in number as the years go by, and sometime by the end of the century, we'll reach saturation."

James sat there, stunned. "Wh-what does that have to do with the guilds committing crimes?"

Miss Walker gave him a pitying look. "You already know the answer, James. This projection is based upon the guilds continuing to pull their weight. If we started to actively persecute every crime they commit, we'd simply not have enough forces to clear the dungeons that keep spawning."

He gritted his teeth, angry at himself for being able to see sense in her words. "Which means we just have to accept them acting like organized crime syndicates, slowly eroding society away until we are nothing but a bunch of fiefs? Do we have no hope, then?"

The woman's eyes softened, and she patted his hand in a show of comfort. "That projection is only expected to come true if nothing changes. Now, the latest studies expect the mana levels around the planet to plateau around midcentury, which means we're not necessarily done for."

That was a huge relief, but if it was true, that begged the question: "But then why? Why don't we slowly deal with the most rotten guilds and leave the righteous ones to help protect the Earth?"

"What makes you think that's not exactly what's going on?"

The question stunned James briefly, but he quickly reached the correct conclusion. "So you're allowing them to basically tie their nooses with their own hands!"

"Exactly. It will take some time, and some crimes are less urgent than others. Guilds like Radiant aren't worth the effort cleaning them up would require." She raised a hand, stopping the complaint forming on his lips. "The presence of Esposito at your confrontation with their thugs should tell you how intertwined they are with Golden Sun, and that is a heavy weight we can't move against lightly."

"So they can continue to siphon off resources from the AA, because they still take less than what would be required to eradicate them," James concluded with a heavy heart.

"That is correct." Then, upon seeing his glum expression, she added, "Still, that doesn't mean nothing can be done about them. If I or other high-rankers were to move against them, it would immediately call Golden Sun's attention upon us. However, if a newly arrived rookie were to somehow find enough evidence of their crimes and managed to subdue them, well, there's a reason why high-rankers avoid getting in the business of those weaker than them."

A smile slowly crept up, James quickly grasping where she was going. "Just as you can't get involved because of Golden Sun, they can't be the first to come into low-ranker business because of you."

Miss Walker stood up, gracing James with an eye smile. "I can see that you've gotten an idea. Now, as a responsible adult, I must warn you not to do anything that would pit you against someone much stronger than you."

"Of course, miss. I would never." *That just means I have to hurry and reach D-rank. Just you wait, Callum Wright. You and your little band of criminals better enjoy your freedom while you have it.*

CHAPTER NINETEEN

Having successfully shown that they could clear an H-rank dungeon by themselves and wanting to keep their momentum, Team 0's members agreed to ask for a new mission before the end of the week.

They were beaten to the punch by Miss Walker. One Thursday morning, she informed them that they would be going back to the sewers, in Manhattan this time, to clear up a newly spawned dungeon.

It would be an understatement to say they weren't particularly enthusiastic about going back into the smelly bowels of New York City.

"Is there really no dungeon available that doesn't involve holding my breath for hours?" Lauren complained. She had spent the two days following the rat dungeon run grumbling about the smell sticking to her hair.

Miss Walker just gave them a wan eye smile, shattering their hopes. "I already had trouble finding you guys a dungeon within your capabilities, something that wouldn't require you to camp out in the wilderness. So no, there is nothing else."

After shutting down their complaints, the masked woman went on to send everyone the file she had compiled on the dungeon. Since it was in Manhattan's sewers, despite being new, there was already a wealth of information.

"It's only crocodiles, as far as we know. Mostly swarms of smaller ones, since they must be newly hatched, so it shouldn't be too hard to deal with. But you shouldn't underestimate them either. Can anyone tell me why?"

Maria sighed, immediately picking up on the subtext. "Unlike the rats, these crocs will probably stay in the water for the most part, so it'll be tough for me to deal any damage."

Miss Walker nodded but was still not satisfied. When she gave James an insistent look, he acquiesced, "It'll be difficult to deal melee damage as well. If they stay in the waters, we'll be hampered, and even if they come out, crocodiles are known for their tough scales."

Their teacher hummed. "Then why would I pick this dungeon for you? It seems like the perfect counter to your abilities."

By now, they were all used to her methods. Miss Walker enjoyed giving them just enough information that they could get to the answer by themselves. That meant she must have already given them sufficient hints.

"Probably because we won't always be able to choose our battles, and getting used to fighting at a disadvantage now, against a new dungeon that hasn't been able to grow enough to truly threaten us, means we won't get as surprised in the future," James finally answered, feeling quite confident in his understanding of his teacher.

"That's absolutely correct. If you want to be spoon-fed easy matchups all your career while ignoring the real dangers to society, you should have gone to a guild. We don't shy away from any challenge here at the AA."

With its beautiful arches and Garibaldi statue, Washington Square Park was always teeming with life, being so close to NYU.

On a dreary Friday morning, just after daybreak, Team 0 was greeted with absolute stillness. The alert had gone off the night before, after one two-foot-long crocodile had crawled out of the sewer cover and tried to take a bite out of a dog.

Luckily, a police officer was nearby and, with a couple of well-placed shots, dealt with the monster. Unfortunately, panic spread quickly, and law enforcement had to declare the park a no-go zone until the appointed AA team could reach it.

Considering the dungeon's proximity to important institutions and the center of the city, the mayor's office sent a note requesting they deal with the problem as soon as possible.

That meant James and his teammates had been forced out of bed while the stars still twinkled; they were taken to the AA building where they changed into their suits before being hustled out to deal with the problem.

"This sucks. Nobody told me I would have to work this early," a yawning Ezekiel grumbled. Despite his usual peppiness, he wasn't a morning person.

"At least they had the decency to buy us breakfast." Daniel shrugged, a Starbucks blueberry muffin and latte on the bench next to him.

James quickly glanced at their two female teammates. They were still in their nonverbal state, though color was starting to return to them as they savored the warm brews. "As far as the police know, no new monster has crawled out of the sewers since the one from last night," he commented, reading the report one overly excited officer had handed him.

Daniel hummed around his muffin, slowly chewing as he considered the information. "That's good, at least. It means they haven't expanded their territory that much yet."

"We might be able to clean this up relatively soon," Ezekiel agreed, throwing his empty cup and dirty napkins in the trash can. "We might even be able to get some sleep before lunchtime."

At that, Lauren stood up, suddenly looking very determined. "Let's go. My bed is waiting for me, and I don't intend to leave it hanging for too long."

Maria gave her a long look before sighing. "All right, let's get this over with."

Since everyone was done, James threw back the last of his coffee, very happy that his higher stats made scalding his tongue a thing of the past, and threw the cup in the trash can, brushing a few crumbs off his skin-tight black-and-green suit.

"We'll do it like last time with Daniel and me going first, and when we call it clear, you can join us. Let's make sure we don't do anything stupid, and we'll go back home before we know it."

After his little speech, James bent down and opened the sewer cover, gesturing for Ezekiel to come closer. "Make me some light, will you?"

The younger boy agreed, and the Manhattan sewers were quickly unveiled as the white built-in flashlights of the suits sent the shadows scattering. Nothing seemed to be moving, so James lowered himself, keeping Thakinetic Awareness active.

He was shortly joined by Daniel, and when they ensured nothing was hiding in ambush, he called the all clear. "Come down. There's surprisingly little smell. Well, my nose might have been ruined by the rat dungeon, but at least this way I don't have to suffer."

Everyone gave a sigh of relief at that. Though they were taught that they should always expect hostile environmental effects, being able to breathe freely was still a great source of comfort.

The team quickly started exploring the sewers, noticing it wasn't too different from the stretch they had already visited. "Well, in Coney Island, we were close to the depurators, which means a lot of dirty things were accumulating. Here, we're far enough that it's still dispersed. Also, most Manhattan skyscrapers have internal cleaning systems, which means most of the job is already done," Ezekiel commented, getting weird looks from everyone.

"Hey, I'm just curious. There are a ton of YouTube videos on this kind of thing, don't you know?" he defended himself.

Before anyone could respond, James lifted a hand. "Incoming, a dozen little ones. Prepare!"

All the levity immediately dropped, and they took their positions. A few seconds later, movement in the waters became visible, even to those without sensory skills, as a swarm of three-foot-long crocodiles made their way toward them hungrily.

They were a bit bigger than the one that had sent Washington Square Park into a frenzy, but they were still not fully grown. As soon as they left the safety of the water, Daniel planted himself before them, an unmovable rock that forced the monsters to go around him.

Taking advantage of that, James and Lauren dispatched most of the swarm quickly while Ezekiel empowered himself and Maria so that their knives could end the little monsters with no trouble. James's punches broke their skulls easily enough, and they had no defense against blades.

"Well, this was easier than expected," Lauren commented, flicking the blood away from her own weapon.

"They're too young to do much to us. But if they were allowed to keep growing unchecked, I don't doubt this dungeon would become a real problem," James said, considering one of the corpses before him.

They're weak enough that a single empowered punch to the skull kills them, but an adult one could probably tank several of them. We need to be careful with the boss, as it might have already grown to be a threat.

He relayed his thoughts to his teammates, who all agreed not to lower their guard. Even if the first fight was easy enough that no one had gotten much closer to the next level, it still paid not to be caught unprepared.

A couple of minutes later, they encountered another similar swarm, which they dispatched with little effort. One of the crocodiles decided to pit its jaws against Daniel's shield and was dogged enough that Daniel was forced to bash it across the head, almost breaking the formation, but he was quick to return to his position that nothing happened.

Soon after the fight, they found something that shook them to their core. Team 0 used their suits' small resistant flashlights to illuminate the way. Their light reached from floor to ceiling, uncovering any secret that might be hidden.

But when James saw the *thing*, he didn't want to believe what his eyes were telling him. "Ez, could you please shine some of your light over here? I think the flashlights are making me see things."

Hesitantly, the boy complied. White healing light illuminated the surroundings and James could see that no, he hadn't been mistaken. It was indeed a foot sticking out of the water.

Everyone let out horrified gasps when they finally saw what he had been so concerned by, and they gathered around it.

"Do you think it's a trap?" Lauren asked, her knives held tight before her.

James shook his head. "I can't feel anything living here. Unless the crocs have suddenly become smart enough to start building things, we might've just found the remains of their dinner."

With some hesitation, he reached for the foot and grabbed it with two hands. James braced himself and pulled, surprised at how light the weight was.

Probably because it was connected to a leg that went up to midthigh, where the bone was sticking out and the muscle was entirely gone save for enough to identify him as a man. The corpse had been chewed up by whatever had killed the poor victim, making for a gruesome sight. All five Awakeners looked at each other in disgust and worry.

Finally, Ezekiel asked, "Do you think we have to go look for the rest of that poor man?"

"No, once we've cleared the dungeon of monsters, we can leave that to the proper authorities. What worries me the most is that unless this person was exceptionally drunk or under substances, he should've been able to run away from the little crocs," James answered, laying the solitary limb to the side of the tunnel, looking at his gloved hands in distaste.

"Which means something big and strong enough to kill a grown man is here," Lauren concluded, looking grimly into the darkness ahead of them.

CHAPTER TWENTY

Since things looked much dicier, the members of Team 0 regrouped to think. Ezekiel raised the possibility of going back up and informing the AA that they found human remains, that they suspected this dungeon might be more dangerous than initially expected.

According to the rulebook, that was what they were supposed to do. But they might not be taken seriously with little evidence beyond half a leg, which probably belonged to a homeless man.

"Miss Walker wouldn't dismiss us though. She knows us and knows we aren't ones to flake off a mission simply because we got spooked!" the boy kept arguing, though it sounded weak even to his ears, given his grimace.

James shook his head. "I don't think we can justify abandoning the dive just because of this. Rather, I think this means we *have* to keep going to find exactly what is going on here."

No one liked it, but eventually they all agreed. If they found any evidence of a monster beyond H-rank, they would immediately leave and report to the AA, but if it was something within their range, they had a duty to fight it.

It didn't take long to find a potential cause of the gory mess. Five minutes after they resumed the dive, James felt something big moving in the waters. It was large enough that it would have worried him even if it had been a common animal; the mana in the dungeon could have mutated an ordinary crocodile into something truly dangerous.

He immediately alerted the others, and they took up position, waiting to see if it would surface. Like the ambush predator it was, it hid until the last minute. It emerged just as it looked like it was passing them by, its mouth wide open and ready to clamp down on Daniel, who was serving as the vanguard.

The creature, though not entirely out of the water, was enormous. Ten feet of its body was visible, while its lower body and tail remained hidden.

It snapped its mouth with a strength James doubted they would have survived, but it was slow enough that, while on high alert, Daniel was able to avoid it.

Immediately, they all started attacking it. A small fireball, emitting enough heat that no one could have doubted its power, smashed into its snout, sending it reeling in pain.

While it was in midair, James launched a devastating kick to the side of its head, concentrating his skill on his foot. The blow sent the crocodile skidding over the concrete path, finally revealing its full size.

Close to twenty feet, the monster had wickedly sharp scales all over its spine. Its teeth were as long as two of James's fingers, and its eyes, glowing yellow even in the dim light, held nothing but death.

That was, until a knife buried itself into one eye. It twisted and coiled around itself in pain as it tried to dislodge it.

Suddenly, the creature slowed down, looking like a great weight had been added to its frame. Knowing that this was the effect of Ezekiel's skill, they all continued their assault.

Another fireball found its target, this time entering the crocodile's open mouth and burning its insides. James dealt the last blow by jump-kicking its head, sending the still-buried knife into its brain, killing it immediately.

A moment of silence passed as all the Awakeners regained their breath. The fight hadn't been particularly long, but the speed and lethality with which the monster moved had spooked them.

"Well, I guess we found a possible culprit," Ezekiel tried to joke, earning some weak chuckles. Yet, the boy's eyes remained affixed on the crocodile's corpse, and James could understand why.

It was, by far, the biggest creature any of them had ever fought. Its sheer size and strength would have been enough to kill any of them immediately, unlike even the rat boss.

Yeah, that one could use skills and was technically stronger, what with the versatility and crowd control abilities it had. But one-on-one, this monster would win anytime if it were allowed close.

It was a different kind of fight when you knew that every mistake might lead to your death. Their suits were made of materials strong enough to withstand the crocodile's bite, but their heads were still uncovered, and if it clamped down on one of their limbs and twisted, well, James didn't like his chances of getting out unscathed.

"Now we have to hope these things don't operate in groups, or we're fucked."

Lauren might be correct, unfortunately. As long as they worked together, they could easily overcome the limitations imposed upon them by this specific dungeon, but if they were forced to fight more than one, things could get tricky.

"Did anyone get a level?" James asked, hopeful that a last-minute power-up might make their chances better. He hadn't, but he was very close to it. The little crocs hadn't given him much, but the big one had filled almost half his needed experience.

"I did." Ezekiel and Maria raised their hands simultaneously, and they high-fived each other in celebration.

While the two assigned their free points, James and the others kept watch, knowing how delicate a moment it was.

Once the two acclimated to their power-up, they resumed their track, though not before pushing the crocodile's carcass to the side of the path.

"We don't want to run back quickly and find this thing slowing us down," Daniel had said, and they had all agreed.

The atmosphere of the sewer tunnel was dark and damp, their every step echoing despite their best effort, except for Lauren, whose Rogue Talent gave her the skills necessary to go unnoticed. In such an environment, they couldn't hope to mask their arrival, but since James could sense presences in the area thanks to Thakinetic Awareness, they'd know if something was coming, nullifying the disadvantage.

Another swarm of little crocs, though this time closer to four feet in size, found them shortly after the two mages were done with their stat points. The monsters charged and tried to bite anything within reach, a tactic which turned out to be more effective when the monsters were stronger and faster.

They had no compunction to stop when their siblings were killed, instead redoubling their ferocity. James was thus forced to come to Ezekiel's rescue, as the boy risked being encircled.

The last of the little monsters was dealt with by Daniel, who took a surprising amount of gusto at smashing them against the wall when they clamped on his shield. "These little buggers are persistent, I'll give them that."

James wasn't listening, however, because he finally reached level 10. It wasn't much of a milestone. Level 50 was much more important, being the cutoff for G-rank, with level 100 being the most critical as the gateway to the second Awakening.

Still, it represented something to him. It gave him a nice round number that showed his increased power. To James, that was enough to be happy. "Hey, guys, I just leveled up. Cover me while I assign my points?"

"Me too. Just give me a moment, and I'll be done," Lauren said, sitting down next to James. They had been told that increasing their stats while standing was dangerous, as muscle twitches could cause them to fall.

Status!

Not only did he level up, but he also increased Thakinetic Empowerment's level! James quickly assigned the points, a smile stretching his lips.

STATUS WINDOW	
Name	James Summers
Age	19
Awakening	1st
Talent	Thakinesis
Title	
Level	10
MP	41/50

STR	10
VIT	8
AGI	9
SEN	10
MND	8
STAT POINTS	0

SKILLS	LEVEL	DESCRIPTION
Thakinetic Empowerment	3	(Active): Utilize your Willpower to temporarily raise STR - VIT - AGI.
Thakinetic Awareness	2	(Active/Passive): Expand your SEN to feel others' wills.
Thakinetic Resistance	2	(Active/Passive): Empower your MND to defend yourself against foreign influences.

With his points assigned to strength and agility stats, bringing them to ten and nine respectively, James was overtaken by the usual headache mixed with muscular twitches, though they didn't last long.

Before he could stand up, his Thakinetic Awareness blared with danger, and he only had time to scream, "Incoming!"

A massive form breached the water, effortlessly bridging the gap between the edge of the platform and the sewer proper. His warning gave Daniel enough time to shield Maria, who was standing next to him.

The massive crocodile clamped down on the shield, ripping it off the Tank's hands and throwing it away.

By that time, though, they had all moved into position, and when it turned to face them, ready to lunge again, it was greeted by a fiery present. The skill was strong enough to scorch its hard scales, making the creature screech in pain. That didn't deter it, however, and it lunged again.

James punched it with all his strength, the urgency of the moment focusing his willpower on the task, aided by his skill level increase. Thus, he was able to blow it away, sending the large creature skidding on the cement platform.

Lauren was immediately on top of it, having managed to go unnoticed up until now, and once again aimed for its weak point. By a stroke of luck, the crocodile tilted its head away at the last moment. It took a gash that didn't even manage to make it bleed.

Another fireball splashed against it, giving the Rogue time to get some distance.

Again, they repeated the same tactic, with Ezekiel slowing the monster down. James dodged a lunge, thanks to Daniel faking a charge, and managed to send the crocodile belly up with a retaliatory kick. With its relatively unprotected side exposed, Lauren made short work of it, her sharp knives opening its belly, making its internal organs spill out.

James directed one last uppercut at its head, the blow crushing its throat and ending the already fading creature's life.

"Ugh, I think I found where the rest of the body is." Maria was pointing directly at where the monster's stomach was, full to the brim with powerful gastric acid and a half-dissolved head.

It took strength not to retch at the sight. The skin was almost gone, and only bits of muscle and hair remained attached to the bone. The skull, however, was unmistakably that of a human male, and it took little imagination to realize the leg they found belonged to it.

"Well, mystery solved, I guess. The other one was innocent," James commented. He used his knife to further open the stomach, careful not to get splashed with the acid. Though his suit was D-rank and should easily stand up to it, he didn't want to get into the habit of not caring for it. Considering his luck, it would give up on him at the worst moment.

"Gah, do you have to do it now?" Ezekiel asked, voice muffled by his hands over his mouth.

"The acid will keep melting it. It'll already be difficult to find out who it was. It might be too late if we leave it for another few hours," he explained, not particularly enjoying the task either.

At least, the encounter managed to get Daniel over the line for his own level-up, so he took a moment to assign the new points while the others kept watch.

We're gonna need it if we want to make it out of here in one piece.

CHAPTER TWENTY-ONE

Manhattan's dank, dark sewers were home to more plant life than James had expected. Seaweed of many different kinds had made their home in the waters, and there was even moss sprinkled in patches all over the platform Team 0 was walking on.

Considering how desolate the rat dungeon had been, it was a pleasant surprise. It gave an otherwise dreary landscape a burst of life.

I wouldn't mind it too much if it wasn't for the murderous crocodiles. Well, I certainly won't be coming back even after we've cleared it, but it's not as repulsive as Coney Island's sewers.

The mere fact that he was seriously contemplating the qualities of different sewers made James shudder. Refocusing, he glanced down at the corpses of the fourth swarm of little crocs they had defeated. Luckily, it didn't seem like they would be getting any bigger than four feet, but they were already plenty dangerous.

Their increased size also meant more agile movement, especially when they jumped from the water. Still, the team developed a successful tactic for dealing with them and managed to get through the assault without any injuries.

"I wonder if we can keep some of this leather and have bags and belts made from it. It's not as cool as a high-rank material, but this vivid green is much better than any other of the same level." Maria and surprisingly Ezekiel had been engaging in that kind of talk for a while now.

They had found out that they were both fashionistas and were spending their downtime wondering over possible combinations of high-quality materials for their next suits.

The ones we have work just fine. I don't think we need to worry about them for quite a while, to be honest. D-rank leather can stand up to anything a dungeon can throw at it until E-rank, and we need some time before we can get there.

"Guys, I think that's enough of a break. We shouldn't waste too much time anyway. Remember, we need to get back up before lunch so I can nap a bit more!" Lauren's enthusiasm was met with a half-hearted cheer.

They had decided to stop for a while, since the constant waves of monsters and the occasional ambush by much larger specimen had been wearing on them, especially after fishing out the remains of a man from a crocodile's stomach.

"You feeling all right, Jimbo?" Daniel's shoulder bumped his as he directed a questioning look his way.

"I'm good. I was just thinking about how long the road ahead of us is. We'll probably need to run a dozen dungeons like this before we can get to G-rank, then a couple dozen more of those to get to F-rank. And then more and more. It'll take some time to get strong." James wasn't foolish enough to aim for the stars immediately, but he wanted enough strength to gain agency.

Daniel hummed, considering his words. "That's true. But it's better to get there doing things properly rather than simply rushing ahead. Levels count for a lot, but you risk getting a weak evolution for your skills if they aren't where they need to be before the second Awakening."

And wasn't that the truth. Skills operated in a slightly different way than the rest of the System. They could only go up to level 10, and once their holder reached the limit of their Awakening—level 100 for first tier, level 200 for the second, and so on—they could evolve into a more powerful variation.

If, for some reason, the Awakener in question didn't bring all their skills to level 10—which could take some time, as they were not something that would rise with simple repetition—they could still evolve them, but they'd get a weaker variant of their normal evolution.

For example, Thakinetic Empowerment, which is already at level 3, is pretty much guaranteed to reach level 10 by the time I hit level 100 and go through my Talent rank-up, if I keep pushing myself. Generally, enhancement skills become a more holistic version, granting their bearer some exotic effects. If I were to go through the second Awakening while it was still at level 8, instead, it would simply become Thakinetic Empowerment II, giving me just a little bonus on top of what it is now.

"You're right," James replied, looking forward into the darkness. "I know I must be patient, but it still grates on me. I can't do anything to really help anyone the way I am now."

Daniel, though not one for long conversations, turned out to be something of a kindred spirit. James didn't know the details, but from little bits and pieces, he had discovered a great injustice in his past, which he was determined to see made right.

That resolve was something he and James shared. An unspoken bond formed between the two, as they discussed possible paths to advancement and ways to accelerate their growth.

The Black teammate was always steadfast in his belief that good things came to those who worked for them. That although human society had long since abandoned meritocracy, if it had ever implemented it, the System changed things.

It made it possible for someone like them, two young adults who hadn't been sure of their future, who could have given in to despair at seeing how fucked up the world was, to have a worthy, respectable career.

Daniel patted him on the shoulder before nodding in the direction Lauren was walking toward. "I'm getting close to level 11, so you must be too. Just think that by the time we clear this dungeon, we'll probably be at twelve, well on our way to thirteen."

James agreed, his determination reigniting. "That's right. Enough moping." Then, with a louder voice, he said, "All right, guys, let's get going. If we dally any longer, Lauren's gonna hog all the monsters and leave us in the dust."

The girl in question grumbled but hid a smile; she wasn't that annoyed. They all gathered their things and were off, walking deeper into the dungeon's maw.

The path gradually enlarged, until it became broad enough that all five could comfortably walk next to each other. Not that they did so, as that would leave them vulnerable, but they appreciated the additional room.

It wasn't long before James felt something approaching from behind and, soon after, another presence ahead of them, waiting in the water. He quickly alerted his teammates, and a grim air came over the group.

"How do we want to handle this? Just concentrate on one while Daniel holds off the other? Or split up?" Ezekiel asked, but Maria had a different idea.

Two scorching hot orbs were forming atop her palms, and her eyes were trained on the sewer line, looking for any sign of movement. "Where are they hiding, James? I have a present for them."

Grasping her plan, he pointed in the correct direction. "All right, force them out, and hopefully give them some nasty burns. Meanwhile, Lauren and I will rush the one behind us. Ez, buff us so we can finish it quickly and come help you with the last one."

No one had anything to say against that, so they took their positions. Maria launched her fireballs, which exploded on contact with the water. A cloud of steam covered most of their sight, but they were already used to operating in low light. The two beasts, as large as any they had encountered so far, emerged from the water with a growl, their forms shrouded in the vapor. Still, their frantic movements made it clear they had been hit, though they were not out of commission yet.

James used his sensing skill to head toward the largest of the two crocodiles, which thrashed halfway out of the water. Before it could understand it was being attacked, he launched a devastating strike to its head, a place he wouldn't have dared to attack had the monster been aware of him.

His gloves, strengthened with D-rank materials, hit a lot harder than his old reinforced pair and allowed him to deal much more damage than his bare hands would have.

The crocodile's skin, however, was resistant enough that it wasn't defeated yet. It reared up and, with a swiftness that belonged to an apex predator, managed to avoid Lauren's lethal strike.

She still scored a gash on its snout, which gave it enough pause that she could get away from a retaliatory strike.

Meanwhile, the other three were keeping the second crocodile at bay with a combination of Maria's fireballs, which it weakened by using its tail to throw water up in the air in a surprising show of intelligence, and Ezekiel's flashes of light and debuffs, which greatly disturbed it. Daniel stood before them, glowing shield held firmly to ward off any lunge the creature might try.

Slowly, both groups were chipping away at the crocodiles. The damage they inflicted wasn't lethal, as they couldn't get close enough, but it was slowing them down. Soon, they'd reach a tipping point and attempt a desperate last move, which was precisely what the Awakeners were waiting for.

Unfortunately, their carefully laid plan went up in smoke when James sensed another swarm heading their way. They had a few seconds before it arrived, and given their current situation, he was afraid they might get overrun.

"Swarm!" he called. "I'm going to leave finishing this one to you!" he then yelled to Lauren, who pursed her lips. She determinedly looked at the monster and nodded; she would take care of it.

Thus, James launched himself deeper into the dungeon, where he could now visibly see the swarm of little crocs. He crossed the hundred feet between them in what felt like an instant, and then everything became a blur.

The little monsters jumped at him from all sides, latching onto the protective suit and trying to bite through. Fortunately, the AA hadn't skimped when buying their gear, which easily held against the combined assault.

James ignored all those beasts, instead concentrating on simply maintaining his rhythm. His punches flew true, and each hit another croc, sometimes simply shooing them away, sometimes stunning them, and, when he got lucky enough, killing them on the spot.

James's mind was blank as he kept mowing down the swarm, hitting leathery flesh again and again, ignoring the aches building up until, finally, there were no more targets.

It took him a second to realize that he had utterly annihilated the swarm before he remembered his teammates' precarious situation. He turned to rush back to them, only to witness Lauren jump on top of the monster that Maria, Daniel, and Ezekiel were fighting, then drive her knife into its brain—an instant kill.

Behind them lay the carcass of the monster James and Lauren had fought. Its blood pooled onto the concrete from the myriad gashes all over its form.

James sighed in relief. When he had felt the swarm approaching, he had been afraid they would be done for, but luckily, they pulled through. *Well, it wasn't just luck*, he thought, looking at his bloody fists.

An itch in his brain distracted him then, and he smiled. With just a thought, he brought the notification to the forefront.

Level Up!
Congratulations, your level is now 11.

Well, no one can say that the rewards aren't worth it. I might get to level 13 by the time we clear this whole thing.

CHAPTER TWENTY-TWO

They ended up having to fight another swarm of little crocodiles, as well as five larger ones before they got to the end of the dungeon. Ezekiel's healing also got a bit of a workout, putting James back into fighting form after he threw himself headfirst into the swarm.

The D-rank suit had protected him well, but it couldn't do much to stop him from bruising after receiving countless bites. Still, he was right as rain after a short healing session, and he was able to take down two big crocodiles.

By then, James was so close to level 12 that it hurt, and all his companions had also leveled up. He assigned his points to strength and agility, bringing them to eleven and ten, respectively. His senses were already good enough that he could feel every croc that got near them, but what he lacked the most was his ability to kill them quickly.

Even when he was buffed by Ezekiel's skill, it still took him four blows to kill one of the larger crocodiles. It was impressive enough for someone who had Awakened not even three weeks ago, but it was still not enough for him.

I realize I have very high standards for myself, but if I don't push forward with this intensity, I'll never become strong enough to change things. Strong enough to show the Radiant Guild they can't do whatever they want with impunity.

Then, James noticed that though their path had stopped expanding, the sewer water deepened until it could easily hide three large crocodiles.

"I think we might be getting close to the boss," he said, making the others perk up.

The fights so far had been pretty difficult, especially since they had come in expecting something closer to the squirrels he had cleared by himself. Basically a den of newborn crocs. Instead, they had been faced with monsters strong enough to easily overpower the mutated rats and a dungeon large enough it couldn't have been that recent.

That meant it had been growing unnoticed for quite a while, possibly even a couple of weeks. How it had managed to do so, James didn't know. Mana readers were ubiquitous these days; even regular law enforcement had them on hand.

That a dungeon could grow for weeks beneath Manhattan without anyone knowing a thing about it was simply impossible. Not with the sheer amount of attention that was on the island.

Which means either a complete failure of the system—which I wouldn't be too surprised about—or someone knew but kept it quiet.

The second option was sinister. He imagined the heart of New York City being ripped apart by a swarm of monstrous crocodiles. It evoked terrible memories of the apocalypse.

Back then, such occurrences had been quite common, and until order was finally fully restored in the city in 2013, they had to live with the constant fear of monster attacks.

Considering just how much blood and tears had been spilled to take some normalcy back, James wasn't inclined to let the "error" slip by unnoticed.

"Do you think we should expect another boss that uses swarming tactics?" Ezekiel asked, drawing James's attention away from his musings.

"With all the little crocs we had to kill to get here, it wouldn't surprise me," he answered, looking at his gloved hands, still coated in a dried layer of monster blood that was slowly peeling off.

It's not like I can clean myself with the water. We're in a sewer, for fuck's sake.

"Either that," Maria interjected, looking around with a distrustful frown, "or it's gonna be an absolutely massive croc. Big enough to swallow us whole. Or it could chew us up. Oh! Or it could try to bring us into the water and drown us there!"

The pretty redhead, it turned out, was surprisingly morbid. James knew she did it to rid her fears, but in these moments, he'd really like it if she managed to keep her mouth shut.

Any retort he might have given was interrupted by a low growl that reverberated through the tunnel. It was deep enough that James felt it in his chest, and it seemed he wasn't the only one to be spooked by it.

"All right, I guess massive croc it is," Maria whispered, though they all heard it.

"You know the drill people. DDD: Distract, Direct, and Deal," James called out, ignoring the Fire Mage's mutterings.

It was a strategy they had agreed upon to fight with the previous boss, though they had been forced into a different formation by the swarm the rat had called. It did, however, work well against the large crocodiles, and it was the best bet they had to take the boss down without any serious injury.

When they were ready, they walked forward, entering the boss's den. There was nothing to demarcate this stretch of sewers as different from the rest beyond the deeper water, but James could now feel a large presence ahead of them.

It was already on dry land, as if waiting for them. As the light of their flashlights finally illuminated it, they all took a deep breath. It was massive, twenty-five feet in length and five feet in height. Its snow-white scales covered its body like armor, and with intelligent red eyes, the boss regarded them calmly.

It was as if it didn't care that they had been slaughtering their way through its dungeon. James felt like it was studying them, curiously taking in their suits.

A low rumbling emitting from its throat was the only warning it gave, and when they made no motion to leave, the creature coiled up.

Instead of rushing forward like they had expected it might, they were hit by a jet of water coming from the side, completely blindsided. The entirety of Team 0 was thrown to the ground, their suits the only reason they didn't suffer damage to end the fight then and there.

Instinctively, James rolled with it and jumped up, knowing that if he allowed the creature to set the rhythm, they would surely lose and become its lunch.

It was a good thing that he did so, because the boss had taken their disorientation to rush them, moving relatively fast for a creature of that size, especially on dry land.

Since he couldn't match its strength directly—and he had to stall it until his teammates gathered themselves and regrouped—James flooded his limbs with Thakinetic Empowerment, pushing twenty points of mana in a single application.

There came a point, after the maximum threshold, when adding more juice to a skill simply wasn't worth it, and he had fiddled with his enough to understand where exactly that point was.

For Empowerment, that was twenty mana points. More than that, it didn't show any further increase. It was still a substantial amount, considering that James only had fifty-five points available.

Still, coupled with his iron determination to grant his friends a reprieve, his strength grew enough that he was able to deflect the boss's powerful lunge. It also increased his vitality stat, so he wasn't immediately taken out of commission when the massive white tail hit him in a surprise strike.

James could only scramble up, desperately dodging another bite he was sure he would have felt, D-rank armor or not. He then firmed his resolve, rolled under another tail whip, and jumped over the boss, raining punches everywhere he could get to.

The monster, however, was clever and immediately rolled, dislodging him. Before it could strike, a powerful blow threw it away from James. It granted him some much-needed air. Daniel nodded at him, having recovered his shield and taking up his position as Tank.

Now that the formation had regrouped, the balance shifted. The boss tried again to disperse them with a water jet, but Daniel interposed himself and, through his skill and Ezekiel's buff, managed to take the hit with only a grunt.

Maria shot several fireballs, aimed more to distract the creature than do any harm, considering how thick its armor was. Thanks to that, Lauren and James were able to close the distance. His punch, enhanced as it was, managed to send the crocodile reeling, and the Rogue took the opportunity to score a series of gashes near its eyes, though the boss managed to avoid any severe damage.

To avoid another jet of water, they were forced to jump back, thus returning to their starting position. "This thing is much tougher than the others. My knives are sharp enough, but I don't have the strength to push them through its armor," Lauren complained.

"First of all, Ez, slow it down. If we can avoid its attacks, we'll be better off than if our hits do more damage. This is a death-by-a-thousand-cuts type of situation. We need to avoid wasting mana, but we can't win in a direct assault." James took charge, seeing that their regular tactics were not working.

Ezekiel obeyed; he released the buffs he had cast on them and turned his attention to the boss. His debuff skill, having leveled up, allowed him to lower a specific attribute, and tanking its agility seemed the most effective way of getting some room.

The crocodile, however, didn't let them be for long. Another jet of water hit Daniel's shield, and he grunted in pain. However this time the attack masked the creature's next move as it charged, sending the Tank flying with its powerful tail. Without respite, it launched forward, trying to clamp its jaws on the Tank's leg.

"It's trying to pick us apart!" James yelled, even as he shoulder-checked the crocodile away from his friend. By then, Ezekiel's debuff had taken hold, finally slowing the boss's speed so they could reorganize.

"I'll keep it at bay. When it gets close, force it back." Maria's fireballs flew true and hit the monster, scorching the outer layer of its armor. It didn't seem to be feeling too much pain. However, under the Fire Mage's continued barrage, it was forced to call upon the waters to form a liquid shield.

The situation, it seemed, had reached a stalemate of some sort. Thanks to the slowing debuff, the crocodile couldn't get close enough, nor did it have enough time to attack with its water magic, while Team 0 didn't seem to manage to inflict lethal damage on it.

The beast, though it looked beat up, was still perfectly capable of fighting, and if they continued this kind of fruitless assault for too long, they'd end up out of mana and at its mercy. James's plan to whittle it down would only work if they managed to do some damage, after all.

The water shield prevented James's first idea, which was for them to continue a long-range assault, using rocks and knives if necessary, thus gaining enough time to prepare something more lethal while damage accumulated. His second, however, might just work.

We have to break the stalemate. If we can do enough damage to hamper its movements and force it on defense, then we win.

"Maria, concentrate your fire on the side of the shield; we need to break through. Lauren, let's aim for its legs. We need to slow it down even more. Guys, try to keep its attention. I'll attack from the other side." That said, James rushed forward, with the roar of Maria's fireballs echoing through the cavern. It turned into a hiss as the fireballs evaporated the water shield.

His blood pumping, energy flowing, James found himself grinning. He knew his life was on the line, as were his friends'. He just couldn't help but enjoy it. He felt alive.

This is it. This is the life I want to live.

CHAPTER TWENTY-THREE

For all that the crocodile was a formidable opponent, and it would have probably swept any of them in a one-versus-one fight, its fate had been sealed the moment Team 0 managed to get its measure.

Unlike the rat boss, it didn't have any support to come to its aid, probably because of its reptilian, solitary nature. Since it couldn't properly leverage its water magic or formidable strength thanks to their teamwork, there was nothing it could do beyond being whittled down.

James believed the crocodile to be smart enough to realize its fate, which was why he wasn't surprised when it tried to break the rhythm they had established by throwing itself back into the water.

It wouldn't run away, unlike other monsters. A boss was born when a creature absorbed an abnormal amount of mana from the Well, and if it survived the process, it gained incredible powers, with the caveat that it couldn't leave. Not because the dungeon was sentient and tried to stop it, but because the mana density outside the central chamber was simply too low to sustain it for long.

They were creatures destined to reign over their kin but couldn't leave their kingdom. That was why they ignored the possibility it would run away; instead, they focused on the likely chance it would go for broke and try to change up the pace.

So when it called upon more water, only to use it as a distraction to reach the sewer, they smoothly changed positions, allowing Maria to bombard it more easily.

Her fireballs were not hot enough to do much harm while it hid below the surface. Still, they could certainly make things uncomfortable for it, and while the redhead couldn't maintain the attacks for long, having almost exhausted her reserves, they had a secret weapon the crocodile couldn't possibly counter.

A mana potion, an expensive item they had received as part of their monthly supplies from the AA, went down her gullet, granting her a second wind. With her reserves restored, the girl was easily able to increase her rate of fire, until the monster was once again forced out of the water.

From there, their death-of-a-thousand-cuts plan resumed; they kept in mind that they couldn't afford to prolong it much since everyone was feeling the drain and mana potions didn't grow on trees. Even an H-rank one, such as the one Maria drank, cost a thousand dollars. Moreover, they weren't easy to attain since guilds tended to buy them as soon as they hit the market.

Fortunately, the boss was only an H-rank creature, though a relatively strong one. Its reserves were not enough to outlast the entirety of Team 0, especially since it was forced to call upon its water shield more and more.

Once it exhausted its mana and physical strength was all that it had left, they moved in for the kill.

James, aided by the debuffs still slowing the monster down, disoriented it with a couple hits, creating an opening for Lauren to get her knife into its skull. The armor there was thick enough that the stab wouldn't kill it. But the boss went into a frenzy as it desperately tried to dislodge the weapon, only to push it in more.

The two melee fighters made some distance, not wanting to get caught in the massive crocodile's death throes. When the monster showed no sign of succumbing, Daniel charged it, his shield glowing powerfully as he bashed it against the knife buried in its head, finally ending the fight.

"Oh, sweet baby Jesus. Finally!" Lauren groaned, dropping to the ground in exhaustion as soon as the notification came. She had been using her skills to nick the boss on every possible occasion, making it wary enough that it hadn't attempted to isolate and kill any of them. Her efforts had been fundamental but also very tiring.

"That thing just wouldn't go down. It must have been almost at the top of H-rank, otherwise it couldn't have lasted so long."

James nodded, agreeing with Ezekiel's assessment. Evidently, the boss's main stats had been strength and vitality, granting it a highly enhanced physique, but it hadn't been fast enough to make use of them. Miss Walker's words about keeping their stats balanced rang with truth once again.

Maria was busy rubbing her temples. Her overuse of mana on top of pushing herself further with the potion came back to bite her in the form of a headache. "God, this suuuucks."

Daniel patted her on the back, commiserating, "Let's pick this place clean and go back to the surface. If we're quick, I think we'll still have a couple of hours before lunch to nap."

That was enough for everyone to perk up. The very early rise, coupled with the unexpected difficulty of the dungeon, meant that they really needed the rest.

"Well, what are you guys waiting for? Let's get this done!" Lauren shouted, suddenly peppy.

James chuckled but got his knife out, ready to start cutting into some crocodiles. "I think it's better if we just bring the whole boss up. Trying to search for its mana stone would take us too long and the materials might be worth a lot, considering it's a crocodile."

Daniel grimaced, knowing he'd have to be the one to do most of the work, but didn't complain. He took the end of the monster's tail in his hands and started to pull. "This is gonna take a while."

Showers were God's gift to mankind, James decided. Many had lost their faith after the System had saved them during the apocalypse in 2012, but he was sure that if the bliss he was feeling continued for a bit longer, his faith would finally resurge.

I swear if they send us down in another sewer, I'll quit. I barely managed to get the smell from my hair . . . At least this one was a bit less stinky. The human remains weren't exactly pleasant, nor was having to dig through a hundred of those little crocs for their stones, but at least we got some money out of it.

His bank account had never been happier. His expenses had also increased as he had to commute daily to Manhattan and, more importantly, buy supplies for their dives beyond what the AA offered. Still, the gains, both material and System-wise, were enough that James felt satisfied with the results of his hard work.

That was another thing he truly enjoyed about being an Awakener. When he worked in retail, even after he gave it his all, the reward was a small bonus at the most. Now, having faced his most powerful enemy so far, he had pushed through level 12 and into level 13. The four stat points burned, and he'd assign them soon enough, but first, he needed to finish cleaning himself up.

Once that was done, James exited his shower in Team 0's private bathroom, slipping into his flip-flops and walking to the hair dryer station. He nodded to Daniel and Ezekiel, who had the same blissful, satisfied expressions he knew was painted on his face.

In unison, they activated the hair dryers, shaking their heads like dogs and using them to remove the stubborn water droplets that clung to them even after one pass with the towel.

"This is the life," James commented later, lying sprawled on one of the couches while still in his bathrobe, a cup of hot tea held in his hands.

"Yeah, if only we didn't have to go through the sewers looking for monsters to live it . . ." Lauren commented, sitting with her legs up in very fluffy-looking pajamas.

After their first dungeon run, where they had all become friends, Team 0's members had decided unanimously to drop the pretenses and enjoy their parlor's relaxed atmosphere. That meant wearing whatever they wanted without fear of judgment, eating as much as they wished to, and sleeping without fear of getting disturbed.

James glanced at Maria, who was blissfully napping on another couch, wearing an eye mask and earplugs. He commented, "Well, I don't think we'd enjoy it as much if we hadn't come from a sewer." When they gave him weird looks, he hurried to add, "Not to say that it's the suffering that makes pleasure what it is, but it enhances the experience, doesn't it?"

"I suppose," Lauren conceded, not looking particularly interested in pursuing that line of reasoning. Instead, she chose another subject. "Do you guys want to add your stat points now, or will you do it later?"

Daniel shrugged. "I already put two in strength; I needed it to carry the damn boss."

They all chuckled at that. James had helped the Tank, especially in the last stretch, but since they had to cut into the crocodiles and extract their mana stones, Daniel had to lug the massive creature around for quite a while.

"I'll do it later. I'm relaxing now," Ezekiel replied, who was busy putting some hydrating cream on his face. "The sewers might be humid, but it's the wrong kind. My skin looks horrible."

"I think I'll do it now," James said, bringing up his status window with a thought, adding one point to strength, one to sense, one to vitality, and the last to mind.

STATUS WINDOW	
Name	James Summers
Age	19
Awakening	1st
Talent	Thakinesis
Title	
Level	13
MP	65/65
STR	12
VIT	9
AGI	10
SEN	11
MND	9
STAT POINTS	0

SKILLS	LEVEL	DESCRIPTION
Thakinetic Empowerment	3	(Active): Utilize your Willpower to temporarily raise STR - VIT - AGI.
Thakinetic Awareness	2	(Active/Passive): Expand your SEN to feel others' wills.
Thakinetic Resistance	2	(Active/Passive): Empower your MND to defend yourself against foreign influences.

The boss fight had shown the importance of not overspecializing, especially at an early stage. The white crocodile wouldn't have won even had it been faster, but it certainly would have made things more difficult for them.

As he progressed, James knew he'd have to bring his two main stats, strength and sense, to a higher level than the others, but that was precisely why he was following the strategy he had decided upon with Miss Walker's help.

At every level, he'd put one point in his main stats and one in his secondary ones. That alone would end up making all the difference he would need, even if, at the moment, it didn't look like much.

Well, to put things into perspective, I'm strong enough that I could have competed in a weightlifting championship before the apocalypse. My eyes can see much farther, my ears are sharper, and even my nose is better. Admittedly, that doesn't help much when it comes to trawling through a sewer . . .

The sensation of muscles and mind rearranging themselves under the System's influence was always weird, but James had almost gotten used to it by now. Unless you banked a few levels' worth of points and added them all at once, there would be no problems, even if you added them while on the field.

He was still frustrated at how far he'd have to go before he could do anything definitive about the Radiant Guild, but progress made him feel better. Slowly but surely, he was getting there.

The time of the reckoning would come before they could realize it was on them, and he'd show no mercy.

CHAPTER 23.5 – INTERLUDE

Leila Walker

Her little team of rookies just achieved another victory. It was especially surprising given that they had been thrown out of bed so early in the morning and been given, if she had to be charitable, incomplete information.

Or deliberately faulty. And I'm going to get to the bottom of this if it's the last thing I do.

Leila marched toward the regional director's office, where she had called an emergency meeting. Though she wasn't technically part of the high brass, her status as a high-ranker meant that people listened to her, and when she was as incensed as she currently was, no one dared stand in her way.

Well, almost no one.

In the middle of the corridor stood Roman Lawson, looking as if butter wouldn't melt his mouth. He was one of the few A-rank Awakeners and her colleague-slash-rival. They were both part of the few elite teams the AA employed to take care of high-level dungeons—specifically, those that spawned too close to cities. She could recognize that he was good at his job.

That, however, didn't make him any less insufferable. "Now, what's this? Our little princess calling an emergency meeting, looking absolutely enraged. It must be something truly cataclysmic. I can't even imagine the weight on your shoulders. Really, if it was something frivolous, you might just get your leave extended."

If you looked at his smug expression, his curated image of a benevolent warrior for humanity fell apart quickly. No matter his handsome features, strong jaw, blue eyes, and wavy dark hair that made so many swoon, this man was a vindictive, petty bastard.

She would trust him with her life in the field, as he had repeatedly proven himself to be reliable, but he was different outside the field. He held grudges; he took pleasure in making her life difficult and annoying her as much as possible.

Leila passed him by, not deigning to stop. "You'll just have to wait and see, won't you?" If Roman wanted to believe she was doing this just because she was spooked for her kids, he was wrong.

There was more at work. Something sinister had happened, and when James had confided in her his suspicions, she just had to go look for who it was that should have been handling that area. Unsurprisingly, the Eclipse Guild had bought the right of first refusal to Greenwich Village.

Things started to fall into place pretty quickly after that. She just had to snoop in on a few conversations in the precinct's police department and the AA itself, and she had all the proof she needed.

Opening the door to the regional director's office, Leila was greeted by the sight of all the top bureaucrats of the building, alongside a few more friendly faces. She tilted her head toward the director, who smiled back, his middle-aged, mild-mannered look hiding a shrewd mind. As always, he was well dressed and sporting a short military-style haircut. His almond eyes took in the whole room without missing anything, and she knew she could count on him to see justice done. As much as the man might be embroiled in politics, he wouldn't let go of this kind of thing when presented with enough evidence.

Then, she greeted a few people, deliberately making rounds so that everyone could see her mingle. Marcus, her old mentor, was present and warmly embraced her.

Joanna, another high-ranker, also showed enough affection to signal that she was on her side, no matter what. Others came to greet her, knowing exactly what they were doing by being seen with her, which she was grateful for, even though it was all just part of political calculations.

They were taking a risk, as this was her first official appearance in the halls of power since the meeting in which she was put on forced leave. If she messed this up, she could hurt them too, but they could rise with her if she managed to make a comeback.

Leila wasn't particularly interested in a specific position, nor was she aiming for more resources to be given to her—though those never hurt. No, she had called the meeting because justice had to be meted out.

Everyone slowly started filing in the adjacent room, where a large table had been set. The massive windows overlooking Manhattan in all its glory had a beautiful view as always, and they gave any meeting held in the room a feeling of importance.

Leila looked for her name and was surprised to find she had been placed at the regional director's right hand. When he noticed her gaze, all he did was raise his glass, swirling the expensive scotch, and nod.

Finally, when everyone had taken their place, even that annoying Roman, they all turned to her. After all, she had called the meeting and they wanted to witness a spectacle. Whether it was a tragedy or a triumph mattered little.

Well, Leila was about to begin something they certainly hadn't seen coming.

She took a recording device out of her handbag, its metallic frame and shining blue mana stone telling everyone that it was the kind employed in high-level operations. The type that couldn't be tampered with nor falsified, that nullified illusions and skills and revealed everything concealed.

Sending a thin stream of mana through it, Leila turned it on, deciding to let the evidence speak.

Above it, a hazy image started forming, the light bending to show the interiors of the very same building they were in, though in a much lower office. It was made easily recognizable by the sign hanging on the wall, which read DUNGEON MONITORING DEPARTMENT.

A man, whom many knew personally for his long tenure at the agency, came into sight, speaking on the phone. "This has got to stop. I can't keep giving you this kind of leeway, or someone is going to come snooping around. Someone I can't do away with."

A few intakes of breath told her that a few of the more clever people were already figuring out where this was going, but for the slowest ones, she allowed the recording to continue.

"I don't care how grateful your leader will be. You have no idea how many eyes are on the Initiative now! If the kids get disappeared like that, we're all going to get it! I have to make it look believable," the same man continued. At this, the regional director shifted forward, the light glinting off his glasses hiding his expression.

"Two . . . No, four thousand. And this has to be the last time you give me this short of a notice. I can't help you if you don't give me the time to work. Make sure not to send your goons snooping around, or they'll be suspected immediately!" After that, the man thanked the person he was speaking with, a gleeful smile on his lips, and hung up.

Before anyone could speak and try to contextualize what they had witnessed, the image changed, showing a police precinct. A uniformed man and a woman were speaking inside an office. His tag read CAPTAIN STEVE ROMERO.

The woman, dressed as a secretary, nodded at her superior's words. "And then the mayor called me! Told me not to make a fuss about it and that they would take care of everything themselves. Which, as it turned out, was getting a bunch of kids and throwing them down the sewers to hunt the crocodiles. Not even at their second Awakening!"

Leila could see that even more people were starting to realize where she was going with this. A few went pale.

"First, we have to only speak with the guilds so that they can keep it all hush-hush and do whatever they want without the AA intervening. Now, we have to let them do everything. It stinks, I tell you," the captain continued, gesticulating. It was obvious that he had been keeping it all to himself for a long time and was finally letting some steam blow.

"And they even sent those people to pick up all our reports! I can tell you for sure that they didn't go to the AA, no siree. The truck went the other way!" the secretary added. She was just as incensed.

"The worst thing is," the man said, driving the nail in the coffin, "I know they just won't let us go now. The kids cleared the dungeon, and they aren't the kind of people to stop just because their first plan failed. They will try to hurt those kids again, and there's nothing we can do about it."

The man's downtrodden face faded, leaving a stilted silence behind. More than one person she considered her political "enemies" looked enraged beyond words. The few who had gone pale made sure to look appropriately angry.

At this point, the evidence of a plot to undermine the entirety of the Dawn Initiative, the AA's most important project, was laid bare before them, irrefutable. It now remained to be seen how many heads would fall.

"Well," the director began, his expression furious. "It seems to me like we have some cleaning to do."

CHAPTER TWENTY-FOUR

One-on-one training sessions were relatively uncommon, but after a dungeon run, Miss Walker took the time to check in on every one of them. The progress they made thanks to the speedy leveling was significant, but it also required some fine-tuning of their tactics, which she worked hard to do.

That was why, one Wednesday morning, it was just her and James in the training room. He was the last to receive a personal session, but he hadn't minded, enjoying the time off with his grandparents. They had gotten somewhat used to the idea of their little boy going on dangerous adventures, but it just meant they appreciated the time they spent together even more.

More than that, James had checked with them about whether anyone had approached them, or even if they just noticed people snooping. Since the guild-affiliated high-ranker had reached out and given an offer—though the benefits weren't nearly as generous as the man had made it seem—James feared for the possible retaliation following Esposito's unsubtle threats. But it seemed that they didn't want to mess with the AA for the moment.

Fortunately, no one suspicious had been near them, at least that they knew of, and so he had been able to put his fears to rest and go back to his routine.

"You have to keep in mind that additional strength doesn't always translate to increased power, if you can't leverage it properly," Miss Walker explained, gesturing to the slime dummy before her.

Miss Walker was a talented and powerful woman, and for all that James suspected that she couldn't be much older than twenty-five, she had enough experience that her words were worth as much as gold.

"Now, you can compensate somewhat at higher levels, especially with a decent agility stat. But for now, you must remember that your position affects the power you can exert as much as using your skill does." As an example, she planted her feet. Twisting her torso, she punched the dummy. It flew back, its absorption capabilities overstrained by her power. Then, she readied herself once more, the dummy back in place. After she took a few steps back, she rushed it. When she threw a hit, one leg was positioned forward, carrying most of her weight. Yet, the dummy didn't budge despite all the momentum she had built up.

"Now, some techniques compensate for this, even without investing too many points in agility, but they don't suit your style. Your strength is in single devastating blows, transmitting enough energy to break through your enemies' defenses. We need to make sure that remains our focus." That was another thing James appreciated about her. Miss Walker was obviously good enough at fighting that if she had told him to adopt a different style, he would have followed her advice, but she respected his decision to stick to what felt natural to him.

"I'm pretty sure that at higher levels, your Empowerment will start showing some interesting effects anyways," she added, and James had to agree, thinking back to his fight with the rat boss. He had surprised it when he countered its shadow whips.

"Do you think I'll need to wait for the second Awakening? My skills seem to level up pretty fast, but I know they'll slow down as they get higher." James had been thinking about that for a while. Level 3 in Thakinetic Empowerment opened a few roads for him, as he felt more in control of the flow of energy, being able to concentrate it more than before.

But was the pace sustainable? Most online guides said that an Awakener shouldn't get used to the speed of their early gains . That way lay only dissatisfaction.

"I don't think you need to worry about that for the moment. Desperately trying to force a skill to level up isn't an efficient way to go about it. You've shown that you're capable of adapting on the fly, both in training and in dungeons. That will serve you much better than any specific plan," she reassured him, her red eyes surprisingly warm.

"Keep in mind that skills aren't the same as your general levels. The experience you get by defeating a monster doesn't translate to 'skill experience'," Miss Walker continued, slightly distracted as she tried to recall something. "There's this fascinating paper I read a while ago. It posited that just as the System rewards us for taking back land swallowed by a dungeon and proving ourselves in fights, it also puts limitations on our path so that we're not tempted to simply become murder machines."

"Otherwise someone could simply go around killing other living beings, without ever thinking about the responsibility that comes with having power?"

Miss Walker nodded, fiddling with a glove strap. "It's not so much that I think the System is sentient and is guiding us in a specific direction like some, but there's enough evidence for built-in fail-safes and purposefully placed limitations that whatever its origins might be, there had to have been some thought about what it would do to a society that received it."

"So you believe it was built with the express direction to serve as a bulwark against mana and its consequences?" James asked, knowing that he was treading on dangerous ground.

Enough crazies had done damage with their outlandish theories, be they based upon old religions that required everyone to renounce the System as a "false god" or the belief that it was preparing the ground for an alien-slash-demonic invasion. Some even started worshipping it, though luckily they didn't find much success.

It was a pretty personal thing to ask, especially to an Awakener, but Miss Walker had been open enough that James felt compelled to ask.

She looked at him for a moment, gauging something. She then breathed out, shaking her head. "Theories that can't be proven are just fancy ideas. Until the System itself gives us something more than its initialization and welcome message, we'll just have to keep our curiosity."

She patted him on the back and turned to face the slime dummy again. "That said, I want you to remember that just because you can handle yourself in dangerous situations with little preparation, you shouldn't make a habit of it. Now, show me how you regain your stability after a charge."

James was just about to leave the training room after his shower when he noticed his mentor was still there, sitting on one of the sofas, staring intently at her tablet.

"Is everything alright, Miss Walker?"

"Hmm? Oh yes, don't worry about it," she answered distractedly. He nodded and made to walk away when she stopped him. "James! Come here for a moment, will you?"

Curious about what she might want, he let his bag drop on the floor and went to sit in front of her. "How can I help you?"

"Do you remember our little talk about the state of things and how my hands were tied?" she asked.

Immediately, James nodded. Scarcely a day went by that he didn't think about it. It was what drove him to push so hard. Despite everything, if he could at least deal with the Radiant Guild, he knew he would be able to sleep much better. It would mean taking his first true step in making a difference.

"There might be some changes to that situation," the masked woman continued. "After you told me that what you found in the crocodile dungeon was much different than expected, I did some snooping."

James grinned, amused at the thought of a powerful Awakener like her doing detective work, hiding in the shadows like in one of his grandmother's novels. "I imagine you must have found something, then."

Miss Walker nodded, seemingly quite proud of herself. "To be honest, this was one of the few times I've seen such a racket being stirred up in the high floors. The regional director had to be reminded he couldn't go and personally hunt down those responsible."

James, being far too low in the rankings, had never met the man. From the few times he had seen the director speak on TV, the man seemed so mild mannered that he had a hard time reconciling it.

"So you got some?" he asked eagerly.

His teacher's weird expression told him it wasn't that easy. Miss Walker seemed satisfied and disappointed at the same time, like a big cat who had gotten its prey but had seen more juicy targets escape.

"I got enough evidence to warrant a thorough search of the Eclipse Guild, but they scrubbed the place down before we got there so only a few people will be incriminated," she answered. "No big fishes, unfortunately, and even those we did get are going to be free for quite a while before their trial ends. Their bails were paid as soon as they were posted."

James deflated a bit, having expected more. He knew he shouldn't be surprised, what with the sheer amount of power and influence guilds had on society, but he had hoped that at least something could change.

"It also means that the AA is on high alert at the moment, which makes it difficult for them to act. The fact that they tried to hamper the Dawn Initiative, which the higher-ups have put so many hopes on, means we'll be getting more resources to ensure everything goes smoothly from now on," she added, which was nice.

At least that's something, I guess . . . Having more resources here means that somewhere else will get less, but it's a constant battle for survival. We can't be too picky.

Seeing he wasn't particularly enthused, she reached over and patted him on his hand. "Now, don't get all depressed on me. I didn't tell you all this just to make you sad."

"Then why did you?"

"Because there's something more to this story," she said, her eyes curving into a smile like a fox. "The Eclipse Guild might have been able to hide most of its transgressions, simply coming out as negligent and having to publicly apologize, but they couldn't do anything for their inside man."

James's eyes widened. Seeing that he caught on to where she was going, she leaned back in satisfaction. "Yes, it's not nearly as over as it seems. That man is currently being left in place because we have a much bigger operation going on. He's the contact with several other guilds, after all."

"You deliberately made them believe they could get away with it this time too. You even let them get their papers in order before you went to search their offices. But why? Do you think you'll be able to get much more than just a few arrests?"

This time, Miss Walker seemed a bit embarrassed. "Well, I can't take credit for that. I was ready to go all scorched earth, but once cooler heads prevailed, we put together a much more devious plan. If we can make them think they're in the clear, they're much more likely to make a mistake. And this time, we'll be waiting for them."

"So you expect them to repeat what they did to us? Give faulty information so that, when we inevitably get maimed or even killed, the Initiative might collapse before it could even start producing results." It seemed quite devious to James, but he supposed that considering how deeply entrenched the major guilds were, the AA would need an operation of truly gargantuan size to hope for a real change.

"That's right. It's not just about the Dawn Initiative's success at this point, and it'll take a while. We'll need your and your teammates' cooperation, but this time, we'll change things, James. Will you help us?"

He couldn't possibly say no to that, could he?

CHAPTER TWENTY-FIVE

Just to make it clear, you want us to go to a dungeon you know might be more difficult than it should be, all because it would help you prove that a few guilds are deliberately providing false information for some reason. Is that correct?" Lauren asked, staring Miss Walker down.

No one could ever accuse this girl of being a wallflower. She really has no fear, huh?

"That is exactly what I'm saying. We project this dungeon to be around the mid H-rank, rather than a beginner-level one as they report. But if I or anyone with real authority goes to take a look, we'll undermine the entire operation," the masked woman replied, keeping a calm tone despite the situation.

Ever since she had explained to the rest of Team 0 what would be happening and their part of it, the tension had been high in the room. It wasn't so much that they didn't want to be involved—they all had a sense of justice, and they wouldn't have joined the AA had they liked the way guilds operated. But deliberately putting themselves in danger in an already unpredictable place like a dungeon was not an easy decision to make.

"And you knew about this?" Lauren turned to look at James, trying to pierce him with her gaze.

He just shrugged. "She told me yesterday. You should've seen the news this morning. A couple of arrests, an apology, and then back to business as usual. If we don't catch them red-handed, they'll never stop."

Of course, he had been sworn to silence on the exact details of the operation. Giving this much information to rookies was stretching Miss Walker's mandate, but she couldn't send them off without saying anything.

"I understand that," Daniel interjected. "But why does it have to be us? I'm sure the AA has enough resources to send an elite team disguised as Team 0. That way, we wouldn't need to be put in any more danger than our profession naturally includes."

It was a reasonable point and something James had thought about himself. Unfortunately, the guilds didn't get to where they were by leaving such wide gaps in their traps.

"All elite teams are currently engaged in important missions, and the remaining high-rankers in the building are constantly monitored. If we step foot outside, they'll know," Miss Walker answered, squashing that line of questioning.

Already, the AA had given them more resources than James had expected them to be capable of. There simply wasn't anything left for them to give without stretching themselves too thin.

Despite how much it annoys me, the AA still plays an important role. They directly monitor the most dangerous dungeons, which can't be left alone for even a moment, and considering the mess south of the border, they're still very much needed. If any of those things breaks containment, it could mean disaster for the whole United States.

In the end, there was no two ways about it. Miss Walker had made it clear that this was a voluntary mission and wouldn't affect their standing, but if they did not take it, it would mean losing an essential piece of the plan they were laying.

The higher-ups were busy dealing with the aftermath of their "raid," calming the waters so the guilds would feel safe in acting again, and that would require showing that Team 0 was not cloistered inside the building.

"The only thing I don't get is why even go through all this trouble if this dungeon might not even be tampered with. And even if it has, if we find proof of it, it might not lead to anything for a long ass time." As always, Lauren was unafraid to say what was on her mind.

James, however, was keeping an eye on the two silent members. Ezekiel and Maria had been very quiet since Miss Walker revealed the plot to destroy the Dawn Initiative. Something was going on with those two, but he couldn't quite pinpoint where they would fall.

"I want to make sure that something is not being misunderstood here," Miss Walker said, getting everyone's attention. "I'm not sending you off to die in a ditch somewhere. Montauk's marine dungeon is well within your capabilities, even if its data were tampered with. I'm only asking you to do this because I know you can."

Lauren sat back, taking in their teacher's words. It was true that they had performed better than expected after all. And a mid H-rank dungeon would mean more levels for them if they could clear it. It would accelerate their growth and the risks associated weren't as great as they first appeared.

Finally, Ezekiel broke his silence. "I'm in. I don't really get how proving that they gave us faulty information again is going to give you the leeway to do anything to them, but I trust you, Miss Walker. If you say we can do it, then we can do it."

"I agree," Maria concurred. "I don't like the idea of basically being used as bait, but I wouldn't be able to live with myself if I let this kind of behavior go on without consequences. We might be able to deal with it, but many others might not."

Miss Walker seemed particularly touched by their show of support, and James was almost certain her eyes had misted for a moment before she composed herself.

Seeing that she was outvoted, Lauren huffed, "It's not that I like the guilds more than any of you. I just wanted to make sure we aren't about to be sent off like sacrificial lambs."

Finally, James understood what she was angling at. Since the "scandal" of the crocodile dungeon hadn't been enough to do anything, at least in Lauren's eyes—she didn't know what had happened behind the scenes, after all—she was afraid that the AA might be deliberately sending them to get maimed or killed, to have a much stronger case.

It seemed Miss Walker had gotten it too, because she stood up and walked over to Lauren. The girl looked at her defiantly, evidently expecting a rebuke. Instead, the masked woman bowed her head. "I'm sorry, Lauren. It wasn't my intention to give you that impression. I promise you I'll never deliberately put your lives at risk."

Lauren stared for a moment before she groaned. "All right, all right, there's no need for all this theater. We'll go, kick some ass, and help you deal with the guilds too. Happy now?"

Miss Walker eye-smiled. "Delighted."

The trip to the Hamptons could have been made by taking the train, but Team 0 had agreed that since they had a driver at their disposal, they should make use of him.

Thus, one sunny Friday morning, James was waiting at his street corner for Mr. Robinson to pick him up, a bag with his suit at his side.

After Golden Sun's offer, everyone who lived on Brighton Seventh Street had known of his status as an Awakener. There was little he could have done to hide it; as the men, shining inconspicuously as they flew off, had been an unambiguous indication that a guild member had come to visit him.

That, however, didn't mean he liked to flaunt it. James didn't feel like it made him any less or more important than anyone else. He knew how people treated Awakeners—a mix of awe, fear, and trepidation that was getting annoying quickly. He wanted to avoid constantly reminding his neighbors of what he was.

"Looking good, James. Your shoulders are finally filling in. You look just like your father."

One person James could have done with having a bit more trepidation at approaching him was Mrs. Johnson. The woman was approaching seventy and had been a widow for more than a decade, having lost her husband and son during the early days of the apocalypse. The pity he felt for her ended there, however, as she wouldn't want it.

He'd known her all his life, and while he had some fond memories of her, he'd appreciate it if she didn't feel entitled to feel him up every time she saw him.

Staying as still as a statue, James tried to get it over with as soon as possible. He would be the last one to get picked up, and if his teammates saw him getting molested by an old woman, he'd never hear the end of it.

"Thank you, Mrs. Johnson. How are you doing today?"

"Oh, just good, baby. Better now that I saw you. Where are you going with that heavy bag?" she asked, snooping for some gossip.

At least she hasn't directly asked me if it's for the AA. This woman knows too much about everyone.

"Just some work-related stuff, Mrs. Johnson. A car should be coming to pick me up soon," he answered, avoiding giving any detail.

"Oh, that sounds lovely. Good luck with your work, then, and be careful out there. You never know."

Used to her ominous goodbyes, James just smiled, feeling as if he was back at Home Depot trying to shrug off an annoying customer.

Seeing that he wouldn't give her anything, she finally left, but not before copping another feel of his arms and giggling to herself.

A couple of minutes later, Mr. Robinson's black van arrived and James felt very grateful that he had managed to avoid the embarrassment. He'd need to keep his head in the game.

He greeted the older man and jumped in the back. "Morning, everyone."

"Good morning," they all replied, and James sat down next to Ezekiel, who lived not far from him.

A stack of paper was soon passed over and he skimmed it, noticing that it was a more in-depth analysis of the dungeon they were about to tackle.

"What's going on? I thought we already had the briefing yesterday?" James asked while his eyes went over the lines, trying to see if there was anything important he had missed before.

Immediately, it became clear that someone must have done a proper exploration of the dungeon to gather that much information—the papers detailed the entire cave layout they were supposed to delve into, alongside an explanation of all the creatures they would have to deal with.

"Miss Walker turned up at my house this morning to drop these off. She said they managed to get some more info, but wouldn't elaborate when asked," Lauren replied.

"Seaweed? Like carnivorous seaweed or monster seaweed?" James asked, still taken in by the information. Then, he registered what she said and turned to give her a look.

The Rogue sighed. "Yeah, I know she must have gone there last night to make sure there wasn't anything crazy because of me. You don't need to look at me like that. I made sure to thank her."

"Good," rumbled Daniel, also busy skimming the papers. "We'll have to rethink our strategy a bit, because I have no idea how we'll deal damage to the monster seaweed. I'd imagine that fire magic wouldn't work either, would it?"

Maria shook her head, looking resigned. "Every dungeon we go to must be somewhere with a lot of water. Damp, dark caves. Never a sunny field for me to burn."

James blinked before deciding to ignore whatever it was she meant. As he read further, he came across an interesting line. "Well, we knew it was crabs, but giant blue crabs . . . Do you think they'll be as tasty as regular ones?"

A groan was the only answer, and James chuckled to himself. He'd taste one, even if he had to bring it back home to boil.

CHAPTER TWENTY-SIX

Located at the tip of the South Fork peninsula of Long Island, Montauk was a hamlet of East Hampton. It had served as a major tourist destination and prized fishing spot for more than a century, holding more world saltwater fishing records than any other port in the world.

It was also home to a US Coast Guard station, which technically should have taken care of the dungeon. Still, considering the poor conditions of that particular military branch, it was no wonder it had been left to the guilds and AA.

If there's a federal organization more underfunded than the AA, it's the Coast Guard. Considering how little the US cares about the rest of the world, and the dangers of crossing the ocean without powerful Awakeners, its duties are just what the Navy doesn't want to bother with.

Generally, the US Armed Forces were quick to take control of any dungeon that sprang up in their vicinity, using them to train their own elite teams. The Coast Guard, however, simply didn't have the prestige nor the money to attract any Awakener of significant Talent, which meant that it was almost entirely staffed by ordinary people.

Even then, an H-rank dungeon should have still been within its capabilities. Guns worked just as well against monsters as they did against humans, as long as they were below C-rank.

But the Coast Guard simply didn't have the influence and political power to attempt to requisition the dungeon from a guild or even the AA, which meant that as long as there was no monster out in the streets actively hunting people, they couldn't do anything.

It was why James was unsurprised to find that roadblocks had been set up. They were made to go through a lengthy inspection, meant only to slow them down and remind them that they couldn't do as they pleased.

Team 0, however, had been taught exactly how to deal with this kind of inter-action; they got through by answering any question the very annoyed lieutenant asked them in monosyllables. He looked to be the typical frustrated military man who had believed he'd have an amazing career facing down cartels and gaining glory but whose path had been irrevocably changed by the introduction of Awakeners in the ranks. His hair was shaved; he had a thin brow and flinty black eyes. He couldn't have been older than thirty, but his stern expression made him look at least forty.

"Do you understand that if anything, and I repeat anything, happens to the people of this town that we have been sworn to protect, even while you are inside the dungeon, the authority will revert back to us?" the man asked. He was tall and would have been intimidating if someone like Ezekiel, who was at least five inches shorter, couldn't tie him up in knots with his bare hands.

"Yes, sir," James answered clearly. The question had been meant to provoke him, but he wouldn't give in so easily.

With a frustrated sigh, the lieutenant finally gestured for them to go ahead, and they piled back into the van, keeping quiet until they were well away from the roadblock.

"What an ass," Lauren commented, getting a snort from everyone.

James had been afraid that she would get too riled up by the seamen's behavior, but luckily, she had managed to keep her snark to herself until they were out of earshot.

"There was no need to make us go through all of that. For a while, I thought they were about to try and test our potions for illicit substances," Ezekiel agreed, also looking very annoyed.

"They were trying to get a reaction out of us. An excuse," Daniel said in a low voice, looking out of the window pensively.

They were prevented from further talk when they finally got to the beach's parking, where the van stopped. "All right, this is as far as I can take you. I'll be waiting for you here the whole time. Good luck," Mr. Robinson said, getting thank-yous from everyone.

The fresh sea breeze, coupled with the absolute silence of the off-season, made the beach look peaceful. Nothing to do with a den of monsters waiting for them to enter.

"Let's get this thing started!" Maria exclaimed, trying to sound cheerful. The redhead had been depressed ever since finding out that, once again, her fire magic would be mostly countered by the environment, but she wasn't one to stay down for too long.

They approached the sea, then followed the shoreline until something became visible in the distance. A natural harbor leading all the way to the bottom of a hill. At its base, the mouth of a grotto.

Thanks to their D-rank suits, they didn't have to fear getting wet, but their movements would still slow down while in the water, so they took up a more defensive formation.

Miss Walker's papers made it very clear that they should expect three different types of monsters. The most common were the giant crabs; they were the size of a large dog with pincers that could easily shear through bone if given the opportunity. These, however, were not the most insidious of the enemies.

The seaweed within the dungeon had mutated and would attack any intruder, and their slimy coating protected them against most direct hits. The usual method of dealing with plant monsters—fire, fire, and even more fire—wasn't applicable because of their constantly submerged bodies.

Maria had floated the idea of trying to boil them alive, but James had shot it down. It had been a valid tactic against the crocodile boss because it was just one creature. Doing it against the dozens of seaweed monsters they'd encounter was simply not feasible.

"Remember, we don't know if I'll be able to pick them up with Awareness since they're plants. So be careful of sneak attacks. Also, try to keep the first you find alive so that we can experiment with different methods," James said as they arrived at the mouth of the cave.

They were standing in knee-high water, which would severely hamper their agility, but even more, it would make Lauren's stealth almost entirely useless.

The last monster of this dungeon was the boss, which was an entirely different can of worms. But they'd get there in time. First, they needed to assess how much they could actually do. It was important they be objective, since risking their lives even further than what they were already doing would be simply stupid.

Once he entered the dungeon proper, James cast out his senses, seeking to find anything hiding in the waters. Sunlight still streamed in through the opening, and deeper in, glowing seaweed seemed to illuminate the way, as was written in Miss Walker's report.

Focusing on his skill, James felt a faint presence ahead of them. It was different than any he had encountered before. Much simpler and entirely single-minded.

Even the average dungeon monster, made more aggressive by the influx of mana, wasn't as focused on one task. James strongly suspected that the being was a seaweed monster. It was simpleminded enough that its only focus was on reaching them. "A monster's coming! I think it's a seaweed!" he called, mana flooding his legs to give him an agility boost.

A long green vine, which looked like a tentacle, soon breached the water. It slammed onto the ground, right where he had been a moment before, with enough strength to break bone.

A second one crashed against Daniel's shield, though he held without much problem.

Lauren sped over, her knives out, and scored a hit. Then she was forced to retreat as the seaweed shrugged off the dismemberment and reached toward her.

The monster wasn't particularly fast, which was why they were able to keep it at bay. A fireball from Maria failed to ignite it and didn't cause enough damage to be worth the expenditure. Therefore, she was reduced to smaller, faster ones whose explosions at least made the vines deviate in their paths.

Thanks to Daniel and James taking the brunt of the creature's attention, Lauren managed to get close enough to its main body and shred it to ribbons, killing it.

The notification identified the monster as [Mutated Seaweed - Whip], which was simple and to the point. It gave them [+50 EXP], which was less than expected, but considering its overall fragility, it felt fair. Their difficulty in dealing with it stemmed more from a lousy matchup than from it being at a high level.

They met two more of the whip seaweeds, this time working together. They didn't have any strategy, but they didn't need it when their simple tactic of using all their "tentacles" at once forced them on the back foot.

Thanks to Ezekiel buffing them, no one took any damage, and Lauren was able to weave through the vines to reach the main bodies, cutting them up and ending the fight.

"I feel like this should be more difficult. But these knives are just so damn sharp that it's almost unfair," the brunette commented, observing the floating pieces of monster.

"Considering how stacked against us the odds are, I'd say we should take every advantage we can get," Daniel responded, having been the one to take the brunt of the whip attacks.

His skills and build made him much more resilient than his teammates, and he usually didn't mind serving as the focal point for the enemies' attention, but that didn't mean he enjoyed being constantly hit.

Their third fight was much different, since their opponent wasn't a seaweed but a real monster. Sensing the crab in advance, James almost let out a breath of relief. He had gotten used enough to fighting creatures that he had been a bit unsettled with the almost brainless seaweed.

The crab was faster than expected as it scuttled around, speeding toward them with murderous intent. Its claws were wickedly sharp, and its armor was thick enough that James doubted Lauren's knives would damage it, even if they got through on sharpness alone.

Fortunately, while cutting and fire magic were out, he knew just the thing to do since the crab was half-submersed in water. James shot forward, Thakinetic Empowerment flooding his limbs with strength.

In a surprising move, he jumped out of the water, his head almost touching the cave ceiling, and fell upon the crab like a meteor, his reinforced boot crashing onto the crab's head with enough strength to crack it.

Not letting the monster have time to defend itself, James hopped off the creature and pushed all his Empowerment into his fist, punching it down and ending its life in one blow.

"Now, this is what you call a fight. None of that whipping nonsense. I don't like monsters without an actual brain," he said, earning snorts of laughter from all the others.

They left the crab's corpse behind. When James requested that Maria boil it—just a little so that he could have a taste!—she refused with a shake of her head and an amused smile.

That levity left them soon after, as they came upon a dozen seaweed monsters strategically positioned around the path. They couldn't avoid any, even if they wanted to.

"This might be a problem," James gulped.

CHAPTER TWENTY-SEVEN

The map was detailed enough to depict all the dungeon's twists and turns, but Miss Walker hadn't written where concentrations of monsters gathered, mostly because they usually roamed around.

The whip seaweeds were stationary enough that James felt she could have easily added their location, but it was too late now.

The strategy they had employed earlier had been one of brute force. They'd take on all the plants could give and thus allow Lauren, the one most capable of dealing damage to them, to cut them up.

That had worked against one or two monsters. Against a dozen, they had to rethink their approach entirely.

"The idea of boiling them alive doesn't sound that bad now, huh?" Maria said, a touch hysterically.

"You'll boil us too by the time they are all dead," Daniel answered, his voice still calm as ever, but his eyes betrayed some apprehension.

James knew what his friend was thinking. This was a terrible matchup for them in a place where they were already stretched to their limits. The average level of this dungeon had to be around twenty, which made it more dangerous than what they should normally attempt. A dozen of the seaweed monsters might just be too much.

"I want to try something," Ezekiel said, breaking the silence that had fallen. "These monsters are very annoying to deal with because they're pretty strong, and the vines give them a lot of versatility, even if they can't move. But James said they're very dumb, right?"

"Yeah, the most simpleminded wills I've ever felt," He confirmed.

A smirk came on Ezekiel's face, devious and impish. "Then what would happen if their mind stat was lowered even further?"

Immediately, they all saw the possible consequences, and James almost slapped himself for not having thought of it first.

"Of course, I don't expect them to just die. But if their simple movements become even more predictable, and their reaction times lengthen, then we might have a chance," the White Mage finished, looking very satisfied.

Seeing that there were no objections, he stepped ahead, standing just slightly behind Daniel in case the plants all decided to attack him at once.

His hands glowed softly as he cast a debuff on every single one. It would have been wiser to test out the theory with one specimen, but since the cave only had one path, they'd need to go beyond this group to find more. It was either try it now on all of them or retreat.

A faint veil descended over the whip seaweeds, their swaying tendrils slowing ever so slightly. James quickly focused his senses, attempting to gauge how effective Ezekiel's spell was. As he reached out with his magical senses, he felt the mental fortitude of the whip seaweeds become even weaker, the threads of their intentions growing duller and less focused.

"It worked," James declared. "They're slower. They're not thinking clearly—if they ever were."

Lauren unsheathed her knife, eyeing the debuffed monsters. "Let's test out this theory, shall we?"

They moved into formation, Daniel taking the lead with his shield at the ready, followed by James, who was prepared to jump forward and intercept any whip that passed through the Tank. Lauren stayed near the middle, ready to lunge forward when an opportunity presented itself, while Maria and Ezekiel remained near the back.

The whip seaweeds, seemingly disoriented, reacted slower as Daniel stepped closer. Instead of the frenzied lashing they were used to, the vines now reached out in sluggish, uncertain movements, as though grappling in the dark.

Maria took the first shot, and her fireball hit true. The explosion, though not severely damaging the plant, sent the tendril rocketing back, and it took several seconds before it got back into position.

Immediately, Lauren lunged forward, her knives singing through the air. She cut down two vines, slicing through them as if they were paper. Even James and Daniel, who had been relegated to being a punching bag, were able to do some damage of their own.

Charging in on the sluggish plants, they rained blows on the monsters' main bodies, stomping and squashing until they were pulped.

They fell one by one, their slower movements and delayed reactions giving the group the needed openings. By the time they were through, the cavern floor was littered with the crushed and severed remains of the whip seaweeds.

For a moment, everyone stood in silence, catching their breaths and relishing the victory.

"That was incredible," Maria said finally, breaking the silence. "It worked, Ezekiel. It worked really well!"

Ezekiel smiled, pleased. "It's not often that one can outsmart a plant." He chuckled. "It took a lot out of me, casting so many debuffs, but if I can get some time to rest before we meet more, I think I can make it."

Daniel cleaned his shield, his eyes meeting James'. "You know, this doesn't make the rest of the dungeon any less dangerous."

James nodded. "True. But at least we have one less thing to worry about, and perhaps a new trick up our sleeves. We're learning and adapting. That's what this is about. We all have our circumstances that push us to get stronger, and this is the way to get there."

They regrouped, checked their equipment, and prepared to delve deeper into the dungeon with newfound confidence. The whip seaweeds had been an annoying foe, especially because of the bad matchup. Still, they had shown that they could overcome even the most unfavorable odds with teamwork and ingenuity.

"I have leveled up," James announced with a grin once he was done reading through the notifications. Fighting against higher-leveled enemies was a fantastic way of speeding up progress, especially since he managed to go from passive bystander, who received only a fraction of the experience, to active fighter.

"Me too," Ezekiel chimed in. "I got a lot more experience than I expected, honestly."

"Well, without you, we wouldn't have been able to do anything here, much less defeat all of them. You deserve it," Daniel said, patting the younger boy on the shoulder.

"I'm close, but since I can't manage to do much to them, it's taking a while," Maria announced, looking depressed that her Talent couldn't be put to use.

"We'll let you have the crabs. Miss Walker's papers said we should come to a shallower part of the cave soon, so your fire will be much more effective." Lauren might not have been the best at comforting others, but it seemed like her promise to let Maria join in on the slaughter did the trick, because the redhead perked up.

James shook his head in amusement, focusing on his stat sheet.

STATUS WINDOW	
Name	James Summers
Age	19
Awakening	1st
Talent	Thakinesis
Title	
Level	14
MP	53/70
STR	12
VIT	9
AGI	10
SEN	11
MND	9
STAT POINTS	2

He put his free points in agility and mind stats, bringing them up to eleven and ten respectively. Having a bit more mobility and brain power in such a restricting environment could only help.

He had been briefly tempted to add to his strength stat so that his punches could deal more damage, but that way lay overspecialization, and he had been repeatedly warned of its dangers.

The mind stat, on the other hand, could give him an edge in noticing patterns and developing tactics. Considering how difficult it was to detect the whip seaweeds, he'd be grateful if he could spend a bit less of his mental strength on that.

Finally done with the upgrades, they moved on, the atmosphere tense but electric with a newfound sense of possibility. They had all been afraid that it would simply be impossible to go through the whole dungeon, thanks to the lousy matchup and the high level, but in a stroke of luck, they now had the upper hand.

The map showed a straightforward path, but the dungeon was littered with enough alcoves that it was a lifesaver. Still, Miss Walker's map proved accurate, guiding them through the labyrinthine underworld without any missteps.

After a few more minutes of walking, they reached a large chamber. At its center was a glowing pool of water, lit from beneath by luminescent mineral. The water sparkled in the dim light, casting strange reflections on the walls.

Since they had been forewarned by Miss Walker's map, they were unsurprised when a giant crab, almost as big as the crocodile boss, emerged from behind a rock.

It's not even the boss . . . Well, I think my crab boil's just gotten big enough to feed all of Brooklyn.

James spied Maria's hands trembling, but the look on her face was one of excitement, not fear; this was an enemy she finally could unleash her full power on.

"Okay, team, let's do this! Daniel, Ezekiel, you guys know what to do. Maria, unleash hell. Lauren and I will take advantage of any opening Maria gives us. Ready?" James called out, energy flooding his limbs.

Everyone nodded, taking their positions.

Maria started the assault. Raising her hands high, she concentrated, her face flushed. Flames flickered around her fingers, growing and swirling into a massive fireball. With a cry, she launched it toward the crab, the spell roaring like a jet engine as it shot through the air.

The fireball impacted with a deafening explosion, steam and smoke filling the chamber. The heat reached even them, but James knew it wouldn't be over so quickly. The false boss—it would have been easy to believe it was the final monster had they not known the truth—was much sturdier than that.

When the smoke cleared, the crab was scorched but still very much alive—and now quite angry. It let out a guttural, clicking noise, its giant pincers snapping in the air.

"Good hit, Maria! It's weakened! Daniel, Ezekiel, your turn!" James shouted.

Daniel charged forward, shield raised, drawing the crab's attention toward him. Ezekiel started weaving another debuff spell, aiming to reduce the crab's reaction speed even more.

As the crab lunged at Daniel, its pincer met the solid surface of his glowing shield. The Tank grunted, digging his heels into the ground as he absorbed most of the impact. He was sent back ten feet but quickly retook his position.

Ezekiel's debuff found its mark, and the crab's movements slowed.

"Now, Lauren!" Daniel yelled.

Lauren was already moving, her knives gleaming in the chamber's luminescent light. She darted around the crab, dodging its slower pincers, and aimed for its joints. Her daggers found their marks, cutting through the tough exoskeleton. The crab screeched in pain, now even more disoriented.

"James, finish it!" she called, sidestepping the frenzied movements with grace.

James grunted, having focused as much mana as he could in his fist. With a jump, he landed beside the crab the moment it turned to chase after Lauren. Taking advantage of its distraction, he threw a powerful punch right to its belly, flipping over the crab. The sight was almost comical.

Jumping back, James slightly regretted his promise to leave the next monster to Maria as he watched her unleash all hell on it, burning the beast enough that its insides cooked. He could have cracked it open from below in a few hits, and it would have felt amazing, but when the smell of roasted crab reached him, he decided it wasn't such a big deal.

The notification telling him he had helped defeat a [Mutated Crab - Giant Guardian] and gained [+350 EXP] was enough to make up for it. He was already almost halfway to the next level, and considering the cave's layout, he was sure he'd have the time to surpass it easily. They were just about at the midway point, and the monsters would only get more plentiful from here.

Now, if only this stupid headache would go away . . .

CHAPTER TWENTY-EIGHT

The swarm of Labrador-sized crabs was easy enough to deal with, especially with how much shallower the water had become this deep in the cavern.

The team allowed Maria to have some fun roasting the crustaceans alive and then was forced to pull James away, lest he crack them open to have a taste.

It wasn't so much that monsters couldn't be eaten. There were entire dungeons left open because of their ability to produce so much food, after all. But stopping in the middle of a dive for a snack was a rookie mistake.

Taking the risk to add stat points was one thing. It was acceptable since more power was always needed in their profession.

Leaving the fragrant aroma with tears threatening to fall from his eyes, James rubbed his brow. His headache was getting worse. He briefly considered whether he might have gotten sick, but with his vitality stat rising, it was unlikely. It was common knowledge that even low-level Awakeners like him would stop getting sick from basic illnesses.

From the corner of his eyes, he spied the others looking haggard too. The fights so far hadn't been particularly taxing, even the giant crab one. And ever since they had found a way to deal with the whip seaweeds, the tension had lowered considerably. But, inexplicably, they still got more and more tired as time went by.

Before he could bring up the problem, another field of plant monsters opened up, and he put it aside for the moment. Ezekiel smiled, happy to directly contribute to the team's victory, and cast his debuffs, bringing the seaweeds' mobility and reaction time to almost zero.

"This is almost too easy. It feels like we shouldn't be able to simply walk up to their main bodies and crush them like this," Lauren groused, even as she hacked at the bulbous center that housed the seaweed's "mind" and mana stone.

"It's almost like getting free levels. I'm not complaining, though." James wasn't one to turn down an easy power-up, so he pushed his mana into his fists and pulped the monsters, eliminating half a dozen by himself.

By the time they were done clearing the path, he had achieved another level, bringing him up to fifteen. His quick leveling speed would take him to his goal of reaching G-rank earlier than expected. James knew they weren't supposed to face such challenging dungeons, but the benefits made up for the dangers.

After putting one point in strength and one in vitality, which brought them to thirteen and ten, James took a deep breath, feeling a bit better with the additional stamina provided by his stats.

"Guys, I think we might have a problem," Ezekiel called, looking even paler than normal. The boy was sweating, but not because of the exertion. His hands glowed a bright white, signaling his usage of a healing spell.

Gradually, he returned to a healthier complexion, but if anything, he looked even more worried. "We're being poisoned," he revealed, stunning everyone into silence.

It took James's brain a few seconds to reboot, until he finally realized what the younger boy had said. Then, he understood why he had been flagging so much despite not doing anything exhausting. Why his head was hurting so much.

"What the fuck?! Is there another monster? Are the seaweeds poisonous? Why didn't Miss Walker tell us??" Lauren rambled in agitation, moving closer to Ezekiel so that he could heal her too.

The White Mage obliged, casting his healing spell over the Rogue and clearing her of any poisoning in a couple of minutes.

"Go ahead, Maria. I just raised my vitality, so I can take it for a bit longer," James said when the redhead looked at him questioningly.

"This is a cave," Daniel stated in a tone of realization. "It's pretty common for there to be dangerous gases in the air. We should have checked before entering." Even as he spoke, he opened his pouch, taking out a field-testing kit. He picked one slip of paper among many and lifted it up as high as he could, which was almost to the ceiling, considering his height.

The paper immediately changed color, going from a pale yellow to a dark blue, confirming Daniel's suspicion. "That settles it. We're in an environment saturated with dangerous gases. We're getting poisoned just by breathing this air."

"We can't just leave the dungeon," Maria pointed out, rubbing her temples as Ezekiel's healing spell washed over her. "You know why we have to clear it, and we should be getting closer to the boss room. If we make it there, we can exit the dungeon and rest before returning tomorrow to clean it up. We have enough allowance to pay for a night out here."

James clenched his fist, feeling the weight of the decision that lay before them. "We can't ignore that these gases might also affect our performance against the boss. If we're weakened, we're vulnerable. And that could turn out to be fatal."

Ezekiel chimed in, "I can periodically cast a healing spell. It won't directly protect us, but it should reduce the rate of poisoning and improve our condition over time. But it'll also eat into my mana reserves."

"Then we better make it quick," Lauren said, her eyes sharpening. "If we clear this dungeon fast enough, we can limit the drain on Ezekiel's mana and our own health."

"There's also the problem that if Ez has to keep healing us, he won't be able to debuff the whip seaweeds as easily. Taking one mana potion is fine, but more than that can be hazardous," Daniel commented as he was being healed.

"Look at the bright side," interrupted Maria, a tiny flame dancing on her finger. "If this poisonous gas was flammable, we'd already have died in an explosion the first time I cast a fireball."

James paled even further, not having thought of that possibility. *We really should have checked before coming inside. We could have died in so many ways . . . Wait, is that why Miss Walker didn't say anything?*

"I think I might have figured out why there was nothing about poisonous gas in the papers," he said, drawing everyone's attention. "Think about it. We know our teacher usually moves through the shadows, and even if she ever comes out, her stats are high enough that this level of poison wouldn't affect her even if she spent a year here."

His teammates' looks of realization told him that they understood precisely what he meant.

"Basically, the biggest danger in this cave comes not from the faulty information the guild that held rights over this dungeon had, but because the one person we can trust forgot we're not nearly as strong as she is?" Lauren's face was a mix of amusement and incredulity, as if she couldn't really believe it.

As amusing as the situation might be, and James was sure they'd tease Miss Walker enough to drive her up the walls, they were still in a more challenging environment than they had first believed.

"All right, look," Ezekiel began, "I can keep us going for a bit longer with my healing spells, but if we're going to do this, we need to be efficient. I say we go for it. If we face the boss weakened, it's going to be dangerous, but we're a good team. We can pull it off."

Lauren nodded, her eyes showing newfound resolve. "I agree. This mission is too important, and the rewards are worth it. I don't want to turn back now. If we appear as too weak, it could reflect badly on the Initiative."

Maria grinned. The little flame on her finger burned brighter. "Well, if you guys are in, then I'm in. Let's just burn that boss down and get out of here."

Daniel hesitated, his gaze flitting to the blue-stained paper still in his hand. Finally, he folded it carefully and placed it back into his pouch. "I say we go for it. We're prepared, and now that we know what we're up against, I think we can take it down quickly."

James felt a sense of pride looking at his team. "Then it's settled. We're moving forward. Ezekiel, conserve your mana for healing and only use the debuffs when absolutely necessary. Daniel, keep up the good work. Maria and Lauren, let's save most of our mana for the boss. And let's make sure to communicate; we don't know what kind of tricks it might have."

As they pressed on through the poisonous cavern, their spirits were high despite the palpable tension in the air. They encountered three more groups of whip seaweeds, though luckily, they were not in large enough numbers that Ezekiel was forced to debuff them.

Without his help, the fights took much longer, and they risked getting injured a couple of times, but through perseverance, they managed to defeat the monsters.

"It's a run against time, but if we hurry too much, we risk getting hurt, and that would mean even more healing than what Ez already has to do to get rid of the poison. We're between a rock and a hard place," James said, looking deeper into the cave, where he felt the first stirrings of another wave of crabs.

"You are so weird." Lauren chuckled, shaking her head. "Why are you smiling like a loon if it's so dangerous?"

"It's fun." The Thakinetic shrugged. "Now prepare yourselves—there's another wave of crabs coming. I count at least a dozen."

"Oh, oh! Let me have a shot at them first!" Maria was already gathering her mana in front of her, a fireball forming. As soon as she spied the first of the monsters, she sent it forth, a bright trail following in its wake.

The explosion was almost deafening as it sent the crabs flying back, clattering noisily against each other and slowing their advance down.

Taking advantage of the moment of confusion, Lauren and James shot forward, turning their skills onto the unprepared monsters. Their spiny armor was strong enough to withstand a couple of blows, but eventually, it cracked, and nothing could protect the soft interiors from the Awakeners' wrath.

They battled with the creatures for a while, being forced to temporarily retreat behind Daniel when they managed to finally use their numbers advantage to their favor. One sharp claw almost grabbed James's arm as he was busy pummeling another crab into a gory mess.

The monsters were big enough that their movements in the cave were limited, and they couldn't charge in a single line. Because of that, with the help of Daniel's skill and Maria's occasional disrupting fireball, James and Lauren were able to whittle down their numbers, until only three remained.

"I'll take the central one," the Tank yelled, his shield glowing brightly. His Bash proved its worth once again, as it managed to crush a crab beneath it, and Daniel ended it with a couple more blows.

Lauren disappeared in midair, only to reappear behind the leftmost crab. With a heave, she pushed from beneath, turning the beast belly up, and she buried her knives into it, ending its struggles with a screech.

With his mad grin still present, James decided to go for the more straightforward tactic and simply evaded the crab's pincer, entering its space. A powerful right hook sent the beast scuttling back, but he followed it with two more hits until the rock-hard shell broke. One last punch blew its brains out, putting an end to the fight. It net him another level, bringing him up to sixteen.

CHAPTER TWENTY-NINE

The fight with the crab swarm was the second to last before the boss room, the last one being with another field of whip seaweeds. It took them a while, but the two stat points James put into sense and mind allowed him to react to their attacks faster.

In the end, Ezekiel was forced to use his debuffs because the risk of getting further injured was too significant, and they all agreed that they had to be close to the end of the dungeon.

With their mental attributes lowered, the seaweeds once again became a straightforward fight. They managed to deal with them all in a few short minutes, shredding the main bodies.

"If it wasn't for the poison in the air, this dungeon would be a cakewalk. I can see how it's more difficult than the crocodile one, what with the massive increase in numbers and the monsters' resistance, but our team is almost purposely designed to deal with it. Much more than what it initially appeared like," Lauren commented as she cleaned her knives.

They sat on a few rocks that rose from the water, close to the entrance of a much larger chamber that they knew to be the boss's, thanks to Miss Walker's map.

Ezekiel was taking the time to heal everyone from the poison gas, since he had decided to drink the mana potion immediately before they went in. His reserves were basically at rock bottom by the time he was done, having been forced to heal and then debuff much more than he usually would have.

He hadn't participated much in any fights the whole dive, but his contributions had been enough for the System to give him three whole levels, showing just how much his help had allowed them to clear the obstacles in the way.

"If those stupid seaweeds weren't so well protected against fire attacks, I would have burned them to the ground without needing to tax Ez so much." Maria grumbled. Her Talent was the least suited to the current dungeon, but at least the explosive qualities of her fireballs had been excellent crowd control against the swarms of crabs. They would have overrun the team otherwise.

Since she had frequently used that specific skill, she had leveled it up; now, she could channel her mana into making the spells hotter or more destructive.

All in all, they gained more than enough to make the trip worth it. The difficulty was much greater than what the initial guild's paper said it should have been, and even Miss Walker's lacked a critical detail, but thanks to their teamwork and dedication, they made it without taking more than a few hits.

"Now for the boss," James said, peering forward in the cavern. "According to Miss Walker's information, we're up against a giant starfish. It can use rock magic, which means we should expect both projectiles and potentially the terrain itself to be used against us."

Ezekiel uncorked the mana potion and took a measured sip, his eyes flashing as his reserves started to replenish. "If it can manipulate rock, it might also have a high resistance to physical attacks. Considering the crab shells' resistance, I would go in prepared for that." He then gulped down the rest of the potion, grimacing at the taste. "I can focus on using my debuffs to lower its defenses, but that would limit my healing capabilities. And we might need those to get back out of here."

"No, you need to keep us healed, especially with this damn poison in the air," Maria interjected. "I can try to focus on offensive magic, although I don't know how well fire will work on a creature in an aquatic environment."

"Fire can still deal significant damage, especially if you can heat the surrounding water and make it uncomfortable. Or you can try to directly damage the starfish," Daniel suggested. "Especially since it uses rock magic. It might give its armor more resistance, but it should mean it benefits less from the surrounding waters."

Lauren slid her knives into their sheaths. "I'll get above the creature by taking advantage of the platforms I can see from here, then harass it and force it on the defensive. Since a starfish's underside is generally softer and more vulnerable, if we can flip it or expose its belly, I can aim for critical points."

James cracked his knuckles. "I'll serve as the primary distraction and bait. If this thing throws rocks, I want them aimed at me and away from you all. Daniel can defend you two." He gestured to Ezekiel and Maria. "But I think we might need his help in attacking this thing as well, so I'll keep its attention away."

Once everyone had been healed fully from the poison gas's effects, they picked themselves up and readied themselves to enter the last room of the dungeon.

Once they stepped in, it became immediately evident why the boss wasn't a water magic user, which would have been the natural conclusion to come to. Massive crystalline growths spanned the whole chamber, reaching as high as ten feet.

Purple-and-blue light reflected off them, the glowing moss and refracted luminescence giving it an otherworldly atmosphere. At its center, the most alien of creatures sat, water barely licking its form.

It was a gigantic starfish with a rocky, calcified surface that seemed to merge with the cave floor itself. As Team 0 entered, it began to stir, its arms lifting as rocks started to float around it, imbued with a magical glow. It had noticed their entrance.

"Here we go," James muttered, and they sprang into action.

Maria opened with a blast of fire, aiming not at the starfish but at the water around it. Steam hissed as the temperature rapidly increased. The starfish didn't even react, unbothered by the attack.

Instead, a dozen fist-sized rocks rose up in the air, levitating for a moment, before they were shot in their direction, forcing them to scatter.

Daniel took the brunt of the attack, his glowing shield not budging as he protected the two mages. Lauren agilely jumped between the projectiles, taking full advantage of the dry platforms to use her stealth skills.

James dodged to the side, his eyes narrowing as he saw the rocks shatter against Daniel's shield. "All right, looks like this one is not messing around."

Taking advantage of Daniel's shield, Maria unleashed another fireball, this time aiming directly at the creature. Surprisingly, the rocky armor of the starfish started to glow red-hot under the intense heat. Again, it didn't emit a sound, as if nothing could affect it, but the sight was encouraging.

"It's working—keep it up!" James yelled, running forward. The moment the boss shifted away from him, its arms rising to craft another series of projectiles, he was on it, his fist charged full of mana, his mind dedicated to a sole intent.

The blow was enough to send the monster skidding backward a few feet, interrupting its spell. Though he was forced to jump back by an arm that threatened to squash him, James smiled. Though it felt like hitting a rock wall, his reinforced gloves were enough to protect his hands, which meant he could attack without fear.

Seeing an opening, Lauren moved like a shadow, disappearing and reappearing on one of the crystals above the starfish. The moment Maria sent another fireball to its base—this time an explosive one—Lauren jumped in, scoring a gash on the armor and quickly retreating.

Ezekiel took the moment to cast a debuff on the creature, slowing it down. He had already helped by buffing them all up, but the starfish's armor seemed to mitigate most of the hits. So, he decided that quickly ending the fight was more important than conserving his mana.

Daniel was the next one to attack, as the boss was busy trying to pin James and Lauren down with a barrage of sharp rocks. His shield Bash skill glowed brightly, enhancing his charge. The monster only had time to raise one arm before the Tank was on it, pushing it back several feet.

This time, the boss let out a warbling sound, and they all immediately realized why. Daniel's attack shouldn't have been enough to truly harm it, but he had attacked precisely where Maria's fireball hit. Even if there hadn't been any visible sign of damage beyond a momentary change in color, it seemed that it had been enough to weaken the structure.

James jumped to punch the starfish's side again, giving his friend the time to retreat, and was in turn helped by Lauren, whose knife severely chipped its armor by hitting it again in the same spot.

"Get away!" Maria screamed and threw another fireball as soon as they all left the monster's vicinity. Rather than tanking it, the boss decided to levitate several rocks in its path, showing a surprising degree of intelligence.

Its distraction, however, allowed James another chance to strike. He leaped into the air, then executed a powerful spin kick at one of the starfish's arms, the force lifting the starfish up, which gave him brief access to the creature's underbelly.

It wasn't enough to flip it over like Lauren wanted, but James made sure to throw one last punch to it, earning another groan.

Smiling in triumph, he didn't notice the stone chip rocketing his way until it was buried in his thigh. The force of the hit blew him back.

James groaned in pain, but thanks to Thakinetic Empowerment, he managed to quickly pick himself up and rolled away, avoiding another barrage aimed at eliminating him from the fight.

It's trying to take me out. It wants to pick us apart one by one so that we can't constantly attack it from all sides, and its resistance might just make it possible. Fuck, that hurts.

James's greatest weakness, he knew, was his complete lack of a defensive skill. Empowerment was usually enough to protect him from stray hits, as it also increased his vitality stat. However, when it came to direct hits from boss-level monsters, he could only dodge them, and since the starfish wasn't the type of melee attacker he was used to fighting, he had let his guard down.

His over-reliance on Thakinetic Awareness bit him in the ass, and James was forced to roll away from a third barrage of sharp rocks, even as it pulled him further from Ezekiel and possible healing.

This fucking thing is trying to box me in between the crystals so it can finish me off.

James, however, wasn't one to give up so easily, and his teammates wouldn't let him fall without a fight. Both factors helped him avoid being crushed to death by a gigantic boulder.

Thus far, the starfish had only used small rocks, so they were taken by surprise when a ten-foot-wide boulder rose to the air. The boss prepared to launch it, with James as the target.

James braced himself, ready to dodge.

However, as it was an H-rank creature, its powers were still limited. When it was hit by Maria's fireballs, which struck its vulnerable spot, it couldn't protect itself.

It made the rocky armor glow cherry red, and the boss let out another warble, dropping its weapon to defend from Daniel's advance.

James took that moment of reprieve to retreat, hobbling back to Ezekiel, who immediately started healing him. Maria stood before them to intercept any stray hits while Lauren and Daniel kept the boss's attention away.

All right, let's get ready for round two.

CHAPTER THIRTY

The moment James was fully healed, he drank a mana potion and jumped back into action, taking over for Daniel, who had been seriously battered by the boss's attacks. He would have liked not to waste the precious brew, but now was not the time to be thrifty.

"It's flagging!" the Tank called out as he retreated, retaking his position next to the two mages. Ezekiel cast a healing spell, restoring his health enough that he could keep going for a while.

"We need to finish this now before we get too drained," James shouted to Lauren, who was busy taking up the giant starfish's attention. She flitted around it, jumping between the crystals, never staying still for more than a moment.

"Let's do this!" Maria's fireball was answer enough, as it exploded right next to the boss, unbalancing it sufficiently that James was able to slip by unnoticed. The moment it righted itself, and brought its attention to the Fire Mage, was its undoing.

Lauren's knives shimmered with the use of a skill, scoring a deep gash on one of its arms, and James punched right below another limb, lifting the entire boss by a couple inches from the ground.

Assaulted from all sides, it tried to shield its most vulnerable parts, calling upon dozens of rocks from all around to cover its underbelly.

That, however, was not their target. Instead of going for the natural weak point, Team 0 had made their own from the beginning. Maria's fireballs had heated up the front armor that its structure weakened, and Lauren's repeated blows had chipped at it until it was almost broken.

Both melee fighters completely ignored the newly formed rock shield, instead jumping to deliver the final blow from the front.

Simultaneously, they struck the weakened area in the starfish's armor. James's punch, imbued with all the mana he could muster, created a shuddering crack, while Lauren's knives, glowing with energy, further deepened the fracture. The weakened armor finally shattered under the coordinated assault, revealing the vulnerable flesh beneath.

Rather than following through, as would have been instinctive, they immediately retreated, barely avoiding the retaliatory barrage of very sharp rocks.

By then, however, the fight was almost over. Maria followed up quickly, her most potent fireball unleashed. The flames roared, engulfing the exposed part of the creature. A muted warble echoed through the waterlogged cavern as the heat seared its flesh, eliciting spasms from its massive limbs.

With one last buff, Ezekiel enhanced their stats so that they could dance around it, waiting for another opportunity. The creature was racked by pain as it blindly tried to hit everything in its vicinity.

The team didn't let up. They continued their coordinated assault, exploiting the opening they had created. James pushed his skill even harder. He flooded his limbs with enough mana that some of it leaked when he finally hit its exposed flesh again, causing even further damage.

Its cooked interiors trembled with pain, and strength had already started leaving the boss. Knowing this was the most dangerous moment of the fight, James carefully timed his assault to avoid any last-ditch effort.

His arm easily penetrated the cavity in the starfish's armor and reached the internal organs. Without meaning to, he unleashed a wave of excessive mana—a result of trying to squeeze a little more from his skill—which left James exhausted.

Luckily, he did not have to worry about retaliation. The mana racked the creature's insides and pushed out of its back explosively, breaking through its rock armor in a shower of fragments.

A ping from the System, unobtrusive as always, told him the fight was over. It was followed by a flood of notifications, which he left to the side for the moment.

This is so fucking embarrassing. I'm stuck. I'm actually stuck inside the boss. Jesus, take me now.

James groaned, trying to leverage his feet against the massive corpse to pull himself out, but his last attack had left him truly drained. It felt like his limbs were made of jelly, and it was all he could do not to slump.

Having received the same notification, his teammates were busy celebrating. It took them a minute before they realized James was still arm-deep inside the starfish, and they all gathered at his side, worried he had gotten hurt.

"What happened, do you feel sick? Is it the poison?" Ezekiel fretted, his hands starting to glow with healing light. James waved him off with his free arm, not wanting the White Mage to waste even more of his mana.

He then took a deep breath and muttered, "I'm stuck."

Looks of disbelief were exchanged, before slightly strangled laughter echoed through the crystalline room. James turned a glare to Lauren, who was trying and failing to stifle her chuckles.

"It's not that funny," he complained, even though he knew it actually was.

"I'm sorry, this is just too good. How in the hell did you manage to get yourself in this situation?" she replied once she had gathered herself, her lips still twitching with suppressed mirth.

"I punched it. What else?" James explained, his voice laced with exasperation. "And now I can't pull out."

"Yeah, I can see that. Something to work on before it's too late, eh, Jimbo?" Daniel added, joining in the laughter.

"But why can't you pull yourself out? You're strong enough," Maria asked, tilting her head in confusion as she stared at his arm, which was shoulder-deep into the starfish.

"It's the explosion, isn't it? It wasn't a skill," Lauren realized.

James grimaced, sighing. "I may have gotten a bit too overenthusiastic. I put way too much mana, overloaded my skill, and now I feel like a newborn baby." He gave a weak tug, to no effect. "Now that we all know, can you guys help me?"

"So let me get this straight," Daniel began, his lips pressed tightly to prevent the laughter from escaping. "Not only did you get stuck inside, but you also blew your load?" As soon as he finished, he guffawed, holding his stomach. Lauren, unsurprisingly, joined in, tears falling from her eyes.

The other two hid their faces, but James could see their shoulders shaking. He took a deep breath and then let go. It was a bit funny, and he'd laugh at it, too, as soon as he was out of the monster's bowels. Maria approached, still chuckling but with a determined glint in her eyes. "All right, let's get you out of there," she said, grabbing his free arm.

Daniel added his own strength to the tug, and with a collective effort and much more laughter, they managed to extract James from the now lifeless husk of the giant starfish boss. He stumbled back, supported by his friends, panting and a little unsteady on his legs, but otherwise unharmed.

"You're never living this down, you know," Lauren said with a smirk as she gave him a supportive pat on the back.

"Yeah, I've resigned myself to that fate," James replied with a weary grin.

As the laughter subsided, the team regrouped, taking a moment to breathe and recover from the intense battle. The boss had been strong enough to require all their combined efforts, and James was sure that if they hadn't been so well trained and capable of covering each other's weaknesses, they wouldn't have walked away unscathed.

"We really shouldn't have made it this far, eh?" Lauren asked, staring at the massive starfish. "No way a team of rookies could take on this thing. Hell, the field of whip seaweeds alone should have sent us packing."

"Do you think that's what they wanted to happen?" Maria wondered. "The guilds, I mean. For us to give up not even halfway through, thus showing how ineffective the Dawn Initiative was?"

Daniel hummed, looking all around at the show of reflected lights. "It wouldn't surprise me if that had been the initial plan, but they wouldn't have minded had we been taken out of the picture entirely."

"They must have known about the gas," James concluded. "Miss Walker can be excused because she probably didn't even step into the cave. She must have done the survey in a hurry, since she said they were watching her. But the guild that had the lease for this thing must have known, and they didn't say anything about it."

He wasn't one to give in to baseless conspiracies, but at this point, it would be more foolish to believe the guilds to be acting righteously.

Their speculations were interrupted by Ezekiel, who seemed worried. "That's another thing we can bring up once we get back home, but for now, we need to leave. I have just enough mana to get us back outside, but if we wait much longer, the poison will start taking effect."

He finally added, "Nobody should come snooping here anyway. I think we can leave it all as it is and come back tomorrow morning." Then he grabbed James and pulled him up.

Walking out of the cave was much quicker than their initial exploration, as they didn't need to worry about monsters since the straightforward path—alcoves aside—made it impossible to have missed any.

It still took them the better part of an hour before they were out and the light of the afternoon sun greeted them. A cold wind picked up, but after the dangers they had faced within the cave, it felt refreshing and benign.

After trudging alongside the shore, they soon reached Mr. Robinson's van, where the man was waiting for them, smoking a cigarette. He put it out as soon as he noticed them, and their victorious, if exhausted, grins told him all he needed. "Congratulations! Has it been a fruitful run?"

"A lot of monsters mean a lot of levels and loot, so I'd say it went better than expected. We just need to rest a bit before we can go back in and pick up the mana stones. Could you take us to a hotel that's part of the AA's affiliate network?" Daniel answered, putting down his shield with a sigh.

"There are a couple nearby that should do the trick. Will you be spending the night as well?" the man asked, his phone already in hand to choose a place.

The Tank nodded. "Yeah, we're exhausted and need to eat and sleep. Since it's the off-season, it should be well within the budget, right?"

"Very well, leave it to me."

Lying down on a comfy bed, much better than the one he was used to, James sighed. *I could get used to this. Actually, why don't I just ask them which mattress brand this is and buy myself one? The one I have at home has to be from the sixties, at least.*

Since Daniel was in the shower and Ezekiel was well and truly asleep, James was left with his thoughts. The dungeon had been more complex than he had expected, but the team's great synergy made it possible for them to tackle it with little trouble, beyond needing to be careful about mana usage.

We would have swept it if it hadn't been for the poisoned air. No questions asked.

Still, for all the complexities and challenges, the rewards were worth it. Looking at his status screen, James smiled. The boss gave him a ton of experience, and since he had been close enough to level 17, it had brought him all the way to eighteen. For a few hours' worth of fighting, it was quite a lot. Especially since most of the EXP in the battles with the whip seaweeds went to Ezekiel, who gained six whole levels.

There's still a long road ahead, but I'm making progress. I'm growing stronger every day, and it won't be long before I can start making an impact.

CHAPTER THIRTY-ONE

fter a refreshing nap, Team 0's members found themselves at the hotel's restaurant, scouring the menu for something that wouldn't land them a meeting with HR, discussing how much they had spent on dinner.

The rooms might have been cheaper, owed to the off-season and few tourists, but the restaurant operated on different margins. They couldn't simply lower their prices because of the little demand, which meant that as much as they might have wanted to celebrate with lobster, they couldn't do so on the AA payroll.

And I'm not about to pay for a meal that can be free. They gave us a budget, and as God is my witness, we'll use it.

"I really don't want to interrupt," came a voice from the table next to theirs, where two people sat—there were only ten other patrons tonight besides Team 0. He looked to be a man in his early forties with short brown hair, wearing a deep blue cashmere sweater and brown pants and loafers, appearing as if the model resident of Montauk. "But are you the team sent to clear the dungeon?"

"We are. Just got done killing all the monsters, we'll finish up cleaning the cave tomorrow morning," Lauren answered, not taking her eyes away from the menu.

A wide smile grew on the man's face, and his eyes sparkled as if he just met his favorite celebrities. "Oh, that's just amazing!" His tone was a bit louder than necessary, but wealthy customers generally liked taking up the room for themselves, so it didn't surprise him.

The man's companion, a beautiful blond woman with large blue eyes and a voluminous chest, tittered in agreement, batting her eyelashes. "So cool," she said, red lips curling with something that sent a shiver down James's spine.

"Oh, please. You must let me treat you to this meal. Marty! Marty, come over here!" The man suddenly stood up, calling for the maître d'. Before any of them could even attempt to refuse his offer, as they rightly should have, he had already decided for them. "These people are my guests, Marty. Put their meal on my tab, no limits!"

Then he turned to face them. "Please just let me do this. The Dalmatian Guild certainly wasn't good enough to clear that dungeon, and if we had to wait for the Coast Guard to move off their asses, we'd have to cancel the summer season altogether."

The man was like a steamroller, evidently used to getting things his way. And since the maître d' hadn't put up any resistance, merely nodding impassively and walking over to the register to speak with the cashier, they had no choice but to accept.

"Well, thank you then. We appreciate it," Lauren said, finally looking at the man. "Could we have our host's name?"

"Oh, how stupid! I'm sorry, I'm just so used to everyone knowing me here. I'm Theodore Clapton II, but you can just call me Theo. Make sure to go for the lobster bisque. Better than the ones I've had in New England, and that's saying something." His subsequent laughter was, again, very loud, but since the man had just offered to pay for their otherwise costly meals, they would just have to put up with it.

Theodore Clapton was the kind of rich man used to buying people's attention and affection but was also lucky enough to have the resources to do so successfully. He evidently liked being the center of attention and monopolized the evening, asking questions about the dungeon, the monsters inside it, and what they had done to defeat them.

He looked so much like a kid in a candy shop that they didn't see much harm, and James didn't stop them. His mana had recovered enough from the foolhardy usage that he could finally use his skills again, and he had swept Thakinetic Awareness through the restaurant as soon as they had entered it.

Theo Clapton was nothing to worry about if his weak will was any indication, but the woman sitting with him would have been dismissed as eye candy if not for James's skill. She was entirely different.

Her willpower blazed to his senses. Though it was hidden behind the carefully constructed facade of a vapid model in her twenties trying to bag a rich man, it rivaled Miss Walker's. Nothing in her image gave her away. Not a twitch out of place. Even her eyes didn't betray her. They didn't wander, her smile never faltered, and she kept her sultry tone steady.

This was a dangerous person, and James had no way to inform his teammates without her noticing.

It was quite likely, he realized, that Theo Clapton was an unknowing patsy. The man seemed genuinely interested in their story and had that fascinated look that people obsessed with Awakeners would get.

It wouldn't be difficult to ask if the two had known each other for long, and James was ready to bet that the answer to that was no.

But this was no time to make assumptions. James's mind raced as he smiled and answered Theo's questions, always keeping half an eye on the blond woman. He noticed how her eyes keenly followed their conversation, even as she acted disinterested and fiddled with her golden necklace, occasionally whispering something into Theo's ear, making him laugh.

As dinner progressed, and they all enjoyed the delectable dishes served in a restaurant so fancy James would typically never approach it, he decided he needed to do something to get across the message that they needed to be careful to his teammates.

It seemed increasingly apparent that she was using Theo Clapton to get close to them, to pry information that James and his team wouldn't give under normal circumstances.

When dessert came, with Theo now regaling his exaggerated tales of bravery in the face of a raccoon invasion at his summer house, James subtly tapped Lauren's foot with his own, bringing her attention to him.

"I love raccoons," he said, willing the girl to understand him. "They remind me of rats, and I love rats. They're cute and cuddly, but have a hidden strength."

A moment of confusion was followed by the realization that he was trying to say something. He couldn't be clearer than that, but at least the message that something was going on arrived loud and clear. Lauren gave a slight nod, indicating she understood.

The others, having picked up from his words that something weird was afoot, closed up, letting the man speak rather than contributing more information.

They finished their meal with forced laughter and polite applause for Theo's tale, and as they were about to get up to leave, the woman stood up and approached them, her walk a sultry sashay that was probably meant to be disarming.

"You guys are just so fascinating," she said, her voice a silky purr. "What guild did you say you were from?"

"Oh, we're not from a guild," Maria answered politely. "We were sent by the Awakeners Association."

"Oh my!" the woman gasped, looking genuinely shocked. "I didn't know they also had teams of beginners. Do they treat you well?"

James felt his skin crawl. He really wanted to get as far away from her as possible, but he kept his cool, not wanting to alert her. "It's a good gig. Decent pay, decent training. Just about what you'd expect."

By now, his teammates all understood that he wanted them to get out of there, so nobody contradicted him.

"Now, I'm terribly sorry, but as you can imagine, we are truly exhausted," he continued, giving Theo and his companion a grateful smile. "We really need to get some sleep. The dungeon still needs to be cleared, so we have work in the morning."

"Oh, you are right, poor dears. We must have kept you up for too long," the woman replied, her lips curling into a smile that didn't quite reach her eyes. "Get some sleep—you deserve it."

The next morning, they had a quick breakfast before leaving for the dungeon, eager to get it over with as soon as possible.

"Now that we're here and we know nobody is listening in, can you tell us what happened?" Lauren asked exasperatedly.

James's teammates had been frustrated the night before when he had kept his silence on why he had pulled them away from a pleasant evening, but they had eventually acquiesced to his paranoia. Considering how strong he suspected the blond woman to be, he felt justified in taking precautions.

Thus, he waited until they were back inside the dungeon to spill the beans, explaining everything he had sensed from the woman and his suspicions about her true intentions. The team listened intently, their casual demeanor from the night before replaced by hardened concern.

"I should have noticed," Lauren muttered, frustration coloring her words. "I let the luxury and the food get to my head. I should have been paying more attention."

"So you think she might have even been a B-rank? Why would such a powerful person waste an evening trying to spy on us?" Daniel asked, not disagreeing with his assessment but confused at the excessiveness.

"She might have been a C- or D-rank, for all I know. I just compared her to what Miss Walker feels like, but then again, she might not be letting out her whole presence, what with her stealth abilities," James answered. "My skill doesn't tell me levels or stats. But I've learned to trust it, and I can assure you, that woman has a will of steel. Nothing like the vapid model she tried to pass as."

"And her questions at the end confirm it. She wanted to know about the AA. Nobody that's not an Awakener cares about the AA," Maria concluded, looking pensive.

James shrugged. "We made it out unscathed, and now we're aware they're spying on us. That's what matters. Let's just be more cautious in the future."

The team nodded in agreement, focusing their attention on the task at hand: cleaning out the remainder of the dungeon.

Hours of meticulous work passed. The team moved with renewed caution, watching not only for residual dungeon dangers but also keeping an eye out for external threats, particularly a blond woman.

They gathered the mana stones with little trouble, the remains of the smashed crabs and whip seaweeds not standing a chance to their dressing knives.

When it came to the boss, they made the executive decision to cut its body into pieces. The starfish was simply too big to fit into the van as it was, and no one wanted to lug it around.

Thankfully, its rocky armor had lost some of its durability, as the monster had actively enhanced it while it was alive. With it dead, James could smash its limbs without too much trouble, and Lauren finished the job, cutting off the attached flesh.

By the time they left the dungeon, it was already midday. They decided to head directly back to New York, not wanting to risk reencountering Theo and his scary companion. Their loot would be enough to refill their coffers to buy more mana potions, especially with the sale of the boss's corpse.

Unfortunately, James was forced to leave behind the giant crabs, having been convinced after a long debate with Ezekiel that the poisoned air in the dungeon had likely seeped into the beasts' meat, making it too dangerous to consume.

They left Montauk with a sigh of relief, gladly leaving behind the annoying Coast Guard roadblock after they had inspected the loot.

More importantly, they discovered a critical piece of information. Someone was tailing them, seeking to learn more about their team and how the AA treated them.

CHAPTER 31.5 – INTERLUDE

Leila

Snooping around New York Harbor wasn't particularly dignified, especially for someone of her rank, but Leila wasn't one to delegate such important tasks to others.

Since her kids just returned from their last dungeon run—and once again managed to get into trouble—she was now free from the guilds' surveillance, at least for a while.

It rankled her, having to move around so surreptitiously, but there was nothing she could do about it for the moment. As much as she would like to confront the sensor who was observing the AA HQ from the Starbucks across the street, it would ruin their entire operation.

Well, it might ruin both. The AA's and mine. Because I haven't forgotten what Golden Sun was doing in that C-rank dungeon, and if I manage to get enough dirt on them, it'll also help the director's plan.

Leila was a firm believer that a secret only stayed secret if just one person knew of it. She had been forced to share with the AA what she knew and yield on pursuing the major investigation on data falsification and corruption, simply because she wouldn't have been able to tackle it alone.

But she had a matter that needed settling with the Golden Sun Guild, and she'd be damned if she gave it up.

It was why she was skulking through the shadows of massive shipping containers, slowly inching closer to where she felt several powerful Awakeners.

Technically, being in the harbor without a permit was enough for her to intervene, but she'd look ridiculous trying to give a B-rank a ticket for trespassing. Especially since they'd be able to say they were investigating some mana disturbance, and she'd be forced to let them go.

No, she needed to gather much more information than the loose collection she currently had. No judge would seriously look at her speculations, and then these bastards would be wise that she was onto them.

The excessive riches she had observed them use could be explained away as simply bad purchases. Their use of subsidiary guilds to control entire boroughs of New York, as negligence in checking on them.

But what she suspected she'd find now . . . Well, that was a different game entirely.

[Wedding Dress of the Princess of Hell] was an extremely versatile skill; it allowed her to blend into the darkness with nary a whisper of her presence, and granted her unmatched defensive capabilities within her rank.

It was the fruit of months and months of grinding in dungeons for the then level 200 Awakener to bring her last skill to level 20; it granted her a powerful evolution. Some had scoffed at her doggedness, but now she could avoid the notice of even the strongest B-rank sensors.

Thanks to her skill, she reached the waterfront undetected, hovering in the shadow world right next to the group of high-rankers she had come all the way there to spy on.

"We should really accelerate our relocation. No matter what your spies say, I know the AA has started waking up. We shouldn't make it easy for them to catch onto us," one of them said, which Leila recognized by the flashy purple suit as Marques Etoile, one of Golden Sun's elite front-liners.

His companions, dressed in less ostentatious but equally expensive outfits, nodded in agreement. The small gathering was an odd mix, but each emanated a palpable aura of power.

"We've already begun moving the assets to the secondary location," another man, his hair slicked back into a sharp silver mane, replied. His tone was calm but carried an edge of urgency. Leila knew him as John Scott, an old special-forces-soldier-turned-Awakener in the early days of the apocalypse.

With so many B-rank elites present, she felt like she struck gold. Of course, the danger was proportionate to the rewards, and if an A-ranker had been present, she would have had to flee the scene as fast as she could. Fortunately, the Golden Sun Guild only had one, and that man wasn't likely to hang around in a place like this.

Only two other people were at the harbor, and she had met both more than once. Bradley Esposito was easily recognizable thanks to his pale blond hair and well-groomed beard, while the other was a woman who went by the name Poison Snake. She was dressed in green and yellow with well-manicured nails, which Leila knew were strong enough to cut through steel.

"Your little power struggles don't interest me. What about the artifacts?" the woman asked, her voice dripping with concern. Her sharp amber eyes scanned the dim lights of the harbor suspiciously. "We can't just leave them here. They're too valuable and too dangerous."

Scott nodded, tapping a finger over his golden pocket watch. "We should really find a different system. I understand the importance of ensuring each shipment is handled well, but we all have pressing duties. We can't have such valuables stay out in the open for so long. The consequences alone . . ."

"Agreed. This batch will be moved tonight by my men. I've already ensured the safety of the routes, and they'll reach a new deposit soon enough," Marques interjected with an air of authority, motioning toward the containers.

A thrill went down Leila's spine. So far, nothing explicitly illegal has been said.

After all, the Golden Sun Guild was known to take part in the trade of high-rank materials and artifacts. But if she could follow them to a deposit, she might be able to get her hands on something more consistent.

Bradley Esposito, who had remained silent until now, spoke up, his voice clear and commanding. "We should make sure that the new location is more secure, and maybe look into hiring more trustworthy personnel. Your thugs might be loyal, but they're done if anyone above C-rank finds them."

The purple-suited man took the insult with grace, merely smiling. "Need I remind you, my friend, that the entirety of this operation is only possible because of my men? Should I mention what happened the last time you tried using your family's network?"

Leila giddily listened in. If cracks were already present, she might not need to do too much to bring their crimes to light.

The squabbling was interrupted by Poison Snake. "I have connections in other guilds, people who owe me favors. They know not to ask questions, and it might make things easier on us if we have scapegoats ready," she said, unbothered by the heated glares her two companions were throwing at each other.

The fact that they were discussing this kind of thing out in the open made Leila think they had been getting away with it for a long time. This brazenness only came about in long-standing, successful operations, and she was increasingly sure this was one of those.

At one point, Poison Snake looked around as if sensing something off, her eyes narrowed and scanning the darkness. They passed over Leila's hiding spot without stopping, much to her relief.

The woman was the most concerned about security of the group, obviously wary of being found out, but Leila didn't think it was because of any guilt or inexperience.

Rather, she seemed the most conscious of how badly things could go if they were found out.

Eventually, the meeting concluded, with the group agreeing to move the "artifacts" that very night. They dispersed, each heading to separate points of the harbor, forming a perimeter.

Leila waited a few more minutes before she resumed her hunt. The discussion she had overheard hinted at several interesting things, but they had been careful enough not to explicitly speak of criminal activity.

However, that didn't stop her from looking for the evidence by herself. Entering the massive, reinforced containers would have been impossible for anyone without a spatial skill, and Leila was sure Golden Sun wouldn't have allowed such a glaringly obvious weakness to stand.

[Wedding Dress of the Princess of Hell], however, operated on entirely different rules. Although it had a spatial component, as long as she didn't materialize she'd be able to snoop around without tripping any sensor, human or mechanical.

Thus, she entered the first container.

After listening in on Golden Sun's leaders' talk, Leila expected to find powerful artifacts and monster parts. Rare, to be sure, but nothing outside the ordinary. The information in her head painted a picture of smuggling valuable objects to avoid taxes and oversight.

Instead, she found something much worse, and suddenly Poison Snake's words made sense. The danger here wasn't simply caused by high-level artifacts possibly being stolen.

Golden Sun was smuggling mana stones in quantities large enough that they should have caused a B-rank Mana Sink all by themselves.

Leila observed with wide eyes the sheer level of wealth on display. There was enough in one container to pay for the annual budget of the AA's New York branch.

The trade of mana stones, especially of this quantity and quality, was strictly forbidden, and was one of the few things the federal government kept an eye on.

Too many times in the early days people had caused dungeons to appear because they had collected a critical level of the precious things.

In just one container, Golden Sun stuffed enough to cause half a dozen Mana Sinks, or, more likely, to forcefully increase an already present dungeon's rank.

That's what they were doing at the bear dungeon. They weren't using such powerful equipment without a reason. They made that C-rank dungeon into a B-rank one!

CHAPTER THIRTY-TWO

Returning to the AA HQ after the unexpectedly long stay in Montauk was surprisingly relieving. James knew the blond woman—she'd given him a fake name, Lucy Bleu—wouldn't have harmed them, at least not directly. But the safety of the AA's solid walls and the presence of more than a dozen high-rankers made him feel much better.

Unfortunately, Miss Walker couldn't stay for long. She listened intently to their report, shook her head in bemusement at all the messes they got themselves into, apologized profusely for having missed the poisoned air, and left.

She seemed genuinely remorseful for her mistake and confirmed that she had sped through the dungeon while in the shadows, thus completely avoiding the toxic gas.

For all of that, she also seemed confused about it. She explained that while more minor environmental changes were expected in dungeons, like the unnatural shadows of the rat den, this kind of complex obstacle was usually found only in D-rank and above.

It was quite lucky, she told them, that Ezekiel realized what was going on so soon. She had a pensive look, and the implication that it might not have been a natural phenomenon hung in the air.

She seemed very busy, though, so they didn't bother her any longer. At least, she promised them a more in-depth review of their dive and all the exciting things that happened while they were out of town.

Without Miss Walker, Team 0 unanimously decided they could take the rest of the day off. Their debrief was done, and they could write the reports at home. While the training room's showers were good enough for a washup, they needed to go back to their own beds and sleep the stress away to truly relax.

So they said their goodbyes to each other and promised to hold off on assigning the stat points, pending a review of their performance.

"I'm hooome," James called, making sure to brush his feet against the porch rug, knowing that his grandmother would have his hide if he tracked dirt in.

"James! Welcome back, love. How did it go?" Rosa asked from the kitchen, where she was busy preparing dinner for his return.

He had called the previous evening to let them know he'd be sleeping out. They'd worry endlessly without hearing anything from him, even if he was technically an adult.

They've gotten used to me being an Awakener surprisingly quickly, but if I don't call regularly, they'll freak out like when I was fourteen.

"Pretty well, actually. We got a good haul in, leveled up a few times, and had a great dinner. I'd say this was my favorite dungeon so far," he answered, purposefully not mentioning the toxic air or the spooky lady who dined with them.

Well, considering that the other three dungeons I went to saw me either confronting my trauma, getting horribly injured, or discovering a dead body, I'd say that this is honestly the best one so far.

Rosa smiled, coming into the living room to give him a hug. She removed her apron, which sported a few tomato sauce stains, and embraced him. "That's good to hear, love. I know how hard you're working and how much it means to you."

James hugged her back, breathing in the familiar scent and finally relaxing. He had been wound up ever since he realized they were being tailed at the restaurant, and while getting to the AA helped, a part of him yearned for the warmth of his home.

They let go, and he dropped his bag to the side, going to sit on the sofa.

"Is that James?" his grandfather's voice called from the second floor as he made his way down to check.

"Just got back, Grandpa." He waved, smiling as the older man took a spot beside him.

"You'll have to tell us all you can about it at dinner. I'm making lasagna. Nonna's recipe," Rosa announced and left for the kitchen, looking determined enough to face a dungeon herself.

"Did everything go well?" Larry asked once she was out of earshot. James understood he wanted to know if he had gotten hurt, but the old man was never good at talking directly about that kind of thing.

"Nobody got hurt badly, and even then, Ezekiel quickly healed everyone. It really went well." He tried to show how sincere he was. And it was the truth; putting aside the nerve-racking dinner, the dive was very successful. The profits alone made it worth it, considering that the AA loot desk had estimated them to earn about five thousand dollars each.

If he kept his growth rate steady, he'd reach G-rank in a couple of months or so, and F-rank in less than a year. That was a breakneck pace, even for prized guild members whose Talents the guilds wanted to nurture.

If Team 0 got to F-rank within a year of the Dawn Initiative, they'd prove that the money the AA had spent on them was more than worth it.

"Good. I know you can handle yourself," Larry continued, eyes cloudy as he looked at the photos on the fireplace's mantle. "But your grandmother worries. She doesn't get that you are too much like your father to stay at home, safe while the world goes to hell."

James barely stopped himself from coughing in surprise. His grandfather seldom spoke of his father and certainly not favorably. He made his opinion clear on his son, calling him irresponsible for leaving a little kid behind to go and play hero.

To hear him compliment him, even indirectly, was surprising, to say the least.

"It's just that I couldn't live with myself, knowing I have the power to make things better. People, real people, are suffering out there," James finally answered.

It was the truth. He didn't think of himself as a paragon of justice. He wouldn't necessarily go out of his way to tackle every problem in the world. But the things he could affect, that he knew should be different . . . Well, he couldn't ignore those.

Larry half-smiled, chuckling lowly. "Yeah, that's what he used to say too. Difference is, you are a kid with your whole life ahead of you. Nothing is holding you back. He had responsibilities that he deliberately put aside because of what he felt was more important."

"Grandpa . . ." James didn't want to bring up too many painful memories, but he didn't know when the next opportunity to ask would come. "Is that why he left for that last mission? Because he felt he was needed more elsewhere?"

It was a question that haunted him for a long time. He could vividly remember, having been eight at the time, his father's kind smile as he put on his armor to go on a mission he would never come back from. More than once, he had asked himself if his father had been forced to go or if it had been voluntary.

He knew his father died because his team hadn't received the reinforcements necessary to hold their position and had been swept aside by a monster tide. His death lay at the feet of the weak and ineffective government that initially chose to abandon so many places all over America.

But that didn't answer the much more emotional question of whether his father had willingly gone on a mission he must have known to be extremely dangerous, if not suicidal.

"Your father loved you, James. That much I can recognize. But after that woman . . . Well, let's say he changed. He became a man obsessed with his duty to the country. He threw himself at everything with a fierceness that should deserve praise if it hadn't been a way to be away from his family."

And that was the crux of the matter, wasn't it? His father had been a broken man who used his duty as a crutch. Or maybe that was too simple a judgment. It was easy to pontificate long after the chaos of the Mana Apocalypse, but in those days, people honestly thought that the End had come.

"Dad was . . . He cared; I remember that much," James said. Thinking of his father always brought about strong emotions, be it determination to solve the causes of his death or mourning for his absence. "He knew that people would die if he didn't go."

Larry chuckled bitterly. "And where did that bring him? I told him many times what would happen. But he didn't listen. He needed to save the world by himself, even if it killed him. And it did."

"I'm not going to die," James said, cutting to the heart of his grandfather's fears.

They were speaking too loud not to be overheard in the kitchen, but since he knew his grandmother shared the same worry that he'd end up the same as his father, he didn't bother to lower his voice.

"You can't know that, James. You have no idea what kind of crooks are out there. The monsters that roam the land are not all so convenient as to have horns," Larry answered, his frown pronounced and eyes shiny with suppressed sorrow.

No tear fell, as he wasn't the kind of man to allow himself such a relief. Larry Summers was a Catholic through and through, self-flagellation and all.

"Of course, I don't know the future. But I have the System. I have friends and a good teacher. I'm not alone against the world," James countered, feeling himself get emotional. It wasn't often that he had such heart-to-hearts, especially with his grandfather.

Before the older man could answer, James stopped him, lifting a hand in the universal sign for silence. Someone with a powerful will was outside, sitting on his neighbor's lawn.

He carefully went to the window, acting as if he wanted to get some fresh air, and spied a nondescript man having a beer with Bobby Mattinsky, the doctor who retired a few years back. His house in Florida had been destroyed by a monster attack, forcing him to come back to New York.

He didn't seem to be under duress as he chatted with the unknown man without a care. James's ears, however, picked up on their conversation; it was inane to be highly suspicious. After all, why would you be talking about the weather for so long?

No, the man was obviously there to do something else. To avoid giving away that he'd caught on, James returned his attention to the living room, bringing a finger to his lips as he spoke, "How's that lasagna coming, Grandma? I'm starving after all that work. There's nothing but snacks at the AA."

Luckily, the two elders caught on without a problem, putting away the heavy topic they had been discussing and smoothly transitioning to table talk.

"I've been told that adding some sugar to the tomato sauce cheapens it, but you just can't get the natural sweetness of the Calabrian ones here. Without that hint of sugar, it's surprisingly bland," Rosa said, setting the table without a hitch.

While his grandfather spoke of some other inane thing, James kept his physical and metaphysical senses on the stranger.

He didn't appear to be doing much, barely bothering to reply to his "friend." Instead, he was surreptitiously glancing at the window James had left open as bait, further confirming his suspicions.

That man is here to spy on me—there's no doubt about it. But if his presence is any indication, he must be at least E-rank, possibly even D-rank if he's keeping his power concealed.

Considering his last encounter with a possible spy, James felt more sure than ever that a network of surveillance had been set up around him, and probably his teammates too.

The guilds, it seemed, were not playing around.

CHAPTER THIRTY-THREE

After spending the entire evening and night keeping an eye on the man, who he was sure was there to spy on him, James arrived back at the AA thoroughly exhausted.

He had been hesitant about leaving his home, not wanting to let his grandparents be undefended while such a dangerous person was around. Still, he eventually decided that it was much more likely that the man would follow him rather than stay behind and watch over two perfectly normal elderly.

James briefly considered the possibility of it all being an intimidation tactic. If someone outside the AA learned about his sensory skill, they might have devised such an intricate way to torture him.

Still, the knowledge that only his teammates and his teacher knew the specifics of his skills calmed him. With Occam's razor in mind, it was more likely that the guilds were keeping a close eye on those involved with the Dawn Initiative to see how and why they were able to keep going, rather than a deliberate way of sending him to the madhouse.

When he finally entered Team 0's room, he was surprised to find that Miss Walker was absent. The woman was usually punctual and wouldn't miss a training session without alerting them.

He checked on his phone to see if he had unread messages. There was one from a few minutes before where she apologized for taking the day off with so little notice, saying that some things she needed to handle immediately had taken precedence.

"She has to be doing something about the guilds' investigation, right?" Maria asked, noticing that he was reading the same text she was.

James glanced at the redhead, glad that at least she seemed to have gotten some good sleep in. "Probably, yeah. I just wanted to see her because I'm 99 percent certain that we're being monitored," he answered.

The Fire Mage paled, and the others turn toward him, silently asking him to expand on that.

"There was an Awakener at my neighbor's house. A decently strong one, who I've never seen before despite living next to him for years." Seeing they didn't seem particularly convinced, he added, "My neighbor's family is dead, and he's well known as a lonely man. He could possibly be a new friend, but they spoke about the weather for more than one hour. I'm not being paranoid."

"You heard them talk about the weather for that long?" Daniel asked gravely.

"Yeah, it wasn't even a good attempt at hiding. I don't know if it was on purpose or just because he was incompetent, but since he somehow convinced Bobby to let him stay on his lawn for so long . . . Something fishy is going on."

Ezekiel gulped, immediately catching onto what he was saying. "You think he was using a mind-altering skill."

James nodded, lips tightly pressed together. Then he noticed a strangely familiar presence approach the training room.

Soon after, the blast doors slid open, revealing a giant man, whom he recognized from his license test at the AA.

"Good morning, children," Marcus Bethany rumbled. "I was asked by young Leila to sub in for today as your combat instructor."

There was some confusion, as no one but Miss Walker had ever taken the role, but eventually, they decided to go with it. Mr. Bethany, as he told them to call him while he was teaching, seemed like a jolly person, and it wasn't like they could say no.

That impression was quickly shattered when he started putting them through physical drills that would have broken hardened soldiers. The man might look like a friendly shopping-mall Santa, if one ignored his height and the rock-hard muscles hidden beneath the fat, but his training regimen was nothing short of brutal. It was a reminder that even the friendliest of faces in the AA could be seasoned and formidable warriors.

"This is nothing! You must be ready to spit blood if you want to see some results! Are you ready to spit BLOOD?!" he roared as he guided them through a grueling run where they were weighed down by purpose-made suits.

"Yes, sir!" they yelled back. They had made the mistake of not being loud enough once, and as punishment, their weights had increased.

Mr. Bethany had a different style to Miss Walker, being much more oriented toward training rather than sparring, but he was evidently experienced as a teacher. He immediately caught on when someone was starting to flag, like Ezekiel and Maria, who didn't put nearly as many points in the physical stats, and lowered the weight accordingly. That way, they could continue to run, he explained with a demonic smile.

In less than an hour, they were all so exhausted that they couldn't even lift a finger, much less have the mental wherewithal to discuss possible spies.

"I can see that little Leila has let you slack off when it comes to physical training. I'll have to talk to her about it," Mr. Bethany said as they were busy inhaling as much air as possible. Their run finally ended once their muscles simply couldn't move anymore.

"B-but why would we train this much if we can just put stat points in?" Lauren finally asked once she recovered enough.

A roar of laughter startled them as the massive man shook with mirth, making the entire room move. "This is why you youngsters are so soft and can't reach the high ranks despite all the advantages you have!" he answered, dropping into a lotus position next to them. "Yes, it's much easier to put points into your attributes and get immediate results," he acknowledged. "But if you only do that, you'll never grasp the full potential of your bodies. Thanks to the System, skills and attributes become inherent to you, but you're not immediately taught how to use them in the most efficient manner."

"But that's why Miss Walker makes us spar so much. She says we'll become accustomed to our changed bodies much faster that way," James interrupted, defending his teacher's methods.

Mr. Bethany grinned, looking very pleased. "Yes, and she's correct. To get used to fighting in a stronger body, there is nothing better to do than sparring." He then raised a finger in admonition. "But, that's not the end-all, be-all. If you never push yourself to the brink of physical exhaustion, you'll never actually know what you are truly capable of!"

Ah, I think I'm understanding now. He means to say that though our stats increase, we might not be using them to their fullest extent because we've never pushed them to the limit, simply seeking to add more points for a quick power-up.

"Does that make a big enough difference to be worth it?" Daniel asked, as always cutting to the meat of the problem.

Mr. Bethany hummed, twirling his well-groomed mustache with one sausage-sized finger. "I'm not saying it's all you must do, but alternating between sparring and extensive physical training will put you above those in the same weight class."

"But will it actually have any effect on our status?" Maria inquired, looking interested. As someone with a Mage Talent, she wasn't keen on wasting stat points on her physical stats. If she could get more out of those she had, it would mean having plenty for her main attributes.

"As you might already know, increasing one's stats without using the System is an extremely long and arduous procedure," Mr. Bethany admitted. "Weeks of effort, if not months, all to receive a singular point. It's time much better used inside a dungeon, where growth is measured in hours."

That much was common knowledge. On every forum dedicated to Awakeners, guides for all kinds of Talents warned rookies away from wasting too much time in the gym. It was simply not worth the effort.

"However," the old man continued, "your status is just a raw display of your stats. It doesn't take into account your mastery of those stats. Two people with the same strength stat may not be able to lift the same weight if one has trained their body and the other hasn't. The same goes for all the other attributes. Training your body and mind to handle these increased attributes makes you able to use them far more efficiently. You're not technically stronger, faster, or more resilient, but knowing how to use your attributes trumps even a minor bump in stats."

That gave them all pause. It was counter to almost everything that was commonly said about the best methods to train, but it was also an intuitive concept.

It's also similar to what Miss Walker taught us about leveraging our strength stat correctly. Two different people with the same stat might not use them the same way, and though on paper they are the same, their outcomes are likely to be different.

"And don't think this is just about physical attributes. Mental attributes benefit from this sort of mastery too. The more you use them, the better you get at using them efficiently," Mr. Bethany said. "Pushing yourself in a safe environment like this, even if it brings you to the brink of exhaustion repeatedly, will help you be more efficient in its use in a real-life situation."

Mr. Bethany, it turned out, was an excellent teacher, despite his draconian methods. He enjoyed pushing his pupils physically and mentally, and then, while they recovered, he'd explain the philosophy behind it.

It was demanding, and more than once, James felt like he might actually pass out, but he pushed through. They all did.

By the end of the day, they were utterly spent, but there was a sense of accomplishment too, a feeling that they had really achieved something. As they limped into the changing room, James couldn't help but feel a grudging respect for Mr. Bethany. The man knew what he was talking about, and James could already see the benefits of his approach.

"We're all going to be sore for a week," Daniel grumbled, but there was a smile on his face too. As the Tank, he had been pushed the hardest in endurance exercises. So much so that James had been afraid his friend would collapse.

Instead, he had risen to the challenge and pulled through. Just like James had done when his limbs had been weighed down to the point that he felt like he was walking around with a small car in his arms. When he had been told to go through a boxing routine like that, James had almost thought the old man was joking, but one look at his deadly serious expression had made him rethink. He had made it, though, and that was all that mattered.

Once they were out of the showers, feeling as if they had been wrung dry, they were met by their teacher for the day sitting on one of the sofas, taking the entire space. "Please join me; I have a couple of things to talk to you about."

Hesitantly looking at each other, they did as he bade. Mr. Bethany gained their respect with his peculiar but effective training methods, but that didn't mean they were any less wary about him. Not many people at the AA earned their trust.

As they all sat down, some sprawling on the floor for lack of space, the large man took a deep breath. His eyes moved from one student to the next, and James felt the full weight of the man's attention. It wasn't intimidating in the usual sense; it was the intensity, the complete focus, that felt so heavy.

"Now," Mr. Bethany started, his voice gentle compared to his roars during training, "I know that this day has been quite the departure from your usual schedule and methods, but I hope you have learned something valuable today."

They all nodded, albeit some more begrudgingly than others.

"You might be wondering why I was brought in today and what's happening with Leila. Let me tell you about the truth behind the Dawn Initiative."

CHAPTER THIRTY-FOUR

Let me tell you about the truth behind the Dawn Initiative."

They sat up straight at that. Though they were the pilot for the project, the name was highly classified. While Mr. Bethany had to be a big shot in the AA for Miss Walker to have trusted him with their training, they were still surprised he'd give them direct information.

"The main component is exactly what you know. A good chunk of money was set aside to build new teams of rookies from the ground up, thus refilling the starved ranks of Awakeners in the agency," he explained, getting nods from all around. "But there's more. You've experienced what leaving everything in the hands of guilds is like. What it means to have no oversight over their operations."

"There's a reason why the federal government has decided to get involved and create this initiative," Mr. Bethany continued. "Guilds have been, in many ways, poisoning the well. Exploiting talents, monopolizing the field, and deciding who rises and who falls. Their power and influence have become too broad and too deep, and it's eating at the very foundation of society."

This was a well-known problem, debated and discussed in whispers and online forums. Everyone had their own opinions on the solutions to the issue, ranging from abolishing the AA entirely to nationalizing the guilds. Still, they all agreed that things couldn't stay as they were, because the balance tilted too far on one side—the guilds'—which would send the whole system crashing.

"The Dawn Initiative is not just about raising new talents. Yes, we want a corps of powerful and relatively loyal Awakeners. But it's not the main reason why the bigwigs in Washington agreed to fund the project." He leaned back, his massive frame making the sofa creak under his weight. "You are, to be quite honest, bait."

And there it is. Well, it's not like we didn't know. Miss Walker was clear that we were being sent into dungeons whose information had been falsified or deliberately let out. At least she was honest with us and even broke rules to check the Montauk dungeon for anything outside our possibilities.

"We already knew that," James said, making the old man blink in surprise. "No one said it directly, but it doesn't take a genius to realize. Miss Walker told us about things happening at the higher floors and that they suspected several guilds of wrongdoing." He was careful not to be too specific.

Mr. Bethany might have proven himself a good teacher and an intelligent man, but as long as Miss Walker didn't personally vouch for him, he'd still treat him with wariness.

"It's good to know you can use your brain then. It will make this discussion easier," The older man responded. "Leila was never one to stick too close to the rules, but I suppose I have some fault in that, being her teacher and all."

"You were her teacher?" Lauren interrupted, looking surprised at first and then pensive. It made sense if one thought about it. Miss Walker would only send someone she trusted completely to take over for her.

"I was. Back when the AA was still a newborn agency, and things were fluid, I led a team of ex-soldiers and cadets who had Awakened. I taught her the ropes and made sure she wouldn't kill herself," Mr. Bethany explained, sounding fond; it was clear to everyone in the room that the old man cared deeply for their instructor.

"Anyways, as I was saying, it's important you understand that the Initiative received the funds it did because of the hidden promise behind it," he continued, looking serious once again. "The chief director's talks with the White House aren't available to me, but I'm ready to bet my pension that he assured them he would retake some power back from the guilds and that you'd be the tool for him to do so."

It wasn't surprising to James that even people ostensibly on their side, like the AA's chief director, would use their future as a bargaining chip to receive more funds. Still, if there was an actual plan behind the mess they were in, it would be better to learn as much as possible. "Does that mean we'll continue to be sent into falsified dungeons? So that the AA can rack up a pattern of similar misdeeds by various guilds?"

Mr. Bethany smiled, pleased at how quickly he had caught on. "That's part of it, yes, though it won't be long before the guilds become wise to that kind of tactic. I wouldn't be surprised if they started keeping tabs on you to find out if you're AA plants there to bring their 'mistakes' to light."

"They already are," James interrupted. That was all the confirmation he needed to know he wasn't being overly paranoid after being spooked by the blond woman in Montauk.

Rather than being shocked, like he had expected him to be, Mr. Bethany looked extremely excited hearing that.

"So they've already started moving more directly. That's good to know." The old man's grin was almost boyish; he seemed to have a lot of fun imagining the next steps.

"The problem with large organizations," Mr. Bethany chuckled, "is that their left hand seldom knows what the right hand is doing. That gives us a certain advantage for now. However, it won't last long. Some guilds must have gotten spooked, and their relative fragmentation allows us some maneuvering space, but the major ones will reel the others back in soon enough. If we can get at least one big fish to eat the bait, it'll mean we can start with the next phase."

It was clear that the old man enjoyed this game of shadows and deception as much as he did the physical training. There was a kind of thrill in the dangerous dance they were playing.

"You'll be walking a thin line. A precarious balance between being the unsuspecting victims and the proactive agents of change. But remember this," he emphasized, leaning forward in his seat, his massive arms resting on his thighs, "the key to your survival and success lies in your unity and trust in each other. We can't guarantee you'll always be safe, but you already knew this would be a dangerous job. However, I can promise you that you're not alone in this fight. Important and powerful people are betting a lot on this, and their resources are plentiful."

Then, he relaxed, his expression returning to the jolly amusement he had presented himself with. "It's a big game, children. The pawns are numerous, and the knights and rooks are always ready to strike. But sometimes, a pawn can become the most powerful piece on the board if moved wisely. Being a small fish often means you can go unnoticed for much longer, until it's too late."

Maria tilted her head, processing his words. "Does that mean that you expect the surveillance to not last long once they have realized we are not high-rankers pretending to be H-rank to screw them over?"

"That's exactly right. I might be wrong, but in the grand scheme of things, they can't be seen as too interested in you. Certainly, your failure would allow the guilds to claw back the little breathing room we made, but they're likely to leave that to smaller, weaker Awakeners. The big shots will turn their focus on Washington, and that is the beauty of this plan."

"With their attention elsewhere, you intend to sweep in. Take out at least one large player," James realized. It was an ingenious plan, especially since it relied on the guilds feeling safe once they had ensured nothing was out of place. Since they were truly H-rank, it wasn't too farfetched.

"And if things go south?" Lauren's voice was calm, but James could see the tension in her eyes.

The old man's face became somber. "In the world we live in, children, there's always the chance that things will go south. And it can happen faster than you think. If it does, your first priority should be ensuring your safety and that of your teammates. You're no good to anyone dead."

Mr. Bethany stood up, his towering frame casting a long shadow over the team. "It's late, and you have another long day ahead. Remember what we talked about, and keep your eyes and ears open. You might be a single cog of this machine, but you are an important one. Keep up with your training, and you'll achieve all you want."

South Mountain Reservation should have been outside their range as it was in New Jersey, but since the entire Northeastern District was headed by the AA's New York branch, they had some privileges others didn't have.

Mostly woodland composed of hardwood trees and hemlock fields, the reservation was a wild place. It had been left to itself since the 1930s, aside from the construction of the recreational complex, thus resulting in few visitors venturing deep enough to notice any changes.

It was a stroke of luck, then, that the ranger corps, during their periodical sweeps of the area, had detected an unusually high level of mana and, after personally checking it out, had found that a dungeon had spawned.

Since it was relatively new, and the power in the air wasn't enough to declare an emergency yet, such a place would normally be auctioned to private guilds. Still, its presence on county property made things a bit dicier.

Normally, the bureaucrats in charge of such departments would salivate at the idea of getting free money in exchange for having one of their problems solved, but this time, the man that should have simply rubber-stamped the Black Crow Guild's request for a lease had rejected it.

He refused their second offer, which was twenty thousand dollars for a renewable lease of ten days. Quite generous, considering it was an H-rank dungeon.

That left a vacuum, as the New Jersey AA department didn't have the resources to deal with such a low-priority problem. That meant it was sent back to the main branch for the district, the New York AA, where it should have been auctioned again, hopefully receiving the county official's consent.

Instead, it was snatched up as soon as it arrived by a masked woman with red eyes, who gleefully went over the process of getting it approved and received confirmation that the park bureaucrat accepted the request.

That whole chain of events led to Team 0, on one early Thursday morning, trudging through the humid woodland, headed toward the dungeon with a hand-drawn map and their mana-detecting device as a guide.

"And you'd think that being rangers, those people would show some more willingness to accompany us, but no. They all had duties to attend to!" Lauren complained, skipping between roots thanks to her enhanced agility.

"Well, you know what they told us. There was a plant monster that wouldn't die even if they shot it several times. If I wasn't an Awakener, I wouldn't want to come and deal with murderous plants either," Ezekiel answered, trying to calm the Rogue down.

"At least this time, I should be able to do something," Maria interjected, sounding gleeful at the thought of successfully setting a monster on fire.

James shook his head in mirth, keeping the mana-detecting device ahead of him and following its indications.

Finally, after a good half hour of trekking, it pinged loudly, signifying the presence of substantial concentrated magical energy for a dungeon. "All right, we're here," the Thakinetic said, setting his bag with the fragile device between a rock and a tree so that it could stay hidden for the duration of their dive.

As soon as he was done, he turned around to check on his teammates when his senses screamed a warning. He threw himself to the ground, barely avoiding what looked like a feathered missile that would have slammed into him with enough strength to break his face.

CHAPTER THIRTY-FIVE

As he rolled away from the hole in the ground, James was able to see the creature that caused it. Pulling itself out with sharp talons was a fist-sized bird with a bright blue feathering and yellow belly. It chirped aggressively, as if it hadn't just attempted to murder him.

Considering the absurd speed at which it had moved, it looked no worse for wear, probably having a high vitality stat as well as agility. Before James could pounce on it, having shaken off the surprise, the mutated bluebird took to the air, coming to a stop on a high branch.

"Holy fucking shit. We are fucked."

James would have usually been shocked at such language coming out of the typically polite Ezekiel, but looking at the dozen birds that were taking residence next to his would-be murderer, he couldn't help but agree.

"Behind me!" Daniel shouted, his shield glowing brightly. Even as he set himself to stand as a bulwark against the tide of dive-bombing birds, they were already launching themselves off the branch.

Maria and Ezekiel managed to get to safety in time, but James and Lauren were not so lucky. Knowing that he risked getting truly injured, the Thakinetic flooded his body with Empowerment. For the first time in a long while, he wasn't channeling it to just his limbs.

A second later, he was hit by three different birds. The strength of their assault threw James like a rag doll. He rolled to a painful stop against a maple tree.

James could feel a pulsating sensation in both his arms, which he had used as a shield. Opening his eyes, he saw that they weren't horribly mauled, thanks to his suit, but they didn't feel great either.

Attempting to open and close his hands proved painful, but at least he knew they weren't broken.

"Die, you stupid birds. Dieee!" Maria's shout brought him back to the present. He looked up, noticing that several of the birds were busy desperately dodging her fireballs while others lay on the ground, unmoving.

James picked himself up, focusing his skill only on his arms. He sighed in relief, glad that the enhanced vitality stat could lessen the pain.

A shadow moving within his senses told him that Lauren had been luckier than him. Her left arm was limp at her side, but beyond that, she looked no worse for wear, and she was busy stabbing those birds that had remained on the ground.

"They can't attack more than once or twice. Kill them before they recover!" the girl yelled, even as she moved to her next victim.

James didn't need to hear that twice and sprang into action. Despite the great deal of pain he was in, he still had perfectly functional legs and made good use of them.

His reinforced boots easily squashed the birds, their high vitality evidently the result of an active skill rather than their base stats.

Daniel was busy holding against the assault of the few still-flying birds, but with Ezekiel's debuffs, they were not a particular threat. They chirped in confusion, evidently not used to their prey surviving more than a hit or two. Certainly not their entire flock's combined assault.

Maria unleashed fire on those that had flown back on the branches but were too tired to fly again. Her spells were more precise than before thanks to the skill leveling up after the fight with the starfish.

"Try to hem them close to the ground!" James called, lifting his foot off another bird's corpse. He tried hard to ignore the pulsing pain in his arms. He had to. Forced to use his legs to fight, he split Empowerment between all his limbs, thus lessening the pain-relief effects of the enhanced vitality.

Maria complied with his request, stopping her direct assault and instead covering the sky in a much thinner veil of fire. Since they'd witnessed many of their comrades get burned to death by those very same flames, the bluebirds flew low, trying to escape the fiery curtain.

Unfortunately for them, they landed directly in Lauren's and James's strike zones. It took them a few passes to get them all, owing to their limited mobility after the first assault, but eventually, they managed to get them all to the ground. Ending the fight was a quick affair.

"Jesus H. Christ. That was so much harder than I thought it would be," Lauren complained, walking to Ezekiel, whose healing skill was busy putting James's arms back into fighting condition.

"That's the problem with walking in without any knowledge. The rangers said they were attacked by a plant, but nothing about dive-bombing birds," Daniel commented as he inspected his shield for any damage. Luckily, being made of D-rank materials, it had held up without a scratch to show for it.

Maria, who had been fundamental for their efforts at hemming the birds in, didn't look that impressed. "They weren't even that tough. We could have dealt with them easily if we had known what to expect."

"Yeah, but the problem is, we didn't know about them. And we won't always get every bit of information about the next dungeon. The cave in Montauk should have taught us that," Ezekiel replied, wiping his forehead after having finished healing Lauren's arm.

James lifted a hand to pause their bickering, Thakinetic Awareness telling him that something that wasn't there now suddenly was. Slowly, he turned to look at where he felt the presence, but nothing stood out to him beyond the usual shrubbery and trees.

"What is it?" Maria whispered, looking around furtively.

"There's something here that I can barely feel. It might be hiding behind the trees," he answered, suspiciously checking the hemlock plants for any sign of mutation.

"James . . ." Daniel murmured, eyes wide. "I think it might be the trees."

As soon as he said it, a root sprang from below and, with incredible swiftness, speared one of the bird corpses, pulling it into the ground.

Immediately, Team 0 took up a formation behind the Tank. They waited for another move, but nothing seemed to happen. Then, just as James was about to propose they attack instead, the earth rumbled and a dozen roots lifted themselves up.

Thick enough to withstand several hits, the mutated tree trunk split open, revealing a gaping black maw. The roots wiggled in the air like tentacles and its fronds shifted.

"Well, I guess we found the plant the rangers were talking about," Ezekiel muttered, clutching his knife a bit tighter, his face pale. The roots slowly snaked toward them, their movements grotesque yet agile for plant matter.

"Maria, do you think you can burn it?" James asked, keeping his eyes on the undulating mass before them.

"Not sure, but I can damn well try!" Maria replied. Flames erupted from her fingertips, forming a whirling ball of fire that she hurled at the open maw. The fireball was met by one of the roots, engulfing it completely.

The tree seemed to shriek in pain, retracting from the heat. The root, shriveled and blackened, fell to the ground, but the monster itself wasn't affected.

Emboldened by her success, Maria sent three more fireballs in quick succession, each promptly intercepted by a wiggling root.

"We need to get the roots' attention and give Maria a clear shot!" James called out, advancing. He grabbed one of the tentacle-like roots, causing it to twist in surprise and then try to spear him through.

He jumped back, dodging the strike, and grabbed onto another. Then he let it go immediately to avoid the whip-like hit. The air whistled as it passed over his head, and since it was the only unprotected part of his body, James was very keen on keeping it away from any murderous root.

I know high-ranking helmets are super expensive and getting a bad-quality one is worse than having none, but we really need to find a way to protect our heads.

Things started moving much more quickly when Lauren jumped in from the other side. Buffed by Ezekiel's magic, they could easily avoid the roots, even though they couldn't do much in return. James tried a couple of times to hit the roots after avoiding their strikes, but the most he could manage was breaking some of the exterior wood up and pushing them away. They were surprisingly springy, moving with the hits and softening the blows enough that they wouldn't break.

However, that had never been their plan anyway. While the roots were occupied with the two melee fighters, Maria finally got a few good shots in, burning the last protective roots.

Hidden behind Daniel's glowing shield, the Fire Mage continued her barrage, hitting the trunk for the first time, making it shriek. The magical flames burned brighter and hotter than usual, and it wasn't long before the rest of the tree caught on fire.

It flailed around, sending burning sparks everywhere and forcing Maria to run containment, for fear of creating a massive blaze. Still, with the tree on fire, they only needed to avoid its increasingly desperate hits until it started breaking down, its roots losing their strength and becoming inanimate.

Team 0 kept their guard up, watching the bonfire, until a notification finally popped up, telling them that they had defeated a [Juvenile Treant].

"That's a juvenile? I really don't want to meet an adult one, then," James commented, somewhat annoyed at not dealing much damage. He had still received some EXP, since Maria wouldn't have been able to kill it without his help—but it annoyed him, having been relegated to support.

Lauren grimaced, wiping her blade clean from the birds' crusted blood. "Let's also make sure to clear this whole area. If one tree mutated, others may have as well."

"Yeah, and more importantly, I couldn't feel it until it started moving. I think they might be in hibernation." James had been shocked and confused at the treant's presence. Even the whip seaweeds had much more willpower than the treant in its hiding phase, making him worry about any future encounter.

His ability to find beings based upon the strength of their will was one of Team 0's greatest strengths and what allowed them to tackle dangerous situations without fear of falling prey to ambushes. If his skill was becoming less useful, it might spell difficult times for them.

Still, a second notification broke him out of his spiraling, and James smiled. Leveling up was always a good way of breaking him out of his funk.

STATUS WINDOW	
Name	James Summers
Age	19
Awakening	1st
Talent	Thakinesis
Title	
Level	19
MP	71/95
STR	15
VIT	11

AGI	11
SEN	15
MND	11
STAT POINTS	0

James closed the window, feeling much better now that he had increased his strength and sense stats again. It was important not to overspecialize, but at times, having a bit more punching power was worth it.

Also, given his fears of being ambushed by the stealthy treants, it only felt right to boost his sensing ability.

Soon after, another such presence pinged his skill. Turning around, James noticed a tree in the distance starting to shift around unnaturally. He silently alerted the others with a hand sign and started to get closer, only to stop in his tracks.

There wasn't only one treant. There were five.

CHAPTER THIRTY-SIX

A large root speared the ground next to him as James dodged, rolling forward. Getting farther into the treant's range might have seemed counterintuitive, but his options were very limited at long distances.

Thakinetic Awareness alerted him to another attack coming from the ground, and James jumped to the side. A root shot out from where he'd just been standing, but it hit nothing.

With three quick steps, he was close enough to the main body that he could do more than just dodge. A branch, larger and thicker than the roots, bent down to intercept him, but his buffed speed allowed him to once again avoid it.

That was close. I felt the leaves brush my suit.

Cocking his fist and firming up his stance, James took the moment to strengthen his arm, focusing on increasing his destructive power.

He had been tempted, for a moment, to use the last-ditch move he had employed against the starfish, releasing enough mana to break through the hard bark, but he first wanted to try his hand at old-fashioned punching.

With a grin, he released the coiled tension.

When his fist hit the treant, the sound resembled a gunshot. It broke through the initial hardwood, coming to a stop three layers deep.

He was then forced to jump back, feeling his hair swish with the wind created by the tree's movement.

"I can take this one!" he yelled, confident now that he could hurt it. It would surely take some time, as the treant didn't seem interested in letting James punch it to death, but since it couldn't really hit him, even when the treant directed its limbs at him, it was just a matter of time.

One more root was added to the mix, but its speed was slower. Rather than being the effect of a skill, it seemed that the monster had hit its limit of how many limbs it could move at the same time. Though it was enough to force him a few steps back, it didn't change the direction of the fight.

James dodged for half a minute before another opportunity opened up. He slipped into the treant's guard and punched hard, hitting the same spot. Wood chips flew everywhere as his fist reached almost midway through the tree, causing the gaping maw to screech in pain.

Again, he leaped back, rolling to the ground and jumping up to avoid roots. In his buffed state, James could sense the path of an attack as soon as the monster committed, and for all its dogged determination, the creature wasn't smart enough to change its patterns, especially since Ezekiel had weakened its mind stat.

The effect of the debuff wasn't as dramatic as with the whip seaweeds, which had barely been able to move after being hit, but it still made the treants predictable enough that they could be dealt with.

Dodging another thick branch aimed to crush him, James was once again within striking range, and he didn't let that opportunity go to waste. His gloved fist, this time, went through the trunk, weakening it enough that it began tipping over.

The monster's warble of pain was cut off when its trunk snapped, the weight of its upper body simply too much.

As soon as the notification of its death came, James turned around and ran toward his friends. The situation wasn't much different than when he had left them, with Ezekiel and Maria hiding behind Daniel, and Lauren flitting around, gathering the treants' attention.

While only one tree had been set aflame, the fires engulfed all four, two of which still unscathed.

Jumping to Lauren's aid, James tapped a few of the wriggling roots, alerting the treants to his presence and giving the girl some breathing room. With the experience of successfully fighting against two tree monsters, James was able to dodge their attempts to turn him into a shish kebab pretty easily, if only thanks to Ezekiel's skill.

Lauren was busy cutting off roots that got too daring, lessening the number of limbs they had to worry about, and since time was on their side, what with the fires spreading all over them, there was no need to risk themselves by getting too close.

It wasn't James's preferred mode of combat, and he couldn't wait until his skills reached a high enough level to let him bulldoze through any mid- to long-range fighter, but when clearing a dungeon, it was important not to get ahead of one's capabilities.

In her lessons, Miss Walker had been clear that even seasoned Awakeners could fall because of hubris. They thought they had fully understood a monster and were killed by a surprise attack at the last moment. "If you can kill them without risking your life, do it. Always do it," she was fond of saying.

Ten minutes later, the last of the treants was burned to death. The clearing was full of broken branches and smoke, but at least they were safe from the tree monsters.

James extended his senses, searching for even the most minor presence, but was unable to find any. "We should be clear here. Still, their stealth abilities are better than what I was expecting, so let's be careful."

The others nodded in agreement, save Maria, who was too busy being giddy about her newest level-up. She had taken the lion's share of the experience, being the primary damage dealer, which had been enough to push her over the line.

James's bar was only at a tenth, even after killing a treant all by himself, but he wasn't particularly discouraged. The dungeon run was still long and he was sure he'd have the opportunity to gain more EXP.

They all took a moment to rest, as they had been forced into back-to-back fights. The treants were resilient monsters, and their roots gave them great control over the battlefield. Thanks to his increased stats, James wasn't even winded, but it was important to pace oneself.

I bet we'll have to spend the whole dive jumping from one fight to the next. This dungeon seems specialized in keeping the tension very high, so I'd expect the birds to come back any moment now.

His thoughts were prophetic. They didn't have even five minutes to relax when a dozen presences flew closer from above the canopy.

"Birds!" James yelled, rising from his crouch and staring intently north, where he could feel the [Mutated Bluebird - Dive Bombers] gather.

"I want to try dispersing them first. If we allow them to reach us on their terms, we won't be able to avoid the initial attack," Lauren said even as she swiftly climbed a tree, her skills working overtime to hide her.

Understanding her plan, James jumped, grabbing onto a thick branch, and pulled himself up. On the ground, Daniel prepared himself, his shield held high and glowing. A Tank's skills were mostly geared toward redirecting damage, and whether that was to themselves, to cover their allies, or away, to bear even more force, was up to their discretion.

Usually, the heavyset young man wouldn't need to redirect the damage away, as his vitality was high enough he could take almost anything an H-rank creature could throw at him, especially when holding his D-rank shield.

However, this time he prepared to do so. He was the only obvious target left in the clearing—Maria and Ezekiel had hidden behind the treants' broken trunks, ready to swoop in once the birds' initial charge was over.

Of course, the plan was for very few birds to reach him at all, even though they never survived contact with the enemy; being prepared was better than getting hurt.

Once the bluebird flock became visible, and more importantly, the monsters noticed Daniel, they quickly flew closer, rising up in the air to prepare their signature attack.

Before they could complete their rise, however, they were beset from two fronts by Lauren and James, who launched themselves from the trees, catching a few and disrupting even more.

Immediately after, three fireballs flew toward the last remaining group, forcing them to change direction midway through their dive, thus reducing the strength with which they hit Daniel's shield. The Tank didn't even budge this time and hurried to take advantage of the bluebirds' disorientation, falling upon them with his full weight.

Meanwhile, James finished stomping on the two birds he had managed to grab and looked up. The rest of the flock was unsuccessfully attempting to regroup. Smaller fireballs were stymieing their efforts and slowed them down so that Ezekiel could nail them down with a debuff, reducing their agility.

Once the birds were forced to the ground, their movements lagging, James and Lauren dealt with them in short order, ending the fight in a much cleaner manner than their initial one.

"Man, it's wild how different fights are when you know what to expect. These things could have easily sent us packing earlier if they had just a bit more vitality, but now we killed them without breaking a sweat," Ezekiel commented. His healing skills had been absolutely necessary to continue the dive; otherwise, they'd be forced to rely on the few very precious potions they had brought along. Using one at the beginning of a dungeon dive was a clear indicator that it was simply too dangerous to keep going.

"It's why the guilds tampering with the information they send us is such a big deal. If a team enters thinking they'll meet long-range monsters but is immediately beset by something like those bluebirds, they'll suffer casualties, maybe even deaths if they don't have a healer on hand," James answered. The sheer brazenness they had to send people to their deaths, just to get more influence, was infuriating.

"All right, let's leave that for later," Daniel warned, looking deep into the forest. "I think we might get some company soon."

Immediately, James activated his skill to check, sweeping the direction of the Tank's gaze.

There, almost hidden under the shrubbery, something was moving. It wasn't a huge creature, smaller than the mutated rats they had killed so long ago, but its form was quite dissimilar. Its presence was like a beacon to James's senses, indicating an animal with an exceptional will.

"Holy crap, that's a badger," Ezekiel murmured.

Indeed, the thing that had scared them turned out to be a stocky, low-slung badger with short, powerful legs. It was armed with huge foreclaws, at least three inches long, and had the distinctive head markings of the species.

It scampered up to them, showing absolutely no fear but no aggression either, and it sniffed around. Stopping before one of the bluebirds, the badger speared it with a claw, held it up to inspect it, and, once it found it acceptable, walked away with its new dinner, all without sparing a glance to the bemused members of Team 0.

"I think that might have been a normal animal, you know," Lauren said, breaking the spell of silence.

"I don't know. It was a blaze to my senses," James admitted, still a bit confused about the whole ordeal.

Normal animals still existed, of course, as mutation occurred only when enough mana pooled to form a Sink. But to find one so close to a dungeon was a surprise.

Maria chuckled, shaking her head. "That little bastard stole our loot!"

They all had a laugh at that. They had been so surprised that a seemingly ordinary animal would come close to them without overt aggression that they let it take a bird. "It stole at least three hundred dollars' worth of materials," Daniel added, mirth evident in his smile.

The moment of levity, unfortunately, didn't last long. A roar, so loud that it made the forest tremble, resounded through the vegetation.

The boss, it seemed, had noticed their presence. And this time, it was coming to them.

CHAPTER THIRTY-SEVEN

Another roar shook the reservation, this time much closer than the last. Since the boss would come looking for them, Team 0 decided to prepare a proper welcome.

"Do we even know if it can get here?" Ezekiel asked as he huffed and puffed while pushing one of the broken treant trunks.

"Bosses usually stay in the deepest areas, but they're known to roam, especially if the ambient mana is higher than normal through the whole dungeon," Daniel explained, holding aloft an entire treant with his arms.

"I think it'll be here soon," Lauren called from where she was crouching on a maple branch, looking deeper into the forest. "It might be some kind of badger, from the looks of it. A very fat one, at least."

Maria snorted. "Like the little guy that stole one of the birds?" The redhead was busy cleaning up the area, taking all their loot to a safe place where it wouldn't get damaged by the coming fight.

"Its angry, ugly cousin. I think it might breathe fire, to be honest. Something is burning where it just passed, but it might be from a different source," the Rogue answered, sounding a bit confused. Her line of sight wasn't exactly clear, so she couldn't give precise information, but it was better than going in blind.

The shaking and rumbling continued for a while, until a weird stillness settled over the clearing as tension built up.

Their preparations mainly consisted of making sure nothing would impede their movements while battling with the boss, which meant removing all the treant trunks and roots and placing them on one side, where they could serve as a last-ditch barrier, in case the boss had wide-area attacks they couldn't deal with.

Beyond that, they built something resembling a kill zone. It wasn't often that they had the time to set up before a fight in a dungeon, and so they had never had the option to use most of their kits, but the retractable caltrops and razor lines could be used to significant effect if given the chance.

Finally, the silence was broken by a low rumbling, which they soon realized came from the north. Trampling through the underbrush with little care, a creature that looked like a mix between a badger and a walrus emerged from the dungeon's depths.

It had thick, coarse fur and was black and white, in the same patterns they had seen in the little thief that took one of the birds. However, its body was massive, at least ten times the size of its "cousin." Its midsection was much larger than average, like walruses.

Sharp, thick black tusks emerged from its maw while cloudy eyes took in the arrangement of forces before it.

It gave one last sound, more like a chuff than a roar, and proceeded to walk into the clearing, its paws heavy against the loamy soil.

"Positions!" Daniel shouted, his shield glowing with power. Each team member swiftly moved to their predetermined spots, circling the clearing, ready to attack from all angles.

The creature halted midstep, seemingly aware of their presence but uncaring. It sniffed the air, its nostrils flaring. The beast's calm demeanor heightened the tension.

James carefully observed the boss, searching for any weak points or behavior that might give them an advantage. The creature's fur was thick and tough, which would absorb most of their hits, and its tusks looked capable of spearing them. But James noticed a soft underbelly and a subtle pulsing within its throat, the probable source of its supposed fire-breathing ability.

"Try to target the throat! We have to stop it from burning everything," James relayed the information to his teammates, his voice tense yet low.

Finally, when it arrived at the middle of the clearing, all hell broke loose. The razor-thin wire—which they had set up by using the dead treants to keep it taut—snapped around its body, digging into its flesh and making the boss bellow in pain.

In response, Maria called up a round of fireballs while Ezekiel debuffed its agility to stop it from escaping the encirclement. The flames licked its fur, singeing the edges but not causing as much damage as they had hoped. "It's resistant!" the Fire Mage yelled, falling back to the secondary role they had decided upon.

When confronted with a monster that could use her same element, she had been told to first assess if it was susceptible to her flames, which was common in the lower levels. If not, she was to make some distance and help by controlling the spread of the flames, using them to confuse and redirect its attention.

A rumble built up in its throat as it prepared to use its fire breath. To prevent it from unleashing the attack, Lauren dashed toward the beast's flank, her dagger poised to strike.

The badger, however, was quicker than expected. Ignoring the sharp wire digging into its flesh, it used its thick tail to swat the Rogue away, sending her flying into the trees.

Still, the attack had the intended effect of stopping the skill from being unleashed. Lauren rolled with the blow and quickly rejoined the formation.

The beast's attention shifted to Ezekiel, its large paws thundering against the ground as it charged. It let out another grunt of pain as it met the field of caltrops they had laid out, the sharp edges cutting deep.

Unfortunately, it didn't seem to feel much beyond initial annoyance as it continued its charge, uncaring of the damage it was doing to itself.

The attack was much clumsier than it would have been, though, which allowed Daniel to take it head-on, preventing the creature from reaching Ezekiel. "Now, James!" he shouted, his shield locked with the creature's tusks, trying to hold it in place.

The Thakinetic took advantage of the distraction, sprinting from his position, his empowered legs propelling him with great speed.

He focused his willpower on his arms, intending to land a solid punch on the creature's exposed throat.

With a loud yell, his fist connected with the equivalent force of a speeding car. It howled in agony, and Daniel released it as it stumbled backward, curling up to protect its ruined throat instinctively.

It wasn't down yet, though. With a low growl, the creature's maw began to glow red. "Scatter!" James yelled, noticing the imminent danger.

They barely had time to move. It released a torrent of flames, scorching the area where the team had been moments before. The trees around them were ablaze, heat rapidly rising in the clearing.

"Fuck yes!" Maria yelled, gathering the spreading fires into one massive fireball and throwing it back at the boss. It exploded on contact, sending the creature flying back into the prepared field of caltrops, which dug into its flesh.

It bellowed again, truly feeling the pain, and slowly righted itself. The creature, though powerful, was clearly exhausted from the accumulating damage. Its movements were slower, limited severely by the razor wire still cutting into it with every move, its breaths ragged. This was their chance.

Lauren used her stealth skills to reach it unnoticed, and before it could truly reorient itself, she was upon it, her daggers precisely aiming for the already open wounds, bypassing its thick layer of hair and skin, inflicting even more damage.

She retreated quickly, avoiding another jet of flames. This one, however, was much smaller than the last, and it gave James the confidence to close in. Charging again with all his energy gathered in his limbs, he quickly crossed the distance, jumped to avoid the last-moment tail whip, and landed a devastating blow on its head, burying it into the ground for a moment.

His Thakinetic Awareness then blared with danger as he felt the beast become more determined, its focus sharpening, and he jumped back, yelling, "It's trying to do something!"

In response to his warning, all the members rushed back behind the fortifications they had built earlier. It had almost seemed overkill at the time, but they had followed Miss Walker's instructions to prepare for every possible situation, and it paid off.

The beast, battered and worn, mustered its waning strength for a last desperate assault. The glint of malicious intelligence flashed in its cloudy eyes as it gathered all its remaining mana. The air around it shimmered with intense heat as its body began to glow ominously.

"Fall back!" Daniel's order boomed through the clearing as the team kept sprinting away from the creature. Its body continued to heat up, with steam hissing from the wounds in its fur, the seething heat within it turning its blood to a charred black.

Just as the team reached the treant trunks, the creature exploded in a massive fiery burst, sending a shock wave of heat and force, the impact smashing into the surrounding vegetation, turning it into instant charcoal. The explosion was loud enough to make their ears ring, even from a distance.

Stunned by the sudden explosion, the team took a moment to regroup. The once lush clearing was now a smoldering crater; bits of burning debris littered the ground, and a thick plume of smoke billowed high into the air.

"Everyone okay?" Daniel called out, his voice echoing through the now eerily quiet forest. One by one, each member of the team responded, confirming their safety.

"That was one hell of a boss," Ezekiel muttered as he wiped soot off his face.

"And one hell of a mess," Maria added, looking at the smoldering wreckage.

Although his friends relaxed, James felt a strange sense of unease. They had fought an almost textbook battle, never allowing the boss to have the initiative and drawing it out into several prepared traps, but his instincts told him something was amiss.

Looking into the cloud of smoke, he concentrated on his skill and was unsurprised to find a presence still blazing within.

"We didn't get the notification! It's still alive!" James called, and indeed, a growl echoed through the clearing.

At the epicenter of the crater, amid ash and embers, the beast was rising again, now free from the razor wire and the caltrops. The heat it had emitted had been enough to weaken the wire, and its massive strength had done the rest.

The explosion had cleared its way too, launching all the remaining traps away.

The boss, it seemed, wasn't done yet. It was slowed down, hobbled and battered, but its resilience was such that even now, it cut an intimidating figure.

"Unbelievable . . ." Ezekiel whispered in disbelief.

"It's still standing . . ." Lauren muttered, her eyes wide as she stared at the burnt yet intimidating figure of the creature.

The beast let out a weakened but determined roar, clearly ready to continue the fight. Heat still emitted from its body, strong enough that James was hesitant to get too close.

Once it was ready, the beast lunged at them with desperation, its movements more erratic, guided more by rage than precision. Its breath, now a plume of sparks and embers, created a field of fire, further igniting the surroundings.

It was slow enough that it couldn't really hit them, and even its skill had been weakened by the battle, which allowed the team to evade its assault. Maria danced through the flames, taking control of the rapidly spreading fires and redirecting them away, obscuring the boss's vision and thus diverting its rampage.

They were at a stalemate, neither with the ability to end the fight, when James had an idea.

Oh, you are not going to like this, you fat badger.

CHAPTER THIRTY-EIGHT

The shimmering heat around the badger boss prevented James from assaulting it head-on, another infuriating situation in which his short-range abilities were mostly countered.

But the truth was, the increased strength Thakinetic Empowerment gave him wasn't limited to punching harder.

With a grunt, James picked up one of the logs he had hidden behind and, keeping the boss's location in mind with Awareness, swung it around, building momentum.

"What the fu—" Lauren's exclamation was interrupted when he let go, the treant's trunk sailing through the air. It hit the mutated badger and bowled it over.

Without a moment of rest, James picked up another log and started swinging in a circle again until the speed was such that, when he released it, the log took to the skies in a perfect parabola and hit the just recovering boss once more.

Seeing that it was almost down for the count, James picked up one last trunk and approached the monster. It looked at him in defiance, still emitting enough heat to deter him from coming close.

Instead, he gave a nod of respect to the creature, as it had shown enough will to live to deserve it, and started whacking it with the trunk, each hit powerful enough to crush the skull of a grown man.

This time, it did not rise.

Only when he received the notification of his victory over a [Mutated Badger - Fiery Fang] did James finally relax, letting go of the log, which thumped against the earth loudly. He allowed himself a smile, satisfied with his work and the rewards.

He had been close enough to level 20 that he had sailed right through it, the boss giving him enough to reach level 21. James now had four stat points to assign and was one step closer to his goal.

"Man, that thing was tough, eh?" Maria said, approaching it with a stick. She poked it a couple of times, letting out a sound of surprise when the wooden branch caught on fire, the boss's corpse still hot enough to burn.

"Badgers are generally very stubborn and resilient, especially the honey badger variety, but this took the cake. It almost ignored all the traps," Ezekiel observed the creature. "We might have to leave it as is for a while. It's too hot to move around for now."

James hummed, looking farther into the woods, in the direction the badger had come from. "It's lucky that we still have a dungeon to clear, then."

Getting some cold drinks was truly an unbeatable feeling after they spent the better part of a day hunting for murderous bird flocks, James decided.

After defeating the boss monster, Team 0 started scouring the rest of the dungeon, hoping to quickly finish it up and return home. Unfortunately, the monsters' territory was quite large. While the treants had been easy enough to identify and defeat, since they really couldn't move much, the birds had been a different problem altogether.

Clearing a dungeon meant completely eradicating the mutated wildlife, or there was a risk the mana would continue pooling in a circular effect and start changing the fauna again, thus spawning another dungeon.

While this was relatively easy to accomplish in places like the Montauk cave, where the entire run could be done in a straight line, in an open forest it meant having to scour every hiding place.

Eventually, however, they managed to find the last flock and easily dealt with them thanks to their tried-and-true strategy of hemming them in with fire and slowing them down with debuffs, making them easy prey for Lauren and James.

All in all, the cleanup after the boss fight netted them all another level, so they couldn't really complain about it, even though they really wanted to.

"If it wasn't for the surprising amount of EXP those things gave, I'd consider them the worst monsters so far," Maria complained. Her role had been providing containment, and though she had dutifully kept up with it, it was obvious she much preferred fighting the treants, against which she could unleash her full power.

"A level is a level," James commented as he opened up his bag. They couldn't take their phones and other things during a dungeon dive, so they left them with the driver, Mr. Robinson. He didn't expect to have received many notifications. His grandparents knew he was working, and the few high school friends he still was in contact with would message him through social media, which he occasionally opened since he Awakened.

Surprisingly, there was a little red icon next to the green message app, showing that someone had, indeed, looked for him.

The moment James saw who it was, he ceased to hear the others speaking. He must have stared at the name at the top of the list for at least five minutes, because he felt a hand shake him. "Oy, everything all right?"

"Yes, sorry. Just heard back from someone I didn't think would answer," he said distractedly, ignoring Lauren's worried look.

As they piled into the car, eager to get back to New York, James felt his phone burn a hole in his pocket. Still, he kept his cool, going through the car ride and then the debrief at the AA while trying not to freak out.

Only when he got back home, reassured his grandparents that everything was fine and that he hadn't been badly hurt, and entered his room, closing the door with its lock, did he allow himself a moment to release his pent-up emotions.

He grabbed a pillow, then smushed his face into it and screamed.

Once he got that out of his system, he dropped onto his bed, feeling much more exhausted than after completing the dungeon.

I should wait a little bit. Make her feel like she did to me.

Unfortunately, those thoughts didn't help him, and he managed to resist for a few minutes before his hand gripped the phone and unconsciously opened the messaging app.

There, still red and unopened, sat Sally's message.

James took a deep breath, steeling himself. The possibilities of what she could say were almost endless, and he didn't want to get disappointed by raising his hopes up.

Hey, James. Sorry it took so long to answer; as you might imagine, things have been pretty difficult. My treatment was expensive, and Dad had to reorganize some things to be able to afford it. I'm better now, and after thinking about it for a long time, I think I owe you more than an apology via text. I'd like to meet you if you can. What do you think of Kaiser Park, at our bench, tomorrow at 10? We could get a coffee and talk.

That was all the message said. James reread it three times, trying to grasp all the subtle implications that might be hidden.

His first thought was that it was high time she answered him and that yes, a simple apology wouldn't make things right. He could understand she had been traumatized, but ignoring him for a month was too much.

His second one was that it was too good to be true. While he would never think Sally would fall so low and lead him into a trap, other people might have.

Any guild member, even the weakest H-ranks, could forcefully take her phone. And he knew someone who would really like to get him somewhere out of the way, alone.

If this is Callum Wright, I swear to God I'll kill him. He might kill me first, but I'll come back and haunt him until he kills himself.

Already, the idea that this was a trap solidified in his mind. James had been through too much to believe this was exactly as it looked. Or he might be paranoid. But was it paranoia when they were out to get you?

With a thought, he brought up his stat sheet and assigned all the banked points, knowing in his heart that he had already decided he would go.

He'd take precautions, like using all his attributes, alerting his teammates and Miss Walker of where he was going and to expect a text from him at certain times, but he'd go.

On the small possibility that this was Sally trying to make amends, he couldn't not try.

STATUS WINDOW	
Name	James Summers
Age	19
Awakening	1st
Talent	Thakinesis
Title	
Level	22
MP	110/110
STR	17
VIT	12
AGI	12
SEN	16
MND	12
STAT POINTS	0

That morning, James woke up very early. It was a rest day since they had spent the previous one fighting through the New Jersey wilderness, and he usually would have luxuriated in the peace and quiet.

He'd sleep until midmorning, stumble downstairs, still not fully awake, and eat enough pancakes to feed a family of four. Instead, he had spent the night twisting and turning, afraid of what he'd find the next morning at Kaiser Park.

He read and reread Sally's message enough times it was imprinted in his brain and he could recite it by memory.

More possibilities came to him, from his once crush needing monetary help to pay for her elixir treatment to her needing to escape an abusive home. She could have been kidnapped, and he was being contacted for ransom. She might have gone insane and decided to assault him with the excuse of apologizing.

All his worrying did, in the end, was make him more tired. He mumbled some excuse to his grandmother when she asked why he looked so exhausted, and started eating, shoveling as much food as he could stomach in, not wanting to worry her further.

When the time for the meeting approached, James sent all five texts he had prepared, one each to his teammates and Miss Walker, and set off.

He'd ignore their requests for clarification for the moment. If he didn't text them about something only they could know about by 11 a.m., they should start looking for him at Kaiser Park, and that was all that mattered.

James sincerely hoped to be proven wrong, but he wasn't so foolish to risk getting ambushed. The situation between the AA and the guilds was tenuous at the moment, and it wouldn't surprise him if some of the less intelligent Awakeners started thinking they could take matters into their own hands.

It didn't take long to reach the park, and since he got there early, he didn't find anyone, as expected. Instead of simply walking to the bench and sitting down, James set up next to the waterfront, behind the running track, and waited.

His sense stat was high enough that even without using Thakinetic Awareness, he could see everyone who entered the park. He observed them further, peering deeper to see if any of them were Awakeners.

No one suspicious came by, though; to be honest, not many people were out and about. A couple of young men were using the track and giving him weird looks, but he couldn't be bothered to explain himself.

He knew his fears could be entirely divorced from the truth, after all, and to someone who knew nothing of what was going on, he'd sound insane.

That was, until something pinged his skill. Entering the park from Bayview Avenue, a presence, more substantial than the rest, stood out to his senses. It was vivid enough that he was sure it must have been an Awakener.

James gritted his teeth and turned to take a look, ready for the disappointment.

He was startled. The Awakener he felt turned out to be Sally.

CHAPTER 38.5 – INTERLUDE

Leila Walker

After holding herself back from rushing in several times, Leila smiled upon finally getting the signal to get into position.

She had been stalking Golden Sun's operations for quite a while and had accumulated enough evidence to make a difference, especially now that she had a good idea of what they were doing and, more importantly, where they were doing it.

The pieces of the puzzle slowly came together after she found the executives at the pier and realized what they were transporting. That many mana stones, especially when hidden from the knowledge of the competent authorities, could only be used for one purpose.

They forcefully increased the ranks of the dungeons they leased and did not report it so they could loot better, higher-quality materials and sell them off to the black market.

So many countries are barely holding themselves together that very few are in a position to refuse to buy such valuable treasures. The risks of being put at odds with the US are minimal anyways since our foreign policy is so isolationist.

Shaking her head, Leila refocused. She was currently stalking a processing plant on the outskirts of Kingston, New York. Close to the Ashokan Reservoir so that no one would casually come by it, a massive complex had been built recently, giving the signs of construction still going on.

This specific center, she had found during her investigations, was one of the main hubs Golden Sun used. It was technically all above board, too, since they did have a license to buy and sell dungeon loot.

Unfortunately for them, little could stop her from reaching the deepest, most guarded parts, and she found even more evidence of absurd amounts of mana stones being collected, alongside high-quality parts that they shouldn't have access to. At least not in that amount.

The higher-ups, especially the regional director, wanted rock-solid evidence before they even attempted moving against a colossus like Golden Sun. So she had been forced to observe, again and again, as they conducted their shady business, using their legitimate front to introduce their illegal loot in the system.

Those they didn't sell overseas, of course.

Lately, however, things had changed. Maybe sensing her impatience, or possibly because he himself was unwilling to let such a massive operation go on for much longer, the regional director had started applying pressure on Washington.

Finally, after weeks of waiting, the green light had arrived, with three teams of black ops Awakeners from the Marines and a detailed plan for what they needed to prioritize and where confiscated resources should go once the operation was wrapped up.

It's not the complete sweep we expected, since the conditions for that aren't ripe yet, but it's something. If we can take out such a massive guild, it'll show the world we're not to be trifled with. It'll also give us the political capital to really ramp up the rest of the operation.

Still, all of this wasn't particularly relevant to Leila. She had received her orders after an initial tense moment, in which it had been uncertain whether she could participate in the mission. Luckily, the director and Marcus intervened on her behalf, giving her the go-ahead.

That meant she needed to think only about taking down a specific target and securing a location. Things she was more than suited to.

All the boring stuff that comes after can be left to the pencil pushers, as long as they don't make a mess. But it'll be almost impossible with the director breathing down their necks.

With her stealth skills unmatched by anyone in her rank, Leila had little trouble reaching her preassigned position. One entire warehouse had been given to her, mainly because it contained only sturdy equipment and an office, where her target was smoking a cigarette and reading through paperwork.

Despite being an extremely illegal operation set to undermine the US government on foreign and domestic terrain, the whole thing ran much like a regular business.

During her long hours of stalking, Leila had seen overseas orders arrive for specific materials on stamped paper letters, meetings being held about productivity, and even HR interventions when too much abuse was being heaped on the workers.

It was a rigid, efficient business, and it must have been going on for quite a while to have reached such a level of organization. The earliest paper she had been able to find was dated January 2022, but that didn't mean much. Until they got their hands on those well-guarded files, they wouldn't know how long the operation had been running.

Leila remained in the shadow world for a few more minutes, impatiently waiting for the rest of the special ops to get into position.

Armed with a dimensional mana transmitter, the signals of which could reach even her own personal dimension, she wasted no time proceeding when the go-ahead message came.

Stepping into the office of one Bradley Esposito, Leila felt a little satisfaction seeing him jump.

As a B-rank Awakener, he had to have some kind of sensory skill, but her own abilities far trumped it.

"Ah, so it's come to this," he said, quickly regaining his cool. A hazy golden mist started spilling from him, condensing into a solid armor. He looked like a medieval knight, though the one thing he lacked was a sword, which soon appeared in his hand.

"What, no surprise, no 'Please spare me'?" Leila groused. She had been waiting to experience this moment for so long, had been denied it again and again, that his composed reaction was a letdown.

"Nothing lasts forever." The man shrugged. "I knew one day something was gonna happen. Personally, I believed the Ten Thousand Eyes Guild would find us first and try to take over, but I guess the AA had to have some last spark of defiance before its death."

Leila smirked, her eyes conveying all her amusement. "It's a good thing it's not just the AA, then, huh?"

She couldn't see his expression, as it was covered by his helmet, but she liked to imagine his eyes popping out of his head. To force the full might of the federal government on the guild, they had to pull many strings and she had to spend many, many long hours accumulating evidence. It was worth it.

"I see," he answered after a moment of silence, his voice much more hesitant. "It seems like we've been outplayed. I don't suppose you'll allow me to leave without a fight, then?"

Leila snorted. After all she had witnessed this man do and what she knew of him, there was no chance in hell she would let him go.

Then, with the feeling of something snapping into place, a glowing white dome appeared in the sky over the compound. "That must be my special ops friends. They really don't want any of you guys to run away, you know."

Apparently done with words, Esposito lifted his sword and got into a stance. Yeah, you're right. Words are for later. Now, give me the satisfaction I wanted.

The golden sword was suddenly in front of her, the mana radiating off it enough to obliterate a C-rank being just from the proximity.

It passed through Leila harmlessly as she dispersed into shadows. Esposito crashed through the office's wall, entering the larger chamber of the warehouse. He looked around for Leila and quickly noticed the darkness pooling at every corner, every crevice, sealing them in.

"You'll have to do better than that if you want to keep me here!" he shouted, power flooding into his sword. He swung it, and a massive arc of golden energy launched forth, aiming to reduce the walls to rubble.

It splashed harmlessly against the shifting shadows, which greedily absorbed every ounce of light they could get.

Like a wraith, Leila appeared behind him, unfazed by his might. Her fist buried itself in his armor, sending Esposito flying against the wall at great speed.

It became quickly evident that little of the original structure remained, as it couldn't have withstood their clash. Instead, it had all been replaced with solid darkness. It twisted into limbs and grabbed onto the man, holding him still.

Then, a glow burned through the shadows, and the guild member emerged, freed from its viselike grip. Silently, he flooded more mana into the environment, succeeding in driving back the encroaching terror slightly.

Leila smiled. If it had been already over, she would have been very sad. Her eyes lit up with power, and a deep red color ignited among the shifting shadows. Embers rotated around her, as if captured in her gravitational well.

Then, she sprang forth, instantly crossing the distance between them, with a sword in her hands. It was a deep black with a red edge, and it clashed against Esposito's glowing weapon, creating a massive shock wave that shook the enhanced room.

Before the man could react, a geyser of flames erupted from beneath them, engulfing the two entirely. He was tossed once more into the air, cracks forming in his once pristine armor.

Again, Leila didn't let him have the time to reorient himself. A large wave of darkness rose up from the ground and grabbed onto him, pulling the man back down.

Wings of the same golden light sprang from his back, beating powerfully to keep him aloft. Esposito grunted with the effort and raised his blade, preparing to deliver a powerful strike.

That was, until a wave of white-hot fire from her sword hit him. The energy released was enough to melt the reinforced building, traveling through the air until it hit the glowing dome, making it flicker.

In the smoldering remains of the warehouse, Leila touched down next to her opponent, who was desperately pushing mana into his charred legs, his breath ragged, as he tried to heal himself.

"I was expecting a bit more, to be honest," she commented before she delivered one last strike that sent him into unconsciousness.

CHAPTER THIRTY-NINE

What the fuck?"

"I can't say that's not the kind of thing I expected you to say," Sally commented, a tentative smile blooming on her face.

"What the fuck," James repeated, still confused about the whole thing. He had spent the past night obsessing about all the possibilities behind Sally's message, and the one thing he hadn't considered was that she had Awakened too.

"Do I look that bad? All the pretty girls you surround yourself with must make me look ugly, right?" she asked, some of her usual impishness coming to the forefront.

When he opened his mouth again, she stopped him. "If the next words out of you are 'What the fuck' again, I swear to God, James!"

He shut up, his teeth clicking. He blinked twice and then slapped himself, rebooting his brain.

"All right. All right, I think I'm good now," he said, blinking rapidly.

"So," Sally began, seeing that he was finally paying attention, "you already know I Awakened, then."

James took a deep breath and nodded. "Yeah, I have a skill that makes it easy to tell."

Sally pouted, crossing her arms. "And here I wanted to do a big reveal. I even had all the words picked!"

He chuckled, feeling as if they were back before everything changed. "You can do it now anyway. I promise I can act convincingly."

"Nah, it wouldn't be the same."

For a little while, they chatted about everything and nothing. It was as if they had gone back to sneaking around Home Depot, stealing a few more minutes of break to keep talking with one another.

Unfortunately, they got a cold splash of reality when James's eye fell on the still-bandaged leg and Sally stiffened.

"It's not a pretty sight, but it's almost fully regrown," she said in a deceptively light tone.

"At least you can walk with it," he answered, maintaining the same disinterested facade. He wanted to ask what she had been through, how she had dealt with the trauma, and how he could help. But he wasn't about to bring up bad memories for her if she didn't do so first.

"Yeah, the doctors say a couple more weeks and it'll be like nothing ever happened to it. I even stopped taking elixirs. Just potions and rest, for now," Sally revealed, her gaze lost in the bay.

"Sounds like things are looking up," James commented. It wasn't that he didn't care, but he felt awkward, not knowing what he could talk about. Technically, Sally was the one who needed to apologize, but it didn't feel right to force one out of her by asking directly.

The specter of her absence, however, still hung over them.

Finally, she refocused, turning to face him completely. "Sorry, I asked you here and now I can't even gather the courage to say anything. I didn't come because I just wanted to see you, as much as I may like it."

James braced himself. Whatever she would say next would change everything, he knew.

"I originally wanted to ask you to come with me."

He blinked, before the implications settled in. "You're leaving."

She smiled sadly. "I am. I can't stay here, James. Too much has happened. Every time I get out of my house, I feel panic rising up. I keep looking back, afraid something is going to attack me."

He sighed. It shouldn't have been so surprising, after all. Not many people liked remaining in the same place they had been mauled. While it wasn't exactly possible to find someplace where the chances were nil, he couldn't begrudge her for not feeling at ease in New York.

"I wanted to ask you to come with me," she repeated. "But I can see that you've already overcome that night. You're probably happy, even."

Tears started forming at the edge of her eyes, but Sally stubbornly pushed them back. If there was one thing James had always admired about her character, it was how strong she was. After what she had gone through, having the courage to leave the house by herself at all was impressive.

"I didn't have much choice. I couldn't let the Radiant Guild get away with it," he answered, though he knew it wasn't what she meant.

Spite was a powerful force, but the truth was that he had never even considered shutting himself in his room and never coming out. It just wasn't him.

"I saw you in the news," she revealed. "They obscured the face, and you were wearing a uniform, but I knew it was you. You went back to the sewers. You cleared the rat dungeon, even."

James smiled. It had taken some time to overcome his hesitation, and he had to take a moment more than once to strengthen his will, but he confronted the trauma head-on. He was proud of that.

"I did. Couldn't really leave it open, right? And Radiant wasn't about to do it anyway."

"See, that's what I mean. You look more fulfilled now than in any other moment. Compared to this, you were a sad, gray person a few months ago. You craved this," she said, vaguely gesturing to his body. He knew it wasn't an accusation, but it sounded like one.

"I . . . I couldn't do anything before, but now I can. I'm growing every day. I'm getting strong enough to finally do something!" he said. He cleared his throat awkwardly at the end once he realized he had subconsciously raised his voice.

"And I'm so happy for you," she said, smiling sadly. "But I can't do that. I may have Awakened, but I can't live like that. I want to finish college, work in a research facility, and understand this new world we live in. Not wade in blood and monsters and . . . It's not me."

"So you are leaving," he murmured, but this time, it was with conscious understanding. Sally was choosing to escape New York, knowing it would tear them apart. And he couldn't stop her.

"So I am leaving," she answered.

"All right, lovely people, gather around!" Miss Walker called as she entered the training room.

The woman was usually cheerful, but today she glowed with happiness, as if a great weight had been lifted.

Quickly, they all sat on the parlor's couches, looking intently at their teacher.

"You might have noticed, these last couple of days, that something was happening here at the AA," she began, sounding very smug. "We talked more than once about the situation with the guilds, and specifically, we spoke of Golden Sun and its subsidiaries, the Radiant and the Eclipse Guilds."

By now, all five young Awakeners had gathered that something had been going on, especially since their teacher had been uncharacteristically reserved with her lessons, aiming to give them tactical knowledge rather than bringing them to the field like she would usually push for.

Seeing their curious faces, Miss Walker eye-smiled. "A few days ago, a massive operation, with the full support of the federal government, took place all over New York State."

She's enjoying this a bit too much. They don't even pause this dramatically on Family Feud.

"Yours truly was one of those high-ranking Awakeners chosen to participate, having provided most of the evidence necessary to move on with the entire operation," she revealed, the tension ratcheting up another notch while they waited to hear the results.

"In seven different locations, raids were conducted by AA agents and special ops members. Most of Golden Sun's elite are now in custody, held in Alcatraz Island's Awakener Penitentiary. Their smuggling and illegal rank-raising operation has been dismantled, and their assets seized."

There was a stunned moment of silence, soon followed by a loud cheer. Maria hugged James before launching herself at Ezekiel, then Daniel and Lauren.

Miss Walker let them celebrate for a while longer, watching with amusement, before she interrupted, "Yes, yes. It's good news. More importantly, this will show everyone that the AA is back in the game and ready to fight. It will also mean much more scrutiny on you, so keep that in mind."

James laughed, not caring one whit about what people would think of him. Golden Sun was down!

"What about the subsidiaries?" he then asked. Miss Walker hadn't said anything about them being involved in the raid, but they were so profoundly intertwined that he couldn't think of them going unscathed.

On one hand, I really wanted to be the one to take them all down, but it might be better this way.

"It wasn't my focus, but I can tell you that some of their top executives were also taken in. Not everyone had enough evidence arrayed against them, but your efforts in proving their falsification of dungeon reports helped a lot."

The smile on James's face dimmed. Of course, he had known they wouldn't be completely destroyed, but he couldn't help hoping. "Will Golden Sun get dismantled, at least?"

"It will. Most of their direct properties will fall under the aegis of the AA until the trial is over, but a judge already sent an order to allow us to seize almost anything. As far as the subsidiaries, they'll be allowed to continue working, if only because most of the evidence against them was of negligence. Following orders isn't an excuse, but it is true that they were kept in the dark about the illegal business of their parent guild," the masked woman answered. It was, in truth, a much more significant victory than James had been hoping for.

Even after contributing to the investigation, he hadn't believed they would actually go through it, subconsciously.

Still, the Radiant and Eclipse Guilds' survival meant he could get his revenge. Obviously, most of the government's efforts had been focused on Golden Sun, so he couldn't expect them to solve every problem. And thinking back to his earlier conversation with his teacher, he realized they couldn't justify using their resources on such small guilds.

It's still up to us, then.

"How did you do it?" Lauren asked, leaning forward.

"You know I can't share too much, but we caught them red-handed several times. It just took a while to organize the whole operation."

Ezekiel hummed, mildly impressed. "Is that the end of it, then? This will surely send a big message across the country, but I thought you wanted to do one massive sweep and take in everyone."

Miss Walker sighed, deflating slightly. "I would have liked to do that too, but this already took a lot of resources. We need to pace ourselves, lest we overextend."

That sounds reasonable, unfortunately. It isn't like the government can unleash the full might of the military on domestic territory. As cool as that would be, people would be up in arms, rightful mission or not. And to be honest, I don't think I'd trust them to do it right.

"So!" Their teacher clapped, regaining control of the conversation. "More on this whole thing will come out in the papers soon. For now, we can finally go back to grinding."

Ah, of course. They kept us in here for so long because they needed to complete the sweeps. They had to make sure there wouldn't be acts of revenge.

"Does that mean we're in the clear? You got them all?" Lauren seemed suspicious; honestly, James could understand where she was coming from. Good news was pretty rare, after all.

"We can be sure no one will target you guys for revenge." Miss Walker's wording, however, hid the truth. She deliberately did not address the second question, meaning someone had likely managed to escape.

All members of Team 0 shared a look, understanding the subtext.

"All right, I guess that's all you can tell us for now, huh?" The Rogue fished with a hopeful expression. When their teacher just kept eye-smiling, she drooped.

"That said, it's time we take a look at your next dungeon. How do you feel about dark forests full of spiders?"

CHAPTER FORTY

H-rank dungeons were something most people considered to be relatively harmless, as long as the monsters within didn't come out. A well-trained team of police officers, armed with rifles and enough ammunition, could clear the whole place with little trouble.

The main problem with such weak dungeons was their high spawn rate, which could overwhelm the Awakeners' ability to clear them up, as well as the risk of their going unnoticed long enough to rank up.

A G-rank dungeon, after all, was a different thing entirely, requiring military intervention to clear.

It was why, when an H-rank one was found at the brink of reaching the next level, they were given priority over some F-rank ones.

Conversely, those on the higher end of the tier were often ignored if they weren't close to evolving. They were stable enough that no intervention was required and were not nearly as lucrative as ones on the brink of ranking up.

"That leaves several H-rank dungeons for you to tackle, now that you've reached a level where you won't get squashed like bugs," Miss Walker had said.

And indeed, at least a dozen relatively stable dungeons had been earmarked for their use in the next few weeks. Most of those had been owned by the Golden Sun Guild, whose holdings were still in the process of being completely disbanded.

Their properties were mostly given to the AA, which included the dungeons they had held for their shady purposes, alongside those they operated legally.

The place they were currently heading to was one of those. Sitting a few miles north of Carmel, New York, a sleepy town of about twenty-five thousand people, was one of those irrelevant dungeons.

Golden Sun had initially earmarked it as a potential moneymaker, what with all the silk they could get from it. They had paid a whopping twenty thousand dollars for a monthlong lease and, after a short inspection, had decided it wasn't worth the effort to develop it.

The spiders produced thread, yes, but it was incredibly sticky, not conducive to making clothes like they had hoped for.

Of course, they could have sent a couple of their Awakeners to slaughter their way in, take all the mana stones, and called it even. Their guild would've recouped their initial investment, and they wouldn't need to justify a loss on their balance sheet.

But why waste an entire afternoon slaying beasts just to receive some crumbs? Thus, it was simply left fallow. They had much more lucrative business to get to, after all.

Still, there's something not quite right. I just can't put my finger on what.

"And so here we are," the local guide said. She was a middle-aged blonde, the kind that became progressively lonelier once her children left the house. This Megan had found a calling as a volunteer guide for the local park, Clarence Fahnestock State Park, and it served as enough excitement to keep her from depression.

She gestured to the darker patch of the forest, where the canopy of trees obscured much of the filtering sunlight. With his high senses, James could see the first webs, strategically hidden to catch unsuspecting prey.

"It's really a pity, but no one wants to risk getting eaten by giant spiders, you know?" Megan continued, laughing to herself at her morbid statement. "We thought that since a big-shot guild like Golden Sun had taken the deed, it'd get resolved immediately, but then it turned out they were crooks. Can you imagine? I could've never. The guy who came to take a look at the spiders was very elegant and charming."

Tuning out the woman, James extended his metaphysical sense deeper. There was the expected unnatural quiet of a dungeon since most wildlife were either eaten or driven away, but even the smallest insects were missing here.

Given its mana levels, it doesn't seem to be pushing to G-rank, but it wouldn't surprise me if the spiders were about to start roaming the forest. They must have already eaten everything within the dungeon proper. Usually monsters self-regulate . . .

"Thank you for your help, ma'am," Daniel said, always the most diplomatic of the group. In short order, he managed to convince the woman to leave them be, as it would become quite dangerous for an average human like her.

"I thought she would never leave," Lauren muttered under her breath.

"All right, annoying WASP aside, we need to get our heads in the game," James announced as he started walking toward the dungeon. "Ambush predators, sticky webs, and paralyzing venom. Let's try not to become spider fodder, people."

"That's if the information from Golden Sun is reliable. I wouldn't put money on that."

James turned to give Lauren the stink eye. They had already been over the issue several times with Miss Walker, but she was too stubborn to give up. He was as suspicious as she was, but bringing it up again wouldn't accomplish anything. They would find out soon anyway.

"Yes, yes, I know. I'll shut up." The girl held her hands up.

James shook his head in exasperation, before something pinged his senses. Immediately, he refocused, and his teammates quit horsing around, following his lead.

"Two big ones. Two hundred feet, one on top of the big oak, the other inside a bush," he relayed.

Against ambush predators like these spiders, Thakinetic Awareness was truly a godsend. It nullified the spider's biggest advantage, turning the fight into a more predictable confrontation.

Carefully, they approached the monsters, not giving any hint of having realized they knew.

When James felt the first one coil up, he lifted one finger, alerting the others, and then all hell broke loose.

Maria's fireball flew true, hitting the sticky web that the bush spider shot, igniting it and pushing it back to its maker.

The second monster jumped from above the tree, fangs poised to sink into James's flesh and paralyze him. Instead, they met Daniel's glowing shield, which easily held against the pressure.

James was upon it before it could reorient itself, fist charged with Thakinetic Empowerment. The hard chitin of its skull held against the first blow, but it still rattled the spider that it remained immobile, flat against the loamy soil.

Another hit in the same spot cracked it, making the beast screech. That sound was cut off abruptly when Daniel drove his shield into the fracture, pulping its brain.

Turning around, James saw that the other monster was down for the count too. The sticky web it had released turned out to be quite flammable, and having it splashed against its body had made it go into a frenzy, which allowed Lauren to quickly drive her knives into it.

Now that the fight was over, James observed the beasts. They were almost pitch black, save for a grayish discoloration on their abdomen. Their fangs dripped with paralyzing venom, and their eight eyes were glassy with death.

The System proclaimed them as [Mutated Hunter Spider - Sentinel], which felt appropriate. These creatures, for all the ease with which Team 0 had dealt with them, were true predators. Their central bodies were as large as the squirrels James battled with so long ago, but their legs made them almost as large as the rat boss.

Shortly after they were done with their initial assessment of the threat level, which aligned with Golden Sun's papers, they proceeded deeper into the dungeon.

Several more of the same ambushes repeated themselves, so much so that it became clear it was the only tactic available to the spiders.

Sometimes, they were lone, larger variants, named [Mutated Hunter Spider - Forager], indicating creatures meant to venture farther out into the forest; it confirmed James's suspicions that the dungeon would have started spilling in short order. Other times, there were three or four of the sentinels, but the result was always the same.

With the element of surprise taken away and without enough strength to damage Daniel's defenses, the spiders simply didn't have any way of harming them.

Maria's fireballs burned any web they came across, and her control was precise enough to harmlessly ignite the sticky mess, even if it caught onto their suits. Any possible discomfort was further eased by their D-rank quality.

They all got a level as they pushed through the dungeon, always being careful of a possible larger ambush. Still, it seemed the spiders were simply not interested in or capable of working together, even though it would have completely changed the balance.

I can sort of understand why the Golden Sun Guild didn't clear this place. The spiders are all so far apart, and they're disgusting enough that it's almost not worth it for us. For them, it would've basically been charity work. Twenty thousand dollars on a bad investment probably wasn't worth bothering with.

Once the numerous webs in the canopy nearly blotted out the sun, casting them in darkness, they activated their built-in flashlights.

Standard teams of rookies would avoid doing so simply because the light could attract larger numbers of monsters, but given the spiders' modus operandi and James's sensory skills, they had little chance of getting swarmed.

After one last ambush, this time by two large spiders, they finally entered a clearing. Webs spanned the entire thing, so thick that the trees beneath them were almost invisible. A strange atmosphere permeated the whole chamber, as if they had stepped into a library.

It was quite evident why the spiders had spent so many resources on this specific place, as hundreds of eggs shined in the reflected light of the flashlights. They were milky white and stuck together in weird clumps, some in geometric shapes while others haphazardly arranged.

Actually, there might be thousands. Jesus Christ, there are so many.

As the light of their flashlights illuminated the whole chamber, a shiver went down James's spine. The sheer number of the eggs was mind boggling, and the consequences of their hatching would be catastrophic.

"Shit. There might be enough here to overrun the town," Lauren cursed, taking in the sight.

"If they all hatched, they would take over the entire reserve. It might be enough to push this dungeon up a rank altogether," James agreed, staring fixedly ahead as he considered the implications.

"We need to kill them all," Daniel concluded, grim but resolute.

"I actually don't think I should just set fire to all of them, for once," Maria added, pale faced. "I can generally control the flames, but this much webbing would ignite immediately. It could turn into a gigantic wildfire."

"The old-fashioned way it is, then." Ezekiel sighed before taking out his own knife. He cast a buff to everyone's agility stats; there was little need to augment their strength to break the eggs. More important was to do so before the boss found them, and they became embroiled in a desperate fight while trapped in the webbed chamber.

With a sigh, James started punching and kicking, crushing the eggs and its barely developed embryos with numbness.

It was somewhat revolting, but he had gotten used to being elbow-deep in monster offals so that he could turn off his brain with little trouble.

Only after the twentieth egg, when a notification blinked at the edge of his sight, did he snap out of it.

He smiled, seeing that he had received a level for killing a [Mutated Hunter Spider - Embryo], which gave him [+50 EXP]. It wasn't that much, but considering the sheer number of unprotected eggs, his mind quickly made the connection.

I think we might have found a way to power-level. There are enough eggs here to get us all at least three more, if they all give this much.

CHAPTER FORTY-ONE

This is great.

As disgusting as hacking through hundreds of spider eggs might have been, James would have done it a million times for the experience points he was getting.

Of course, being [Embryos], they gave very little compared to the fully grown versions, but the numbers added up. After a couple hundred broken eggs, he had already gotten three whole levels!

It was enough to be worth a dungeon run all by itself. Since thousands more remained, he could very well see getting all the way to level 30 just from this room.

"We really struck gold, haven't we?" Lauren cheered, even as she tried to remove some of the muck that clung to her gloves.

They had given up using knives soon after they began, resorting to fists and, in Daniel's case, his shield. It was just a numbers game, after all, and they needed to be as efficient as possible before they got found out by the boss monster.

"It's not like we're being greedy either. Think of the mess that would have happened if all these eggs hatched," Maria agreed, her fist buried into another embryo.

Once she took her fist out, she ignited a small flame, quickly burning off anything sticking to her.

"It's so not fair you can do that. Ugh," Ezekiel groused. As the least physically oriented of the group, he was the one suffering the most from a lack of stamina, but at least he could use his buffs to make up for some of it.

"Keep going, guys. The sooner we finish here, the sooner we'll get to kill the boss and be done with this place." As he was the only one not using his bare hands, it was easy for Daniel to say that.

Half an hour later, they took a break. Having achieved another two levels for their efforts, they wanted to at least add the stat points to make continuing with the massacre easier.

Status.

STATUS WINDOW	
Name	James Summers
Age	19

Awakening	1st
Talent	Thakinesis
Title	
Level	29
MP	125/145
STR	21
VIT	14
AGI	14
SEN	20
MND	14
STAT POINTS	0

Even when he braced for it, the surge of power still caught James off guard. Fourteen stat points was quite the number, after all, and he was forced to the ground, twitching as if he had been electrocuted for the first time since he'd added to his attributes in his room.

His mind expanded as it was forced to understand more, process more data. His body flexed and changed, muscles tightening and growing with new strength. His organs contracted with the energy and returned to doing their job more efficiently, pumping blood faster and bringing more oxygen to his cells.

All in all, James received the most significant bump in power in his life, all because he had been lucky enough to find a spider hatchery.

He picked himself up slowly, testing his body with great care.

His hands effortlessly flexed with enough strength to powder the eggshells he grabbed, whereas before he had to push himself. His eyesight, which had been good enough to perceive things in the dark, now saw the hatching chamber in all its monstrous glory. He could smell the blood, the dirt, the humidity in the air, like never before.

After walking up to a particularly large cluster of eggs, he punched forward, his arm easily clearing its whole length, killing five embryos in one shot.

"Oh, yeah," he whispered to himself with a satisfied smile. He crossed the midway point of H-rank with absurd speed, considering the average time was four months.

He turned around, having felt Lauren try to sneak up on him, and found her pouting. "It's not fun if you keep putting points in your sense stat."

He chuckled, noticing how silent her steps had become. With great agility, augmented by her skills, the girl was becoming a right terror, and it wouldn't be long before she'd be a ghost on the battlefield, flitting between enemies and delivering lethal blows without being noticed.

"This place is amazing," he said, looking at the hundreds of eggs still intact. It would truly have been a disaster if the dungeon had been left fallow, but James could only be grateful that the Golden Sun Guild's prospector hadn't gone deep enough to find the hatchery, otherwise they would have no doubt hogged it all for themselves.

Well, it wouldn't have been worth much to them, but their subsidiaries would have loved it.

"Can you believe what they were sitting on?" Ezekiel asked after he was done with his own twitching. Just the increased mana was a game changer for him since his healing spells were so costly. It would allow him to contribute to the fights much more, rather than keeping in reserve in case someone got hurt.

"If we could find a couple more dungeons like this, we'd get to G-rank in no time," Daniel joked. His powerful physique became even more impressive. Some fat still covered his muscles, but it only made him look more robust, and his forearms were as big as Maria's legs.

"Yeah, maybe there are more in the other dungeons we got from Golden Sun," the redhead agreed with a laugh. Since her build was mostly based upon her firepower, her body didn't change much, but she moved more fluidly now, her increased agility important to let her dodge melee fighters.

"All right, guys," James interrupted. "Enough rest, let's get this done and go find the boss."

As much as he would have liked to extend their pause, he was already getting worried. Good things didn't come without a caveat, and the absence of dungeon's strongest creature was making him suspicious.

This is the perfect spot for it to rest. We should be around the central point of the spiders' territory, so I don't get how it's not here yet. It's not like we've been particularly quiet.

With hundreds more eggs to go, even with their increased stats, they would have to work for at least another thirty minutes, probably more before they were done, and he really wanted to get this job over with.

Unfortunately, just as he was about to restart the grind, he felt his fears be realized.

A massive creature, much larger than the crocodile boss had been, was scuttling toward them with great speed.

"The boss is coming!" he yelled, abandoning the cluster of eggs to make for the chamber's center, where they quickly regrouped.

Daniel raised his shield, which was glowing brightly with his skill. The light it gave off, coupled with their flashlights and newly enhanced senses, was enough for James to finally see the creature he was sensing.

His nightmares manifested, a dozen feet tall and twenty feet long. The spider boss was as big as an elephant, and its fangs clicked with enough strength to shear one in half.

Its eyes, unlike the dumb, almost mechanical look its subordinates had, shined with malicious intelligence.

As soon as it fully entered the chamber, it let out a screech, seeing the mess they had made of the eggs.

The sound was powerful enough to make them all wince and cover their ears, even though no skill had been used. Without wasting time, the boss charged, and they were in a battle for their lives.

Thanks to his increased stats, James's Thakinetic Empowerment granted him even more power, so he took it upon himself to try and act as bait, leaving the rest of the group behind.

He charged right back at it, and was met with one massive leg, its wickedly sharp tip rushing to spear him through.

Its speed was such that he was forced to abort his run, instead rolling away from it, and then again to the left, when another leg punched into the ground just a few inches next to him.

Meanwhile, the spider's maw descended on Daniel, clamping on his shield with the strength of a hydraulic press. There was little the Tank could do to avoid getting it ripped away from his hands, and with a swift motion, the shield was thrown aside, clanging against the wall of trees that made up the chamber. The boss spider then turned its many eyes on Maria and Lauren, lunging toward them with its massive fangs bared.

Lauren, swift and agile as she was, managed to dodge just in time, rolling away from the monstrous arachnid. Maria, on the other hand, was not so lucky. She unleashed a torrent of flames at the creature's face, which made it shriek in pain, but she couldn't avoid its momentum.

It crashed into her, sending her flying off into the sticky webs with enough strength to crack the branch she landed on. She screamed but managed to keep her cool without lighting up something.

Had she done so, they would have gotten trapped in a flaming hell with the spider, and she was not yet good enough to control that amount of fire.

Ezekiel acted quickly, his healing spells flying through the air to envelop Maria in a warm light. The healing energy mended her wounds as she pushed her skill to prevent the spread of the fires. Maria burned off the webs sticking to her and broke free, leaving behind only the scorched scent of burnt spider web.

The team was now in full defensive mode, their earlier success with the eggs forgotten. The monstrous spider moved with a frightening agility that belied its size. Like deadly spears, its legs stabbed at them from all angles, forcing them to be constantly on the move.

Daniel, now unarmed, went to grapple with the creature's legs, trying to divert its attention and give the others an opening to attack. His strength was enough that he managed to maintain his hold on the limb he grabbed, and James's constant attacks held its attention, keeping it away from running the Tank through.

James, realizing they needed to coordinate better, shouted over the din, "Ez, lower its agility! Maria, focus your attacks on its eyes! Daniel, hang on while Lauren finds your shield!"

As they followed his orders, James found an opening after a fireball made the monster turn around to protect its eyes. He rushed in, his empowered fists slamming into one of the spider's massive legs, sending cracks sprawling across its exoskeleton. The creature reeled, allowing him to press the attack. Even a monster of this power felt the weight of his hits. Since this wasn't the kind of situation in which he could justify holding back, he prepared to unleash as much mana as he could, in a replica of his final move against the starfish.

It was a gamble, he knew, but he could see the writing on the wall. If he allowed the fight to go on much longer, they'd lose. The spider was simply too strong, too fast, and too resilient.

It has to have reached G-rank. Fuck, I knew this would happen. It was really too good to be true.

"Found it!" Lauren yelled, throwing the shield like a frisbee to Daniel, who jumped off the monster's leg to catch it. He did so just in time, because that very same leg tried to skewer him soon after, though it couldn't penetrate the D-rank equipment.

With the spider distracted, James ran forward, using a rock as a springboard to jump. He soared through the air, his enhanced strength allowing him to easily reach the top of the creature's body. The moment he touched down, he punched.

I don't have the right balance, and there's no leverage, but this attack doesn't need any of that. Eat this, bitch.

CHAPTER FORTY-TWO

James's fist glowed in the dimly lit chamber, illuminating the monstrous creature completely for the first time. Its eyes, two of which were positioned high enough to glare at him hatefully, reflected an understanding. It knew it was about to die.

A massive wave of power left James, a hundred points of mana concentrated into his fist and released down into the spider.

He heard a loud *crack!* over the roar of adrenaline, as the hard carapace broke under his ministrations. Light flashed through the fractures as mana wreaked havoc on its insides, and an ear-splitting shriek resounded through the dungeon, making the trees shudder.

The spider thrashed wildly in agony, attempting to throw James off its back. It spun and convulsed, but he held on, driving his fist again and again into the gaping wound he had created.

He felt the fluids of the creature's entrails splashing against his skin, hot and viscous. Despite its desperate flailing, the monstrous arachnid's movements gradually slowed, and the light in its many eyes dimmed.

With a final decisive blow, James thrust his fist deep into the spider's body, the hot rush of its ichor gushing all over him. The creature gave a shuddering twitch before its legs buckled beneath it, collapsing to the ground with a tremendous *thud* that shook the chamber.

The others, battered but not broken, gathered around as James disentangled himself from the fallen beast, his breathing heavy, shaking his arm to clear it of the creature's innards.

"That thing was not H-rank," he said, jumping off it.

"Early G-rank, you think? We probably wouldn't have made it if we hadn't found all the eggs before. Without those stat points, I don't think I would have managed to avoid it," Lauren commented, her knife flashing and burying itself into the boss's closest eye.

It had become a habit of hers, to make sure the monsters they killed were truly dead, even after they received the System notification. The Rogue claimed it was only a good habit to have since some very high-rank creatures with illusion skills could fake their death.

James didn't think they had anything to worry about, considering that such creatures were recorded to be at least B-rank, but it wasn't like she was doing anything bad. The badger boss had given them a right scare, after all.

"Uhm, guys," Ezekiel called their attention, his voice strangely high pitched. "Why does the notification say [Mutated Spider Matriarch - Newborn]?"

Swiftly bringing his own prompt up, James saw that his friend was telling the truth. "What the fuck? How could that thing possibly be a newborn? What kind of monster would even give birth to it?" he said, stunned.

Thud! The loud sound made them all jump in fright and turn to the entrance.

James felt his heart beat madly in his chest, as he hadn't noticed anyone approaching with his passive sense. Activating Awareness, he cursed himself for being so loose with his scout duty. He immediately detected a massive presence coming toward them.

First, though, his eyes fell on the thing that made the noise.

The light of their flashlights revealed a strange creature lying sprawled at the entrance of the incubation chamber.

It had the bulbous body of a large spider, three times the size of the small ones they had fought in the dungeon but quite a bit smaller than the one they had just defeated. But instead of the fanged maw one could reasonably expect, it had the torso of a woman attached to it.

White hair and a generous, uncovered bust gave her a fair appearance, marred only by her lower half and the eight eyes that crowned her brow.

"An arachne," James whispered. A beast known and feared among Awakeners for being as intelligent as—if not more than—humans and capable of hatching plots to capture territory. Its individual strength was that of a B-rank, but since its power lay in the strategic usage of its monstrous progeny, it was considered an A-rank threat for its ability to take over large swaths of lands in a short amount of time.

It was a being they had absolutely no hope of defeating. Something so strong that even just its presence should have sent them to their knees.

"Is it dead?" Maria asked, her eyes glued to the still form of the arachne.

"I think so," James answered, not feeling anything from where he was standing. His eyes, however, were trained on the chamber's entrance. A very alive and powerful being was approaching, and he had no idea what to expect.

"It is," a deep voice answered from where the presence should be.

Stepping into the light was a man. He was seven feet tall with well-developed muscles, bare chested save for a sleeveless fur coat that was left open.

He had long wavy dark hair and a wild air, enhanced by a fanged earring that glinted in the light.

"Did you kill it?" Daniel asked, keeping a wary eye on the man.

The new arrival, however, didn't answer. Instead, he kept walking toward them, making them ready themselves for a fight they couldn't win.

With a rumbling sound, he passed by them, not sparing a glance at the massive corpse of the creature they originally believed to be the dungeon's boss.

It took James a moment to realize that the man had been laughing at them. "Who are you?" he questioned, his muscles still tensed as his mind ran through scenarios and escape plans. They were drained, wounded, and facing an unknown entity that radiated immense power.

Again, he was ignored. With long strides, the massive man finally reached the end of the chamber, where the last few clusters of eggs were stashed.

With a gesture of his hand, a wave of bronze mana annihilated the webbed wall, eggs and all.

James heard a strangled sound from beside him, which he knew had to be Lauren. Those eggs might not have been worth much to someone capable of killing an arachne, but for them, they represented several levels without the need to be in danger to gain them.

However, not one member of Team 0 said anything, watching as the man stepped into the cavity he had created in the webbed walls. The difference in power between them and someone capable of killing an arachne without a wound to show for it was simply too great.

A minute later, he emerged, a red stone of some kind clutched in his fist. He was looking at it pensively, apparently unsure what to make of his find.

Finally, he reached them again, and this time, he stopped.

James had just a moment to realize something was about to happen as he felt a flex in the stranger's will—the kind he recognized from Miss Walker's aura resistance training. Then they were being crushed against the dirt, an immense weight appearing in their minds.

The sensation was unbearable, like being smothered in the shroud of bronze energy, each thread woven with domination and power. Their bodies were pressed to the cold ground, and they could only gasp for breath, their limbs unresponsive under the oppressive force. The chamber seemed to dim further, the light from their still-glowing flashlights now a mere flicker in the man's crushing presence.

James clenched his fists, dirt digging into his fingernails as he tried desperately to fight off the monstrous aura. His muscles twitched with the effort, and he could barely gather a coherent thought. Still, with a single-mindedness that was becoming familiar, he slowly started being able to move. His last remaining mana flooded his body, lessening the aura's effects; though he still couldn't stand up, he pulled himself into a kneeling position.

"Speak not unless spoken to." The command was not loud, but it echoed in their minds, a blade of authority that cut through the suffocating silence. The man's eyes, an uncanny shade of molten gold, scanned over them dispassionately.

Releasing the pressure with a negligent flick of his wrist, he observed as they scrambled to their feet, gasping and clutching at their throats, their eyes wide with terror and confusion.

"What do you know of the owners of this dungeon?" he asked, his voice low.

None of them tried to lie, knowing they could do nothing to stop the man from getting what he wanted.

"It was the Golden Sun Guild's," James answered. When a wave of the man's hand prompted him to continue, he added, "There was a big raid, and most of their properties were confiscated by the AA. Since their papers and the mana radars said this was an H-rank dungeon, it was given to us to clear."

"Golden Sun has been raided . . . Has the slumbering giant finally woken up?" the man murmured, more to himself than them, a slight frown marring his rugged features.

"The . . . giant?" James ventured, his voice shaky. His body was still racked by the occasional tremor after being subjected to the man's aura, but he did his best not to make it show.

"The Awakeners Association." The man's gold eyes fixed on James, making him feel like an ant under a magnifying glass, small and insignificant. "Has it moved against Golden Sun?"

"We're not privy to the details," Maria stammered from where she stood beside James. "We're just an H-rank team."

A grunt of understanding came from the man. He seemed to ponder over their words for a moment, his eyes never leaving them. The silence stretched painfully. "You were lucky I was in the area and felt something was amiss," he finally said.

"Was . . . Was the arachne hiding in the dungeon?" Lauren asked, gathering her courage.

"It was. However, for all its cleverness, a creature of that power wouldn't appear naturally. Not here, where the AA's eyes can still see," the man answered, tossing the ruby-red stone in the air.

Without conscious thought, James focused his senses on it and immediately recoiled away.

Despite being a rock, the thing held an immense amount of power, and hidden within it, noticeable only because of his Talent, there was an ugly, twisted mind.

"Oh? You noticed?" the man asked casually, coming to stand before James.

"What . . . That thing is evil," he answered, shocked at how an inanimate object could have such a clear will.

"Mmm. You are still too weak to know the truth," the stranger said, his golden eyes piercing James to the depths of his soul. "But you might become useful some-day. If you ever get to B-rank, I'll come find you, kid. You'll learn the truth of this world then. For now, you'd all do yourself a favor if you forgot what you saw here. Take pride in defeating a level 57 creature as H-ranks and leave it at that."

Without letting anyone get a word in, the man stepped past them, moving much more quickly than before. He grabbed the arachne's corpse, hoisted it over his shoulder as if it weighed nothing, and walked into the darkness, disappearing even from James's senses.

They all remained silent following his departure, until their madly beating hearts calmed down.

"What the absolute fuck," Lauren murmured.

For once, no one had anything to say to that.

CHAPTER FORTY-THREE

After stumbling out of the spider dungeon, the members of Team 0 took a moment to reorient themselves.

The battle with the [Mutated Spider Matriarch - Newborn] had been difficult, but the meeting with the mysterious man had completely drained what was left of their strength. Withstanding his aura alone had been enough to push them to the brink of unconsciousness, and James knew he had held on so well only because of his skill, Thakinetic Resistance.

Luckily for them, the powerful stranger had the decency to finish the job, killing all the remaining spiders in the dungeon. If he hadn't also taken away a couple of levels by destroying all the remaining eggs, they'd feel truly grateful.

"I feel like we can't really complain that much, considering how lucky we were in finding the eggs and not getting nuked by the arachne," Ezekiel commented, exhausted but relieved to be out in the sunlight.

"I'm still not done processing all that happened in there," Lauren responded.

"We came so close to dying," Maria whispered, staring far off in the distance. "There really was nothing we could have done had that man not intervened."

James pressed his lips together, agreeing with the sentiment. His killing of the gigantic spider might have been a great accomplishment for an H-rank Awakener, but that didn't mean anything against the might of a B-rank monster. They would have died, plain and simple.

They continued their trek in silence, slowly exiting Clarence Fahnestock State Park. They left everything behind, from the mana stones to the valuable corpses. Even if they still had the strength to take them, they couldn't have.

After the mess with the arachne and the mysterious man, they needed to alert the AA, which would send a senior team to investigate the scene. The appearance of such a powerful monster in an unmonitored dungeon wasn't something to be taken lightly, after all.

Even the sleepy agency would have no choice but to get off their asses and thoroughly investigate how they had missed it. Of course, most of the blame would fall on the Golden Sun Guild, but since it was already in the process of being dismantled, they wouldn't be able to use it as a scapegoat.

Miss Walker alone would probably want to push for an in-depth investigation.

This was supposed to be a simple dungeon for them to level up, a mission away from the guilds' influence. Instead, what should have been a routine operation had turned into a near-death experience with monsters beyond their rank and a man who carried a power they could barely fathom.

The sight of Carmel's church in the distance was more soothing than James would have liked to admit. It meant they were reentering their world, filled with its own monsters, of course—political, economic, and societal—but it was a world they knew how to navigate.

"Do you think that man will be angry if we talk about him?" Ezekiel asked, his voice filled with uncertainty.

"I don't know," James replied, expression grave. The stranger seemed indifferent to their existence, only interested in the red stone he had found within the depths of the spiders' lair. "But we have to report everything to the AA. If he's a threat, it's their job to deal with it."

They all nodded in agreement. Even if they were just low-ranked members, they were still part of the organization tasked with monitoring and managing the supernatural elements within the United States. It was their duty to report such an encounter, and the responsibility would then pass to those higher up the chain.

James pulled out his phone, glad that it finally had some signal. He immediately called Miss Walker, the only person in the AA he knew was undoubtedly on their side.

The phone rang three times before the woman answered, "Yes, James, is everything okay?"

"We're okay, but a lot's happened. You need to send a high-level team here. There was an arachne that was killed by an unknown man. A very powerful one," he reported, keeping his response short and to the point.

A beat of silence was followed by a long sigh. "Come back to the headquarters immediately; I'll handle everything else. Good job getting out of there alive." And she hung up.

James looked at his phone, chuckling at the abruptness. "All right, guys. Let's get out of here."

Reaching the AA HQ took longer than expected, as New York traffic created a bottleneck at the entrance to Manhattan.

James was almost tempted to just get off in the middle of the road and walk from there, but one look at his teammates' exhausted faces told him he wouldn't have company.

Their disheveled appearance and dirtied uniforms would have stood out too much amid the crowd of city dwellers.

He noticed Maria clutching her arms, as if in an attempt to hug herself. Her eyes were haunted and lost, and he couldn't help but bump her shoulder with his, offering comfort. "We made it out," he whispered, a reassurance for the both of them.

"Yes." Her voice was barely audible over the noise of traffic. "Yes, you're right. We made it out."

She fell back into silence, but she kept her shoulder pressed against his in a silent request for support, which he gladly obliged.

The moment they arrived at the AA, they were waved in through the subterranean garage by a uniformed individual whose presence flared with power. Evidently, they were being expected.

As soon as they got out of the van, they were hustled through the labyrinthine maze of corridors by two more uniformed agents. They took an elevator, different than the public ones they used to access their training room, and arrived at one of the upper floors, where they finally got to their destination.

A set of blast doors opened with a *hiss*, revealing a conference room with all the bells and whistles, coupled with refreshments on the side.

What captured James's attention, however, were the three people sitting at one end of the twelve-seater table: his teacher, Miss Walker; her own mentor, Mr. Bethany; and the last was a nondescript man, who he knew to be the most powerful person in the room.

"Welcome, Team 0. I'm sorry that our first meeting has to be under these conditions, but rest assured that I have carefully monitored your growth," the regional director Alfred Meyer said, gesturing for them to take a seat.

As they shuffled into their seats, one of their two guides entered the room with them while the other took post outside, closing the door behind him. The former walked over to the refreshment table and poured several glasses of water, bringing one to each.

"Thank you," James murmured, now truly feeling the exhaustion of the day.

James found it difficult to meet the eyes of the director. There was something unsettling about the man, as if he wasn't what he appeared like. His vision kept telling him that he was a harmless middle-aged man, to whom he shouldn't pay that much attention, while his skill and instincts screamed that he was very dangerous.

To prevent the budding headache from worsening, he focused on the glass of water in front of him.

"Please tell us everything," Miss Walker said, breaking the spell of silence.

And so they launched into their retelling of their dungeon dive. They were interrupted several times with questions about the mana detection tool's results, the webs' density, and the eggs' consistency.

When they finally spoke about the battle with what they had believed to be the boss, James spied a glint of pride in his teacher's eyes. It wouldn't make the news, not with all the mess that followed, but it was truly an impressive accomplishment.

"And then I felt a massive presence. Bigger than anything I ever felt before," James said, which made the three executives sit up. This was what they were genuinely interested in.

"The corpse was thrown through the entrance. And just when we realized what it was, he walked in," he added, trying to recall every little detail about the man.

"It has to be said that James's skill hasn't failed yet. It's possible to hide from it at a high level of stealth," Miss Walker interjected, gesturing toward herself. "But nothing has managed to falsify its results. If he says he felt the man was stronger than me or Marcus, I believe him."

James smiled in thanks, grateful that she'd go out of her way to give credence to his words.

The director just nodded, willing to accept his expertise.

"And he was just interested in this red stone?" Mr. Bethany asked, his eyes glinting with curiosity.

"Yes, sir." Ezekiel nodded. "He didn't seem to care about us at all, though we found several smaller spiders dead after we left the chamber. He couldn't have considered them enough of a threat to fight them, so he might've wanted to ensure we'd get out."

The largest man in the room waved that away negligently. "Bah, better not to make assumptions. He might just be a very thorough man. I know I never liked leaving jobs half-done."

"Mr. Summers, could you describe his aura as clearly as possible?" the regional director suddenly asked, his voice calm but carrying an undercurrent of tension.

James nodded "Yes, sir. It was . . . overwhelming. Like a tidal wave, but not malicious or aggressive. It was just immense. It felt like the weight of a mountain bearing down on me without effort."

Director Meyer hummed, leaning back in his chair. His fingers rhythmically tapped against the armrest. "Did he say anything? Any indications of his intentions or affiliations?"

"Just that we were too weak to learn the truth of the world," Lauren answered, sounding a bit miffed. "He said that if James ever got to B-rank, he might contact him."

At that, the attention of the three high-rankers shifted to James, and he answered the unspoken question. "I managed to withstand his aura a bit more than he had expected, I think. And he was surprised I was able to feel the evil within the red stone."

"Evil is a strong word. Do you mean that there was a thinking mind entrapped within it?" Miss Walker followed, red eyes trained on his.

"Not so much a thinking mind, as there was a craving, a strong determination about what direction the energy contained had to take. Just enough mental energy to have resolve. It didn't feel like it had thoughts, at least," James explained, feeling frustrated at his lack of details. He had been dead tired and not particularly focused on the stone, after all, and he could only recall so much.

The room fell into a tense silence, the implications hanging heavily in the air.

"It's above our pay grade," Mr. Bethany concluded with a hint of dry humor, trying to alleviate the weight in the room, but his eyes were serious as they met each theirs. "We'll have to escalate this to the national office."

The director stood up, his posture radiating authority. "I commend you all for handling such an unexpected situation with bravery. Rest now, and let the agency handle the rest. We will keep you informed of what we can tell you as we unravel this mystery. For now, you've earned some rest."

They all murmured their thanks as they stood up and filed out of the conference room.

James's mind was a mess as he tried to make sense of everything that had happened. One thing, however, kept popping up. None of the three seemed surprised to learn that the powerful man had been there for the stone.

CHAPTER 43.5 – INTERLUDE

Leila Walker

Leila watched her brave little team of rookies file out of the conference room, the blast doors shutting behind them with finality.

"It was the Sin of Pride, wasn't it?" she asked, even though she already knew the answer.

The description James had given them fit what they knew of the S-ranker to a T, and it was just like him to stroll through America as if nothing could bother him.

"We must first confirm a few things, but it's safe to assume it was him," the director answered, looking much grimmer now that there was no need to keep up the facade.

"I think this is one of the very few instances we can be grateful that *that man* was around," Marcus rumbled as he smoothed his mustache.

Just the thought of what might have happened to the kids had they met the arachne by themselves . . . It sent a shiver down Leila's spine.

I've lost dozens of comrades to the unending tides of monsters, but I genuinely don't know what I'd do if they were killed. I'm self-aware enough to recognize I have truly gotten attached.

"Yes, it would have been a disaster on more fronts than just losing a promising team, as much as it would have hurt us. Had the arachne been allowed to set up for much longer, we might have had a repeat of the early days."

Leila clenched her jaw. The director's words brought back memories she preferred to stay buried in the recesses of her mind.

"We might have had to saturate the area with artillery. Just call it a loss and glass it entirely. It wouldn't be worth the loss of life necessary to retake it," her mentor mused, seemingly thinking of the exact same episode she had.

"Well, while it's too soon to call it a complete victory, I doubt the Sin of Pride would leave the job half-done, so I think we can avoid discussing the complete devastation of a stretch of domestic soil." The director stood up, walking over the windows to observe the hustle and bustle of Manhattan below them.

"How did he know, though?" Leila asked after a moment of silence as they all contemplated what could have been. While she was grateful the worst hadn't come to pass, she had no idea how the usually reclusive man had learned of such a situation when even the AA's devices hadn't noticed anything.

"Sloth might have told him. She would definitely know if she cared to turn her gaze away from the Mariana Trench," Marcus answered. He might very well be correct, but Leila didn't think they should immediately shelve the problem by accepting the most straightforward explanation.

Noticing that she wasn't convinced, the large man added, "You think he might be getting more involved. But why now, after all this time?"

She shrugged. "I'm not privy to his thoughts, but it seems to me that we'd commit a mistake if we simply ascribed his actions to Sloth. She might be the mastermind behind their group, but she's also very much preoccupied with other things. I doubt she has the time to scout the American countryside for every little variation in expected mana levels."

The director hummed in agreement. "That's good thinking. Assuming is what got us into this mess in the first place, after all. Better to be safe than sorry."

Marcus snorted, making the room shake. "What got us into this mess is that the special ops are only good at frontal assault. Best people in the world if you want to capture or kill someone, but ask them to do anything else, and they fall apart."

This was an old argument of his, as he had very little faith in the military's supernatural branches after the mess they made in the early years of the apocalypse. However, Leila felt it was a bit too harsh. "It's not really their fault, though. The rangers used the proper equipment; it's just that no one could have anticipated an arachne being there. I'm not saying this incident has no culprits, mind you, but assigning the blame so widely only means we'll have no one to point to in the end."

Because she'd worked with the special ops in the assault against Golden Sun and, more importantly, been the one to conduct the preliminary investigation, Leila was well aware of just how many things those bastards had their sticky fingers on.

She understood the military was spread thin and had to focus on the big players, so some situations could and did slip through the cracks. "In the end, the Golden Sun Guild is the one who was messing with the mana levels in dungeons to gather better materials. There was some negligence on others' part, but the fault lies squarely with them."

"True, it's just . . ." Marcus sighed, a heavy sound full of past frustrations. "We got too close this time. All of this could have been avoided."

The director turned from the window, his face calm and composed. "Perhaps, but it wasn't. All we can do now is ensure this doesn't happen again. Improve our scanning and detection methods, investigate how the arachne managed to avoid detection, and learn from this. It's not often that we get to put our hands on one of their nests. The Sin of Pride might have taken the body, but we should be able to find some interesting information."

Leila nodded. "I'll try to pry as much as possible from the kids, see if they remember additional details."

"As for Pride . . . This really isn't for us to handle. Washington will decide what to do with this information, even if I suspect they'll simply share it with the loyal guilds, make sure the S-rankers on our side know what to expect," the director added in a serious tone.

The three sat in silence for a few moments, each lost in their thoughts about the future and the potential developments this incident could spur.

Finally, Leila said, "Do you think Towers will go hunt for him? At this point, it might be better to leave Pride be. Even though he's gotten his hands on a Shard of the Aby—"

"ENOUGH!" Marcus roared, mana spilling into a corona. "Do not pronounce that name here! This place is secured only as much as you can trust the bureaucrats to keep their noses to themselves."

Chastised, Leila apologized, "I'm sorry, I wasn't thinking." It wasn't often that she needed to admit her faults, but in a room with just her mentor and the director, she could do it. It was true that she had almost said something dangerous, after all.

"Yes, let's avoid names and speculations that might cause unrest, especially here," the director seconded with a stern look. His mana surged momentarily, as though to neutralize the effects of Marcus's outburst, ensuring that no trace of their conversation was left lingering in the room's energies.

"You are right, though," Marcus said, pulling back his energy as he took a deep breath. "Towers and his group might seek him out if they learn of this. As it is, the situation is too volatile. An S-ranker with that thing is not a situation we want to handle lightly."

"Towers was always too much of a Goody-Two-shoes. Since he's been forbidden from entering The Caldera and the Chinese have been relatively quiet outside their borders, he's been itching for a big win," the director commented, taking a sip of his water. "Still, he's not stupid, for all that he presents himself as a meathead. Even if he can find Pride, and that's a big if, he's not likely to attack him on sight."

Leila considered the possibility of those two monsters fighting for real and shuddered. An S-rank Awakener wasn't just a stronger A-rank, after all. They were existences on a different plane entirely, and the difference between the two highest ranks was closer to that between A and C.

Those two going at it would be like several nuclear bombs going off at the same time.

We can't really ignore Pride getting his hands on a Shard, but it might be better if Towers doesn't find him. The consequences of their fight . . . Better not to think about it.

The director spoke up again, bringing Leila back from her dark thoughts. "For now, our course of action will remain internal. Let's clean up our backyard first, improve our surveillance, and understand where we went wrong. We might be able to use the arachne's presence to increase the surveillance on other guilds' dungeons, even though they weren't directly involved with Golden Sun." A satisfied smile ghosted across his features, there and gone so swiftly that it might have been her imagination. Leila, though, knew the man too well. Even in the depths of despair, he would always find a way to eke out a small victory.

"And the rookies?" she queried, her mind shifting back to her students. "Should I brief them on the situation? James at least should know who is keeping an eye on him."

Marcus and the director exchanged a brief glance, a nonverbal communication passing between them. After a pause, the director nodded. "Inform them all, but keep it limited and controlled. They are still young and unseasoned. There's no need to throw them into the deep end of one of the planet's greatest crises just yet."

"And caution them on the extreme confidentiality of this matter," her mentor added, his tone gruff but concerned. She knew he also had a soft spot for the kids.

Leila nodded, standing up. "All right, I need to get a handle on the situation on the ground first. I'll inform you if I find anything worthwhile." That said, she left the room, sinking into the shadows at her feet.

She had a job to do.

CHAPTER FORTY-FOUR

"All right, kids, before we do what I know you must be itching to do and assign all those sweet points you got from defeating the newborn matriarch spider, I need to talk to you about a few things," Miss Walker announced once they had changed into their training suits and had taken a seat on the parlor's couches.

While James would have been desperate to get to the juicy part, at the moment, he was much more interested in what his teacher had to say.

The other day, they had been quickly dismissed once it was clear they didn't know much, but the three executives' reactions to their story made him very curious.

James had several theories about the mysterious man who saved them and what the red stone he had taken might be. Ranging from plausible theories—a powerful Awakener, guild affiliated but low-key, noticed the increase of mana and the artifact stolen by the arachne—to absurd ones—a humanoid monster was trying to infiltrate society, and the red stone was a meteorite containing forbidden energy.

In the end, he decided to shelve them, at least temporarily, until he could speak with Miss Walker about it. She'd at least give them some more information. And since a couple of days since their dive had passed, the preliminary investigations should be done.

"You're probably curious about what happened in that spider dungeon, eh?" she asked, getting deadpan looks.

Chuckling at their expressions, Miss Walker continued, "All right. How much do you guys know about the S-rank?"

Silenced by the non sequitur, they took a moment to answer.

Finally, Maria said, "They're the most elite Awakeners in the world. There are less than a hundred in total, and they can be considered one-man armies by themselves."

That was the most common understanding of an S-rank. The best and greatest humanity had to offer against the unending tides of monsters.

Miss Walker nodded, pleased. "Yes, that's mostly correct. And as you might know, most of them are connected to extremely powerful guilds or even directly to countries. The US Armed Forces has a few on contract, though they don't disclose the exact number."

The masked woman stood up and paced before them in a show of uncharacteristic nervousness. She was deep in thought as she carefully chose her words. "But what most people don't know, and some choose not to acknowledge, is that there are a few S-rank Awakeners who walk a different path. They do not align themselves with any guild or pledge loyalty to any nation. Some of them aren't even known to the public."

The blood drained from James's face as he made the connection. *So there is a reason why he was so unconcerned with us. He literally has more power in his pinky than all of Team 0 combined, several times over.*

His thoughts raced, but he stayed silent, allowing Miss Walker to proceed with her exposition.

"The man you encountered in the dungeon the other day is one of these more elusive S-rankers. Not that much is known about him, nor can I reveal more than the basics of what we do know, but I can tell you something: he's very powerful and his actions, though often seemingly erratic, are calculated and purposeful," Miss Walker explained, pausing momentarily to let the information sink in.

"So he went there for the stone. He must have known about it beforehand," Daniel wondered out loud.

Miss Walker sighed, dropping down on her couch. "Probably, yes. But as you might imagine, he's not exactly around to ask questions. That stone wasn't just any artifact. But I can't, and won't, go into details about it now. It's a topic that goes way above your clearance and should remain so."

Maria shifted, uncomfortable yet inquisitive. "But, miss, why would he save us? If he is as powerful as you say, why didn't he just go in before us and take the stone?"

James nodded in agreement, adding, "Yes, and why did he bother eliminating the arachne? He could have just retrieved the stone and left."

Miss Walker leaned back, crossing her arms, her gaze distant as she considered her response. "We believe . . . that he, despite his complex morality and questionable methods, has some semblance of a code he follows. He may act in his interest, but that doesn't always mean he is indifferent to others."

She then locked eyes with each of them, her tone dropping to a serious note. "But don't mistake that for benevolence or assume he is an ally. That man and his partners are not to be trifled with or sought after. They are dangerous and, more often than not, a deadly risk to those who encounter them."

"His allies? So there are more like him?" Lauren, always quick on the uptake, asked.

Their teacher sighed, looking around the room pensively. Finally, she reached a decision, and her mana flooded the space. Shadows lengthened and the lights winked out; they were enshrouded in darkness.

All throughout this process, Team 0 remained calm, if only because they trusted their mentor.

Satisfied with the results, Miss Walker turned to face them. "Sorry about that.

I'm really not supposed to tell you this, but having met one of them, and especially since he expressed interest in you, James, it would be foolish not to tell you what to expect."

Seeing that she had their full attention, she went on, "The man you met is known to the high brass as the Sin of Pride. Now, while that might sound like an edgy nickname, he has well and truly earned it. He's a monstrously strong Awakener known for regularly clearing upper-tier A-rank dungeons by himself. The feat that made him famous was the solo battle against an S-rank dragon in the Siberian wilderness. Unnecessary, by all standards, since the monster never left its territory, and it created a burnt wasteland where nothing can grow. But it proved his absolute strength. He's dangerous."

The rookies absorbed the gravity of what Miss Walker was revealing. James felt his pulse quicken, sharing glances with the others that mirrored his own disquiet.

She continued, her low voice echoing in the dark room, "Not only Pride, but there are six others—collectively known to the few who are aware as the Seven Sins. Each has capabilities that could rival small armies. But unlike armies, their motives and operations are entirely enigmatic. A force, undeniably capable, that moves in the shadows of our world."

"Is . . . Am I in danger, then? If this Pride is interested in me?" James asked in trepidation.

Miss Walker regarded James for a long moment before responding, "Danger? Perhaps. Interest from one such as Pride doesn't come lightly nor without reason. But the exact nature of it . . . I can't say for certain."

James clenched his fists, the memory of those piercing, inscrutable eyes analyzing him in the dungeon returning with vivid clarity. He felt a shiver of anxiety, yet paradoxically, an exhilarating rush of adrenaline coursed through him.

Daniel, ever the practical thinker, interjected, "Should we be preparing to meet him again, then, Miss Walker? Is there a protocol or something for dealing with these Sins?"

Sighing deeply, Miss Walker nodded. "A fair question, Daniel. Protocols exist, but they're intended for much higher ranks than yourselves. What I will stress to you all, however, is caution. If you encounter Pride or any of the Sins again, do not engage, do not confront. You observe, you avoid, and you report."

Maria furrowed her brow. "What about the AA and the guilds? Are they doing something about these people?"

"Again, this isn't something you need to be worried about. You're so low on the ladder, far from having the power to do anything, that it would sound insane to many that Pride took an interest in one of you." She sighed, red eyes lost in the darkness. "However, I feel it's only right you should know that the guilds, the military, and the AA have organizations and divisions that monitor and try to understand the movements and motivations of the Sins. But it's a dangerous game, and thus far, they've managed to elude any meaningful interactions or confrontations."

She clapped her hands, and the shadows rushed back toward her, revealing the brightly lit room, just as they had left it. "Now, let's get to your development."

Status.

STATUS WINDOW	
Name	James Summers
Age	19
Awakening	1st
Talent	Thakinesis
Title	
Level	31
MP	155/155
STR	21
VIT	14
AGI	14
SEN	20
MND	14
STAT POINTS	4

SKILLS	LEVEL	DESCRIPTION
Thakinetic Empowerment	5	(Active): Utilize your Willpower to temporarily raise STR - VIT - AGI.
Thakinetic Awareness	4	(Active/Passive): Expand your SEN to feel others' wills.
Thakinetic Resistance	7	(Active/Passive): Empower your MND to defend yourself against foreign influences.

The most significant change, beyond the absurd level growth they had achieved by killing the spider eggs, was that his skills had all shot up.

It wasn't a shocker that Thakinetic Resistance reached level 7 after James suffered under Pride's aura and managed to not succumb completely.

Of course, he didn't use even a fraction of his power, but considering the sheer difference between us, it was still enough to make the leap.

It wasn't often that H-rankers met an S-ranker, after all. Surviving the experience was more than enough.

His Empowerment skill getting to level 5 was more surprising, but even then, he had been pushing his skill in all sorts of manners. Mana felt much more malleable now, and he could allocate it to specific body parts without issue.

I wonder how much easier the overcharged punches I've been doing will be. They're not necessarily part of the skill, after all. More like a consequence of it. It'll probably get reflected in the second Awakening possibilities.

Thakinetic Awareness was trudging along. James would keep pushing the sensing skill, which he still considered to be his greatest asset, but it wasn't easy. Stealth skills generally operated under different rules, making them easy to pierce in most cases.

Only high-level skills like Miss Walker's could hide from him, but again, those worked under different rules. Being in a separate dimension made one quite hard to notice, after all.

Maybe the next tier of the skill will give me more options in that regard. Still, it's crazy how much we all depend on it.

His four free points went to the stats mind, strength, vitality, and sense. The surge of power was much more manageable, especially compared to what he had gone through after the killing spree in the spider hatching room.

"Man, it really sucks that he had to take those last eggs too," Lauren complained, mirroring his own thoughts. While getting two whole levels from the spider matriarch would be more than good enough, they could have earned at least a couple more if Pride hadn't destroyed the remaining clutches.

"You guys don't know how good you had it. Finding a hatchery like that is almost impossible. They only happen when higher-tier monsters are around to protect them, making it far too dangerous for rookies to attempt," Miss Walker interjected.

James hummed in agreement. It was true, after all. They had been terribly lucky. So lucky, in fact, that something stank.

The explanation about the Seven Sins evoked a memory inside him. Something he had been more than willing to lie forgotten.

A curly-haired woman, standing tall, her smile kind. Her auburn locks caught the light, distracting James from what she was saying.

"So they need me in Siberia for a while. I shouldn't be too long if nothing new crops up, dear heart."

That was all he could remember.

CHAPTER FORTY-FIVE

Animal conservation had been a well-respected pursuit even before the apocalypse, but with mana wreaking havoc on creatures around globe, maintaining healthy populations of ordinary specimens had become a much harder job.

High-tech equipment was needed to control the ambient energy levels, alongside the occasional evacuation when the possibility of a dungeon being born increased. Dedicated biologists and animal-rearing experts conducted complex operations to prevent excessive mana from mutating the wildlife.

It was why James had been surprised to learn that a dungeon had formed in Long Island near the William T. Davis Wildlife Refuge. Considering that the dungeon was close to the refuge and its highly trained professionals, it was unlikely that a mistake had been made.

He was correct, it turned out. The dungeon hadn't spawned in the refuge, which would have been normal, but in one of the houses nearby.

Between Mulberry and Park Avenues, a few buildings had been left abandoned, as was common in the suburbs. Great cities like New York would always be well protected, but its suburbs didn't receive as good of a service, especially in the early years after the apocalypse.

One of these houses, it seemed, had been the epicenter of a Mana Sink. Not enough power to change anything beyond its limit, luckily, but the well-tuned detectors employed in the reserve had caught it quickly.

Unfortunately for them, that dungeon was then assigned to the Golden Sun Guild, which would typically conduct a sweep and, if nothing of worth was found, would give it to their subsidiaries.

This process was disrupted, however, by the dismantling of the organization following the raids and subsequent court orders. That left several smaller, low-priority dungeons, such as the Mulberry Avenue one, unattended.

It's unfortunate, but even after they caught most of Golden Sun, it's not like things changed that much. Yes, there's less overt criminality now, and whatever it was they were doing has been stopped, but the AA is still short staffed. We still need to auction most dungeons to private guilds.

Thus, three-quarters of Golden Sun's dungeons were given to more reliable organizations, while the rest were split between the special ops and the AA.

Coming out of Mr. Robinson's black van, James laid his eyes on the dungeon. His team had been taken off the roster for a few days, owing to the legitimately dangerous situation they had found themselves in. Plus, they needed to get accustomed to their more powerful skills and bodies.

Now, however, they were ready to get back to the grind.

"I doubt we'll get as lucky as in the spider dungeon. But if we can eke out a couple of levels from this thing, I'll consider myself satisfied," Ezekiel said from where he was busy tying his boots.

"Never met anyone as mana hungry as you, Ez." James laughed. It was the truth. As a White Mage, Ezekiel could serve as a force multiplier all by himself, but his skills all required an enormous amount of power to operate, forcing him to rely on mana potions, which could have undesired effects down the line if one took too many.

James's chuckle echoed amid the eerie silence of the desolate suburban area as his eyes flicked toward the decaying house at the end of the street. The muted, dark windows gazed back like vacant eyes. It was an unusual sight to associate with the formation of a dungeon, these domestic shells of a world gone by, now playing host to creatures born of mana and chaos, but it still happened sometimes.

Lauren strapped her daggers to her sides, contemplatively looking at the neighborhood. "This place has really become a shithole, hasn't it? I remember coming around these parts when I was a kid. It wasn't pretty, but nothing compared to what it is now."

Daniel, adjusting his shield and checking his equipment, nodded in agreement. "It's much worse than it should be, I think, because it's so close to the reserve. People just don't want to be close to possible dungeons." Then, looking at the creaking fence door, he added, "Even though this place isn't screaming danger like that spider dungeon, we can't let our guards down. Since it's so concentrated, this dungeon might have created some unique monsters. Let's proceed carefully."

The overgrown garden, which once might have housed flowers or vegetables, rustled ominously. Without much wind to move the grass, they could only conclude that something else was in there.

"Go away!" A frail old woman emerged from a nearby house. She clutched at her shawl, pulling it tighter around her as if to shield herself from the spectral chill of the place.

Mindful of what might be an abandoned person whose mental health was likely in a bad state, James addressed her gently, "Ma'am, we're here to make sure nothing comes out from this dungeon. We mean you no harm. We'll resolve this problem and be on our way."

Her wild gaze was drawn to the darkness of the house's entrance, which seemed to absorb all light. "The family that lived there . . . The Winchesters, they were ruthlessly murdered, and their spirits have never found peace. This isn't just a dungeon—it's their graveyard!"

Lauren's gaze softened with a mix of pity and understanding, casting a gentle glance toward the elderly lady. "Can you tell us more about them, about the Winchesters?" she asked with a coaxing tone.

"The girl . . . She was always disturbed. Strange," the woman began, itching to share the story. "She made friends with bad people. They'd come around once in a while, with their tattoos and drugs. She went down a bad road. In the end, she brought her whole family with her."

Drug problems were an unfortunate reality, and as one might expect, living through the apocalypse only made them more common. "So they were murdered by a gang?" James asked.

Her gaze shifted to him with a disquieting focus. She answered, "They were. Their remains were left there for a week before the police finally came by to clean it up. I know the dungeon is here because of them. I know it."

They all looked at each other. Incorporeal spirits were not an impossible thing, but they were usually of high rank. And they did not have stealth skills like the arachne, meaning their mana alone would have significantly lifted the ambient reading.

Still, such a tragic event could explain why this house specifically turned into a dungeon, and not one of the other abandoned ones. Strong emotions could direct mana, after all.

"Very well, thank you for the information, ma'am. We'll proceed with care, and if anything of the sort turns out, know that we have a White Mage with us." James pointed to Ezekiel, his hands glowing white on cue.

The woman gasped softly, a relieved smile breaking through the haze of sadness and desperation. "Oh, that's fantastic. Please, please free this place from its curse."

"Don't worry, ma'am. We'll be done quickly," the youngest of the team reassured, angelic smile firmly in place.

The woman finally left, muttering to herself how glad she was that finally someone would exorcize the place.

When she was finally out of earshot, Lauren chuckled. "Do you think she might realize that you don't have the skills to do anything of the sort?"

Ezekiel shrugged. "Hey, it's James that said it. And it's not really a lie. I am a White Mage. It's just that it'll take until my third Awakening before I get anything close to that level of power."

"All right, I think it's time to get inside. While we shouldn't expect spirits, it's true that a tragedy of that level might influence the development of the dungeon, so let's be careful," James said, taking point.

Since Thakinetic Awareness had leveled up, he could sense more with better precision, now able to discern the nuances of a being's intentions.

Focusing his skill on the abandoned house, he immediately noticed the presence of several plant monsters. Their minds were weak, but they burrowed deep—their intentions seemed less inclined to immediate, direct harm and more toward slow ambushes.

He relayed this to the rest of the team, and Daniel took out his testing kit. After he waved one of the papers in the air, it quickly changed color, turning to a burnt orange.

The Tank quickly consulted the pamphlet. "Paralysis and hallucinations. Since it's in the air even outside the dungeon proper, it might explain why that old lady seems so bizarre."

"Should I just burn them?" Maria asked, always eager for a bit of pyromania.

James shrugged, looking at Daniel, who sighed and took out another slip of paper. This time, it didn't react, showing that the gas in the air wasn't flammable.

"Go ahead, but try to keep it contained," James finally said, extending his senses deeper into the building while Maria let loose a torrent of flames.

Things were moving inside, scurrying between the floors, hiding in the rooms and basement. Since it was such an unconventional dungeon, they'd need to rethink some of their tactics, but he felt confident they'd make it.

A few minutes later, the lawn was entirely burnt, not a blade of grass in sight. Once they crossed the now empty lawn, they arrived at the door, which easily broke into splinters under James's kick.

The interior was a portrait of decay, with timeworn furniture and moth-eaten curtains draped like specters in the darkness. The house opened directly into the living room, a strange occurrence in a 1960s construction. Some of the floorboards were waterlogged and looked like they'd break under the slightest pressure.

Creaks echoed through the entire building. It was one strong gust away from falling apart.

Yet, amid the rot and ruin, an uncanny semblance of life persisted. A meal, now a moldy mess, was still on the dining table, perhaps left behind in the family's last moments of terror.

James's skill resonated with the quiet and hidden life forms. Their intent mingled with the more malicious crawl of monsters. Other things scurried in the dark above them, their forms indicating insects and critters overgrown thanks to the mana. One group in particular—long and sinuous, with brutally simple minds— caught his attention. When they didn't move, he kept looking around.

His gaze lingered on the remnants of a family portrait, the faces scratched out by some violent entity or desperate act.

Lauren leaned closer to observe what looked like a small child's drawing pinned to the crumbling wall. It depicted a happy family; yet it was obscured by dark, amorphous shapes. The incongruity between the naive art and the lingering malevolence of the dungeon caused a shiver to go down her spine.

Suddenly, three centipedes, as long and thick as an anaconda, came out of the kitchen, pincers dripping with venom. They scurried toward the team.

Without the need to speak, Team 0 all set up around the table, forcing the creatures to face them separately.

Daniel's shining shield caught their attention. With a screech, they attacked, ignoring the trap they were caught in. James and Lauren swiftly crushed the two closest ones from the sides with a single brutal hit, while the Tank allowed the last one to try and bite into his shield. It was too late when it realized it couldn't, as a mighty bash crushed its head.

"Nothing else seems to be coming," James announced, shaking his fist to clean the centipede brain stuck to it.

A couple of minutes later, Ezekiel's voice sliced through the oppressive silence. "This place is too damn creepy. Insects I can kind of get, but these drawings are not normal. Do you think someone lived here after the murders?" he asked, staring at the same portrait that had captured James's attention.

A distant, muffled cry echoed through the hollow recesses of the dilapidated structure. The team turned in unison, hands tightly gripping their weaponry, bodies instinctively sinking into a combative stance.

It came again, a sorrowful wail, tinged with an undercurrent of simmering rage, shaking the cracked window panes. Their eyes locked with shared acknowledgment—this dungeon wasn't just a den of monsters. Something else was inside with them.

CHAPTER FORTY-SIX

So, this place may actually be haunted, after all.

James wasn't one to give in to superstition and baseless fears, yet he couldn't help but make the sign of the cross. He might not be a devout Christian, but some things were never really forgotten.

"Yeaaah, I really don't like this place," Lauren murmured, clutching her daggers tightly. "James, what the fuck was that?"

As much as he would have liked to answer, he couldn't. Nothing stood out to his senses beyond a few more insect monsters scurrying around, primarily concentrated in the basement, and a small but fierce beast in the master bedroom. The whole dungeon had a weird atmosphere, and while he knew it could be a simple suggestion, James thought, for just a moment, that there might be something to the old lady's theories.

"The only things I can feel are regular monsters. Mostly big ass cockroaches in the basement," he answered, sounding as concerned as she was.

"Then we should go investigate those." Daniel was a bastion of calm. In the weeks they had known each other, James had yet to see anything truly shock him, which he appreciated even more now. Having someone keep a level head was very important inside a dungeon.

Shaking off his fears, James refocused. "You're right. If something is in here, we'll find it. We just need to keep clearing the rooms."

So, they started moving toward the stairs that led below, where the darkness pooled. Even under the light of their flashlights, only a few feet were visible, the rest swallowed by the unnatural shadows.

Still, James trusted his senses enough. Even his regular ones told him that about a dozen monsters were scurrying in the dark, preparing to attack anything that might enter their territory.

Taking point, since he was the only one who knew where they could come from, he stepped on the creaky staircase.

This really would be easier if it didn't look so much like a horror movie. Why do dungeons have to be always so dramatic? How about a nice open field with nothing to ambush you? What happened to fighting with honor, looking at your opponent in the face?

James successfully distracted himself from the fear when he walked off the last step. As soon as his foot touched the floor, a screech echoed through the basement, and several presences converged on him.

Long black antennae—at least four feet in length—emerged in the low light of his flashlight, quickly followed by a massive body. The carapace had to be six feet, made more intimidating with its bloodred markings. Beady eyes showed no mercy as the cockroach charged him, scuttling forward with an open maw, ready to make a meal out of him.

James did what any rational person in such a situation would do and kicked the thing with as much force as possible while yelling obscenities.

He pumped mana into his leg to create a small explosion on impact. The cockroach, blasted by the concussive force of James's kick, flew backward, colliding into its kin that were pouring forth from the dark recesses of the basement. The other creatures hissed and reeled, momentarily disoriented by the sudden violence that had been visited upon their peer.

James increased his flashlight's power, illuminating the vast space and revealing more chitinous bodies scuttling about. The reddish-black hue of their shells glistened under the struggling light, creating an eerie scene.

Lauren, appearing like a ghost, darted forward, her daggers slicing into the carapace of another advancing creature with a viciousness that betrayed her current feelings. Greenish ichor spilled from the wound, pooling on the concrete below as the creature's legs twitched, its death throes a grotesque dance.

"Ez, stay behind and prepare to debuff them when you get the chance," Daniel called, stepping forward, his shield raised and glowing, placing himself between the oncoming swarm and the two mages.

Maria, however, had other plans. A fireball soared above their heads; it was hotter than usual as she concentrated its power to prevent an explosion. It wouldn't do to send the whole house crashing on their heads, after all. The fireball hit the vanguard of the swarm and immediately killed them, melting their heads in a gory display.

"Can't really be more disgusting than it already is, anyway," James commented to himself, even as he stepped forward, intercepting another of the monsters.

The basement transformed into a chaotic battlefield, with each step forward met by the clashing of steel on chitin and the squelching of punctured exoskeletons.

The overwhelming metallic scent of cockroach ichor mingled with the acrid stench of burnt carapace, filling the room with a choking atmosphere. The light, combined with the shadows cast by the scuttling swarm, made the walls look alive, the darkness pulsating with malevolent intent.

Daniel, with his shield glowing an ethereal white hue, swung mightily, bashing one of the creatures and sending it spiraling into its kin.

However, in a surprising maneuver, a few cockroaches took flight, their wings whirring menacingly.

The basement ceiling wasn't high enough to grant them much space to move, but the surprise element allowed them to avoid another fireball.

Just as the biggest of the swarm started to glow red, its markings lighting up as it prepared to do something, a dagger penetrated its skull, ending its flight unceremoniously.

"Let's get this shit over with," Lauren muttered, jumping high to slash at the last remaining cockroach in the air. It screeched, opening its maw to try and take a chunk out of her, but before they could clash, another monster was thrown at it, sending it tumbling down.

"Sorry, the wings were kind of freaking me out," James commented, fists dripping green.

"Get down!" Maria yelled. Her hands glowed with a fierce orange red, her eyes intense with concentration. Casting a wide arc of flame that singed the remaining few, careful to keep the heat and force controlled to avoid damage to the house's structure, she managed to push them all together.

With the enemy clustered together, James jumped in, fists charged with a large amount of mana. He released a wave of power as he punched through the closest one, pulping the remaining three in one hit.

He grunted with the effort but unlike the last few times, he managed to retain his strength. Even though it wasn't a proper skill, more like the bastardization of one, this kind of explosive punch was becoming increasingly useful as it expanded his arsenal with a mid-range option he severely lacked.

The last roach, which had been far enough not to get swept up in the flames, was quickly ended by Lauren, who threw her remaining dagger into its mouth, punching through its brain.

"Anything else in here?" Daniel asked, shield still up and ready to block any incoming attack.

"Not that I can tell," James answered. He had learned to rely upon Thakinetic Awareness, and if it said nothing was within the basement, he'd trust it. The upper floors were a different thing, as the weird atmosphere of the house seemed to conspire to confuse him, but he was confident they had gotten everything down here.

They still gave one last cursory sweep, as the regulations dictated for an enclosed dungeon, to make sure nothing had escaped their notice, but beyond the disgusting muck and dirt, they found nothing alive.

"So it's only the upper floor that's left. Still nothing about what made those sounds?" Ezekiel asked, sounding worried.

So far, nothing they had encountered could be a serious threat to them, but the creepy feeling of the house, coupled with the tragic story the old lady told them, made it seem scarier than it should.

"Just some more insects. I think there might also be a cat, but it's a normal-sized one. Doesn't seem to have been enlarged by mana," James answered after turning his senses above them. It was still fuzzier than he was used to, but at least he was getting something.

"There's only one question left, then," Maria said, standing over the roaches' corpses. "Who did this?" There was a red residue, like dried paint, on her finger after she swiped it on a monster's carapace.

"It's not their natural color?" Daniel was surprised for the first time. Even he couldn't maintain his aplomb when confronted with this: something with at least a modicum of intelligence was in the dungeon.

"It's not. It can't have happened too long ago either because the cockroaches mutated when the Sink started. Something or, more likely, someone has been here," the redhead replied, sounding grim.

In unison, they all turned to look up. Weird sounds had been coming from the upper floor for a while, and while they could attribute them to the creatures James could feel scuttling above them, this kind of action required some intelligence.

"If there's someone here, it would explain why the photographs and the portrait were scratched. That's not the kind of thing murderers usually do. Certainly not for drug-related causes," Lauren added, lips pressed tightly together.

James cocked his head, quickly understanding where she was going. "So you think someone related to the family that lived here still haunts this place? If there's a spirit, we need to leave immediately."

The girl shook her head. "No, not a spirit. They're not interested in stealth despite being incorporeal beings. You'd feel it if there was one. I just think it's someone."

"But someone able to spoof James's skill is not a person we can take on by ourselves. They'd need to be a high-ranker!" Ezekiel countered.

It was true that so far only very powerful people had been able to avoid his detection, but just like he could bypass most stealth skills thanks to his unique Talent, others could likely do the same to him. He said, "We can't discount that there is a person. They might be using a spatial skill, and if they're technically not here, I can't feel them."

Grimly, they all decided to explore further but with increased caution. So far, all signs pointed to a skilled stealth user being in the dungeon with them, but since they hadn't shown themselves, they could only assume they'd be hostile.

Walking up the stairs and back onto the ground floor, James kept his senses peeled for any movement. The house kept creaking and groaning, and the scuttling above continued uninterrupted, but nothing to show a person's presence.

However, when they got to the living room, they found incontrovertible proof that, indeed, there was someone else with them.

The table, which had laid broken in the middle of the room, was now beside the centipedes' corpses. The broken glass had been swept away, and the chairs that blocked the entrance to the upper floor had been stacked together.

"Fucking hell. All right, whoever you are, you better come out now!" Lauren yelled.

No response came, save for the creaking of broken things.

"I don't like having to play this kind of game," Ezekiel complained, clutching his dagger. Having the least directly offensive options, he was the most vulnerable of the group. And by now, James knew him enough to know of his desperate fear of jump scares.

"Yeah, I can't deny that this is exactly the kind of place you'd expect a big, ugly ghost to haunt. Maybe a demon? Seems a bit cliché, to be honest."

But James couldn't deny being a bit unsettled. It was the second time in a row, inside a dungeon, that his most prized skill wasn't working as intended. He could only hope it wasn't anything like the arachne that was waiting for them.

"All right. Let's get this over with," he said, moving toward the staircase.

An ominous wail from above answered.

CHAPTER FORTY-SEVEN

The wailing is a bit cliché," James muttered, even as he scoured the building with his senses. There was something not right about the whole dungeon. The obvious signs of presence, the deliberate screams made just to scare them off.

It was exactly the kind of thing one would expect in a haunted house if they didn't know how real spirits manifested.

"I think we're dealing with someone with very little knowledge of the outside world," he said out loud, getting a grunt of acknowledgment from Lauren. She seemed the most spooked of the team, evidently not liking the gloomy atmosphere. "Why?" she asked.

"Because," Maria interrupted, "this isn't how a real dungeon operates. It's not until D-rank that truly intelligent monsters appear, and they certainly aren't the kinds that would be found in this dump."

"But something is going on here," Ezekiel argued, looking at the changed room. From the damaged photographs to the painted cockroaches, it was evident that an intelligent being was there with them.

"There is; that's why I said someone with very little knowledge of the outside world. I have a strong suspicion about who it might be," James answered.

He started walking toward the staircase, ready to get the mystery over with.

As soon as his foot touched the first step, another ghostly wail resounded through the house and a blue wisp of fire appeared at the top.

"This is getting ridiculous." With quick steps, James reached the second floor. He didn't allow the thing time to react and he punched it, his fist encased in Thakinetic Empowerment.

Just like he expected, he felt very little resistance and the wisp dissipated in the air. More than that, no notification appeared, confirming his belief.

"Yeah, this is no haunted dungeon. There's a person here, and they're trying their best to scare us away."

Once the others reached him, they stepped into the creaky hallway, careful not to get ambushed.

James kicked in the first door and jumped back, allowing dog-sized spiders to fly by. They were much smaller than the ones they had dealt with in the forest, but their fangs gleamed with thick venom, and he very much wanted to avoid experiencing its effects.

A dozen more monsters followed the first two, flooding the hallway with their clicks and hisses.

With two quick steps, Daniel interposed himself between the monsters and his team, his shield glowing. Behind his protection, Maria crafted a fireball.

The cramped space made it difficult for them to move properly in formation, but it also forced the spiders to stay clumped together, making it very easy for the Fire Mage to hit them all with one spell.

A blazing inferno roared through the hallway, incinerating the venomous spiders instantly. The smell of charred exoskeletons filled the air as the team cautiously proceeded forward, James in front.

The house wasn't a mansion, but it wasn't small either. They needed to sweep through five more rooms, two bathrooms included, before they could get to the last one, where they were expecting to find out the truth.

They sidestepped the burned spiders, with Maria extinguishing the flames to prevent anything else from catching on fire.

Another wail, this time sounding much closer, made them pause, but when nothing happened, they resumed their march.

The second room, where James could feel several more monsters, turned out to be a bathroom. Clustered together in the bathtub, three massive centipedes—just like the ones they had fought below—screeched angrily at the intrusion.

Not wanting to get boxed in by the more maneuverable insects, James once again retreated to the hallway, letting them come to him.

He sidestepped the first, knowing his teammates would handle it, and ignored the last, having felt Lauren get into position behind it. His opponent clicked its mandibles menacingly, aiming to get at one of his legs.

I'm gonna give you exactly what you want.

With a grin, James pushed mana into his right leg and kicked it, hard.

It tried grabbing onto it, but the strength behind the blow folded the creature in half and launched it back into the bathroom.

Now unafraid of getting swarmed, James stepped in behind it. Though damaged, the centipede managed to resume its attack after a moment of dizziness. Again, he allowed it to get close, but he didn't try to stop it this time.

The monster's mandibles clamped down on his calf with enough strength to shear it off. Luckily, he had the protection of D-rank armor to stop it, though he still winced at the pressure.

Since the centipede was busy trying to amputate him, he took advantage, punching down on its already messed-up side. The blow was strong enough to cut it in half, and James's gloved fist penetrated through the floor like paper.

Still, the beast didn't let go. Even in its death throes, its grip on his leg only tightened further, and he was forced to grab onto its mandibles and forcefully open them.

It took James almost a minute to get free. When he did, he tossed the twitching remains back into the bathtub, massaging his leg.

All right, that might not have been my most brilliant idea. The armor stopped it from doing any damage, but it still hurt. Ugh, when I get to the fucker who's playing pretend with this whole thing, I'll show them.

Just as he rejoined his friends, another wisp appeared, this time brighter and more corporeal. It was accompanied by the now expected ghostly wail while hovering in the middle of the hallway, blocking their path.

"What even are these things?" Ezekiel complained.

Maria snorted in disdain. "It's not fire, I can tell you that much."

Still holding his shield at the ready in case the wisp tried something, Daniel chipped in, "I think it's supposed to be a spirit in mythology. Like, in graveyards." Noticing the looks he was getting, he shrugged. "What? I like retro games. They're pretty common."

James shook his head and walked up to it. "Hey, if you want to tell us anything, how about you stop hiding and come talk to us? As far as we know, you haven't done anything too illegal beyond entering a dungeon without a permit."

Considering his first foray into the profession had seen him do just that, he was inclined to be charitable. If the person behind the gloomy atmosphere stopped the charade, that was.

He waited for an answer, but he sighed when it became apparent it wasn't coming. His punch easily plowed through the apparition, but this time, he felt something flicker while dispersing it.

He stopped, placing a hand on the wall, and concentrated.

By now, his teammates were used to his demeanor and waited for him to come up with something. The spooky atmosphere quickly lost its scary factor, and they all just wanted answers and to get it over with.

James sought those answers, scouring the building again for another hint of what he had felt, but nothing revealed itself.

"Damn, I thought I had it. For a moment, I felt like someone was here, but then it disappeared."

"We'll just have to get to the last room," Daniel consoled him, sounding about as done as he was.

With a sigh, they resumed the dive. The next few rooms hosted several insect monsters, transformed from their base forms to something more powerful and intimidating, but nothing close to the cockroaches they fought within the basement.

James's annoyance was palpable, his motions becoming brusquer, his senses stretched to their utmost in hopes of discerning whatever trickster hid behind the fake haunting.

The team moved meticulously, professionally clearing the rooms just like they had been taught by Miss Walker. For rooms that were too cramped, they wouldn't enter but made enough of a racket that the denizens would chase them into the hallway, where they could be more easily dealt with.

In the larger room, the one adjacent to the master bedroom, hid a dozen more centipedes, though bigger and meaner looking. They fought inside the room, not wanting to be cornered from behind should whatever was in the last room come out.

James had learned his lesson not to let the insects get too close, and though he didn't employ his explosive punches, he still managed to keep the monsters at bay while the others attacked from the back.

As always, Ezekiel's buffs and debuffs proved immensely useful, granting them absolute superiority over their opponents.

"This is definitely not a newborn dungeon, but it feels almost too easy," Maria said as she finished crisping up the last centipede.

"Yeah, I didn't wanna say anything, but beyond the creepiness, this hasn't been nearly as hard as the ones before," Lauren agreed.

Thinking back to their previous experiences, James snorted, "It's not like it has to always be as difficult as what we've been through. Sometimes, a dungeon is exactly as difficult as it should be."

The girl snorted too. They had all gotten so used to their information being manipulated by various guilds that the one time they got a dungeon within their possibilities, it felt too easy.

"It's still too early to say," Daniel grunted, keeping his eyes on the door.

Now that they were done with the centipedes, and James could only feel a presence in the last room, they refocused. They managed to eke out a level after fighting everything the house had thrown at them, which they quickly used to boost their stats in preparation for the boss fight.

James made the unorthodox choice of increasing his sense and mind stats in the hopes that whatever skill the person in the last room was using, he'd be able to pierce through.

That done, they collected themselves and walked up to the door. It looked ordinary, just like all the others, but James could feel one strong presence inside, alongside the general fuzziness of the dungeon but amped up.

Without hesitation, he kicked the door in, stepping through to reveal a strangely preserved room.

Everything looked to have been left exactly as it once was. On the nightstands were a pair of glasses, an open book, and even a bottle of water. Not a speck of dust marred the scene, as if someone had meticulously spent hours every day making sure it would be perfect, waiting for the owner to return.

On the bed was the presence James had felt from the beginning, which he had tentatively dubbed the boss of the dungeon.

Instead of the significant changes mana usually inflicted on low-level creatures, this one seemed almost entirely unchanged from its original form.

A tawny cat, with black rings around its eyes and a swishing tail, observed them from where it was perched. Its eyes glowed green in the light, giving it an otherworldly air.

"Is that . . ."

"That should be the boss," James answered Ezekiel's question. Despite its small size, he could feel a powerful will from the animal, and while it didn't seem overly aggressive, it wasn't an average cat anymore, what with the way its paws glowed softly.

It stood up, hissing lowly in warning. Evidently, the miniature boss did not appreciate having its territory invaded, made obvious by the extending of its claws.

Wickedly sharp, they tore into the sheets as it coiled up. Daniel immediately activated his skill, preparing to intercept the creature, when someone interfered.

"Miss Dalloway, you shouldn't treat guests like that," a disembodied voice said, calming the cat down.

The torn sheets repaired themselves, and several wisps appeared in the air, illuminating the room further.

Then, as if to disprove any theory they had come up with, a spectral figure appeared above the cat. A young woman with brown eyes, beautiful and doe-like, smiled at them. She wore a bloodied, torn white dress.

Her completely ruined throat and see-through appearance made it obvious she was not alive.

CHAPTER FORTY-EIGHT

So, there might be a ghost after all.

Looking at the see-through apparition, James could sense a feeble will in it. It was unfocused and even less noticeable than a plant monster's.

However, once he was over the initial shock, his brain started working again. He knew two things. That spirits were high-level creatures not found in H-rank dungeons, and that they never bothered to hide their presence.

When he put two and two together, it became apparent that what he was looking at was not what it appeared to be, as much as it might seem like it.

Still, he didn't say anything, playing along. "I suppose you'd be the girl who was murdered here, then?"

His voice was calm and conversational, as if he were meeting an acquaintance for the first time in a while. The others picked up on it and relaxed slightly, knowing how acute his senses could be.

The smile the ghostly girl graced him with was macabre, if only because of her appearance. "Yes, I'm that Greta."

Despite not having known the name, James still indulged her. "To think you'd still be here, haunting the place of your death. People still talk about your tragedy!" he said, technically not lying. He'd never heard of her before, and he doubted her story had been more than a blip in their chaotic world, but it seemed she enjoyed thinking of herself as a famous victim, so he'd go with it.

Her smile took a satisfied tilt, and she giggled happily. "Oh yes, I knew it. But you must tell me, what did they do to those monsters that killed me? Hanging? Execution by firing squad? Oh, maybe old-fashioned drowning?"

James had frankly no idea, but considering the gruesome end most gangs that didn't fold into guilds had, it wasn't hard to lie. "Shot to death."

Greta clapped happily, sitting down on the bed next to the cat and sighing in satisfaction. "I always knew justice would be done—I just can't believe people would turn this house into a mausoleum to honor me! You can't imagine how dreadfully bored I was for all these years, with only Miss Dalloway to keep me company."

The cat, the apparent dungeon boss, meowed loudly at her name being called before returning to licking her paws, apparently unconcerned with their presence.

"Now that you know that, I don't suppose you'd be willing to let go? We still need to clear this dungeon," James said. Though he didn't expect the apparition to agree, he would try to solve things without violence.

Diplomacy wasn't his best skill, but with intelligent opponents, one should always try to find another way. If that didn't work, well, he had his ways.

Greta's ethereal form flickered, a brief look of contemplation shadowing her spectral face. "Let go? And what, leave my beautiful home? Now that I'm just starting to have fun?! I just became able to manifest again!"

The cat ceased grooming and fixed her glowing eyes on James; the previous mild interest transformed into a focused stare.

Maria's voice wavered, yet she stepped forward, placing a reassuring hand on James's shoulder. "Greta, don't you want to rejoin your parents? Staying here must be lonely."

That was, apparently, the wrong thing to say, because the girl's expression twisted, hate overtaking her features. "My parents?! If it wasn't for them, I would still be alive! Nothing would have happened if they had just listened to me when I told them to give me the money!"

By the end, she was screaming, the entire house shaking. For a moment, the apparition of Greta seemed to waver, becoming translucent, before gaining solidity once again.

Having felt another of the flickers, James turned his gaze to the walls, and his theory strengthened further. There was something weird about the whole house that went beyond it being a dungeon.

"It wasn't your parents who killed you, Greta," Ezekiel interjected, sounding incensed. "The gang members who hurt you are dead, and this place is a danger to all your neighbors. You need to let go."

The ghost girl laughed, but it lacked her previous mirth. It sounded hollow, defeated even. "Let go? There is nothing for me. Nothing but the cold, eternal dark. At least here, I am remembered. At least here, I am something."

"Ah! I think I get it now," James interrupted, running a hand over the wallpaper. Everyone turned to face him, and he smiled, feeling like a sitcom detective at the end of an episode, as he was about to reveal the real murderer.

"You see, it's true that Greta was killed here. Even more surprising, this is actually the real her," he said, gesturing to the spectral entity.

"Initially, I believed it might be an illusionist playing tricks on us, trying to scare us away so they'd keep the dungeon for themselves. But now that I met her, I'm convinced there's no conscious trickery on her part."

Daniel, the most observant of the group, had a look of realization at his careful choice of words, but he kept his silence, letting him have the big reveal for himself.

"That fateful night, when her family was attacked, Greta Awakened," he revealed, and the others finally understood where he was going. James continued with his explanation, however, because the real audience wasn't his team. "The wounds they inflicted on her were simply too much, and it should have killed her. That was, if her Talent couldn't sustain her life outside of her body."

Now shedding the appearance of explaining to the whole group and facing only the spectral girl, he concluded, "That night, you used your newfound powers to transfer your consciousness into the building itself. A unique variation of Druid or Psychic if you ask me."

The girl was shaking her head in disbelief, unprepared to accept the truth. "No, they killed me! You have no idea what the cold, lonely dark was like for all these years. I just gained back my mind!"

James smiled. The last tassel fit in perfectly. "That's exactly what makes me think you didn't truly die that day. Spirits aren't creatures known to wait for so long. They're flighty and unpredictable. They wouldn't have waited here for someone to explain what happened after their death."

"The Sink gave her enough ambient mana to recover beyond what was needed to sustain herself," Ezekiel realized.

Instead of soothing Greta, the knowledge seemed to ignite a fiery turmoil within her. Her transparent eyes glowed fiercely, emanating an eerie light as the surroundings darkened.

"No, I don't believe you!" Greta's voice turned shrill, echoing through the dilapidated house. "This is my place, my sanctuary of remembrance! You won't erase me!"

As Greta's spectral form convulsed with denial and anguish, Miss Dalloway stood up, a low growl building up in her throat.

Although Miss Dalloway was the size of a house cat, the will within her blazed fiercely, and James took up a stance, expression grim as he prepared to fight.

He had hoped it would be unnecessary, but the poor girl seemed too far gone. Greta was beyond consoling. Her wails intensified, and the house itself seemed to groan and shudder under the weight of her anguish. The furniture rattled, windows cracked, and an oppressive force descended upon the room.

They were left with no choice.

Daniel's shield blazed with light as he took up his position, intercepting a lunge from Miss Dalloway, which made him grunt.

The cat, undeterred, bounced off it and tried another attack vector, making for James. Flooding mana into his system, he met her charge with one of his own, bowling the beast over but not seriously injuring her.

A blazing hot fireball passed over his head, aimed at taking Greta out of the fight entirely.

Unfortunately, it passed through her as if she were an illusion. But when it touched the wall behind her, scorching it entirely and blowing a hole in it, she wailed in pain.

When Maria saw her fireball's effect on the girl through the wall's destruction, her eyes sharpened in realization, and she quickly shared her insight. "Her consciousness is bound to the house! Damaging the structure hurts her!"

Simultaneously, Ezekiel's hands glowed with his buffing spell, granting all his teammates much-needed agility, which allowed them to move better in the cramped room.

In the midst of their offensive, the team neglected to account for Miss Dalloway, who, despite her diminutive feline form, erupted with a spectral roar that rippled through the room. Translucent tendrils of energy lashed out from the beast, raking across Daniel's shield with surprising ferocity, causing him to stagger back, his protective energies flickering.

Before the cat could continue her assault, James was on her. "Destroy the house!" he yelled, avoiding a spectral tendril and catching the beast midair with an enhanced kick, shooting her through the broken door and into the hallway.

While his teammates did their best to demolish the building, James grappled with the boss, exchanging a flurry of blows and sending her flying down the stairs.

He stopped at the top, looking at where Miss Dalloway was painfully picking herself up, and decided to end the fight as quickly as possible.

The wails and sounds of things breaking continued in the background, and he really needed to get back to his friends.

He moved back two steps and charged his legs. With a grunt, he took off, jumping off the staircase and closing the distance, falling like an angry meteor on the tawny cat.

For just a moment, James saw her pupils dilate as she watched the approaching death before she condensed her spectral limbs into a shield.

Unfortunately for her, they didn't do nearly enough to save her.

James released fifty mana points' worth of power through his feet, blowing away Miss Dalloway's protections. Unfortunately, the cat's vitality stat wasn't sufficient to survive the blow. His foot pulped her, crushing the beast against the floor, which broke apart.

The force of the explosion made it look like a bomb had gone off in the living room. More than half of the wooden planks had been blown off, cluttering the remaining space.

James spared one last look at the loyal beast, which looked very little like anything now, and climbed out of the hole he had made. He ran up the stairs and reentered the last room.

The walls around it had been blown away, the cause evident as he watched Daniel pull himself out of the crumbled remains of one.

Lauren and Ezekiel were active trying to hem Greta's flickering image, keeping her busy as she threw furniture at them. It only added to the confusion as they danced around the projectiles.

Maria, meanwhile, was holding a marble-sized orb of fire between her hands, looking very proud of herself. "I can blow this bitch up whenever we want," she said once she saw him panting with effort.

James sighed, used to her pyromaniacal tendencies, and yelled, "Let's jump out—Maria's gonna burn it down!"

He received grunts of confirmation, and the others moved to the edge, where the walls used to be. Then they launched themselves out to the ash-filled garden, an acrobatic display made trivial by their enhanced stats and Ezekiel's buff.

Once the other three were out, James grabbed Maria by the waist, hoisted her over his right shoulder like a sack of potatoes, and made to jump.

Greta's scream reached him just as his feet left the floor. "Cowards! Run away before I kill you all!"

Any ensuing profanity was drowned out by the sound of Maria's spell going off.

James barely had the time to soften the landing, shift Maria to the front, and shield his back with mana when the wave of fire reached him.

CHAPTER FORTY-NINE

Little of the house's top floor remained from the conflagration. That, in turn, led to the collapse of the foundation, and the whole thing came tumbling down, raising a large dust cloud.

Through Maria's intervention, once she had picked herself up from where she and James had rolled to, the fires were swiftly contained. It took her several minutes to extinguish them, but the mere fact she was able to do so was evidence of her massive growth.

When she had first joined the team, she had barely been able to conjure a dozen fireballs. Now, she could control an entire house fire, though with a lot of effort.

"I have the notification. We got her," Ezekiel said from where he lay sprawled on the ground, looking at the collapsed dungeon.

James hummed in agreement, pulling up his own. As expected, an alert told him he had killed [Greta Winchester - Tormented Human], which confirmed his theory. The girl hadn't died in the technical sense. Her mind had jumped from her body to what she was most familiar with—her home—when she Awakened her Talent.

Unfortunately, after years of being alone by herself after the brutal murder of her parents and her own suffering, she had been too far gone.

Her death, coupled with the death of the boss—a [Mutated House Cat - Haunted Guardian]—pushed James up two levels, bringing the total from the dungeon up to three.

After the first few fights, he had been afraid he might only get one, but the last two enemies had been much beefier than expected, and he had defeated the boss by himself.

The creature had been limited by the small environment and massive size difference, making it easier for him to leverage his stats, but James decided to pat himself on the back for once.

He had grown a lot too, and his victory was proof that he was on the right path. *It will take a while before I'm ready to tackle the Radiant Guild, but I'm starting to see the light at the end of the tunnel.*

"Poor girl, she really was given a bad hand by life," Daniel mourned, saddened by the loss of life. James couldn't help but agree. For all that they hadn't had a choice, given how deranged Greta had been and the consequences of leaving the dungeon uncleared for much longer, it still was a pity that they couldn't have reasoned with her.

"Bah, she was given a second chance and instead spent it wallowing in self-pity and despair. You heard what she said about her parents. That girl was a lost cause," Lauren spat, disgusted.

The Italian American girl was known for never holding back, but this instance seemed more personal. James cocked an eyebrow at her, silently asking if she wanted to expand, but she just grunted, turning to look at the collapsed house.

"You! I told you not to go in! And look what you did! My poor roses are covered in dust! Covered!" a familiar voice yelled, and they turned to see the old lady who warned them of the tragedy before they went in. She looked absolutely incensed.

"Ah, fuck."

After a long conversation with the crotchety woman, which ended with them handing over a crisp hundred-dollar bill to finally get some peace, the members of Team 0 had to spend a good part of the afternoon sifting through the rubble to find the monster bodies, so they could collect the mana stones.

Despite how much James would have liked to just leave the place behind, gathering them up was not done simply because of their monetary value.

If not properly handled, that concentration of mana could result in another dungeon spawning, which would be a red mark on their file.

It took them longer than they would have liked, but they still completed the task within the day, and after a quick briefing at the AA HQ, where they showered and changed, they were let go, with strict orders from Miss Walker to take the next day off.

As was often the case, James had taken the metro back to Brooklyn alongside Lauren. Ezekiel, who lived close to him, had been picked up by his older brother to go to a family dinner, leaving the two of them alone.

Usually, the Rogue wasn't one for long silences, but she had been uncharacteristically quiet for a while, and James had a strong suspicion as to what might have caused such a mood.

Wary of being too direct, as he knew how touchy she could be, James decided that he could at least try to get her mind off whatever it was that had brought her so down.

"That dungeon was so creepy and disgusting," he casually commented, observing Lauren's will fluctuations with great care. "A drink might be needed tonight. What do you think?"

She gave him a side look, not fooled by his act, but after a moment of silence, she sighed. "All right, let's do this. It's better than going home, anyway."

That decided, they got off at Brighton Beach station, the closest metro station to One Eleven, a beautiful and stylish bar close to Manhattan Beach.

The cool night air ruffled their hair as they silently walked through Brighton Beach Avenue, enjoying the moment of quiet.

Sounds of music and laughter became more prevalent as they got closer to the bar, heightened further by their enhanced senses.

By the time they got there, the place was almost packed, with dozens of young adults trying to enjoy their night, drinking their problems away to the tune of some good music.

"I always get the coconut piña colada," James admitted, getting a snort from Lauren.

"Yeah, you're the type to go for fruity drinks, aren't you?" she shot back, a grin worming its way on her face.

James rolled his eyes, playing along with the banter. "Well, my palate is sophisticated enough to appreciate the finer things in life. I don't see why I would have to suffer drinking some of that swill people pass off as alcohol. No whiskey for me, thank you."

She chuckled, and the atmosphere lightened as they slid into a cozy booth in the corner, away from the thick of the crowd but close enough to absorb the lively energy of the room.

Their server, a somewhat harried girl their age with frizzy hair and a bandana, stopped before their table, eyes silently begging them to be quick with their order. She barely remembered to check for ID, and her eyes widened like saucers when she saw the AA-issued ones. That alone was enough to be allowed alcohol.

"Two coconut piña coladas," James decided for the both of them, earning him a slap on the arm from Lauren.

She spoke up, "Don't listen to this idiot. Make mine a whiskey sour, please."

The server offered them a tight smile, thankful for the straightforward order, and disappeared into the throng of people.

Lauren's eyebrows quirked in mischief. "Sophisticated palate, huh?"

James smirked. "Impeccably so."

The playful conversation cracked the veneer of Lauren's icy mood, but James could still see the shadows in her eyes, the lingering ghosts of whatever had rattled her earlier.

He leaned back, sipping his drink when it arrived, and allowed the music to fill the silence, giving her the space she needed. He didn't want to push her immediately, as that would simply see her clamming up again, but he'd gladly listen to her woes if she wanted to open up.

For just a moment, it looked like she might crack and speak up, but she took a fortifying sip of her drink instead. The moment passed with her jaw clenching.

James sighed but decided he would at least let her have a relaxing night. If she ever wanted to confide in him, he'd be there for her, but now didn't seem the right time.

"Any thoughts on what you'll go for during your second Awakening?" he asked, rousing her back from her mood.

Lauren hummed, "It really depends on what options I get. I know it's going to be more stealth based, but I'd really like to get some range. It's been really annoying having to hold back when enemies had skills that made mine useless. I need some variety to avoid being countered so easily, but I guess that's the same for everyone."

James nodded along, knowing perfectly well what she was talking about. He had only recently developed a way to attack without resorting to close combat. Still, since it wasn't a skill, it was inefficient and too intensive to use as anything but a finishing move.

"Well, basically all Talents gain some more versatile skills during the second Awakening, right?" He got a nod of agreement. "So we should only have a little while to go for that, if we can keep up with our growth rate."

"If only we could find a few more dungeons filled with eggs." She laughed, shaking her head. "That would push us to F-rank in a flash."

"It would make things easier, yes," James agreed, smiling. Their luck had been a mix of rotten and amazing, with very little in-between, which made him hope that despite all the obstacles they had to face, they would at least be met with a few more lucky breaks in the future.

"What about you?" she asked, propping her chin on her hands.

James hummed, "I think some range would be good for me too, yes, maybe being able to use my skills on weapons . . . Most of all, I'm just genuinely curious about what the System will offer me. With all the crazy things we've been through, we should get some good rewards."

Especially after meeting the Sin of Pride. If surviving that encounter doesn't count, I don't know what will.

However, he didn't voice those thoughts, choosing to swirl his drink and take a sip. He enjoyed the coconut flavor. The alcohol content wasn't enough for him to get drunk, what with his vitality stat being twice as high as an athlete's, but that didn't mean that drinking didn't serve its purpose as a social lubricant.

"Frankly, I'd be surprised if—" He stopped midsentence as several presences, strong enough to be Awakeners, entered the bar. Casually turning around to look, he immediately confirmed his suspicions.

He recognized one from Callum Wright's group among the five who had walked in. He didn't know the guy's name—he wasn't sure he had ever heard him talk—but he had been present at the confrontation at the rat dungeon's entrance, which made him an asshole in James's book.

He sat back and lowered his voice, making sure not to be overheard in the din of chaos around them. "At least one Radiant Guild guy, thirty feet behind me. The bald one."

Lauren's mouth tightened, and for a moment, it looked like she was about to get up and do something about it, but luckily her common sense won and she relaxed back in the booth. "He's G-rank, isn't he?"

James nodded grimly. "Yeah, and he feels like it. The people with him, too, are around that level."

"So we can't do shit."

"We can't do shit," he agreed. Despite all that, however, he wasn't discouraged. Sensory skills, especially before the second Awakening, were quite rare and he doubted the Radiant goons would have one. Especially one sophisticated enough to recognize the two of them.

"Do you wanna go now?" Lauren asked, evidently thinking the night had been ruined, but James smiled back impishly.

"We're already here, and I can overhear some of what they are saying. What do you think of staying a bit longer to see if they drop something interesting?"

The Rogue shrugged, apparently okay with his plan. She stood up and walked to his side of the booth, sitting beside him despite how tight the space was.

"What? I wanna listen too," she said, grinning.

Fortunately, their curiosity was satisfied soon after.

CHAPTER FIFTY

So I don't know how long we can go on like this. I told the boss we needed to accept Ten Thousand Eyes' offer, but he seemed reluctant. I think he might still be hoping for the executives to get out of jail, but from what I heard, there's little chance of that happening."

James and Lauren shared a look before they resumed their eavesdropping. They were sitting quite close to each other, looking no different than any other amorous couple in the establishment. Since their faces weren't visible, they could overhear the Radiant members talking with impunity.

They really are dumb. Who even talks about this kind of stuff out in the open? Well, I guess things have been going their way for so long that they got sloppy.

"Bah, we all know that the government was salivating at the thought of finally getting their hands on one of the major guilds," one of the others scoffed, taking a long sip of his beer. "They're not going to let go of the very first win they got in years."

A round of mumbled agreement followed and James nodded as well. Even without Golden Sun getting caught red-handed, they still wouldn't have an easy time getting out of the mess they were in.

When the first raid occurred, after the falsified crocodile dungeon, they must have thought they were untouchable since nothing happened to them. That was why they had fallen into the AA's trap.

"The boss is probably still in contact with some of them. He can't just give up," the thug, the one he recognized, said.

"Yeah, but this way, we'll just be swallowed up. Our guild's been legally set free, but we don't have the resources by ourselves to hold our territory, and the sharks are circling," the first one answered.

It was difficult to picture what the speaker looked like, but from his voice alone, the man sounded older and more experienced than the twenty-something-year-olds that made up Callum's group.

"If nothing big happens within the next few weeks, we'll have to make a choice," the same man continued, sounding like he very much didn't want to.

To be part of the Radiant Guild, one had to be a talented Awakener, which meant he shouldn't be underestimated, but his age stood out. He might have recently received the System, but he causally spoke of "telling the boss" things like he was more experienced.

A third member of the group, previously silent, spoke with a calm, calculating tone. "Look, we either ally with Ten Thousand Eyes and salvage what we can, or we go down in flames. It's survival versus principle here. I don't know about you, but I'm not about to give up all we achieved because I'm too proud."

Tense silence lingered among them before the thug he recognized mumbled, "I didn't sign up to be a martyr. If allying with Ten Thousand Eyes gives us some breathing room so that we can reorganize, I'll take it."

The older man agreed, "As distasteful as it is, I'm with him. We can't just hold on by ourselves, and I doubt Golden Sun is going to send anyone to help us. You've seen what Eclipse is doing anyway."

"Pah! Those bastards are selling themselves to the highest bidder just because they have better territory. It won't be long before they've all been divided and conquered by the larger guilds, stripped of all the dignity they once had," the third member spat, bitterness seeping through every word.

It seemed to James that not everything was as easy as it appeared between the guilds. They usually presented a united front when speaking with the AA or the public, but everyone knew they must have had a cutthroat game of give and take behind the scenes. Now he had confirmation.

The older man's voice rose slightly. "I'd rather not throw in with the Eyes. We all know what they're capable of after Buffalo, but if it's between that and losing everything, then what choice do we really have?"

The sounds of clinking glasses and muffled chatter from other patrons continued to fill the room, creating a semblance of normalcy in stark contrast to the gravity of the conversation being held.

The clandestine information gathering was soon interrupted as a tall, enigmatic figure approached the Radiant members. To James, the figure felt like a distant storm, its might restrained but ready to be unleashed.

This person is dangerous.

He gripped Lauren's hand beneath the table, his eyes communicating that someone new had arrived. She didn't miss a beat, lifting her hand to caress his cheek and bringing her head next to his.

"What's going on?" she murmured against his skin, giving the impression of a young couple incapable of keeping their hands to themselves.

"Tall guy who just entered. He's strong," James replied, barely audible even at the distance they were at. He couldn't afford to risk being overheard by the man, who must have a very high sense attribute—given his impression, the man must be at least D-rank.

"You're discussing sensitive matters in an open space," the man admonished, his voice as cold as ice.

Panic, palpable and raw, wafted from the Radiant members as they scrambled to their feet, hastily vacating the premises under the stern gaze of their superior.

Silence had fallen in the bar, as everyone understood they had a powerful

Awakener in their midst. The man grunted, taking out ten crisp hundred-dollar bills and placing them on the table his subordinates had just left.

"For the commotion," he said, nodding to the trembling server, who let out an "Eep!"

Then, he turned around and left, probably to follow his men.

Lauren's eyes gleamed with a mix of excitement and caution. "Do you think that's . . . ?"

James nodded subtly, his eyes still on the door where the tall man had exited. "Must be. I didn't think we'd see the leader of the Radiant Guild tonight."

They waited a few more minutes, ensuring the dangerous aura had indeed left the vicinity before they, too, left the safety of their hidden observation spot. The two appeared just like any other couple exiting the pub after a cozy evening.

The chilly air bit at them as they stepped into the darkness, but it was a welcome contrast to the tense atmosphere they had just left.

"They're backed into a corner," she murmured low enough that only James could hear. "People become either the most dangerous or the most cooperative when they're desperate."

James's jaw clenched, mulling over the same thoughts. He had a personal grudge with the Radiant Guild, but even he could admit to a certain level of competency in the way they operated. Not in how they protected the people, no. But their illicit dealings were covered up well enough that even during the sweep of their parent organization, they weren't touched beyond losing a few people.

That said, they couldn't possibly operate in the same manner as they used to before. Golden Sun wasn't directly involved with their day-to-day operations, but they offered an umbrella of protection from scrutiny. Their presence prevented any other major guild from setting its sights on their territory.

"Should we have followed them?" Lauren asked, worriedly looking toward Coney Island Avenue, where the guild members had disappeared.

James shook his head. "We were lucky enough that they arrived after us and that our position made it difficult to see us. If we tried to follow them, they'd find us out immediately."

She grimaced, bothered that they had to let go of such an interesting source of information. "And the big guy had to be a high-ranker, right?"

He nodded. "D-rank, at least. Most of their members are G-ranks, but they also have a few E-ranks. Since he's probably the boss, I'd say minimum D-rank."

Silence hung between them as they contemplated their next move. I sincerely doubt the AA doesn't already know of this, but they must have decided to let go of the smaller fish to get the big guys.

Thinking back to his conversation with Miss Walker, James decided that even if he went to her with this information, there wasn't much she could or would do by herself.

It wasn't like guilds were forbidden from buying out smaller ones, and though the Awakeners had spoken of sensitive subjects, they hadn't outright admitted to anything illegal, thanks to the timely arrival of their superior.

Lauren brushed a strand of hair out of her face. "We need to do something. The Radiant Guild coming under Ten Thousand Eyes would reshape the city's underground, and if we allow them to go scot-free, we'll never get rid of them."

James nodded, fingers tapping rhythmically against his thigh. "In a way, this is the best option. If they refuse to submit and choose to hold their ground, the inevitable conflict that'd ensue will tear apart the neighborhoods under their control, not to mention the number of civilians that might get caught in the crossfire."

"A gang war," Lauren murmured in realization.

James nodded grimly. While the individual power of the Radiant Guild wasn't enough to make too much of a mess before the AA fell on their heads like a brick, they could still make life difficult for regular people.

"So we cut off the head of the hydra, and there's already another ready to take its place," Lauren commented bitterly.

"The Ten Thousand Eyes Guild is relatively stable, has taken part in many operations to reclaim territory from monsters, and has never had public scandals." James read off from his phone. The guilds' wiki pages weren't to be taken word for word, as they were subject to censure and influence, but they reflected the general public's opinion.

"So if Radiant goes under them, it'll be even harder than it is now to get rid of them completely," Lauren concluded.

He hummed, thinking of all the possibilities they had. "The real question here is exactly that. Can we afford to wait for them to go under a new patron?"

"You want to take them down now," she stated, sounding halfway between surprised and amused. After all, he hadn't tried to hide his contempt for the Radiant Guild.

"I would very much like that, but we need to find a way that doesn't involve us facing the boss," James answered. Already, Callum and his goons would be a stretch. Adding the powerful Awakener they had seen tonight . . . It just wouldn't be possible.

But if we allow them to go scot-free now, they'll simply continue what they are doing. I don't care if they weren't directly involved with Golden Sun's illegal operations; I know they're crooks.

"We don't have that much time. A month at most, before they crack under the pressure," Lauren added, tapping a finger on her lips.

The fact that she hadn't tried to push him away from his harebrained idea made James smile. He had made some very good friends.

"A month . . . I think we can make it in a month. Getting to G-rank shouldn't be too hard if we do double the dives every week, and once we have the stats, I sincerely doubt any of them could match us," he said, already thinking of how to convince the others and, more importantly, Miss Walker, to push so hard.

"Yes, we can get to G-rank. But what about your little F-rank friend? And the boss? An Awakening tier is a different thing entirely from a few levels." Lauren brought up the biggest obstacle.

James, however, smiled like a cat that got the canary. "I have no intention of fighting the boss directly. But we don't need to do that, do we? We just have to push the last card, and the whole castle will come crashing down."

CHAPTER FIFTY-ONE

Lying down on his bed, James watched the filtered sunlight dance between his fingers. Since it was a rest day, he would get scolded if he went to the HQ to get some training in, but after his declaration the night before, it felt weird to spend the day lazing around.

He tried to play some games like he used to before he Awakened, but his attention kept drifting away. His reaction time was miles ahead of what it had once been, and the excitement from gunning monsters down was gone after fighting them in real life.

He considered texting his friends, both old and new, but he was gripped by a nervous energy that wouldn't allow him to simply spend the day enjoying himself.

Therefore, he ended up turning to one of his other habits: sleuthing through forums dedicated to Awakeners in the hopes of getting some inspiration for his own path.

He had already memorized most guides that could apply to him, which was a lot, considering how his Talent seemed to be the amalgamation of several more common ones. Still, there was always the hope that someone would post something interesting.

One thread in particular captured his attention. Antares was a website known for its extraordinarily long and rambling discussions where field experts mixed with complete noobs to discuss the most inane things, but once in a while, something interesting came up.

One specific thread about the "willpower projection capacities in high-rankers" sounded very much like what he was doing. He was initially disappointed to discover that it was simply a fancy way of saying "aura," but he stuck around out of curiosity, which paid off.

A certain Dr. Robert M. Mulliger had published a paper on the subject, positing that it wasn't so much that people suddenly gained a new power after their third Awakening, when they gained the ability to impose their aura upon weaker beings, but rather that it was a new expression of the power they always had.

That paper went unremarked for months until an Antares user named StarryEyes found it and wrote a thread on it, speculating that Dr. Mulliger's conclusions meant that all Talents were simply an actualization of a person's natural inclinations. Not that a person's character might influence their Talent, but that humans always had the capability for it, which finally manifested when mana arrived on Earth.

Such an absolute statement, without any solid proof, obviously brought a lot of ridicule and rage, with many other users dismissing the whole thread as bait.

James, however, read between the lines and immediately sought out the original paper.

Dr. Mulliger's work was dense, filled with jargon and scientific methods that James barely grasped, but he scoured through the files with great interest. If it could ever be proven, it meant that the potential for supernatural power had always existed in humanity and that the existence of mana had brought it out, only to be co-opted by the System. Not that the System itself had gifted the Talents to humans.

It had profound implications, both for the present and future, but until proof was found, it would simply remain an interesting bit of speculation. Still, a few questions lingered.

What if all Talents were, StarryEyes speculated, inherently capable of affecting the outside world because the user's will could only be expressed in a specific way? Or, even if that definition didn't exactly fit everyone, could it still be applied to him, given his unique power?

A reply from user ShadowWalker was at the top of the thread because it mentioned a "rumored" underground lab that was trying to create Awakeners synthetically, bypassing the System somehow. Many scoffed at the comment, and it received a flurry of downvotes, with the users branding it as a ridiculous conspiracy theory.

It was absurd, James knew, but something about one of the replies made him pause.

Antares had a verification process for its users—if they wanted to tie their real identity to their profile, they could, though it wasn't commonly done since the beauty of Antares was the anonymity. For Awakeners who got verified, they could release official statements.

Not many did so, preferring to leave all PR-related matters to their guild, or the AA. Still, some liked the notoriety that came from interacting with the general public, especially if they had a high enough rank.

ShadowWalker wasn't verified as an Awakener. But someone else who replied to them had.

Ember—a widely recognized name among those who paid attention to the news—was a high-ranking independent Awakener whom guilds often approached for recruitment, but he steadfastly maintained a solitary stance. He was known to operate in the Atlanta metro area, taking care of dangerous dungeons that the guilds left fallow.

* * *

Ember, with his glowing orange verification checkmark, had responded to ShadowWalker: *Opposite direction. It's not humans who are fucking with the System.*

This short and cryptic message sent shivers down James's spine. It was obviously meant to debunk the conspiracy theory, but it had a galvanizing effect, spawning an entirely different thread, which was shortly locked down by the moderators. Dozens of users took it to mean that something shady was going on.

Ember didn't respond, his profile showing that he hadn't accessed the site since the comment, but the absence only made people more curious.

Could the System be experimenting with humans? Was the government extracting powers from Awakeners to give them to others? It was impossible to know, but speculation abounded.

Wait, does this mean what I think it means? Is he saying that the System is the bad guy here?

It sounded . . . farfetched. Without it, there was little doubt humanity would have fallen. But Ember was not someone to spout nonsense.

Closing his computer, James sighed. He didn't learn much from the rabbit hole he had fallen into, but at least he got a few ideas to try out.

While it was impossible to gain skills beyond those granted by the System during an Awakening, one could still get better at and find new ways to operate them.

Just like what Mr. Bethany had told them about attributes, skills could also benefit from dedicated training beyond simple usage. His Talent was peculiar, but if it truly was a pure manifestation of his willpower, as the name suggested, and not just a straight enhancement type, then perhaps there was more he could draw from it with proper understanding and experimentation. He thought of what high-rankers did with their own aura.

The similarities were obvious. He had a skill made exactly to counter the suppression, after all. That meant that he could draw inspiration from the greats.

Thinking back to the most egregious examples, James looked at the poster above his desk. Towers, the Son of War, was an S-rank Awakener known to be among the world's most powerful.

Videos of him mowing through mobs of powerful enemies received dozens of millions of views online, and James had watched a few enough times to be able to replay them in his mind.

Towers's tactics were simple enough, at first glance. He used his overwhelming physique to bulldoze through the crowds, and from there, it was a slugfest as he swung his enormous warhammer to significant effect.

The strength of his blows was such that even powerful A-rank monsters were pulverized, turned into a fine red mist by the passage of his mighty weapon.

But at times, when he was needed elsewhere or when one of his companions required his help, he'd unleash a wave of power that washed over his enemies and broke their minds.

It was aura in its finest form. An attack so raw and intense that nothing could withstand it. But more than that, he could selectively prevent his companions from being hit.

That was what James was interested in. That level of control was absurd if one considered aura a simple AOE skill.

Not even great mages like the White Crane could boast such precision. That meant aura was something else entirely. A power closer to what he was doing than an extension of specific Talents.

If Thakinesis operates the same way that aura does . . . It should mean I have a much, much higher ceiling for control and versatility.

In a way, he had already confirmed it. His exploding blows, where he'd push significant amounts of mana into his limbs and release it all at once, were not something normal Warrior-type Talents could accomplish.

His Talent was meant to be limited to close range, at least before his second Awakening, but he had bypassed that entirely. And to continue breaking down the preconceived ceiling of his abilities, James had to look beyond the established wisdom.

Was mana simply the method through which his inherent ability manifested? Had humanity been like a man who thought himself blind, only to realize that he had been living in darkness?

James extended his arm, fingers splayed wide, focusing on the air around him. He attempted to mold it, not with the physical application of his power, but with sheer intent. Nothing happened.

He frowned, concentration knitting his eyebrows.

Again, he tried. He willed strength to flood his limbs without directly moving his mana. But even the simplest, most basic application of his power escaped him. His frustration grew, but then, from the depths of his vexation, a thought nudged at him.

Aura, Thakinesis, all the powers Awakeners wielded . . . they weren't physical. They didn't operate under the same laws that ruled over physics and chemistry. No, they were both less and more; a mingling of the tangible and intangible, bridging the corporeal world and something else.

Perhaps James had been thinking of his power in too much of a linear, physical way—that is, as a mere manipulation of forces or energy. But if Dr. Mulliger's paper held any water, and if there was any truth in the speculations of StarryEyes and even in the cryptic statement of Ember, then maybe Talents were truly more about will made manifest rather than a set system of rules dictated by the physical world or the System.

He thought about how Towers would let his aura flare—it was never with strain or physical effort but with resolve, a potent, indomitable spirit that refused to be quelled. This overwhelming force wasn't simply energy exerted but an expression, a declaration of his will forcing everything in the vicinity he considered an enemy to bend to it.

Closing his eyes, James didn't try to move the mana in his veins or attempt to physically manipulate anything with his mind. Instead, he gathered his thoughts, resolve, and will, focusing them into a single point of undeniable intention.

The room remained silent, undisturbed, yet something within him shifted. His thoughts didn't scatter as they usually would have. They remained steadfast as his firm purpose let him stay on track.

He opened his eyes and stared at his outstretched hand. There was no visible change, no tangible evidence of any progress. But something in the air seemed different. It was as if, for a fleeting moment, the world around him had paused, acknowledging his will before moving on. His hand felt a tiny bit stronger for a second, but looking at his status showed no mana had been used.

This wasn't a breakthrough in the traditional sense. James hadn't unlocked a new power or discovered a hidden application of his existing one. But in that moment, he'd glimpsed something beyond the structured, regimented logic of the System.

A sensation lingered, a minuscule touch on the edge of his awareness. James had tapped into something great, and though he couldn't draw from it yet, at least not in a manner that could be useful in real life, the knowledge of its existence filled him with a calm and determined hope.

James had little doubt that his selections for the next Awakening would be affected significantly by the discovery.

CHAPTER 51.5 – INTERLUDE

Alfred Meyer

So, just to make sure I understood right, you want to send your team of rookies, the same team that somehow managed to get themselves into trouble at every dungeon, into one of the few stable H-rank ones we have. And you want to keep them there for weeks, so they can farm experience and return as G-ranks," Alfred Meyer, the regional director, said as he massaged his temples, looking at Leila in askance.

"And!" he continued, raising a finger to silence her rebuttal. "You're requesting this knowing that they'll attempt to bait the Radiant Guild into attacking them once they come back, so that we have an excuse to completely remove them from play. Do I have that right?"

Leila huffed, amused at her kids' sheer balls and the fact that she was going along with it. "Yes, that's about what I'm asking. I know that stable dungeons are pretty rare, especially massive H-rank ones like the one in Saratoga Springs. But we've invested so much into Team 0—it would be a waste to allow them to be crushed now."

The *thunk* that Alfred's head made against his desk was loud and expressive. "Then why are you allowing them to go against the Radiant Guild at all?" he mumbled.

"Somehow, they got into their heads that since it managed to avoid scrutiny during the Golden Sun debacle, the higher-ups consider it to be beneath their notice, and so they have to take things into their hands," Leila answered, tone deliberately casual.

From the glare the balding man gave her, it didn't seem to have worked.

"Let's dispense of this mummery," he finally said, sitting back in his chair with a defeated sigh. "Do you think they actually have a chance at not getting killed? Are you trying to use them as bait to intervene yourself? You know we can't be too overt at the moment, as we're using so many of our resources to prevent other guilds from filling in the Golden Sun–shaped void."

Leila got comfortable on the leather chair. "All right, let's talk plainly. Alfred, I know you have a ton of things on your hands right now, but the kids aren't letting go of this one, and I think it might be an opportunity to do something about those thugs."

Alfred Meyer was many things: an Awakener, a retired marine, and someone who had once dreamed of making the world a more just and good place. He was very much aware of what idealism and recklessness could lead to, having lost many of his companions to them, but it was precisely because of that that he had something of a soft spot for the rookie team.

I could let them in. They've gotten to a level where they won't just die immediately, and I suppose it's worth speeding up their progress as much as possible, even if it would mean a decrease in revenue for a while . . . But I can't give in too easily.

"You do realize that Saratoga Springs' dungeon is one of the few money makers we have at the New York branch?" he asked, sounding more exasperated than he was truly feeling.

Leila nodded, her expression firm, not the slightest hint of wavering in her gaze. "Yes, I do. But Alfred, consider this—Team 0 has an untapped potential that's way beyond the economic losses we'd suffer from sending them into Saratoga Springs. They've shown themselves to be an important asset several times. Without their help, we wouldn't have been able to prepare the groundwork for taking down Golden Sun—and more than that, they've come out successful even in the toughest circumstances."

Alfred's fingers tapped against the desk, a contemplative rhythm that echoed in the otherwise silent room. "Leila," he began, his voice lined with sincerity, "I want the best for Team 0. And I'm worried. Their potential . . . they could do so much good, more than they understand. But I fear they may be too reckless and eager to throw themselves into danger. And it scares me that we might lose them too soon. It would be a terrible loss, not just in terms of the wasted resources, but because I'm so sure they'll be great in the future."

Leila leaned forward, expression softening. "They are kids, yes. But they're also Awakeners who had to face circumstances greatly beyond them. Any other guild team of the same rank wouldn't have made it as far as they have. They won't be alone in this, Alfred. I'll be with them every step of the way. I won't let them be snuffed out so easily."

Alfred looked into her eyes and found an unwavering resolve within them. He sighed, knowing that holding them back would be futile. "Fine, but Leila, you keep them in check, and you make sure that they all come back."

Alfred stood on the rooftop of his HQ, looking out over the expansive city. His thoughts were interrupted by soft footsteps behind him. When he turned, he saw Chief Director Harris approaching. The woman, tall and well built, almost towered over him.

"Alfred," the chief director greeted in her typical stoic manner.

"Director Harris," he responded, offering a nod.

The two stood side by side, staring into the vast, sprawling metropolis below them. Even at night, New York was busy, like a beehive ensuring it would survive the coming winter.

"Team 0 is going to Saratoga Springs," Harris said, her voice void of emotion yet carrying an undercurrent of inquiry.

"They are," Alfred admitted without hesitation. "They need to level up quickly, and they have a score to settle."

Harris nodded, her gaze never wavering from the view before her. "You know what's looming on the horizon, don't you, Alfred?"

He hummed, his grip on the railing tightened. He felt the steel bar give in. "If the Sins are moving, it means things are starting to happen. We knew it wouldn't be long before this peace we've won would be tainted, but I hoped it would be a little longer."

Harris turned toward Alfred, her eyes revealing a glimmer of the burden she bore. "The situation in Mexico has gotten worse. We expect that even the last few holdouts will be overrun soon enough. India's managed to regain a semblance of organization, but the loss of the northwest has weakened them. We can't count on them to play the policeman of Asia alone. And you know what mess China is in."

"So we need to open up again. But you know how opposed the general public is. Have you found a way to sell it?" Alfred asked, letting go of the crumpled fence. He watched it bounce near his feet with a blank expression.

"This isn't the kind of operation we can undertake without the public finding out. Despite how isolationist the world has become, news still travels very fast. The moment our boots touch the ground, everyone will know," Harris replied, sounding tired. "We need to gain the approval of Congress, and to do that, we need Americans to want it."

Alfred's jaw tightened at the notion. Gaining approval for an overseas operation, particularly in the fraught and fragile world in which they now existed, was an uphill battle. "I presume you have an idea on how to swing it? You're not one to walk into a storm without a plan."

Harris nodded slowly. Her eyes reflected the twinkling lights below. "We're still considering our options, since there's some time left before we have to step in, but our means are limited by the political will in DC."

He scoffed, annoyed even at the mention. "When are they ever useful? So, are you thinking of a propaganda campaign? Or directly allowing an attack on American soil?"

Despite the bubble of powerful wards surrounding them—they knew it'd prevent any recording or eavesdropping—Alfred saw the chief director's shoulders tense.

"Those are heavy words, Alfred," she murmured.

"I don't enjoy this. You know I don't, but things will get much worse if we don't start setting up now. We'll be next if we allow chaos to take over Asia," he answered just as softly.

"This is why I didn't want to take this job, you know? Why I thought you'd be much better at it than me," Harris wondered out loud, wistful for a peace she knew she'd never have.

Alfred scoffed, "I would've been terrible. I'm good at the cloak-and-dagger stuff, but put me in front of a bureaucrat I have to convince, and I'll find myself holding back from strangling them."

"Looking at us, one would think the exact opposite." She laughed, a new determination in her eyes. "You, the mild-mannered middle-aged man, and me, the fiery and burly warrior. But we're both the kind of creatures ready to do anything if it means the survival of America, aren't we?"

"This is very little compared to what we've already done and what we'll have to do." His words were cold but just as determined.

CHAPTER FIFTY-TWO

The AA local base was a far cry from the New York branch's polished and well-funded facilities. Closer to a miner's camp than a hub for Awakeners, it was distinctly pragmatic and work-focused.

Teams here were not draped in the latest gear or experimenting with newly developed magic. They were men and women, covered in dust and eyes weary, focused intently on the extraction process, their energies attuned more to the minerals than to the pursuit of ranks and recognition.

Awakeners of G-, F-, and E-ranks, often overshadowed by their more illustrious counterparts, found their niche in a system that prioritized economic growth over rank ascension. The local teams, while perhaps lacking the glamorous missions and dynamic adventures of their New York peers, were a tight-knit community bound by a shared understanding of their tangible and immediate needs over abstract, distant threats.

The Saratoga branch was one of the few local AA offices allowed to ignore dungeons surrounding their territory. Their mandate was one: to extract as much as possible from the herds of mineral horses without upsetting the dungeon's balance. They were dedicated to it.

The operation was highly lucrative, producing much more than a comparable mine with a much smaller crew. The peculiar stability of the dungeon, which had never once attempted to grow beyond its rank, also allowed them to have a secure, regular income.

These Awakeners were entirely different from those James had met in New York, but that didn't mean they were worse. No, if anything, James found them altogether pleasant.

If only the dungeon's environment was as nice . . .

The smell of sulfur was thick in the air, so much so that they were given masks to wear to prevent any possible problem from inhaling too much.

"Sure would have been nice to have this kind of equipment back in Montauk," Lauren grumbled, adjusting the straps beneath her hair.

They were in a private room at the AA provincial center, a room which they had been gracefully granted by the local director, a thirty-year-old man with dyed white hair and star-shaped contacts.

Despite his peculiar appearance, Emmanuel Branch turned out to be a competent Awakener, standing at C-rank—more than enough to handle anything the local dungeons could throw at him, unless something requiring special attention from the HQ came up. With an affinity for a unique branch of magic—the ability to control crystal—he had been given command over the extraction operations of the Saratoga mineral horse dungeon.

He didn't raise a fuss after being thrown out of his work site for an indefinite period. He even pointed out where Team 0 could get the equipment necessary to delve.

"I don't think we should expect this kind of organization anywhere else," Ezekiel responded, carefully regulating the tightness of his own mask, which muffled his voice. "This is more a commercial operation than a regular dungeon. It's crazy that they're even allowing us to use it without a strict time limit."

"That's because the higher-ups know we'll end up killing ourselves if we don't get a few more levels." James chuckled, completely unbothered. He had been the one to push Miss Walker the most, after all, directly stating that he would begin operations against the Radiant Guild anyway, and that if the AA wanted to prevent the waste of resources his death would cause, they'd better step up.

"You mean you'll get us all killed," Daniel grumbled, though James knew he wasn't particularly mad. They had discussed his and Lauren's findings the past couple of days and had ended up deciding together that asking for help from Miss Walker, at least in regards to the preparations to take on an entire guild, would be better than just pantsing the whole thing.

Their teacher had been initially reluctant to go along with their whims. But after a long conversation in which they impressed upon her their seriousness, she had come around and had promised she'd leverage her position with the director to wrangle some help from the AA.

She ended up delivering more than expected, granting them unlimited access to one of the most valuable low-rank dungeons the agency had.

James had been afraid they'd get a cold reception, having basically kicked out the local teams, but that wasn't the case. Director Branch had warmly welcomed them and explained that most of the Awakeners working under him were less interested in grinding and growing stronger and more dedicated to making money to support their families.

Team 0's arrival had made it so they couldn't access the dungeon, as it would be reserved for their own efforts, but their pledge to let the locals keep the majority of the minerals they'd get had been enough to quell any protest.

Yeah, I bet they don't mind having a few weeks of paid vacation. But at least this way we won't have to dance around other teams, and this dungeon is expansive enough that it's almost impossible for one team to clear in the time we have.

Despite the director basically giving them carte blanche, James was very aware that they had less than a month to move. Two weeks, if they wanted to be sure they'd have enough time to take Radiant out.

"Guys, here's the deal," he began once he was done dressing up. "This is quite different from our previous experiences, being in an entirely open field. We've all looked at the papers they gave us, but the important things to remember are to avoid the largest herds, attack quickly without too much noise, and leave the battlefield once we've confirmed the kills. We can get the materials out later since they won't degrade with time."

They all nodded, shoulders straightening. It was an unusual scenario for a dungeon dive. The objective wasn't to strike down every creature in sight but to strategize and ensure their actions did not disturb the delicate equilibrium maintained by the mineral horses.

The horses lived and roamed within vast crystal fields where there had once been open farmland. Their forms glistened with embedded gemstones and rare minerals.

The beasts themselves were magnificent, awe-inspiring creatures. They moved in herds, their coats glimmering under the sunlight, a mystical glow that seemed to defy natural explanation. Some grew horns, making them resemble unicorns from fairytales, while others had geometric patterns all over their bodies.

A soft haze permeated the dungeon, limiting their sight to a range of roughly two hundred feet, even with James's enhanced senses.

In a way, that makes it easier not to be swarmed, as other herds will have difficulty locating us, but I'll have to keep Awareness activated. I wouldn't want us to have to fight our way out of here, attracting more and more horses until we get overwhelmed.

Before leaving the team to their task, Director Branch led them to a vantage point, providing a sweeping view of the mineral-rich fields below.

His eyes, accentuated by the starry contacts, twinkled with a mix of respect and pragmatism as he gazed upon the herds. "See," he began, his voice enthusiastic about their adventure.

"The mineral horses, they're smart. They don't attack humans unless provoked, but once you disturb one, you disturb them all. A herd will move as one, and if they perceive you as a threat, they'll coordinate in a way that might surprise you. They manipulate the minerals in their bodies to create armor, spears, and even temporary shelters. That's why a thoughtful approach works best here."

Lauren observed keenly, her eyes flicking between the director and the serene yet somehow unsettling sight below. "So, how do the local teams manage to extract enough minerals without causing a stampede?"

Emmanuel smiled. "Precision and patience. We have folks who can read the creatures, predict their paths. We isolate the herd we've chosen to take, ensuring they're far enough from others that interference is impossible, and take them down fast. We also never take too much at once, as they can feel the balance be upset and start roaming in much larger groups. It takes weeks for them to settle."

"Seems like a risky operation. We're here to power-level, basically . . . Won't that lead to us upsetting the balance?" Daniel asked, narrowing his eyes at a particularly large stallion, its mane a cascade of rubies and obsidian, moving grace-fully among its kin.

The director turned to him, his expression somewhat inscrutable, before a soft sigh escaped his lips. "You all are the anomaly in a system that works, but your need outweighs the risk. If what you're doing wasn't deemed vital, do you think they'd let a team of rookies play in one of the AA's most profitable dungeons?"

He paused, letting the rhetorical question hang in the air. "We understand you're not here for profit, but while you're in Saratoga, respect the balance we've built with these creatures, respect the land, and try not to wreak havoc on our livelihood."

Emmanuel bade them farewell after a few more words of advice and caution-ary tales about prior incidents, leaving Team 0 to gaze out at the vast gleaming expanse.

The fog gave the whole dungeon an otherworldly feeling, as the filtered sun shined down on the crystalline growths, making them reflect the light in myriad colors.

James observed the closest herd, deciding they would be good enough for a first attempt. "The only monster I'm worried about here is the red stallion. If we can take it down immediately after surrounding them, we can finish this quickly."

Lauren nodded as she took her gleaming knives out of their sheaths. "With the fog useless thanks to our masks, I can probably do a lot of damage without being noticed. It should mesh very well with my skills, and I'm pretty curious about how much EXP they'll give us, considering how smug Miss Walker was when she sent us here."

Daniel snorted, picking up his shield and walking down the hill. "If we want to make a dent in the absurd amount of experience we'll need to get to G-rank, we should start soon. I don't know about you guys, but I still would like to sleep in a bed rather than out here in the fields."

Entering the fog for the first time, James was grateful for the generosity of the Saratoga branch. It was more than just protection from the harmful gas in the air; the faint smell that tickled his nose told him it would have been unbearable without the mask.

The team split up, each taking a different cardinal direction, intending to box the small herd in, determined to end the fight before it could truly begin. This time, Daniel volunteered to play as bait. In a smaller environment, James could generally do it more efficiently as he had more mobility, but here, they needed the beasts' attention to be squarely on the Tank, and his large figure would serve much better.

He placed himself squarely before the herd, making enough sound that all the horses turned to face him. The stallion snorted in warning, its muscles rippling, making the rubies shimmer.

The creature was close to seven feet in height, all corded power and fierceness.

Its gaze settled on Daniel unerringly, understanding the unspoken challenge. It moved to the front of the herd without haste, leaving deep imprints in the soil.

Once it took an opposite position to the Tank, it neighed loudly, stamping its foot with enough strength to make the ground shake, and charged.

CHAPTER FIFTY-THREE

Daniel met the stallion's charge head-on. Considering the difference in mass and momentum, it would have normally been a terrible idea, but the Tank's skills and build were oriented to absorb powerful impacts, so he did just that.

The horse's obsidian hooves smashed against Daniel's shield with a loud *crack!* Unfortunately for the creature, however hard its minerals might have been, the D-rank equipment did not budge.

At the same time, seeing that the major threat was occupied, the others jumped into the fray. Maria's fireballs scattered the rest of the herd, allowing Ezekiel to nail them with agility debuffs, which let James and Lauren get in close.

The horses had an unsurprisingly tough hide, resistant against both blunt force and piercing attacks. Though confused and weakened, they fought hard, using their mineral growths as weapons and even conjuring some wholesale. Dangerous shards flew through the battlefield, which had descended into chaos in a few short seconds.

Feeling the willpower of his target coalesce into a specific direction, James lunged, his gloved fists clashing with the crystalline spires that emerged from the ground, summoned by one of the horses.

Sparks flew with each parry, the structures resonating with eerie musical chimes upon impact. But, while the minerals were sturdy, they weren't unbreakable. James's quick reflexes and Lauren's well-timed strikes worked in tandem, chipping away at the natural barricades.

Lauren, twirling her dual daggers, wove through the herd with a dancer's grace, every move precise, every slash calculated. She made use of the ambient fog, disappearing and reappearing in a different location, scoring large gashes on the horses, making them neigh in pain and causing even more confusion.

Maria's fire magic added another layer to their attack. It wasn't just about direct damage. She manipulated the flames to herd and funnel the horses, controlling their movements and ensuring they stayed in check. The one time one filly seemed to be making a break for it, she made the ground explode with a well-timed fireball, sending the monster rolling into James's range.

He took advantage of the opportunity, charged fist crashing into its head, sending it into oblivion.

Ezekiel's role was quintessential. His hands radiated a soft white aura as he cast spells, aiming to maintain the team's vigor while hindering the herd. Every now and then, a horse slowed its charge or made a misstep, clearly affected by the debuffs he cast, which gave James and Lauren the openings they needed.

Through it all, Daniel kept the stallion's attention to himself, charging it down the moment it appeared to want to come to its herd's rescue and holding strong against its increasingly desperate attacks.

The battle raged with intensity despite how little time had passed since its inception. Flames licked the air, mineral shards glittered as they broke, and the rhythmic beats of hooves against the ground mixed with the chorus of clashing weapons and spells going off.

Lauren would divert a horse's attention, leading it into James's path. He'd deal a significant blow before she would gracefully end its life, circle back, and move on to the next target. Once James scored a hit, his blows breaking bone, it'd either end a horse's life or send them on a collision course with Lauren's sharp knives, which she would bury in their skulls.

Standing atop a slight incline, Maria had a panoramic view of the battlefield. The heat waves rising from her spells gave her an ethereal glow, like a guardian deity presiding over the battle below. She noticed a group of the horses attempting to regroup, and with a snap of her fingers, a wall of flames rose, partitioning the battlefield and cutting off their escape.

Ezekiel remained in the background, but his presence was undeniably significant. Whenever one of his comrades suffered a cut or bruise, his magic was there to heal it. He also bolstered their vitality, making them feel invigorated even as the battle wore on.

And Daniel, the steadfast bastion of defense, never faltered. Every time the stallion tried to breach the front line or head for the others, he was there, an immovable object in its path. The two of them, Tank and stallion, were locked in their own private duel, a test of endurance and determination. If the beast dared run for it without paying due attention to its opponent, it would pay dearly, which made it frustrated and wary.

As the battle continued, the herd began to diminish. One by one, they were killed, which decreased their collective ability. It gave James and Lauren a much easier time in drawing close now that the crystalline growths didn't threaten to skewer them at every step.

But with the herd thinning, the stallion's desperation grew. Each time it attempted to counter or rally its dwindling forces, Daniel was there to thwart it, glowing shield raised, feet firmly planted.

There was a fire in the stallion's eyes, a mixture of anger and desperation, as it witnessed its herd being defeated.

Sensing the opportunity to end the confrontation as its willpower started to falter, James signaled to the team and they began to tighten their circle around the stallion. Maria's flames became walls that guided and limited the beast's paths. Ezekiel's debuffs concentrated on it, slowing it down considerably and diminishing its strength.

Lauren disappeared into the fog. Her gleeful laugh echoed as she prepared to give the final blow; the sound was the only indication the stallion had of her presence.

The beast reared, whinnying loudly, its obsidian hooves sparkling against the backdrop of flames. As it landed, Daniel charged it down, his entire body empowered by a skill, and knocked it off balance.

Maria hurled a controlled fireball, targeting the mineral growths around it. She broke its defenses, which allowed the others to close in.

The heat was intense, the air thick with the smell of melting minerals, musk, and the blood of the dying horses.

In the final moments, as the stallion lay weakened, its breathing labored, James couldn't help the surge of respect he felt toward it. This was a proud creature that had battled with vigor and skill against Daniel and had to witness the end of its herd, unable to do anything to stop it.

He knew it would be just another stepping stone in his and his friends' growth, but he had a feeling he would remember it.

With three quick steps, James was next to it, his fist glowing with mana. He released it all in one blow, breaking the horse's ribs and sending it skidding backward, directly in Lauren's path.

The girl wasted no time ending the majestic creature's suffering. It let out one last mournful neigh, and then it was over as two sharp knives buried themselves in its skull.

Silence descended upon the field, interrupted only by the distant crackling of Maria's flames and the heavy breathing of the team.

With a sigh, the redhead waved a hand, lowering the fires until they were extinguished, revealing the scene of a massacre.

"Somehow, horse monsters seem much worse to kill," Lauren commented as she pulled her knives out of the stallion. "It might just be me, but I didn't mind killing the spiders, even the eggs. Horses make me sad now that the high of the battle is over."

"It's definitely not the same thing," Ezekiel agreed. "I know these things wouldn't hesitate to kill a human, just like any other monster, but I'm so used to thinking of horses as noble creatures that it still sucks."

Daniel, on the other hand, seemed quite glad that they had killed them all, dropping on the ground in exhaustion. "Easy for you guys to say—you didn't have to avoid that murderous bastard for the whole time."

They all had a chuckle at that. It was true, after all, that the Tank had the worst role in the fight.

"Let's see exactly how much these guys give." James finally said, curious about how much EXP they had earned. Miss Walker had lobbied hard to send them to the Saratoga dungeon, after all, and she had made it clear that it would allow them to reach their goal much quicker than simply going on their scheduled weekly dives.

"Jesus!" James yelled, seeing the flood of notifications he had been subjected to. *Status!*

STATUS WINDOW	
Name	James Summers
Age	19
Awakening	1st
Talent	Thakinesis
Title	
Level	36
MP	65/180
STR	24
VIT	15
AGI	15
SEN	24
MND	19
STAT POINTS	0

The entire battle couldn't have lasted more than ten minutes, which, while longer than most normal swarm-style fights, wasn't nearly enough to justify two whole levels.

"Yeah, I think I get why Miss Walker was so insistent we come to Saratoga," Lauren replied. She was in a daze as she watched her own status window.

"It's not as much as the spider eggs gave us, but it's a lot more than any monster group has earned us before," Ezekiel agreed.

They had known there was something peculiar about this dungeon since so many G- and F-rankers were here, even though they didn't seem particularly interested in grinding levels.

I just thought they spent some time as part of other guilds before coming here as a form of retirement, but it might be that they just always worked here and gained so many levels just from killing the horses.

"If we can hunt down a couple herds per day, we might get to our goal within two weeks." Maria murmured, still surprised at the sheer amount of EXP they got.

James hummed, sitting down next to Lauren. "These horses were definitely stronger than most monsters we fought, both individually and as a group, but it feels like a bit too much. Where is the rest of the EXP coming from?"

"The stallion probably gave the majority of it," Daniel commented. "It's a mini-boss, like the giant crab we fought in Montauk. Only, there's one per herd.

That, coupled with this many strong monsters . . . It's no wonder they sent us here to farm levels."

"That makes sense. If every herd is led by a mini-boss, it's basically like fighting half a normal dungeon all together. Yeah, I can see it now."

"And we couldn't come here earlier because the horses fight pretty well together. We're good enough to disrupt their flow now, but we would've gotten mowed down a few weeks ago," Ezekiel added, thoughtfully looking at the dead monsters. "They're big and sturdy and they all can use some magic. To be honest, I would consider this dungeon on the border to G-rank. Especially with just how vast it is. I think it would take us weeks of concerted effort to clear it all."

"Makes sense why the guy at the local AA wasn't that worried about us over-hunting the beasts. I think I'll be good to go in another half hour, but Ez will probably need more to replenish his mana after he's done healing us, and it'd be a pity to waste potions here." James shook Ezekiel out of his daze. The curly-haired boy went around the group, taking care of all the scrapes and bruises the battle had given them.

Despite how overwhelming their victory had been, everyone showed signs of having been hit at one point, from small nicks on Maria's face from when her fireballs had connected with one of the crystalline weapons, to James's bruising all over his body, as he'd been forced to roll around the rough terrain.

His suit protected him from the worst of it, but he'd been through the thick of it, fighting against the frenzied horses and taking several blows to get close enough.

Still, no matter how battered he was, James found himself smiling broadly. Not only had he found a good place to gain power quickly, but he was closer than ever to getting justice.

CHAPTER FIFTY-FOUR

can see that you guys have been enjoying yourselves," came a familiar voice from the shadows. It startled Team 0 out of the daze they had fallen into.

Having just returned from their second-to-last dive in the Saratoga dungeon, they were all exhausted, both mentally and physically.

Miss Walker walked out of the darkness behind the rec room's door, eye-smiling at her students. "Have you been making good progress, then?"

Gathering all his remaining strength, James sat up. "We're almost there."

"Oh? So G-rank is in sight, eh? That's good, because if you want to have a shot at taking down the Radiant Guild, you should hurry up. They're starting to crack under the pressure, and I'd expect them to accept Ten Thousand Eyes' offer within the next few weeks," the masked woman revealed, drawing groans from everyone.

Already, the self-imposed mission presented several complicated steps. Adding in a time constraint only made things more difficult.

Well, it's not like we didn't know, but it still sucks. If we were to keep grinding here for a while more, I bet we could get to F-rank in a few months. Maybe a year, considering the gap in necessary experience . . .

Ezekiel, now sporting a thoughtful frown, rubbed his temples. "We did learn a lot during this time, miss. We managed to sync our movements better and create multiple combination attacks for every situation. Also, we established good tactics to cover each other while in the open," he recalled their recent experiences in the Saratoga dungeon.

Gesturing to James and Lauren, he continued, "I've found that concentrating my buffs on James, while Lauren serves as distraction, has great results. He can capture an entire herd's attention that way, and we can whittle them down in the confusion."

James added, "Maria and Daniel developed a hammer-and-anvil strategy. He corners and engages the beasts, ensuring they're focused on his shield. Meanwhile, Maria unleashes a concentrated stream of fire, melting through the creatures' mineral constructs, rendering them vulnerable to physical attacks. This makes it possible to quickly sweep through a herd. It was actually what we did today. We got three whole levels out of it."

Miss Walker hummed, seemingly happy with their explanation. "That's good to hear. Developing different tactics for the same enemies is important, because it'll give you more flexibility fighting similar monsters." Then, she clapped once. "That said, I'm more interested in the numerical gains. How much more do you need to reach G-rank?"

They all looked at each other before James answered, "One last dive, and we'll all be there. Lauren and Ezekiel have actually already passed level 50, so by this time tomorrow, we should be done."

Miss Walker eye-smiled again, satisfied and proud. "Good job, kids. I know it's not easy to keep fighting again and again, every day for weeks, but you're almost there. Just a little push and we can get out of this smelly little dump."

Poisonous mists hung over the plains southeast of Saratoga, but that morning they were thicker than usual.

As they had spent the last few weeks trawling through it, Team 0 didn't need directions or a map to know where to go. They had systematically cleared the herds closest to the edges since they were the weakest and most isolated.

Lately, however, they had been delving deeper, taking on numerous groups. James's brazenness in acting as bait and Maria's fiery walls seemed to do the trick in convincing the horses to follow them away from the dungeon's center and into the more sparsely populated rim, where they could battle it out to their hearts' content.

Today, however, they were determined to aim for one of the biggest fish. Only once, through the whole experience, they had been forced to retreat. That happened when they'd gotten a bit too cocky and decided to fight a herd where it was, rather than leading it into an isolated spot.

The herd ended up calling over another group, larger and stronger, which forced them to disengage and retreat to avoid a genuinely dangerous situation. The massive emerald-studded stallion and its mares worked in unison to prevent any sort of teamwork on their part, and their individual strength was such that they couldn't try and take them on without risking casualties.

The defeat of that day left a sour taste on all their tongues, and they agreed that they'd go look for that specific herd as their last fight.

From that day, they had pushed hard, raking in the levels and bringing their skills to the next step. All in preparation for this one fight.

They entered the deep recesses of the dungeon, and the ambient light dimmed, refracting through the many translucent mineral formations scattered throughout the area.

The tableau their target was in was especially foggy, limiting their vision. Their plan, however, didn't need their physical senses to work.

James would coordinate their movements all through the fight. Because of their last experience with this specific herd, they knew to expect great teamwork and powerful attacks meant to scatter and pick them off one by one.

Team 0 approached cautiously, with Daniel at the fore, his shield held steadfast. Maria's fingers twitched with suppressed energy, ready to invoke the destructive blazes she had learned to control so well. James, muscles taut and ready, kept his mind tranquil, entirely focused on the coming fight.

Ezekiel murmured beneath his breath, white light subtly caressing and empowering each team member, while Lauren, nearly a shadow, melted seamlessly into the fog.

As they got within a hundred feet, the emerald stallion lifted its head, multifaceted eyes gleaming with an intellect and malice that seemed antithetical to its stoic exterior. It neighed a resonant, crystal-like sound, alerting the herd to the intruders.

Without hesitation, Daniel surged forward, his shield a bulwark against the cascade of crystals that threatened to smash into them.

He held steady through the barrage, though they knew it was only a distraction meant to allow the beasts to get close. That was why Maria, with a slightly deranged grin, called upon her element, a spiral of fire materializing before her. With a fierce command, it plunged into the cluster of mineral horses, creating a cacophony of shattering crystals and anguished neighs.

Despite their robust, mineralized exteriors, the intense heat caused fissures to snake across their forms. Yet, they persisted, unyielding in their onslaught.

Again, another tassel of their plan moved forward as Lauren emerged from the fog, brandishing her knives, the blades whispering through the air as they found their mark, exploiting the fractures created by Maria's firestorm. She focused her hits on the stragglers, those that had been hurt more by the redhead's attack, taking them out of the fight entirely while the rest continued their charge, heedless of their comrades' fate.

Ezekiel's light brightened further as he cast more buffs on James, who lowered his head and charged forward, meeting the monsters' assault with his own.

James's fists, empowered by the buffs and his intense willpower, collided with the first of the mineral horses, creating a shock wave that reverberated through the expanse.

Such was the power of his first blow that he sent the leading mare flying back into her herd, head completely crushed, arresting the majority of the charge at once. He didn't allow them to reorganize and attacked without mercy.

With every strike, James broke through another layer of crystalline defenses, killing another beast, but each strike also drained him. He was acutely aware that the herculean stallion was still on the offensive, heading directly for Daniel.

That, too, was part of their plan. Their first fight's tactic had served them well, after all, and there was no need to change it here, since they managed to divert the entire herd from charging the Tank down, which the herd had done during their previous encounter.

Daniel moved with military precision, placing himself squarely in the stallion's path, until the very last moment, when he shifted to the side with surprising agility for his bulk, his shield glowing brightly with the Bash skill, sending the beast crashing to the side in one hit.

Through beads of sweat dotting her forehead from the intense heat she manipulated, Maria maintained a conflagration that separated the herd from their leader, preventing any monster from interfering. It sowed even more chaos. Her flames danced and twirled, licking at the mineral horses, further exacerbating the damage they sustained from James's and Lauren's incisive strikes.

However, the emerald stallion wasn't to be underestimated. It righted swiftly and charged again, thunderous steps shaking the earth, its eyes fixed squarely on Daniel. Despite its armored body, it moved with a grace and speed that belied its size, its multifaceted eyes reflecting not only the light from Maria's fires but an unnerving calculation.

That was the moment they had all been waiting for. James yelled out, "Switch!"

And the curtain of flames opened up, allowing the Thakinetic and Lauren to pass through, while Daniel and Maria went to deal with the scattered herd. Their duty was done as they managed to break the stallion away from its companion, severely weakening its defensive options.

Indeed, James had observed that despite its massive offensive capability, the horse much preferred to let the mares deal with the coming attacks. This worked well in their herd, since they moved as one, but when a more intelligent opponent found a way to separate them . . .

Lauren flitted through the fog, her knives flashing in the filtered light, slick with blood. Her blows weren't enough to end the massive creature, and more than once, she was forced to retreat lest she be impaled by an emerald spike, but they slowed it enough that James was able to complete his own attack.

Having dumped over a hundred mana points into his fist, he felt himself straining to keep hold of it. His mind crushed that little part of him that complained about the difficulty of it all, and he instead ran at the stallion, swiftly closing the distance.

Ezekiel's buffs granted him enough agility and grace to dance through the emerald spikes, never slowing down until he was right before it.

James's eyes locked with the horse's. An unspoken challenge passed between them. The stallion, undeterred by the stealthy assailant that continued to harass it, charged at James, its hooves crashing down with a force that seemed destined to end him.

His empowered fist met the crystalline hoof, causing a massive explosion as all the stored mana was released at once.

James was sent flying back, painfully rolling on the gem-littered ground, until he stopped against a rock.

He pulled himself up with no little effort, ready to take on his enemy again should it be needed, but his senses told him he wouldn't need to. Indeed, the beast was lying on the ground, wheezing in agony as most of its lower half had been blown off by the last blow's strength.

Two daggers shot from the mist and cut off its throat. Its struggles ended, lifeblood spilling freely. The light soon left its multifaceted eyes.

Despite their victory, however, the fight was not over. The remainder of the herd, free from the stallion's domineering control yet enraged by its fall, regrouped and charged as one despite Daniel's best efforts to keep them separated.

Maria, her energy nearly spent, conjured one last desperate firewall, but its strength was only enough to burn the first two mares.

Ezekiel stepped forward; a serene calm overcame him despite the impending doom. His hand traced an arc before him, white light illuminating the fog.

And then, silence.

The horses, whose thunderous charge had threatened them so just a moment before, were moving as if in slow motion, barely faster than a regular person walking.

"What the fuck are you waiting for? I can't keep this up forever! Go kill them!" the White Mage yelled, sweat profusely falling down his brow.

They complied, swiftly ending the fight once and for all.

In the ensuing silence, as they all struggled to regain their breath after the herculean effort, James smiled, looking at his status screen.

Oh yeah, baby. That's what I'm talking about.

CHAPTER FIFTY-FIVE

Team 0 returned to the local AA. After all, there was no sense in sticking around and getting attacked by stronger herds in the dungeon.

They weren't afraid if that happened, since they had ascended to G-rank, their set goal. But with the compounding exhaustion after weeks of daily grinding, it was better to avoid taking unnecessary risks.

Once they had left the dungeon's premises, Miss Walker had appeared. She clapped her hands, delighted with their accomplishments, and led them back to their temporary accommodations. She had been waiting for this moment for a while.

"Not only have you guys surpassed the expectations set on the Dawn Initiative, but you blew my own predictions out of the water! To be honest, it reminded me of the old days when there was nothing to do except fight constantly; nowadays, I've never seen rookies like you achieve a rank-up in so little time," their teacher proudly announced.

Maria smiled, raising a fist in victory from where she was lying sprawled on the couch. "I can't say that it's been a walk in the park, but it wasn't absurdly difficult, if you don't consider the few times we almost died . . . Well, actually, it might have been that difficult."

They all had a laugh at that. It was true, after all. They had to go through many, many dangerous situations—several of which they shouldn't have survived, by all rights—to get to where they were now.

Just the spider dungeon alone should have been our tomb. If it hadn't been for Pride . . . Well, we wouldn't be here today.

"Now, before you assign your spoils and truly enter the next rank," Miss Walker said, interrupting the festive mood, "I think we need to talk about strategy for the coming operations. I know you guys are very proud of your achievement, but you should consider that the AA is still a leaky mess. We can reasonably expect this information to get to most major guilds within a few hours, minor ones like Radiant in a day or two. Also remember that while G-rank is a big step up from H-rank, you will also be dealing with F-ranks. That means people that went through their second Awakening. The less you face them directly, the more likely your plan is to succeed."

Daniel grunted in understanding. "So you think we shouldn't take the test or even announce our accomplishment until after the operation with the Radiant Guild."

Miss Walker eye-smiled. "I can't possibly have meant that," she said in an exaggerated fake tone. "As a good agent of the AA, I can only recommend you take the test as soon as possible and inform the correct authorities of your accomplishments." Then, she became serious. "It'd be a good idea to use every advantage you have at your disposal. Despite the Radiant Guild being a smaller organization now that its backer is gone, you're still far too weak to take it head-on. You must remember that your mission is to lead them to ruin, not fight them all."

Before any of them could get a word in edgewise, she stood up, shadows pooling at her feet. "I need to get back now to ensure I have plausible deniability. If I don't see you cross the threshold with my eyes and you don't tell me, I won't be able to report it. Just remember what your role is supposed to be."

That said, she was swallowed by the darkness, disappearing as if she had never been there.

They all looked at each other briefly before Lauren's chuckle broke the silence. "You can never tell what that woman is going to say."

"Yes, but she's also right. We know for a fact that the Radiant Guild has several people in its employ who far surpass us, even after all we've done here. We need to keep in mind the plan. Bait them into acting illegally, maybe have them admit to a few crimes, and possibly get their boss involved so that Miss Walker can swoop in and save the day," Daniel added, rubbing his stubbled chin.

James nodded, despite how much he would have liked the more direct approach. "I know I'm the one with the most grievances, but the rational part of me knows that a straight-up fight isn't our best option here. We have to be smart about taking them down. That means we've got to act like the weaker prey they think we are, while always being one step ahead."

Maria leaned forward, eyes blazing with excitement at the thought of participating in such an important operation. "We've been gone for weeks. They'll expect us to be a bit stronger, but if nothing gets reported by Miss Walker, they won't expect us to have gained this much power or skill in such a short amount of time. We should be able to use that to our advantage."

So they planned. Each member of Team 0 brainstormed, connected ideas, and explored every avenue for executing their subversive strategy. They discussed various schemes, from spreading disinformation about their weaknesses to setting traps where the Radiant Guild would be tempted to attack them—Team 0 would exploit the guild members' volatile nature.

Daniel scribbled down a few points on a piece of paper, constructing a crude map of potential confrontation points within Brooklyn. "We need to guide them to a place where they feel they have the upper hand, yet everything is actually under our control. But to do that, we first need to get their attention. We'll probably have to walk around their territory long enough to ruffle their feathers, maybe even be overheard talking shit."

The discussion veered into the lay of the land as they determined which locations would be optimal for their deceptive strategies. Maria suggested several locations—such as the waterfront—where fire wouldn't cause irreversible damage but could still be utilized as an effective tool. Lauren noted a few shadowy alleys and abandoned buildings where her stealth could play a pivotal role, wanting to assault an entire team and spook them.

In the end, after a couple of hours of strategizing, they reached an agreement. The plan had several moving parts, and they left some space for maneuvering on the fly, should things happen, but the core of it seemed solid to all of them.

Lauren leaned back, flipping a knife skillfully between her fingers. "Now, it's just a matter of executing it flawlessly. We lure them in, enrage them enough to lose sight of what they're doing, possibly by preying on their weakened state now that Golden Sun is gone, and we should have a strong enough response to warrant Miss Walker's intervention."

"Cool, I think we can be happy with what we have now. Let's sleep on this and see if something new pops up, but otherwise, I think we can go ahead and finally cross into G-rank," James said. His excitement rose.

Status.

STATUS WINDOW	
Name	James Summers
Age	19
Awakening	1st
Talent	Thakinesis
Title	
Level	51
MP	231/255
STR	35
VIT	19
AGI	19
SEN	35
MND	20
STAT POINTS	0

The sheer difference in power between now and a couple of weeks ago—before he had set foot in the Saratoga dungeon—still left James stunned.

Yes, he realized that his punches were more powerful since it took only a couple of direct hits now to kill a mineral horse, whereas at the beginning, it had taken him four or five.

His eyesight was better than ever, allowing him to see even in near complete darkness. He could taste and smell things more accurately than before, and his love for food had only redoubled since new flavors had opened up to him with the increase in his sense stat.

But the numbers on the floating blue screen made it all more real. He had surpassed the first true roadblock in his career as an Awakener.

Getting G-rank wasn't of the same importance as attaining F-rank, as that would mean Awakening again, but it still signified the largest drop off in numbers.

Yes, most professional Awakeners reached F- or E-rank before stagnating after a few years of hard work. However, the vast majority of the people who received the System never went beyond their first couple of dungeon runs, too scared of the possibility of dying.

G-rank was the watershed between those who completely squandered the chance they had been given and those who decided to do something with it.

Skills.

SKILLS	LEVEL	DESCRIPTION
Thakinetic Empowerment	8	(Active): Utilize your Willpower to temporarily raise STR - VIT - AGI.
Thakinetic Awareness	6	(Active/Passive): Expand your SEN to feel other's wills.
Thakinetic Resistance	8	(Active/Passive): Empower your MND to defend yourself against foreign influences.

The past couple of weeks had been hard for more reasons than simply having to fight against strong monsters. Death always loomed like a shadow, but James had long since gotten used to it.

No, what had really pushed him and his skills so much was the intensity of the battles and having to constantly throw himself into new ones, day after day, without a moment of rest.

The way his Thakinesis worked, after all, was that it originated from his willpower, actualizing through his mana into skills. Which meant that the more he was stressed and pushed through it, the more it would grow alongside him.

Powerful monsters had broken his limbs, only for James to heal and jump back into the fray, pained to see his friends getting hurt because of his absence. It had pushed his Thakinetic Resistance skill, alongside the constant alertness he had needed to maintain.

That helped with Awareness as well. Scouring through the poisonous fogs in search of new enemies, having his companions all depend on his skills . . . they had all contributed. Just like a piece of steel being forged, his mind and soul had been pushed to the limits, only to come out stronger than before.

All that effort granted him one singular point in his mind stat. Weeks of struggles as he pushed himself to his limits, strategizing and adapting on the fly. It was all worth one point.

There was a reason why Miss Walker had told them that it just wasn't worth it to train their bodies to gain stats, after all. It was an extremely inefficient use of time.

Still, Mr. Bethany had explained how it would be worth pushing themselves to gain better mastery over their abilities.

We'll have to do that once we finish the Radiant Guild. Really get acquainted with our new powers. But for now, this should be more than enough.

Their plan didn't require them to face the stronger members directly after all, so getting to G-rank, with all the high-quality equipment the AA supplied, should be enough.

Slowly, they rose from the comfortable couches, filing out of the rec room and giving their goodbyes to the local staff, who saluted them with a mix of relief and sadness. The outsiders were finally leaving, but that meant their vacation was over.

The team got much more out of the training trip than they had originally expected. Since Team 0 had pushed so hard to reach the next rank, they had gone through many more herds than expected, netting everyone a nice sum.

James gave one last smile to the wildly waving group of Awakeners and got into Mr. Robinson's van. He was ready to take on everything that would come his way.

Radiant Guild, Callum Wright . . . I'm coming for you.

CHAPTER FIFTY-SIX

Seated in a Thai restaurant at the intersection between Sixth Street and Fifth Avenue, James carefully maintained the pretense of enjoying his meal. The drunken noodles weren't bad, per se. In fact, they were quite good. But keeping Thakinetic Awareness active as he waited for their target made it difficult to savor the dish.

The others around him seemed to have no trouble on that front, trusting him to alert them when it came time to begin their performance. Clothed in their dungeon garb, they were easy to identify as Awakeners.

With Ezekiel, Daniel, Lauren, and Maria all engaged in casual conversation, occasionally erupting into loud laughter, they painted a picture of a carefree group unwinding after some minor conquest. The aroma of spicy curry and the tang of lime filled the air; Brooklyn's evening bustle enveloped them in a warm, ambient noise that shielded their true intentions.

Inside, though, their senses were sharp, eyes flicking subtly toward the entrance every so often, ears straining to pick up anything unusual in the thrum of conversations surrounding them.

James's magical senses were stretched out, feeling for the familiar energy signature of a specific person.

For their plan, they had decided to position themselves as weak prey: in a public space, they'd openly talk about their enemy, providing an easy target, and bait them into a confrontation under Team 0's control.

James had to once again use Miss Walker's access to classified files to choose his victim. He finally settled on one of the newest entries in the guild, someone he had noticed around these parts more than once.

After what felt like an eternity, James sensed it—a shiver of an energy signature that tugged at his awareness. The Radiant Guild member he had chosen, one known for his tendency to eavesdrop and report back to his superiors, was approaching the restaurant.

Carter was a low-ranking Awakener with an overinflated sense of importance. Yet, he had a deeply rooted fear of being unnoticed by the higher-ups in the guild.

Considering how badly things were going soon after he had joined up, James believed him to be desperate to score some points with the more experienced members.

With a subtle movement, he brought up his napkin over his mouth and nose, sneezing three times in the prearranged signal. The others didn't twitch.

Lauren was the first to shift the conversation, her voice taking on a sneering, confident tone. "I really thought the Radiant Guild would have put up more of a fight. With how they strut around, you'd think they'd at least try not to get disappeared the moment Golden Sun isn't here to cover their asses."

Daniel chimed in, his voice louder than necessary. It carried through the ambient noise of the restaurant. "Yeah, and have you heard the rumors about them getting swallowed up by the Ten Thousand Eyes Guild? It's like they've become nothing more than a small fry."

"Ha!" A mocking laugh escaped Maria. "I almost feel bad for them. From being one of the most feared guilds in New York to becoming just another subsidiary . . . How far the mighty have fallen."

Well, they were always just another subsidiary, but they strutted around the place like they owned it, so it's better to play along and pretend that they really once were what they thought they were.

The bait was set, and Carter, seated a few tables away at the nearby bar under the guise of enjoying a cold beer, pricked up his ears, evidently listening in.

The notion of his guild having no recourse but to be gobbled up by another was humiliating and threatened his tenuous position within Radiant. Who knew where he'd end up, after all.

James had chosen him precisely because of this. He knew Carter needed to relay this information—that other Awakeners were openly talking shit about them—back to his superiors immediately.

The subsequent actions of the Radiant Guild would likely be aggressive, possibly rash, making them malleable to Team 0's orchestrations.

Ezekiel, playing his part with a smirk, added, "And to think, soon they'll be nothing more than a footnote in the books of Ten Thousand Eyes. Just another way to expand their growing hold over the city. A once proud guild reduced to mere minions. It's really pathetic."

Carter seemed to hardly believe his luck. He slapped some money on the counter and hurried away from the restaurant, widely grinning at having found a target for his superiors. He probably envisioned himself being praised, perhaps even promoted, for bringing this to the attention of the guild leaders.

As he scurried away, eager to deliver the intelligence, James subtly nodded to his teammates, signaling that the first phase of their plan was successfully in motion. Now, they needed to prepare for the inevitable backlash.

"There's no doubt he'll relay this to his superiors, and knowing their pride and the state of the guild, they'll come looking for us," James surmised, his eyes sharp with anticipation. "But we can't be careless now. If we hang around for much longer, it'll be obvious that we were waiting for them to show up. We have to get them to lower their guards for the plan to work."

The others all agreed. The initial part was in motion and things would start happening quickly, but they needed to remain in control at all times if they wanted the operation to end successfully.

We won't get another chance like this.

The next day found them wandering around the same Thai restaurant, though they chose not to dine there to avoid giving the game away. Instead, they decided to go for drinks, until James sensed Carter once again poking his mousy little face around.

Team 0 retreated from the bar, their movements nonchalant and lighthearted, though they were coiled with tension. They strolled through the borough; the streets of Brooklyn were well lit and lively, undisturbed by the violence that was about to happen. The hum of traffic and echoes of happy chatter formed a subtle symphony of city life.

James's Thakinetic Awareness spread out, a sixth sense feeling for the presence of any Awakener.

They slowly made their way toward Prospect Park, walking openly and conspicuously near the Thai restaurant first, just long enough to stoke the curiosity and bravado of any possible pursuers from the Radiant Guild.

Finally, others started appearing in his range and James had the confirmation that Carter had done his job. Several people from different directions converged on them but kept their distance, allowing Team 0 to slowly meander toward the park.

James quickly cataloged the aura of each pursuer, gauging their capabilities. His mind rapidly translated the intensity and fluctuation of their energies into an understandable metric. Willpower wasn't necessarily the best unit of measurement, but the intensity with which it shined did give a fair measure of someone's power.

G-rank . . . another G . . . H . . . H . . . and another G.

The energies were moderate, nothing that Team 0 couldn't handle. James informed his team through covert hand gestures and twitches, a language they'd developed to communicate silently.

As they sauntered toward Prospect Park, he brushed his fingers across his left eyebrow. *Five pursuers.* Then, he discreetly touched his wrist and ear, which signified their tails' ranks. His team, alert and attentive, caught his signals, immediately understanding the strength and number of the adversaries lurking in the shadows.

Although smarter, more experienced Awakeners would smell the trap, the Radiant Guild had very few of them, nor would they be available for this kind of punitive action. The G- and H-ranks shadowing them were too blinded by an opportunity for retribution and career advancement.

They saw a straightforward mission: confront, challenge, and obliterate Team 0 in a vehement display of guild loyalty and power.

Lauren flicked her hair in a vain manner. *Message received and understood*, she conveyed to James. She also kept an eye out in case someone had a stealth skill that interfered with James's Awareness, but she didn't seem to find anything.

Their path was deliberate, leading their pursuers away from the dense urban area and toward Prospect Park's open and dimly lit environs. At night, the park offered a serene juxtaposition to the bustling city life they had just navigated. The quiet rustling of trees and faint murmurings of the few visitors painted a starkly different scene.

The people quickly noticed the Awakeners. When they saw another group following Team 0—the guild members didn't bother to hide now—the civilians swiftly packed up and departed, sensing the tension in the air.

Team 0 continued forward, their steps calm and measured, beckoning their pursuers into the metaphorical spider's web they had woven.

The once lively park became a secluded battlefield, with lights from nearby lampposts casting long shadows upon the ground as nature unwittingly staged itself for an impending conflict between unseen forces.

The five Radiant Guild Awakeners, drawn into the calm, dark expansiveness, felt a temporary, illusory glee, for they believed they had cornered their prey.

James felt their energies draw nearer, all with a clear, shared intent. These people were not here to give warnings. No, violence drummed strongly in their minds, alongside a need to prove themselves to the world.

Just as James had expected, this Radiant team was made up of insecure Awakeners who were mostly kept in the dark about the actual situation in their guild. But they could sense the downslide. That frustration needed an outlet, and he was more than glad to provide it.

The tranquility of the park, now bereft of any ordinary visitor, was pierced by what should have been the sudden and dramatic appearance of the Radiant Guild members, emerging from the shadows with a boisterous, albeit forced, confidence.

It should have been a sign when Team 0 didn't so much as twitch at their presence. That alone should have told the hooligans they had been expected, but by then, they were too drunk on their own supply.

"Good evening, gentlemen," James said. His voice echoed through the silent park. The sheer assuredness in his tone should have been another sign, but again, it was disregarded.

Young, dumb, and frustrated as they were, the Radiant members only took it as false bravado.

"You AA dogs really should learn to read a fucking map. This is Radiant territory and you can't just walk around here saying whatever shit comes to mind, especially not about us," one of them said. It was one of the G-ranks, and his slicked-back hair and crumpled white shirt gave him the appearance of a wannabe mobster.

Hs probably trying to replicate the Golden Sun guys. At least they had a bit of style. This is just pathetic.

"Do you understand? Answer me when I speak to you!" the same guy yelled, apparently not liking how James kept his silence with a slight smirk stretched on his lips.

"There is no need to yell," Daniel interjected, equally amused. "We can hear you just fine. What is it that you want with us?"

That, if anything, seemed to enrage them even more.

"Are you dumb? I fucking told you already! You can't talk shit about us, especially in our territory. There are consequences!"

Lauren, never one to take such verbal abuse for long, scoffed derisively, "I'd like to see you try, bitch."

CHAPTER FIFTY-SEVEN

Aren't these guys from the AA? Should we be doing this?" one of the Radiant members asked. Considering their guild's precarious situation, it wouldn't be a good idea to get on the agency's wrong side.

Unfortunately for him, his companions weren't enlightened.

The leader of the group, the G-rank who had verbally assaulted James, turned to face him, overtaken by rage. "Shut the fuck up. We can't let these assholes get away with talking shit about us, or we'll never get any respect. Ever."

His words quelled any dissent, and the thugs spread out, slowly circling Team 0 as if to tell them there would be no way out.

"You people really love being dramatic, huh? An ambush at night in a park is almost too cliché," James sarcastically commented, drawing snorts from his friends.

The eerie calm Team 0 was showing seemed to unnerve some, but after the earlier browbeating, no one dared say anything, even if it was slowly becoming evident that not all was as it appeared.

The Radiant thugs' leader was a robust figure with a wild mane of hair and piercing eyes. He stepped forward and raised his hand to summon a translucent energy blade from thin air. It crackled and hummed, illuminating his smug face. "I can't wait to hear what kind of jokes you'll make after I'm done with you."

Beside him, a slender woman with raven-black hair manipulated the fountain water, which writhed around her like serpents, waiting for a command. Another member, a lanky young man with glasses, started to hum. Sharp, ethereal chains encircled him.

The remaining two took their cues from their comrades. One, a bald behemoth whose muscles bulged, transformed his hands into massive stone fists. The last one took out an extendible baton, seemingly a more common variation of Warrior.

For all their bluster, Team 0 remained unfazed.

Lauren winked at James and whispered, "Elemental Talents and Warrior variations. Predictable. Let me handle the woman." In a blink, she vanished into thin air, her innate stealth skills rendering her invisible.

Maria rolled her eyes, her fingers dancing with anticipation. "Let me warm up a bit." Flames encased her hands, then flared out and sent an intense heat wave across the park. It cast menacing shadows in the park; they flickered and distorted the face-off.

Without waiting for a signal, the leader lunged at James, energy blade whirring menacingly.

When James drew upon his willpower, his fists ignited with strength. He deftly sidestepped the leader's lunge and delivered a punch to the side of the blade, his reinforced gloves easily crushing the construct, sending shards of light everywhere.

Daniel stepped in front of Maria, acting as a human shield. The massive stone-fisted Radiant member attacked him with a punch that would've shattered boulders. But Daniel was a Tank in every sense of the word. He absorbed the blow without needing any skill or his shield and retaliated with a powerful shoulder charge that sent the man tumbling.

Amid the chaos, the water snakes shot at James, keen to do damage and even the odds. But James dodged. There was a *crack!* as the snakes broke the stone pavement.

The attack, however, at least managed to grant the leader some time, which he took to conjure up another blade.

Ezekiel's hands glowed a soft hue of white as he enhanced Lauren's agility and speed. Boosted by the Mage, Lauren deftly maneuvered through the shadows and struck. The water user shrieked, hit in the back of the head by the blunt end of Lauren's knife guard. With that, one threat was neutralized.

Seeing the situation quickly spiraling out of their control, the young man with the ethereal chains aimed at Maria. Perhaps he thought the Fire Mage was a key threat.

The chains surged forward with incredible speed, seeking to bind her and remove her fiery offense. Maria, however, was already prepared. A swirling flame barrier encased her; they melted the chains upon contact and turned them into nothing more than glowing embers.

James glanced over at the last thug, the one with the extendable baton, who had remained on the outskirts, trying to find an opening.

But before James could address him, Lauren took care of the threat. Like a wraith in shadows, she appeared behind the man and, with a swift motion, kicked the back of his knees, causing him to buckle. In an instant, she disarmed him of his baton and held him at knifepoint.

After watching his teammates be taken down, the thug leader roared in frustration. "Enough of this!" With a motion of his sword, he summoned multiple energy blades, which hovered around him, ready for launch.

Unfortunately for him, this was real life, and no one in their right mind would allow him to take his time to craft his final attack. Maria took this chance to aim a fireball at the leader's feet. The small explosion sent him flying back, disrupting the attack. Awry, the blades landed scattered throughout the park.

The female Mage, though dazed from Lauren's surprise attack, started to gather her wits. The water from the fountain began to rise, swirling violently. It formed a defensive barrier around her while simultaneously lashing out at Team 0 in an unpredictable, amorphous manner.

Ezekiel reacted swiftly and buffed everyone's agility. It allowed them to avoid anything more than a glancing hit until she exhausted her reserves and decided to concentrate on defense.

Daniel's opponent came back for round two. While the behemoth was likely stronger in raw stats, Daniel's experience as a Tank made him versatile. He planted his feet firmly, taking on a defensive stance. The ground beneath his feet cracked under his pressure, showing that if needed, Daniel could become an immovable object.

The Warrior charged, but Daniel—showing his cunning—merely sidestepped and tripped him, using his momentum against him. The behemoth crashed face-first into the ground, the sheer momentum of his charge sending him sprawling on the stone path, leaving him momentarily stunned.

James, having neutralized the leader's second attempt at retaliation, turned his attention to the chain wielder. While the man's chains had been damaged by Maria's fire, he quickly summoned more. But this time, the chains were cloaked in a dark energy.

Not wanting to take any chances, James closed the distance quickly, his fist crashing like an angry bull into the Conjurer's construct.

Since he knew to expect a more powerful chain thanks to his Thakinetic Awareness, he pumped enough mana to cause an explosion. The caster staggered backward, trying to raise his chains defensively, but James was relentless. With a powerful uppercut, the thug was sent sprawling.

Lauren moved to assist Maria, who was engaged with the leader. The two battled it out in a flashy show of power as he cast more and more blades of light, which were countered by fireballs and waves of flames.

Using her stealth abilities, Lauren took advantage of his distraction and approached from behind. She slashed at his legs—not deep enough to cause lasting harm, but enough to hamper his movement.

This gave Maria the perfect opportunity. She thrust her hands forward, casting an explosive fireball next to him, sending him flying back, skidding on the ruined stone painfully.

The stone-fisted giant once again attempted to stand up and rejoin the fight, but a brutal blow to the chin from Daniel sent him back down, this time for good.

With just the Water Mage left, Team 0 converged on where the liquid dome protecting her still churned, though its intensity had lessened.

The girl was unwilling to come out and face them, but they didn't have many options for how to deal with her beyond just waiting her out.

"I could try to heat up the water. That should make her realize it's over quickly enough," Maria suggested, a small fireball coming into being above her hand.

James waved her off exasperatedly. "Let's try not to boil her alive. That would give them the moral high ground after all our hard work. No, I'll stay here with Lauren to wait until she's consumed all her mana, which shouldn't take too long. Ez, check on the others with Maria to make sure no permanent damage has been done and heal them up a bit if necessary." Then, turning to the dark trees in the distance, he added, "Daniel, a little rat is hiding in the bushes over there."

With a smirk, the Tank walked off in that direction, looking very much like a big feline stalking his prey.

The others jumped to action too, rounding up the injured and, in the case of the leader, healing him to prevent serious consequences.

Lauren scratched her head sheepishly at that. "I think I might have gotten a bit too excited. It's just that it's our first fight since we came back, so I'm still not 100 percent in control of my new strength."

James gave her a look, seeing her unrepentant smirk. Since Ezekiel was there to patch him up, though, there was no need to discuss the issue further.

A couple of minutes later, the water dome was finally released, revealing the raven-haired Awakener struggling to stand up. The defiant expression on her face would have been more heroic if she hadn't just taken part in what should have been a punitive mission, so James felt very little remorse as he roughly grabbed her, pulling her to where he could feel Daniel holding a struggling Carter.

The mousy-faced boy had apparently decided to hang around, possibly to enjoy the spectacle, but given how he was gibbering in terror, he hadn't taken the result well.

Pushing the tired girl into a sitting position next to her unconscious companions, James finally addressed her, "You realize how stupid this was, right? If you had actually beaten us up, we could have called upon our superiors, and you don't have Golden Sun's protection anymore."

The Water Mage remained silent while the little spy kept twisting his hands and looking around at the broken battlefield in horror.

"Well, it doesn't really matter anyway. They were way too weak to do anything to us," Lauren commented derisively, not having to exaggerate much.

The others all chuckled. It was true, after all. Despite being newly minted G-ranks, Team 0 had very little trouble handling a group that had some experience. The G-ranks, at least, should have put up more of a fight.

There's a pretty stark difference between us and them. Not just in equipment, though it helps. But it's obvious that their guild only cares about those who climb the ranks quickly and gives minimal resources to those still in the early stages. Considering how they've had free rein over new Awakeners for so long, it's not a surprise.

But things were starting to change. The AA, spurred by the Dawn Initiative's success, would likely open their coffers to build up new teams. New Awakeners would soon have more options open to them.

Still, to get to that future, bad apples like the Radiant Guild needed to be removed from the board, and to do that, their plan had to continue.

Putting on a superior smirk, James added, "It doesn't surprise me, though. For a guild to hold Callum Wright as the standard, it had to be a shithole."

The Water Mage clenched her jaw. James felt sure the message would arrive where it needed to.

Now, let's see if the fish takes the bait.

CHAPTER FIFTY-EIGHT

The group of Radiant Awakeners finally woke up thanks to Ezekiel's healing spells. Knowing they couldn't do much after being beaten so severely, they left after promising terrible retaliation.

In any other case, James would have stopped them there and made sure they understood they couldn't get away with threatening anyone, especially someone who had just beaten them up, but since that was the entire point of this encounter, he let them go.

Then, Team 0 had to wait until the AA urban repairs team arrived, since they couldn't very well leave the broken park like that. Thankfully, Miss Walker had signed off on enough budget for this mission that they didn't need to worry about paying out of their own pocket.

That done, they went back to their own homes to get some sleep in, knowing that the following day would be one of great excitement.

It was unsurprising, then, that James found everyone in their training room bright and early the next morning, eager to get the show on the road.

They all looked at him as he came in with a pumpkin spice latte, to which he shrugged uncaringly. "What? I like it. It's like drinking pie."

"That's exactly why it's an abomination. Pie is to be eaten, otherwise the calories you take in won't give you the satisfaction that makes them worth it," Lauren replied vehemently.

"Guys," Daniel interjected exasperatedly, "I don't think that's the most pressing question today."

"Still nothing," James answered the unspoken question. He had reassured the others that, since he had called Callum out, he would be the one to contact him, but he had yet to do so.

James wasn't particularly worried. Knowing Sally's ex, it wouldn't be long before a message arrived. Likely within the next few hours, even.

The others deflated at his proclamation, having spent the night waiting for the big day.

"We should go over the plan one last time, kids. Things change at the last moment, and it's important to have your options be clear," came Miss Walker's voice. The shadows coalesced into her form.

She adjusted her uniform's straps, with an emblem of AA embroidered on the pocket. As she walked to the center of the parlor, her heels clicked authoritatively on the floor.

She cleared her throat before continuing, her piercing red gaze scrutinizing each member. "I've just returned from a high-level meeting. The brass is watching this operation with keen interest. They believe the outcome will serve as a stepping stone, an experiment of sorts, if you will."

Maria frowned. "So what are we looking at, miss? Do they want us to change our approach? Is it likely that they leaked something?"

The older woman shook her head with an eye smile. "I've made sure nothing could interfere with this operation from above. It's all on you, kids."

James felt a shiver go down his spine and decided it would be better not to ask what exactly she had threatened their superiors with.

"Give me the rundown, James," Miss Walker said, and he shook himself out of his contemplations.

"We want Callum Wright out in the open by himself. Given the disparity in rank and our recent show of strength, he'll likely take the bait of facing Team 0 alone, if only to restore the Radiant Guild's tarnished reputation. He'll want an audience, but I'm pretty sure I can goad him into fighting us one versus five," James said, turning on a sleek tablet. He swiped to display a detailed city map and pointed to a series of highlighted locations. "We'll have to wait for his message, but I expect one of these places to be where the confrontation will happen."

They were all spots where he had met the man, with the old rat dungeon's entrance being the one he believed to be the most likely.

Ezekiel raised an eyebrow. "Those are all open spaces. Lots of potential for collateral damage."

It was an issue they had already gone over, but they needed to be as thorough as possible. Flexibility was good, but some things needed to be ironed out early.

James smirked, "Exactly. We're not just baiting Callum; we're pushing his pride to make him think he has the upper hand. The more public and open the confrontation, the more he's likely to bite. It's the only way I can be sure he'll agree to face us all together. Besides, if he chooses the rat dungeon's entrance like I suspect he will, it would mean a place far away from most citizens but close enough that the AA can get there quickly, if and when their presence is needed."

Miss Walker leaned forward, her keen interest evident. "Once Callum takes the bait and we have our confrontation, what then?"

James shrugged. "We fight him. Ideally, we defeat him. Show the Radiant Guild and any other potential troublemaking guild that rank isn't the be-all and end-all. That strategy, intelligence, and teamwork always have their place. That the AA has the resources necessary to turn even rookies like us into powerhouses able to take on Awakeners of a higher rank—and more importantly, a higher-tier Awakening."

Miss Walker nodded in satisfaction. "Very good. And once Callum Wright is out of the picture, you anticipate that the Radiant leader will have to intervene, right?"

"Correct," Daniel answered. "He will most likely be monitoring the whole thing, but interfering with such a low-rank fight would be humiliating if not absolutely necessary. The only thing that could possibly push him to action is . . . Well, he'd have to silence us to ensure their reputation doesn't suffer even more. It'd be a death blow and open them to unsustainable pressure from major guilds."

Miss Walker chuckled, her eyes glinting with mischief. "And that's when I step in. While you kids are talented, some things require a touch of seniority."

James nodded. He couldn't deny that a part of him, however much he suppressed it, would like to be the one to take down the Radiant Guild by himself.

But to do that, it would take years before he had the power necessary to face the guild leader. And considering how precarious things were now, he wasn't likely to have that time.

That meant using all resources available now, which included Miss Walker and the full weight of the AA.

Despite how much it's mocked for inefficiency, it still has several high-level teams, and when they want to bite, they demonstrate they have teeth. Golden Sun didn't fall on its own. It's not the perfect revenge I would have liked, but it's something.

"Now, the two weak points I can immediately notice in this plan are Mr. Wright falling for the bait and agreeing to fight alone, and the guild leader interfering, but I imagine you have something since you are so certain, right?" the teacher asked James.

He did. "I know Wright. He won't be able to resist showing off, especially since it's against me. He's had to keep his hands to himself several times, but he won't miss this opportunity now that we've beaten up his guildmates." Then he sighed, feeling much less confident about the last part. "As for the leader, I've only seen him once in person, but from what I have managed to find on him online and in the AA files, he's someone that takes honor and PR very seriously. He must be under a lot of pressure, given how weak they appear right now, and it seems only logical that he'll try to step in when we humiliate them further."

Miss Walker's gaze sharpened, looking beyond Team 0. "There's one last thing we need to address. The aftermath of this operation is crucial. With the Radiant Guild gone, there will be a power vacuum in Brooklyn. We can't afford a repeat of what happened in Queens last summer."

Maria winced. Everyone knew about the chaos that had ensued when several minor guilds and independent Awakeners fought over territory, causing significant damage to both the Awakeners and the city.

It wouldn't surprise me if she'd been involved in that mess. Every time it's referenced, she makes a face, and her reaction to us being under surveillance tells me she has her own fair share of problems.

Daniel chimed in, "We need a plan to secure the borough. If we just defeat the Radiant Guild without thinking of what comes next, we're setting ourselves up for disaster."

James nodded in agreement. "We need to ensure that the AA directly fills that void. This operation could be a double win—not only taking down a problematic guild but also increasing our influence in the area. I guess I wouldn't mind if the Bastion Guild stepped in, but it would be much better for us to take control. I don't think such an opportunity will repeat itself anytime soon."

Miss Walker looked pleased. "Precisely. The brass sees this as an excellent opportunity. They're ready to deploy resources to hold and stabilize Brooklyn after the Radiant Guild falls. But we must be ready to assist and guide the transition. Stability in the aftermath is paramount. If the director and his advisor see that we can handle this effectively, it will pave the way for further trust and more significant operations in the future."

Daniel leaned forward, interest clear on his face. "So it's official. We're not just taking down a guild. We're essentially setting up a new order in Brooklyn, right?"

Miss Walker's eyes half-closed, expressing her amusement. "Why do you think so much leeway has been allowed? I can only push those old fogeys so far by myself. If we manage to do this, we'll prove again to the entire Awakener community that the AA isn't just an old relic but a force that can adapt, evolve, and still dominate when necessary. And while once can be happenstance, twice is much less likely to be dismissed."

James took a deep breath. The weight of the operation felt heavier now, but also more significant. He should have expected that since things were going too smoothly. *Obviously, they wouldn't allow us to do this if they didn't think there could be something to gain for the AA at large. I'm still too naive.*

Ezekiel, who had been silent for a while, finally spoke, "What's the backup plan if things don't go as expected? We should be prepared for any curveballs." The White Mage seemed by far the most worried about the whole thing, owing to his limited offensive abilities and likelihood of being immediately targeted.

Miss Walker reassured, "As I said, I'll be there on standby if things get too dicey. And the AA has several teams ready to be dispatched immediately once it's over. They won't be able to intervene beforehand, since that would make it clear that this is an entrapment operation, and that could weaken the case against Radiant in front of a judge, but I'll be there."

At that moment, James's phone dinged, drawing everyone's attention to him.

He would usually keep it on silent, but he had turned on the notifications for a specific social media app. If their target had to contact him, he'd get in touch through that platform.

His predictions turned out to be correct, because a blinking notification from one Callum Wright told him, *Meet me at the abandoned lighthouse by the old rat dungeon. Bring your teammates and no one else. We're going to settle this like men.*

As he lifted his phone up so the others could see, James felt a devilish smile grow on his lips.

Yeah, we're gonna settle this once and for all, all right. Just not the way you expect.

CHAPTER FIFTY-NINE

After sunset, few people were out and about in the semi-abandoned western-most point of Coney Island.

The area had once been a gated, private community since the late 1800s. Then it turned into an open neighborhood with the influx of people fleeing the suburbs for the safety of the city. When those same people moved into new neighborhoods, it went into decline.

Enhanced by the twilight, Coney Island Lighthouse looked somewhat haunted. Its former neighbor, an eco-plastics company, had also been abandoned, and while the rat problem had been solved by Team 0, it wasn't a particularly inviting place.

James and his companions fearlessly walked into the semi-empty parking space, ready to get the ball started once and for all.

At the center of the lot, standing tall with an aura of arrogance, was Callum Wright. Flanking him were members of the Radiant Guild; they formed a half-circle of observers—among whom James recognized the five his team had pushed around the other day—with Callum as the focal point. It was evident that he had called for a gathering to witness the impending showdown.

The low light gave the whole confrontation a noir feel, but James made sure to keep his senses peeled in case an ambush was in the works.

Callum smirked as he saw James approaching, his eyes briefly flitting to the others who were not too far behind him. "Didn't think you'd show," he taunted.

Unfazed, James retorted, "Couldn't pass up the opportunity to show you up, Wright. After all, it's about time someone put you in your place."

A murmur spread among the Radiant Guild members. They exchanged glances, clearly not expecting James to be this bold in front of the F-rank.

"You think you can go around Brooklyn talking shit about us, and then ambush one of our teams? With no consequences?" Callum's voice dripped with disdain, his eyes narrowing. "Do you think that just because you didn't take the G-rank test yet, we wouldn't know you've been power-leveling?"

"Oh, good job." James clapped sarcastically, injecting as much mockery as possible in his tone. "You realized we're not just H-ranks after we destroyed those idiots."

Callum's face reddened and his fists clenched. The taunts struck deep into his pride. "You're playing a dangerous game, Summers."

"Am I?" James asked, tapping a finger on his lips as if doubting the veracity of the F-rank's words.

James was very aware of the disparity in strength and the perilous situation they were in. Alone and surrounded by greater numbers, among which he could feel at least two more F-rankers—this should have been the worst-case scenario.

Instead, James could barely contain the excitement he was feeling. He had daydreamed about this moment. But to have his revenge, he needed to be careful. Fumbling the bag now would be terrible.

James stepped closer, voice cold. "Here's the deal, Wright. One-on-one, we all know you'll beat me. It would surprise no one if you took that road. But against all of us? I doubt it. So, how about it? Show everyone here that you're not just a big talker hiding behind your guild's skirts."

Callum laughed, but there was a hint of rage in it. "Do you think me so stupid to fall for it? I have you in the palm of my hands now, Summers. There's nowhere to hide; no one is gonna save you."

He didn't seem particularly interested in falling for the bait, but James hadn't been talking to him. He had known from the beginning that it was a long shot to convince him directly.

But seeing the crowd murmur, he knew he had gotten his hooks in. Now he just needed to push a little more. "So this is what you have come to," he announced solemnly. "The once great Radiant Guild, forced to duel a team of rookies just to defend their honor. It doesn't surprise me that people feel free to badmouth you in your territory."

Ignoring the fact that he had been the one to badmouth them, he could see the first stirrings of discontent with Callum's conduct in the group.

His teammates stayed silent throughout; they knew James was much better suited to dealing with Wright than any of them. The only reason he would accept a five-on-one fight, after all, was if it were personal.

Among the guild members, a tall, lanky fellow with dark curls spoke up. "You heard the man, Callum. Is this what we are doing now? Dueling kids in the shadows, scurrying like rats?" From James's observation, this was one of the two other F-ranks present and he didn't seem to mind putting Callum on the spot.

A few others murmured in discontent. It wasn't so much that they were above this kind of behavior, having done much worse, but the situation they were in did paint it as a desperate attempt to maintain their guild honor by silencing Team 0, where once they would have simply done so in the open, without fear of retaliation from anyone.

Callum's face darkened with fury. His ego was taking hit after hit, not just from James but from his own people. "You're questioning me in front of this vermin?"

It was interesting to James that there seemed to be some friction between the Radiant members, but he should have expected it. With the way things were going, the rats would be looking to jump the ship. They were probably still hanging around because of their leader. Plus, no other organization had started making individual offers, concentrating more on absorbing the whole guild.

It was just a matter of time before that happened, however, and James wouldn't be surprised if the high-rankers had already noticed guilds putting out feelers.

James sensed the perfect moment and pressed on. "Come on, Wright. You claim to be an F-ranker. Surely you can handle us by yourself. Or are the rumors true? That your ranking is nothing but a front? That you're just a paper tiger?"

Of course, there was no such rumor. He just invented it for the occasion. But James did have a few suspicions about the speed of Callum's ascent between the ranks, and it wouldn't surprise him if some palms had been greased.

There was a collective gasp from the Radiant Guild members. James's words cut deep, and the implications were clear. If Callum backed down now, his reputation, and by extension the guild's, would be in tatters.

He can't really back down from that. I'm pretty sure he's not particularly beloved, and considering the precarious situation Radiant is in, he can't afford to let something like this go unpunished.

Callum glared at James, his face a mask of pure hatred. "You're going to regret those words, Summers."

"Prove me wrong, then," James said, leaning in slightly. "Take us on by yourself. Show your guild that you're not just a big talker, but worth the position you hold."

The lanky F-ranker from the Radiant Guild, clearly enjoying the situation, decided to push it further. "You know, Wright, I've heard some of the same rumors. Of course, I'd never believe them, but putting them to rest right now would be a good idea." He flashed a malicious grin.

The crowd's unease grew palpable. More whispers and murmurs spread, and the looks on some members' faces shifted from uncertainty to something akin to anticipation. They were clearly curious to see if Callum could back up his talk with action.

None of them believed there was anything Team 0 could do to get away. And if their fate was sealed, well, they might as well have some fun.

Lauren finally broke her silence, stepping forward with a smirk. "Maybe you're all talk after all. Big muscles, big ego, but when push comes to shove, you hide behind your minions." Her voice was calm and measured, every word dripping with sarcasm. She hadn't forgotten the looks he and his cronies had given her.

Being insulted by a girl in front of his men seemed too much for him to bear, and James had to suppress a triumphant smirk as he saw victory come close.

Callum's nostrils flared. The combined pressure from James's team and his guild members started weighing on him. "Enough!" he roared. "I'll take you all on. I'll show you why I'm the pride of the Radiant Guild and why none of you should dare stand against me!"

The entire parking lot was abuzz now. The Radiant members quickly created an open space for the impending battle, forming a ring of spectators.

Callum took a deep breath as he positioned himself at the center of the make-shift ring, trying to radiate a semblance of confidence. But even from afar, the tremble in his hands, the light sweat forming on his forehead, and the darting glances at his guild members told a different story. He didn't seem afraid, but it was evident that he was unnerved.

It wasn't the kind of look one would expect in someone certain that he'd be able to win easily. For a moment, James seriously contemplated the possibility that Callum was truly just a paper tiger and that his rank had been, if not falsified, substantially inflated, but he pushed the thought away. He'd find out soon enough, and underestimating him now would be a big mistake.

Ezekiel leaned in to whisper to James, "You sure about this? He's cornered and unpredictable. He looks like a wild animal."

"We got him where we want him," James whispered back, eyes never leaving Callum. "And we've practiced for this." Turning back wasn't an option anyway.

He knew that what Ezekiel and the others were worried about wasn't necessarily this fight, but the following one. To give their operation the credibility it needed to stand up against a judge's scrutiny, Miss Walker would have to time her entrance so that she'd arrive after the Radiant Guild's leader intervened. The timing was the scariest bit.

Facing against Callum was already a hazard. Taking on the leader would be impossible for them. Thus, they needed to not only defeat the incensed Awakener before them, but they had to do so in a way that would require intervention from his boss and then survive the man's attention.

The lanky F-ranker decided to officiate, perhaps feeling a little responsible for the unfolding situation. "When I drop my hand, the duel begins. No interruptions from anyone. We see this through to the end." He looked directly at Callum, his meaning clear: no crying foul or running away now.

His presence hadn't been expected, but James felt grateful. One of his fears had been that others would interfere once things started to look bad, but if this guy wanted to help them, he'd take it.

The tension was thick. The guild members, all watching intently, held their breath. Callum's reputation was at stake, and with it, that of the entire Radiant Guild.

"When I'm done with you, the only shit you'll be talking is the one that comes out of your mouth after I rearrange your guts," Callum said darkly.

James couldn't help but let out a snort, surprised by the obviously unintended double entendre. His teammates coughed, trying to cover their mirth, and he saw several others in the crowd trying to stifle their amusement.

"Is that why you've had it with me since the beginning? You should have just asked me out," he replied with a grin.

A low growl built up in Callum's throat, and from his flinty eyes, James knew there would be no more banter.

The referee raised his hand high. The world seemed to fall silent, every sound drowned out in anticipation. With a swift motion, he dropped it, and the fight was on.

CHAPTER SIXTY

For all that James had come to strongly dislike Callum Wright, he wasn't so blinded that he would underestimate him. Yes, he was arrogant and spoiled. He had likely used his family's connections to help his career and had an overbearing, annoying personality.

But those things didn't make him any less an F-rank. He might not be among the best, but going through his second Awakening made him impossibly strong for a single G-rank to fight.

That was why, the second the fight started, James let go of any and all attempts at mockery. Making your opponent angry would always be a valid tactic, but that was only applicable when you didn't risk getting smushed into paste from an angry [Knight Banneret].

I'm so glad we could access his file before this. I don't think I would've liked facing him without a good plan.

Wisps of energy rose from Callum's skin as they coalesced over his clothes into a true armor set. From a mana-steel helmet with an intimidating luminescent plume to a full-body silver plate mail that shined under the dim streetlights of the parking lot, he looked like a knight from the past, ready to trample over any adversary.

The Knight Banneret Talent allowed him to manifest his mana into a tangible defense and offense. As the armor pieces clicked into place, James could feel the weight of Callum's determination to crush anyone who had embarrassed him.

He took a deep breath and clenched his fists. This was it.

Mana surged in his veins, scorching hot under the pressure of his willpower. Months had passed since James had been wronged, but not a day went by that he didn't think of it. The mad dash to power, taking part in increasingly dangerous dives . . . They had all been to bring him to this moment. His eyes locked onto Callum's, trying to read his movements before they even began.

With a smirk, Lauren vanished into the shadows, her stealth skills making her nearly invisible in the dim light. During the last few weeks, her growth had mostly been focused on honing her concealment and her ability to deal lethal blows. Her crowning achievement was her killing a mineral stallion before it realized it was under attack.

Those skills would get a workout now, considering how many eyes were on them, but to succeed, she needed to just slip away from Callum's attention.

Maria stood a few steps behind James, her hands radiating with red-hot mana. With a flick of her wrist, she could send a wave of flames toward an enemy or create a wall of fire to shield her allies. The limited space disfavored her, not allowing her to show off her most powerful conflagrations, but it also prevented their opponent from easily dodging.

Ezekiel, as always, kept his distance, knowing he'd be immediately targeted if he allowed himself to get too close. His buffs would spell the fate of the encounter, as well as his healing spells.

They didn't expect to be able to stick too many debuffs on the Knight Banneret since his skills should protect him from the worst of it, but it was still fundamental that he be ready to heal anyone that got hit too hard, which would certainly happen.

Daniel, the team's Tank, moved to the front, his broad physique acting as a catalyst for the enemy's attention. His shield, made from the toughest D-rank materials, could withstand even the most brutal attacks. He'd have to rely heavily on his equipment's quality to stop Callum's assaults.

Callum, seeing Team 0's formation, let out a chuckle. "So, you've come prepared. Good. It wouldn't be fun otherwise." With a swift motion, he summoned a massive sword, the blade more tangible than the rest of his armor set.

That's a real weapon. Not a skill, but likely D-rank equipment too. Shit, I should have expected this.

James gritted his teeth. "Let's do this."

With a roar, Daniel charged forward, his shield raised to take the first blow. Callum, with surprising speed for someone in full armor, met him halfway. His sword struck the Tank with such strength to send him flying a dozen feet back, immediately showing the difference between the ranks.

James took this as his cue and dashed forward, trying to keep their opponent's attention away from the others by aiming a powerful punch at Callum's side. But the knight was quick. Callum parried James's attack with his sword. The force of the blow sent James skidding backward, but he quickly regained his balance.

Lauren, seizing the opportunity, moved silently to position herself behind Callum. She threw a knife aimed at a gap in his armor. The blade flew true, but Callum, sensing the danger, twisted just in time, the blade grazing past him, leaving a mere scratch. The Rogue had known how difficult it'd be to actually hurt him, but her effort still allowed James and Daniel to reposition.

From a distance, Maria directed her channeled energy, hands glowing bright red. With a fierce shout, she unleashed a torrent of flames. A massive fireball hurtled toward Callum. The heat was so intense that the very air around it shimmered. The Knight raised his sword, pumping mana into it, and with a swift motion, he slashed through the fireball, which dissipated into a burst of sparks and smoke.

At that moment, Ezekiel cast his buffs and a soft light enveloped his team-mates, increasing their agility and vitality stats to better handle the confrontation with someone so evidently superior.

Daniel, now reinvigorated, charged once more. As he closed the gap, he swung his massive shield like a battering ram, aiming to knock Callum off balance.

However, the Knight was prepared. Using his sword, he deflected the shield's blow. That left the Tank open for a retaliatory kick that folded him in half.

Before he could do more, James was on top of him and pierced through his defenses with a fist brimming with mana. The hit rang the armor like a gong, disrupting the skill's effect thanks to the large injection of energy.

Although it wasn't enough to injure him, Callum grunted in pain as he skidded back a few feet.

James, sensing an opening, lunged forward as he tried to prevent the Knight from recovering. The air swooshed with every punch, the armor flickering even more under the disturbing effect of James's mana. Callum parried and dodged, but James was relentless; he landed a few solid hits that caused the Knight to stagger.

However, the F-rank was far from defeated. With a roar, he unleashed his Talent's true power. His armor shined even brighter and the air around him became dense with mana. With a gesture, he sent out a shock wave of energy that knocked James back several feet.

An AOE skill of that magnitude would require several seconds of effort for a G-rank, but he cast it while under duress, and from the looks of it, he wasn't even slightly winded.

Lauren, using her agility, managed to dodge the shock wave and quickly closed the distance, her knives ready to strike as she tried to gain some time for her team-mate to recover. But Callum was quick, having expected it, and caught her wrist in a viselike grip.

She struggled, trying to free herself, but his strength was overwhelming. The girl barely had the time to push off the ground and attempt to cushion the blow before she was sent flying with a kick, rolling to a stop next to the circle of leering Radiant members.

The crowd hooted and shouted encouragements as Callum took the upper hand.

To prevent him from ending the fight then and there, Ezekiel stepped forward to cast several debuffs on the Knight.

Of course, he knew they wouldn't be nearly as effective as they should be—it was the entire reason why he hadn't started by using them—but it did allow Lauren the time to scramble away from the approaching danger.

As the crowd quieted, distant laughter and screams coming from the Coney Island rides echoed through the area, a sharp contrast to the tense atmosphere in the parking lot.

It was evident to all that despite putting up a decent showing for a new G-rank team, they weren't about to magically close the gap to the second Awakening. Still,

Team 0 rallied, forming a circle around Callum, who stood there with a smirk, confidence in his victory unshaken.

All at once, the silence was broken. James and Daniel shot forward from opposite directions, trying to force the Knight to keep his attention on them while the others worked out something.

Ezekiel took the moment of reprieve to quickly heal Lauren. While her suit had protected her from organ rupture, she would still be out of the fight without help.

As the Knight deflected and parried James's and Daniel's blows with relative ease, despite being slowed by the debuffs, the temperature started rising again. Maria's hands contained a condensed fireball powerful enough to resemble a bomb.

Suddenly, the ground shook as Callum charged his AOE skill, his armor glowing. He sent the two harassers flying back and quickly closed the distance with the Fire Mage, sword held high and ready to put her out of the fight, possibly forever.

Before he could bring his weapon down, a blinding bolt of light hit him. The Knight roared in pain and annoyance, which gave the redhead the time to retreat.

Ezekiel scurried back, not wanting to be in the path of his rage, but built up another attack. Just like what he had done against the rats in the nearby dungeon, he forwent his healing ability to concentrate his mana into making the bolt as luminous as possible.

It wasn't something that could turn the tides by itself. But definitely enough to allow Maria to release her own magic.

Crack! The fireball hit Callum's armor, exploding into a roaring inferno that blocked everyone's sight.

The redhead kept feeding the spell mana, her hands trembling as she sustained it well beyond what it should have been capable of.

Still, it was all for naught. With a thunderous *boom*, Callum unleashed his ability. A massive wave of energy erupted from him, aiming to obliterate anything in its path. The parking lot trembled as chunks of asphalt flew into the air.

The Radiant members were forced back by the intensity of their companion's rage, not having the luxury of high-level equipment to protect them. Only the lanky F-ranker, who had been silently watching the fight unfold, was unmoved. Gusts of air swirled to protect him from the debris.

Once it was all over, the parking lot resembled a bomb site. The asphalt had been torn apart completely, revealing the sandy ground below. Smoke lingered in the air, which made it difficult to see what was going on, even with enhanced senses.

James picked himself up from the ground after the explosion had sent him tumbling. With Thakinetic Awareness, he quickly located Callum.

He was still standing at the epicenter. His armor slowly knitted back together after having been subjected to repeated abuse. His helmet, which had once covered his face, now lay at his feet. So he bent down to pick it up.

When he rose, James was unsurprised at Callum's murderous expression.

Fuck. This is a bit harder than I hoped.

CHAPTER SIXTY-ONE

Taking another one of Callum's shock waves was out of the question. The last one had already done a lot of damage. More importantly, James strongly felt that if they allowed the Knight to dictate the pace, they'd lose any hope they had of snatching a victory.

This meant turning the AOE attacks into a useless waste of mana. Signaling to the others, James took a deep breath. He ran toward Callum, then stopped when the other started glowing again.

Rather than being discouraged, however, James grinned. Because a small fireball nailed the F-rank in the chest, making him stumble back and grunt in pain. Immediately, James resumed his approach, then clocked Callum with an enhanced punch in the stomach, disrupting his armor to seriously threaten him.

Instead of following through, he retreated. Callum was preparing, he observed, to unleash his area skill. When Callum released the shock wave, it was weaker than the previous. It washed over James, making him stumble, but he was otherwise unharmed. At the same time, Lauren threw a knife, aiming for the gap he had created.

It failed. With his large mana pool, Callum simply flooded the surroundings to prevent anything from touching him, but it was evident that it wouldn't be a viable tactic.

So Team 0 kept their distance while occasionally attempting to get close and inflict a blow, only to be stopped by the stronger Knight. That, in turn, opened the way for another long-range attack, which would force him to blast a shock wave. The cycle continued.

F-rank Awakeners had enough mana to keep wasting it for a long time, but considering that James estimated each wave to cost at least 50 mana, Callum had to be more careful the longer they drew it out.

But what struck James was Callum's breathing: it was becoming ragged. It was clear that continuously pumping mana into defense and his AOE skills was draining him, both physically and mentally. His initial bravado was fading as it dawned on him that he might actually lose if he didn't get it together.

Daniel observed the changes too. Aiming to unbalance Callum, he deliberately said, "He's getting tired. We need to keep the pressure on, and it'll be over soon."

A cornered animal is at its most dangerous. We should expect him to lash out and try to break the encirclement soon.

They had prepared for this exact eventuality, planning out their options and even simulating it with Miss Walker's help. This was their one chance of winning, since, despite how much they could try and tire him out, if Callum calmed down, he'd realize they were more likely to tire before him. Especially if he stopped with the shock waves and started attacking them directly again.

Just as predicted, with desperation evident in his eyes, Callum lunged directly at James, his sword gleaming wickedly. James braced himself, ready to intercept the attack with his gloved fists. He'd trained for this moment and knew that if he wanted to avoid getting skewered, he'd need to at least deflect some of the blow's power.

Still, his role here wasn't to heroically defeat the F-ranker by himself. He just needed to create an opening for the others to exploit.

He shifted his feet, trying to move with the sword. But Callum was quick. His blade pierced through James's defenses and bit into his side.

Lauren took the moment to throw another knife at Callum's exposed neck. While it didn't hit its mark, it managed to graze his cheek, causing a thin stream of blood to trail down his face. The distraction was enough for James to pull away from the blade's dangerous edge.

Stumbling back, blood oozing from his side, James fell to the ground. The severity of the wound was evident; if not treated immediately, he would be out of the fight. Despite the high-level materials his suit was made of, it could only prevent him from being cut in half. After all, it was up against another D-rank weapon and F-rank strength behind it. Eyes wide in horror, Ezekiel sprinted toward James, his hands glowing with healing magic.

Daniel, realizing the direness of the situation, stepped in front of the injured Thakinetic, his shield held high, ready to intercept any further assault. "Maria! Cover us!"

The Fire Mage, anger evident in her eyes, let loose another torrent of flames, this time not aiming for Callum but at the ground around him. The asphalt and sand melted under the intense heat, creating a boiling barrier that temporarily trapped the Knight Banneret.

While Callum struggled with the inferno, Lauren capitalized on his distraction, her stealth allowing her to get close without him noticing. With a swift motion, she landed a solid kick behind his knee, and Callum stumbled into the lava. The heat seared him and he let out a scream of pain, giving the team a moment of respite.

Ezekiel, in the meantime, reached James. Placing his hands over the wound, he channeled his mana. As the wound began to close, a soft glow enveloped James, rejuvenating his energy. The White Mage's skill with healing magic had grown by leaps and bounds lately, thanks to all the broken bones and cuts he had to heal during their forays in Saratoga.

That served him well now, as he was able to quickly put James back on his feet.

Still, the fight was not over. The Knight picked himself up, ugly burns all over his exposed skin. They had managed to prevent Callum from getting the upper hand even as he tried to break the encirclement, but now they needed to capitalize.

Daniel did exactly that, pushing forward and attracting attention to himself. James moved in synchronization with him, ready to exploit any openings the Tank could create.

"Keep him off balance!" James shouted to the team. "Don't give him a chance to breathe."

From a distance, the crowd jeered and shouted, watching the battle unfold like a sport.

"Come on, Wright! Is that all you got?" someone yelled, causing a stir among the spectators.

Feeling the pressure from the team and the crowd, Callum roared in frustration, summoning most of his remaining mana for one powerful skill. The ground shook from the concentration of energy emerging from him, the very air trembling.

Where he once had a classical armor, it now began warping under the strain, the skill not made to support so much power. Still, he kept on pushing until it solidified again. Horns and cruel lines made up the new armor, giving Callum a much more intimidating look.

Lauren, sensing the impending danger, disappeared into the shadows while Maria prepared to unleash another wave of fire. Ezekiel hurried to refresh the buffs, knowing how dangerous the situation was.

But it was Daniel and James who charged forward as they attempted to stop whatever it was that he was doing. The Tank, shield first, slammed into Callum, pushing him off balance. He had to quickly retreat, avoiding a powerful sword swing. It had gone too wide, James noticed, because the new armor limited the Knight's movements.

This gave him the chance to unleash a series of rapid punches, each empowered by his willpower. With every blow, there was a dull *thud* as Callum's armor dented from the damage accumulated all over.

It should have been a powerful defense, yet it was still susceptible to disruption. Rather, it was even weaker since the skill had been strained so much. James's powerful mana only compounded on the weakness and led to the armor's quick destruction. Callum swung his sword desperately, trying to get some space.

He managed to achieve his goal, but it was already too late. Large pieces of his armor flaked off, floating into the air and vanishing, the power that made them too unstable to sustain.

Since he sank the vast majority of his mana into it, he, too, could understand how precarious his situation was. His skills were out of the question now, and Callum would have to rely entirely on his powerful stats.

That might have been enough, but panic took over as he continued to swing his sword erratically, trying to keep everyone away.

The crowd was forced to widen the circle; they didn't want to come under fire for drawing the erratic F-rank's attention.

James gave the referee a look but saw that he didn't seem particularly interested in stepping in. Instead, he appeared to be suppressing a grin, enjoying his rival's pitiful end.

As Callum, overwhelmed and desperate, lunged toward James one last time, Maria unleashed a precise beam of flame, targeting his feet and sending him tumbling down. Callum let out a scream. His sword fell from his grip and clanged to the ground. As the heat dissipated, he staggered up, beaten and with a defeated look in his eyes.

James took the opportunity with glee, feeling a smile sprout unbidden. *I've been waiting too long for this. I'm not going to let you go now that I have you. This is for Sally, bastard!*

He pulled back his fist and punched. The feeling of his gloved hand connecting with Callum's temple was highly satisfying, and he was sure he'd remember it for a long time.

He didn't use as much mana as he could have, not wanting to actually kill him, but he didn't hold back either since the Knight was an F-rank.

The blow was strong enough to send him skidding a few feet until he rolled to a stop, knocked out cold for everyone to see.

The parking lot was filled with a deafening silence. Team 0 had somehow managed to win against an F-rank Awakener, a feat very few believed possible.

The quiet was soon broken by the sound of someone touching down behind the crowd, and from the aura blazing at full force, James realized who it was that had just arrived.

The Radiant members parted as a tall, muscular man stalked their way. He wore a well-made trench coat, which did little to hide his robust build. His eyes were dark as he took in the situation.

"You," the man growled, pointing at James and his team, "have brought shame and insult upon my guild. The disrespect you've shown will not be forgotten."

James, still catching his breath, stood strong against the pressure of the man's aura, his eyes filled with defiance. "We fought a fair fight. It's not our fault if your guy couldn't stand up to the challenge."

"Kid, don't insult me. You know very well what the situation is like. You've deliberately set up this confrontation so you could humiliate us even further. This isn't something I can let go," the man replied, glare intensifying.

The crowd, who had looked to still be recovering from the abrupt end to the fight, tightened into a circle again, preventing any hope they might have had of escaping.

The guild leader, however, turned his gaze on his own men. He looked equally, if not more, enraged. "As for you . . . The fact that you even allowed things to come to this sickens me. Five rookies by themselves were able to utterly shame us, and none of you tried to do anything about it," he reprimanded.

The F-ranker that had served as referee gulped but found the courage to reply, "Mr. Mettermeier, you know that interfering in the fight would've been even worse. Callum agreed to fight them by himself!"

"Then you should have stopped him then and there. What kind of idiot goes along with such an obvious ploy?!" was the incensed comeback.

Shaking his head, the Radiant leader looked at Callum's still form. "Someone pick him up and take him to a healer. I don't want to waste a potion on that idiot."

Then, he turned to Team 0 and grimly addressed, "Kids, don't think too badly of me. Unfortunately, there's no other choice. Any last words?"

CHAPTER SIXTY-TWO

Yeah, maybe we should've rethought this part of the plan. Now that I'm here standing before him, it really doesn't look plausible to last for long.

The Radiant Guild leader wasn't someone Team 0 could hope to take on. Already, they had been quite lucky in their fight with Callum, who was at least a whole rank below the man glaring at them.

"You realize this isn't the kind of thing you can just sweep under the rug by killing us, right?" Daniel spoke up, breaking the tense silence that had fallen.

The man grunted, expression twisting in distaste. "Don't misunderstand me. I do not enjoy killing kids, nor would I be doing this were the situation stable, but you're damaging us in a perilous moment, and if it gets out, we'll be under even more pressure." As he spoke, he took off his gloves, throwing them over his shoulder into the crowd of his men, who scrambled to catch them before they could fall on the ground.

Loosening his tie, he sighed, "My name is Francis Mettermeier. You should at least know the name of the man who kills you. For what it's worth, I'm sorry it had to come to this."

Despite the genuine sorrow in his tone, he showed absolutely no hesitation in his motions. This was a man who had killed many, many times and who wouldn't flinch at doing so again.

"You know we are with the AA, right?" Lauren asked, trying to buy some more time. Maybe he'd reveal something that could be used in the trial. They all knew Miss Walker would interfere when things started to become dangerous, but there was a real possibility of someone getting seriously hurt before she got here.

A low chuckle rumbled through the parking lot. "The Awakeners Association has their hands full with things far more important than this. I don't doubt that there will be investigations into your disappearance, but you'll be forgotten before long. It's happened before, and it'll happen again."

"Are you saying you've killed AA agents before?!" James asked in a strangled tone. Their goal had been to make the man admit to crimes, but he hadn't expected him to be so upfront with it.

Mettermeier shrugged uncaringly. "A few people went missing; who can say what really happened to them? Monsters are everywhere, especially since the one agency tasked with controlling their spread isn't particularly good at its job."

Lauren scoffed in disbelief. "You have a lot of courage to say that, considering how much more difficult you make our jobs! Just the sheer amount of fake readings you give us almost doubles the response time!"

The man chuckled, amused that she had the balls to confront him so directly. "You kids are funny. It's too bad that you won't leave here alive. As for the false alarms, unfortunately, it's just the cost of doing business. Every guild plays this game, little power moves to gain the upper hand. Yes, we might've given false alarms a time or two to get more time to consolidate our grip on the territory, but who hasn't?"

James saw this as an opening. "So you admit to manipulating dungeon information? That's a violation of the contract you have with the AA. You've not only endangered civilians but also other Awakeners who rely on accurate dungeon information for their livelihoods."

Of course, he was talking about himself and his teammates. Their forays in the rat and crocodile dungeons had been mired by false information, making them much more dangerous than they should have been.

Mettermeier's eyes narrowed. Irritation flashed across his face. "You think you can pin me down with such trivialities? It's a dog-eat-dog world out there. Only the strong survive. If we hadn't done so, others would have swooped in. And I can promise you something: I'm not about to let all my hard work, raising the Radiant Guild into what it is now, go to waste."

The crowd around them shifted approvingly, though James could spy a few uneasy faces. Not all of them were as convinced there was a need to kill them, but none dared gainsay their leader, making them all equally guilty in his eyes.

And the eyes of the law. He's explicitly admitted he wants to kill us and to have falsified dungeon information. I think this might be enough to get him a long sentence . . . Please hurry up, Miss Walker.

"You won't be able to get away with it any longer," Ezekiel interrupted, trying to push for more. "Now that Golden Sun has been disbanded, you don't have a patron anymore. It's just a matter of time before you're brought down."

Mettermeier, surprisingly, smirked. "Ah, the Golden Sun Guild. They were a tool, a stepping stone. Useful while they lasted, but hardly essential to our long-term vision. They were laid low as much as they flew high. The legend of Icarus should have taught them something. And as for our patrons . . ." He waved his hand dismissively. "Power attracts power. There are always those willing to invest in the future. Once we've passed this rough patch, our control over Brooklyn will give us a much better leveraging position."

"Ah!" The sound left James's mouth without him realizing it. He finally understood the incomprehensible position the man had maneuvered his organization in. "You're actually looking to get bought off by another large guild so that the authorities will focus on them, leaving you free to slowly expand your empire."

The man hummed in acknowledgment. "Almost. Well, you're still closer than anyone else, to be fair. Even some of my own lieutenants haven't gotten that far." Despite his appearance as a straight talker, it seemed that he still enjoyed hearing himself speak. "You see, the secret of this business is not becoming all-powerful— without the right Talents, that's impossible anyway. No, true victory comes from the slow creep of influence. Covering more and more territory, absorbing more fresh Awakeners so that they can bolster our ranks and keep our growth going. That can only happen if everyone's eyes are elsewhere."

Mettermeier, it seemed, was highly ambitious. He knew when not to push too hard, which made him very dangerous. More so than most high-rankers who flew too close to the sun and whose fall came quickly and brutally.

James felt gratified that he had pushed for this operation so much. If the man had been allowed to operate unchecked, he had no doubt he would have become a real thorn in the side.

Instead, they now had the opportunity to clean the board entirely. They'd take down a mid-sized guild with ambitions to become a significant player. It'd be a vital PR victory to the AA.

That was, if Miss Walker would hurry up and save the day. Because her continued absence was starting to make James wonder if things had gone sideways on her side. She should have more than enough to take Mettermeier in, after all.

Worry was becoming more evident in Team 0's members, as nobody swooped in to protect them, and that didn't go unremarked. The Radiant leader chuckled, eyes glinting. "I see you are starting to realize."

There was a sinking feeling in James's gut, and he frantically reviewed all he knew of the operation, trying to find where things might have gone wrong.

There was nothing that came to mind, as they had managed to achieve all their goals smoothly . . . too smoothly, in fact.

"You let us get here," he said in profound realization.

Mettermeier's chuckle transformed into full-blown laughter. "Yes, I knew from the beginning, when I first heard that an AA team was talking shit about us in Brooklyn, that something was going on. It didn't take long to confirm that your teacher had also taken her leave from the headquarters this evening, so I put two and two together."

Team 0 exchanged worried glances. The weight of the situation pressed down on them, made even heavier by the smug satisfaction evident on Mettermeier's face. If he had known about Miss Walker from the beginning, it meant that they had walked into a trap, thinking they were the ones setting the trap.

James swallowed. The dryness in his throat became more pronounced.

"Where's Miss Walker?" Maria demanded, her voice quivering but defiant.

Mettermeier gave her a chilling smile. "Your precious teacher is likely already dealt with. I called in a favor, you see. There's a particularly powerful Awakener I know who owed me one. I thought, why not now? He has her handled. And as for the rest of you . . ." He waved a hand dismissively. "I'd hoped Callum would be enough to deal with you without having to step in personally, but things have gone a bit too far. I guess the old adage is correct: if you want things done right, you have to do them yourself."

James felt his heart plummet. This was bad. This was really bad. Miss Walker was their trump card. She was their failsafe. Without her, they were sitting ducks.

"We won't go down without a fight," Ezekiel growled. He had a wild look as his worst fears were realized, but he also seemed determined to make the Radiant Guild pay for every pound of flesh they took. "We'll make too much of a mess for you to cover up."

"You kids are just an afterthought," Mettermeier said. "The real problem will be covering up your teacher's disappearance, but it wouldn't be the first time a high-ranker tried to take on a new dungeon by themselves and disappeared in its depths. I know of several that were never declared dead for this exact reason, after all."

As Mettermeier continued to gloat, James tried to think of a way out. They couldn't just stand there and wait for the inevitable. The man hadn't mentioned the teams that were on standby; they were to be dispatched after the initial operation to take control of Brooklyn and clean up any pocket of resistance. Still, James wasn't sure Team 0 could afford to wait for them to notice that something was going on.

He had full trust in Miss Walker's capabilities, and unless a true powerhouse had been sent to face her, he was sure she'd be able to defeat them in time. The problem was, time was short.

Despite how much Mettermeier seemed to like hearing himself talk, he was no idiot, and sooner or later, he would end his cliché villain monologue and actually deal with them.

That moment, unfortunately, came sooner than he would have liked.

"All right, that's enough. I allowed you to stall for a while, but I do have things I need to get to. You created a lot of work for me." The man's tone was much harder now.

A slight wind started picking up as the crowd of Radiant members widened the circle once again, wary of being caught up in anything their leader might do.

"Albert! Barrier!" Mettermeier called. The F-ranker that had served as referee stepped up and lifted his hands.

James considered trying to break the encirclement, but he knew that anything he tried to do would easily get countered by the Radiant leader. He could have easily dealt with Team 0 in but a moment, but it looked like he wanted to make a show of it, probably to reaffirm his position to his men.

As the glowing purple barrier settled around them, James shared a look with his friends, knowing that this would be the hardest battle of their lives.

We can only hope she comes for us quickly.

CHAPTER 62.5 – INTERLUDE

Leila Walker

Despite how well things had been going, Leila was never one to lower her guard at the last moment. Too often, she had seen seemingly perfect missions go to hell when people became convinced that the danger was over.

That caution saved her life. She had been observing the lighthouse parking lot from within her shadow dimension, even though she was far enough to not be noticed by any but the best sensors, when a disturbance in the air made her take notice of her immediate surroundings.

No one without a powerful spatial skill could try to harm her, but that didn't mean it was a good habit to let enemies attack freely.

It was why she made sure to dodge the sword that came for her from seemingly nowhere. Already, the fact that the point of contact between her dimension and the real world had been located sent alarm bells ringing. On top of that, her instincts screamed. She didn't want to get caught up in the seemingly mundane sword strike.

Leila rematerialized a dozen feet away, still on the same rooftop but far enough that she could take in exactly who it was that had attacked her.

"Tsk. I can already tell this is gonna be annoying," a deep male voice said.

Her enhanced sense stat was high enough that she could see his features clearly, despite the darkness shrouding the battlefield. Her mind ran through countless memorized profiles until she stopped on one. "Andre Zan. To what do I owe the pleasure of the First Swordsman of the Broken Tower coming to visit me?" she asked, keenly observing every movement.

He was a tall, thin man with sharp features and hard, cold eyes. A long, straight nose and a full beard, coupled with a well-tailored black suit and tie made him look more like a notary than the powerful Awakener she knew him as.

"The Broken Tower is long gone, girl. Nothing but foolish dreams. I'm an independent now," he revealed, shifting into a sword stance without hurry. He held his weapon directly pointed at her, the sleek blade gleaming under the faint moonlight.

The sword itself was nothing special. Just B-rank mana steel forged into the hardest and most resilient weapon possible, without any other magical powers.

No, the real danger came from the sheer ability the man had in wielding it.

A master swordsman before the apocalypse happened, Andre Zan had taken his skills to their upper limit, achieving incredible feats without a drop of external mana being used.

"Then why are you here? Surely you know that it's a death sentence to go against the AA so directly," Leila asked even as she shifted her weight, preparing herself for battle.

The shadows all over the rooftop broiled under her will. They shifted and geared up for a battle she was sure would require her best. "You could have chosen any other job. Why this?"

"I owed Mettermeier a favor," he said, not sounding particularly put off. "It's not personal. Just business. And to be honest, I've always wanted to see how the famed Leila Walker would fare against my blade."

Despite how much she would have liked to question him, Leila realized that the more time she wasted, the more likely her kids would be in trouble.

He's probably been told to stall me if he can't kill me. I need to finish this quickly.

All at once, the shadows rose up and covered her. Zan closed the distance in the blink of an eye, sword gleaming with the intent to cut her down then and there.

Leila's own blade—which emerged from her dimension with a flex of her will—met it with a resounding screech of metal. As she moved with the blow to prevent him from leveraging his greater reach, the moonlight illuminated her form, making the assassin momentarily falter.

She wore an ever-shifting dress made of shadow, which tastefully hugged her curves. Modest but hinting at more. A veil covered her face as if she were ready to walk down the aisle, but her red eyes shined through. She looked regal and eerie.

Her sword, on the other hand, glowed a muted red, like lava flowing down a volcano.

"The big guns immediately, huh?" Zan asked, retaking his stance. She didn't bother to answer.

The two circled each other on top of the empty building, sizing each other up. The wind howled around them, carrying with it the distant sounds of the city.

They clashed again in the middle of the rooftop, the power released cratered the cement. Jets of flame followed every swing of Leila's sword, forcing the older swordsman to retreat lest he be horribly burned.

His skill with the blade, however, was still superior to hers, which allowed him to not lose much ground. He shifted like a leaf in the wind, always in the perfect position to menace her.

Her abilities were enough to prevent him from getting any serious blow in, but Leila started to get frustrated as they kept clashing fruitlessly.

Her keen senses told her that if she just kept pushing, she'd slowly gain the upper hand. Her magic was an unbridgeable gap, and considering that Zan was known for his disdain of the practice—something that had likely confined him to B-rank forever—she just needed to leverage it. He'd tire from dodging all her multidirectional attacks, and she'd finally be able to win.

But it wouldn't happen fast enough. Already, precious time had been wasted, and she had no idea what the situation was like in the parking lot, where her kids were facing enemies much stronger than them.

She needed to end this, quickly.

Saying a silent prayer for the mess she was about to make, Leila gave up any notion of restraint and started flooding the environment with her mana. Hundreds of points were expended to raise the temperature until the rooftop could have been mistaken for a furnace.

"You're going to bring the whole building down!" her would-be assassin shouted over the groaning of the foundations.

Leila was well aware of that, and she was glad she had chosen this specific place for her observations; no one lived here, as it was slated for demolition. Her mana could still cause massive, irreparable damage to the nearby buildings if she sustained it for long, but she had no other choice.

With the ground so hot, the swordsman was forced to jump around, never staying still for long.

Taking advantage of this, Leila gathered all her shadows and, with a scream of rage and frustration, released them in a massive wave.

Already limited in his movements, Zan could only bring his sword before him to try and cut through the powerful energy coming his way.

Unfortunately for him, that wasn't her only avenue of attack. Under her command, the boiling-hot floor rose up.

Trapped between two equally dangerous attacks, the swordsman retreated to get some distance, kicking off the air and jumping high in the sky.

Without waiting for her attack to finish, Leila shifted back into her dimension, then pushed hard to reach the parking lot and prevent a massacre.

Her speed was enough that the assassin, having been forced away, couldn't catch up, even if he understood what was going on. With another kick, he shot toward her like a bullet, swearing loudly, knowing he had allowed her too much space.

On any other occasion, Leila would have taken the time to make sure he was dead before she left, but time was of the essence.

Still, just as she was coming into direct sight of the lighthouse, the whole building, which she was technically connected to through her skill, exploded.

A trap had been set up to prevent her escape. She had known this was a possibility but hadn't expected it to be so blatant.

Though she wasn't hurt in any way, thanks to her ability, her speed slowed down that Zan managed to catch up.

His sword shined in the moonlight, aiming at her back. The very air parted before it. A finishing move of some kind, she thought. He wanted to exploit her surprise. The rubble from the rubble had just settled as he reached her.

Just when it was about to pierce through her back, bypassing the shadows protecting her form, she fell apart, unraveling like a puppet made of cloth.

With a slick, wet sound, Andre Zan's head fell to the ground, shrouded by the dust cloud he had caused with his traps.

Looking less like a human and more like a monster of fire and shadows, a queen of her elements, Leila barely gave it a glance. Her entire body was covered in darkness, and her eyes and the wedding dress's decorations shined an eerie red.

The obstacle taken care of, she sped toward her students.

CHAPTER SIXTY-THREE

As impending doom approached, James could only firm up his resolve; he'd make his end as difficult as possible for Mettermeier.

He had known from the start that this operation could end in his and his friends' deaths. Still, he had deliberately ignored it, thinking that their hard work and preparations, in the end, would see them triumph.

As overwhelmed and defeated an enemy might seem, you should never underestimate them; it was good practice to have more than one escape plan. That was a lesson he wouldn't forget anytime soon if he ever made it out of here.

Now, the Radiant Guild leader strode toward them, confident for he could kill them with a flick of his wrist. And James could only regret his recklessness.

Not for himself. He didn't particularly care. Not that he wanted to die, of course, but he went in with the full knowledge that it was possible. But he had dragged the others with him, and he felt responsible for them too.

Not much mana remained in his system despite his attempts at stalling for as long as possible. But he still had enough for one attack.

I'll have to make it count.

James closed his eyes, feeling time slow down. There was a minuscule chance that he could deal enough damage with an unexpected blow to give the others an opening, and he would do everything in his power to get it.

When he opened them, his heartbeat slowed. There was no time for fear, no time for excitement. Every fiber of his body coiled up as he gathered as much energy as possible. The moment he noticed his enemy's attention shift, he pushed it all to his legs.

James crossed the distance faster than he ever had before. At his speed, everything seemed to be in slo-mo. He noticed Mettermeier's eyes widen in shock at seeing him so close.

His eyes had barely narrowed in concentration when James was there and, with all the desperation and focus he could muster, poured all his energy into his fist. James punched, hoping beyond reason to hurt the man.

Mettermeier's hand came up to block his blow. Dismayed, James didn't allow it to stop him. The second it connected, he released all the accumulated mana.

Time resumed its course, and James was blown back with the force of the resulting explosion. He rolled to a stop against the broken cement, grunting with discomfort, and gathered himself.

He had gotten a blow in, but James didn't need his senses to tell him it didn't do much beyond stunning Mettermeier.

He picked himself up, helped by two large hands. He gave a fleeting smile of thanks to Daniel, before refocusing on the most powerful enemy he had to fight so far.

When the sea breeze blew away the dust cloud, James was chagrined. His desperate, last-minute attack hadn't dealt as much damage as he'd hoped.

Mettermeier was still standing. He shook his hand as if to clear away an annoying sensation. There was only the furrow his feet had left in the cement after being blown three feet back. Though it was a bit impressive, James realized, with a sinking feeling, it wasn't nearly enough.

He expected the man to gloat, maybe even taunt them a bit more before he started on his execution, but Mettermeier's eyes remained focused on the spot behind them, the same direction he'd been glancing at earlier.

Unwilling to turn his head away from the enemy, James instead sent his Awareness scouring behind them. What could have shocked Mettermeier that he took a hit from someone three ranks below him?

The moment he found it, a laugh escaped him, and his shoulders relaxed. "Jesus, miss, you barely made it."

At that, all his friends turned, expressions of stark relief and joy at seeing their teacher emerge from the shadows. She looked somewhat harried but no worse for wear.

The woman, in her usual black-and-red uniform, walked without a hurry, red eyes entirely focused on the man who would dare kill her students. She passed through the circle of Radiant members, who hurriedly parted the way for her. Then she tossed up the item she'd been holding in her hand.

It was a man's severed head, the neck wound entirely cauterized. His expression was one of concentration and worry, as if the man had been executing a difficult maneuver and had been taken by surprise.

James did not recognize him, but it took little effort to realize this was the man Mettermeier had spoken about. The high-ranker meant to stall and kill Miss Walker so that the Radiant Guild could sweep everything under the rug.

Now less secure, Mettermeier ground his teeth and tried to assess his chances.

Hell yeah. Now, you can get a taste of your own medicine.

All the adrenaline, which had been keeping James up, drained away. Given the amount of energy he'd spent, particularly with the last attack, it was no surprise that he started swaying in exhaustion.

Lauren was there immediately, grabbing his waist and supporting him. James gave her a grateful smile. He had truly pushed himself to the limits, and there would have been nothing more he could have done had Miss Walker not arrived.

"It's over," the woman commanded. She didn't raise her voice, but everyone heard and felt the finality of her words. When she released her aura, it pressed down on everyone, rooting them in place. No one could even think of escaping.

For Team 0, it felt like the caress of a worried mother. They had gotten so used to this kind of presence, thanks to the extensive training the woman put them through, that had it been less protective, they wouldn't have suffered.

The others, however, fared much worse. The Radiant members fell under the pressure; their bodies were pressed to the ground and unable to so much as twitch. The few F-ranks present were forced to their knees, horrified by the full might of a top-tier B-rank fighter.

The shadows of the night lengthened until they surrounded the parking lot, creeping toward them like an unavoidable sentence. Fires flickered in and out of existence. It was eerie.

As the main focus of the teacher's aura, Mettermeier could barely stand, though he seemed to be having trouble breathing from the way he clawed at his throat, eyes wide in fear.

Miss Walker kept the pressure up for a few more seconds until no space was left untouched by her shadows. The whole group gasped in relief when it ceased.

For several seconds, there were only the sounds of deep, ragged breaths and coughs.

"Your crimes are well beyond what's needed for me to act. However, since you've disclosed your intent to trap and kill an AA team, it grants me the authority to do this," she said, capturing everyone's attention.

"The Radiant Guild will be disbanded here and now. I hereby revoke all your licenses, and I'll take you into custody so that you may be judged by a jury of your peers. You have the right to remain silent."

Before anyone could try to say "Not all of us were on board" or "We were coerced into coming!" the shadows swiftly swallowed them, much to their horror. Then they were dragged into the darkness.

Less than a minute later, the parking lot, once the site of a desperate battle, was empty save for Team 0 and Miss Walker, who walked up to them. Her hand gripped the air before producing a tray of replenishment potions. Both health and mana potions, James recognized.

"Sorry for the delay, kids," she apologized.

Giving a glance at the severed head, still visible among the shadows, Ezekiel grimaced. "It looks like you had something to take care of before you got here."

Miss Walker eye-smiled, much more relaxed now. "It was surprisingly annoying, but nothing I couldn't handle. They had some idea that we were coming, however, which means that my work isn't nearly done."

Someone at the AA had leaked their plans. And she was not about to let that go unpunished.

"He didn't know about the other teams," Lauren added, still holding James up and passing him two potions.

Their teacher hummed as her eyes narrowed. "Yeah, I noticed. Zan didn't either, which tells me it was either done at a lower level, or that someone among the higher-ups deliberately leaked only part of the plan."

Gratefully drinking down the two brews, James felt strength returning to his battered form. The artificial taste of the potions was unpleasant, and he knew he wouldn't be able to take them again for a little while, having drunk two together, but it was worth it.

When he stood up, he felt his brain start working again, and he put two and two together. "You think someone tried to sweep the board clean. By leaking the information, they could have gotten us killed, which then would have led the other teams to show no mercy to the Radiant Guild, removing anyone who could possibly know something."

The others turned to Miss Walker, who confirmed James's theory with a nod. "I don't have the certainty, but it does look like that. It's why I restrained myself and didn't kill that man right where he stood," she explained, gesturing to where Mettermeier had been a few minutes before.

Then an explosion went off near the other side of Coney Island. A startling, enormous *boom!* that could be felt all over the city.

The shock wave reached them soon after, leaving them all stunned, as they watched a massive plume of smoke rise into the sky.

"We need to lea—" Miss Walker's words were drowned out by another, closer explosion. There was no time to speak.

Shadows rose up and grabbed Team 0, dragging them into a jumbled, confused world where things moved extremely quickly.

In less than four minutes, they emerged from the central hall at the AA HQ, where people were running around, some armed to the teeth while others panicked.

"Head up to our room; you'll be safe there. Don't speak to anyone that isn't me, Marcus, or the director about what happened tonight," Miss Walker yelled over the chaos, ushering them toward the elevator. "You did your job well. Now, it's time for the adults to start pulling their weight. Try not to get into any more trouble before I come back to pick you up."

With that, she was gone.

When James looked out of the glass entrance, he saw a barrier—much sturdier and more energy intensive than what was usually present—flicker into existence. *It's not just our little operation that's been going on tonight*, he realized.

He was grabbed by Lauren, who started hauling him toward the elevator that the others were holding open.

As the doors closed, cutting off James's sight, he could only hope that Miss Walker and the others would get things under control.

About the Author

Persimmon is the author of *Awakener* and the Sapiens series, originally released on Royal Road. He has written fantasy stories for more than a decade and more recently began to specialize in the gamelit and progression fantasy subgenres. His work centers on themes of magical experimentation and adventure as well as exploration of the human psyche.